One Amber Bead

a novel by

Rebecca Thaddeus

Plain View Press
P.O. 42255
Austin, TX 78704

plainviewpress.net
pk@plainviewpress.net
512-441-2452

ISBN: 978-1-935514-78-7
Library of Congress Control Number: 2011929486

Cover art: *The Necklace*, 1909 oil painting by John William Waterhouse
Cover design by Pam Knight

Reprint Permissions

STARDUST
Words by Mitchell Parish
Music by Hoagy Carmichael
Copyright © 1928, 1929 by Songs Of Peer, Ltd. and EMI Mills Music, Inc.
Copyrights Renewed
All Rights outside the USA Controlled by EMI Mills Music, Inc. (Publishing) and Alfred Publishing Co., Inc. (Print)
International Copyright Secured All Rights Reserved
Reprinted by permission of Hal Leonard Corporation

STARDUST
Music by HOAGY CARMICHAEL Words by MITCHELL PARISH
© 1929 (Renewed) EMI MILLS MUSIC, INC. and SONGS OF PEER LTD.
Exclusive Worldwide Print Rights for EMI MILLS MUSIC, INC.
Administered by ALFRED MUSIC PUBLISHING CO., INC.
All Rights Reserved
Used by Permission of ALFRED MUSIC PUBLISHING CO., INC.

DON'T SIT UNDER THE APPLE TREE (WITH ANYONE ELSE BUT ME)
Words and Music by CHARLIE TOBIAS, LEW BROWN and SAM H. STEPT
© 1942 (Renewed) CHED MUSIC CORPORATION and EMI ROBBINS CATALOG INC.
All Rights for CHED MUSIC CORPORATION Administered by WB MUSIC CORP. Exclusive Print Rights for EMI
ROBBINS CATALOG INC. Administered by ALFRED MUSIC PUBLISHING CO., INC.
All Rights Reserved
Used by Permission of ALFRED MUSIC PUBLISHING CO., INC.

I GET A KICK OUT OF YOU (from "Anything Goes")
Words and Music by COLE PORTER
© 1934 (Renewed) WB MUSIC CORP.
All Rights Reserved
Used by Permission of ALFRED MUSIC PUBLISHING CO., INC.

For Evelyn Zdunek and Maria Stolarek

with love and admiration

Acknowledgements

Where to begin? I have so many to thank.

Certainly my writers' group. Thank you Olive and Dan Mullet, hosts extraordinaire, for years of support, advice and amazing soup. And thank you to the other members of our group: Phillip Sterling, Kelly Thompson, Steve Ross and Susan Morris, for always letting me know when I'd gone astray.

Thank you to other readers who offered various and useful perspectives: family members Becky Maholland and Barb Brice; my book group, Jeanette Fleury, Alice Bandstra, Maryanne Heidemann, Peggy Peterson, Bonnie Golder, Michelle Christner, Susan Fogarty, and Joanne Dew; and friends Christine VonderHaar and Shirley Lerew.

Thanks to those who made this third generation Polish-American's Polish readable: Eva Copija, Tom Stoffer, Sandra Kemperman, and Katherine Piwinska.

Thank you to those whose stories and descriptions took me to places I never actually visited: Halina Anna Copija, Mitchell Zdunek and Ted Stolarek. Thank you to those who unwittingly served as models for two very important characters: Thad Stolarek and Nancy Kaszyca. And a special thank you to Mike Maholland.

I also owe a debt of gratitude to all the writers whose words have thrilled, delighted, provoked, informed, enlightened or saddened me, as well as a special thank you to Susan Bright and Pam Knight, who helped transform a dream into a reality.

Contents

Doppelgänger[1]

Somewhere she must exist. My other self,
lost twin I've never met, only imagined:
the mirrored image of a familiar stranger.

Smoking a cigarette in a Krakow bar,
walking along a gray dock in Gdansk,
hanging laundry in a cramped yard—anywhere

between the Tatra Mountains and Baltic Sea.
A mere roll of the dice that I'm here
and she's somewhere else, someone else

with my face, pale skin, hair streaked
blonde on brown. So many of my family
decided to stay in the Old World

it's amazing I cropped up in the New.
Surrounded by microwaves, CD-ROMs,
enough guilt to fill a baseball field

because of a simple act of birth that placed me
in the suburbs south of Cleveland and
not in a town across the river from Oswiecim.

A toast to my other half: may we each have
a long life on opposite sides of the world;
may we never recognize each other on the street.

—Linda Nemec Foster
Reprinted with permission

---

1 From *Amber Necklace from Gdańsk*, LSU Press, Baton Rouge, 2001.

Bialek Family Tree

Wladislaw Bialek	m.	Sofia (Zosia) Kusiakiewicz
1885-1958		1896-1936

—————————————————————/\—————————————————————

Henryk	Evelina m. Mikosz Sienko	Andrzej	Stephania
	(Eva, Evie) (Mickey)		(Steffie)
1918-	1924- 1920-	1930-1936	1936-

————————————/\————————————

Penelope (Penny)	Margaret (Peggy)
1948-	1950-

Czarnecki(a) Family Tree

Stanislaus Czarnecki	m.	Bronislawa Kusiakiewicz
1892-1944		1894-1944

—————————————————————/\—————————————————————

Marek	Stanislaus (Stasiu)	Jadwiga (Jadzia) m. Roman Kaminski m. Alfons Zadora
1913-	1921-	1924-1985 1909-1963

————————————/\————————————

Marek	Magdalena
1952-	1954-

Zadora Family Tree

Eugene Zadora	m.	Danuta Malek
1885-1930		1892-1942

—————————————————————/\—————————————————————

Jan	Tadeusz	Jozef	Pawel	Anton (Antek)	Apolonya	Alfons	Eugene (Gienek)
1910-	1911-	1915-	1918-	1920-	1924-1941	1925-	1927-

Sofia's Journey: April 5, 1912

Barely tall enough to see over the railing, Sofia Kusiakiewicz surveyed an eternity of black: black sky, almost devoid of stars, stretching far above her, black water, its gentle swells rocking the ship as if to lull it to sleep, stretching deep below her. In three years the Kronprinz Wilhelm, with its two masts and four heavy stacks, capable of reaching a speed of 22 knots, would see far different service; it was destined to sink fifteen Allied ships in 1915. But for now its mission was benevolent—bringing over 1500 immigrants to their promised land.

Sofia felt torn between two worlds: the New, which she would not actually encounter until the next day when the cruiser docked in New York Harbor, and the Old, which at this late hour embraced her heart. Peering eastward toward her home, she wondered what time it was in Niedzieliska, what Mama and Tata were doing, if her sister Bronislawa felt well. Was it dinner time, with the family gathered around the old cherry table and Mama bringing in a big pot of bigos? Was it daybreak, with Bronislawa dashing to the outhouse, her morning sickness overtaking her yet again?

Mostly Sofia wondered whether she had made the right decision. True, many from her village were coming to the New World—three on this ship alone. And once Bronislawa had married and brought her new husband into the Kusiakiewicz family home, where the young couple were to begin their lives together, things had not been the same.

Bronislawa's wifely responsibilities had left little time for the childish amusements she had earlier enjoyed with her younger sister. And Sofia had seen little in Bronislawa's new life that would inspire her to follow her older sister's path. Sofia yearned for something different than the life she saw ahead of her on the small family farm.

Still, here, on a large ship pitifully dwarfed by the immense ocean in which it bobbed and swayed, her desire for adventure was not nearly as compelling. Here, she was homesick. Here, she longed for her Mama and sister, whose advice would surely help her with the decision she would soon need to make.

The next morning gray mist enveloped the harbor as the ship entered its wide expanse, about to complete yet another transoceanic journey. Wladyslaw Bialek, tightly holding Sofia's hand as they stood with many others on the deck, peered through the mist for his first glimpse of the famous statue about which he had heard so much. Finally, "There, there, Zosia. To the left. You can see Berthold's statue. Look. The torch!"

"Yes, I begin to see it." Sofia squinted hard in the direction Wladyslaw pointed but could only see a tall, narrow black shape standing out against the enveloping gray.

"Our journey is done." Wladyslaw grasped her hand tightly in his own. "Will you now answer the question I have asked so many times, moja droga?"

Sofia smiled up at him shyly, traces of teardrops glistening on her ruddy cheeks. "Wladyslaw, we are so young. Everything is so new."

"All the more reason for you to say 'yes,'" he insisted. "A new beginning for us, in a new and wonderful country." Emboldened by the drama of the moment, he placed his arm around her shoulder. The crown of her head, circled by heavy dark braids tied with bright red ribbons, barely reached his chest.

"We hardly know each other," she answered, shuddering slightly beneath her heavy coat. She felt the rugged solidity, the suppressed energy of his body.

"I know all I need to know of you, moja droga. I know of your beauty, your strength, your character, your kindness. I have learned much about you during this long journey."

"Oh look," Sofia cried out, her cheeks reddening further at the praise. Wladyslaw looked away to where she pointed. "The statue. There. I can see it better now." As dawn broke through the heavy veil of mist, revealing the Stature of Liberty more clearly, others on deck exclaimed as well.

"Yes, it is there to welcome us, my clever one. Do you wish to change the subject?"

"No, but what of my cousins in New York? I am to be with them. My cousin Janek has already found a job for me, working with him."

"In a factory, Zosia. Working many hours a day, harder than you did at home. Is this why you came to America? Come with me, to Chicago."

"To work in a factory there. . ."

"Yes, maybe for a little while. But Zosia, we are now in the land of opportunity, and I am a man who takes advantage of opportunity. You, moja droga, will stay at home and raise our beautiful children."

"Yes," said Sofia, "the land of opportunity." She wondered how many children he had in mind, what kind of house. But she only smiled at Wladyslaw, who towered magnificently above her, his steel gray eyes peering intently into her own, his thick thatch of sandy-colored hair tossing jauntily in the breeze.

"And I will get an education, Zosia," Wladyslaw continued. This was something that stirred Sofia's soul. She herself was an educated woman, having completed four years at the church school in Niedzieliska, and Wladyslaw had been a student in secondary school when the threat of conscription into the Prussian army had sealed his decision to emigrate. "There are great universities in Chicago," he continued, obviously encouraged by the interest he discerned on her uplifted face.

"University?" Marriage to a man who had attended university was something to which she had never dared aspire. "Anyone could go to university in this country?"

"Yes, in America, this can happen. In America, anything can happen. I will become a doctor. Or, maybe, my little one, a professor. How would you like that? To be married to a professor? I shall grow a long beard, to show myself as a man of distinction."

"Oh, Wladyslaw," Sofia laughed softly. "How you dream."

"This is the land of dreams. Share my dream with me. What do you say?"

11

Chapter One

Jadzia, Niedzieliska, Poland

April, 1941

"Ouch, too tight!"

"Well, you want to look beautiful, don't you?" taunted Apolonya. She secured the thick chestnut-colored braid she held in her hand with a tiny scrap of satin ribbon, much faded from its original crimson. Then she lifted the heavy braids with one hand, pointing with the other toward Jadzia's distorted reflection in the old dresser mirror in Jadzia's grandmother's bedroom. "Are you sure you don't want these in a crown? They would look much more attractive."

"Not today," responded Jadzia, eager for release from Apolonya's hands. Normally Apolonya, her best friend in all of Niedzieliska, was a gentle hairdresser, despite the challenges presented by the thickness and obstinate curl of Jadzia's tresses. And most days Jadzia loved nothing more than to give herself over to Apolonya's ministrations of brushing and combing and styling. Other holidays Jadzia would request a crown—that most elegant hairstyle, with thick braids woven into an intricate circle around the head and decorated with colorful ribbons. But this Easter, it was as if the whole country's mood could be felt through the roughness of her friend's hands.

"Does your family have enough for dinner?" Jadzia ventured. Few families in Niedzieliska, Jadzia knew, would experience the traditional Polish Easter of years past, with trays heaped with hams and sausages, baskets of carefully etched eggs, several types of pastries, and the traditional lamb molded of butter gracing the table. Yesterday, when the women of the village had brought their baskets of holiday food to the church for Father Jozef's blessing, only the most meager and coarse foodstuffs were on display: a loaf of rye bread, an egg or two, a cabbage, potatoes, perhaps a small slab of bacon. But still, no one in the village was starving—at least not yet.

"Yes, we will eat." The firm set of Apolonya's jaw discouraged further discussion of this topic. As Apolonya turned to finish her own preparations for the day, slipping an old white muslin dress over her head, Jadzia noticed how the dress, though several inches shorter than local fashion dictated and much yellowed from many washings, still slipped easily over Apolonya's slim shoulders and hips. Like a yearling deer's, Apolonya's growth had been concentrated in her extremities: her long, slim legs and arms had become willowy. With white/gold tresses now bound in a crown of braids, she looked to Jadzia like an angel, albeit one wearing a somewhat tattered and faded robe. But what was bothering her so much today?

"Have you heard anything from your brothers?" Jadzia asked.

Apolonya frowned, raising one eyebrow suspiciously. "You saw Alfons and Gienek yesterday, I haven't heard a word about Jan or Tadeusz since I was a little girl, and I imagine that Jozef and Pawel are either in England or fighting somewhere in France." She added through her teeth, "You do remember that I have no other brother."

Jadzia tried to look as though she were paying serious attention to the buttons she was fastening on the bodice of her dress. "Yes, I remember. I guess I was thinking about Jozef." Jadzia's whole family had supported the decision of Apolonya's mother to disown Antek, her next oldest brother, who had been recruited by the German army, and to dictate that his name never be mentioned again. As always, any thought of Antek—of his blonde hair, his tall slim body—made Jadzia's heart skip a beat.

Still, Jadzia thought, looking at Apolonya's downcast eyes and the set of her jaw, it must be difficult for her friend; even if she never spoke of Antek, did she no longer think of him and wonder where he was, if he was well? She could imagine no offence grievous enough to cause her parents to disown her own brothers, Marek and Stasiu, or to forbid her to speak their names ever again.

Jadzia sat on one of the family's two remaining chairs to fasten the laces of her boots. When she had brought the chair into her grandmother's room, she had looked with longing at the changes in the sitting room. The room had been stripped of most of what had given it distinction. *Tata* had had to sell Mama's china service early in the war. The china cabinet had looked barren without its display of plates lavishly decorated in delicate pink roses, but then the china cabinet itself had been sold just two months later, along with the long cherry table and most of the chairs. Mama's shrine to the Black Madonna of Czestochowa still remained, but now just one candle placed on a tin plate glowed dimly before it.

Still, her family was far luckier than most. They were together, still in their home. They had enough to eat and were able to gather sufficient firewood to keep warm. They would be farming this year as always, and although the sight of German soldiers patrolling the streets in town was alarming, very little in their area had truly changed in the two months since Herr Mittenberg had commanded the residents of Niedzieliska to gather in the town square. She and Apolonya had whispered their fears about the reason for this summons during the two hours the villagers were forced to wait for Mittenberg's arrival. They had huddled together in a sharp breeze from the north, their desire to stamp their feet against the cold thwarted by inches of mud created by an uncharacteristic February thaw. Jadzia had feared deportations or perhaps an execution: rumors about such occurrences happening more frequently in other villages had circulated for weeks before.

Her greatest fear that day had been for her *babcia*, who seemed to think that advanced age or her status in the village would exempt her from recriminations for speaking against the Germans. True, *Babcia* had only spoken to a few people, but Jadzia knew that in any foreign occupation, no one outside immediate family or dearest friends should be trusted.

And she had had other reasons for concern. Her grandmother's comings and goings were always erratic: *Babcia* was the town's midwife, and babies seldom came exactly when they were expected. But often in the past months, *Babcia* had been gone for hours, even overnight, at times when no baby had been born in the village or surrounding countryside. And what of the six loaves of bread that Mama had made two weeks ago? Later that evening, when Jadzia had searched for a crust for Cesar, their ancient hound, all six loaves had vanished.

Finally Herr Mittenberg, flanked by several soldiers, had strode into their midst, a vision of German military couture. His polished boots and long leather coat, fashionably cut to show just three inches of his breeches, were impeccable, despite the cold mud that spattered everyone else's attire. His ever-present iron cross shone over the closed collar of his tunic, and a peaked visor covered what the villagers who had seen him hatless knew was a rapidly balding pate. Despite his short stature and tendency toward portliness, he carried himself with the arrogance of a man who considered himself among inferiors.

Father Jozef, the only man in the village learned enough to speak German fluently, had translated. Mittenberg harangued the crowd interminably about their shortcomings: food that had been hidden, hesitation that signaled reluctance in following orders, a general lack of respect sensed by his soldiers. He then proceeded to nail on the church door his one-page directive to the people of Neidzieliska, expounding further on its commands and warning of grave consequences to anyone who dared ignore them:

26 February 1941
To: Polish people of Niedzieliska
From: Hans Mittenberg, Representative
*   General-Gouvernement of Galicia Province*

These directives are to serve as a reminder to the Polish people of Niedzieliska of their duties and responsibilities to the General-Gouvernement and its representatives.

All citizens of Niedzieliska are in all matters under the sovereign authority of the provisional government. All orders given by Director Hans Mittenberg or any of his representatives are to be followed immediately. Failure to do so will result in immediate death.

All citizens over the age of 12 are to carry with them at all times proper identification, which will be produced at any time it is requested by any authority of the provisional government or the military. Failure to do so will result in immediate arrest.

No citizen shall have on his person or in his abode any of the following banned items: any firearm or any other item deemed to be useful as a weapon; any radio or radio equipment; any anti-German written material, or any material which was issued by or supports any supposed claims of legitimacy by any government body other than the General-Gouvernement, or any material written in any language but Polish or German. Discovery of such items will lead to immediate arrest.

No citizen shall assist any Jew by delivering foodstuffs or other materials to the local Jewish community or by attempting to hide Jews or assist in their illegal exportation to other countries. This behavior is considered a seriously anti-social act against the Fatherland and will result in immediate death.

While many villagers initially feared this directive signaled more difficult times ahead, that day was the last most of them saw Mittenberg, who melted back into the town hall where he had taken residence to wait out the end of the Polish winter. Within days even the most fearful villagers had returned to their old ways, paying little attention to their occupiers. For most of the adults, this was just one more among a series of occupations, just one more foreign government with which to contend.

"Do you need some help with that necklace?" asked Apolonya, seeing Jadzia lift a string of amber beads the color of filtered sunlight out of her grandmother's oak jewelry box.

"Yes. *Babcia* said I could wear her amber beads to church today." Jadzia held the beads up toward a sunbeam streaming through the room's east window. The beads glowed, now lightening to the color of butter where the sunlight caught their translucence. *Babcia* had offered to sell them at market, but since they were her last remaining keepsake from her own mother, Jadzia's father had refused to allow her to part with them.

As Apolonya bent to fasten the necklace, Jadzia caught the reflection of their faces in the mirror, Apolonya's gracefully tilted above her own shoulder. At eighteen, the girls' appearances contrasted even more than they had as children. Jadzia had the dusky coloring of Tartar invaders of centuries earlier: heavy chestnut braids framing a round face with dimples punctuating each cheek. Skin the color of weak tea with milk. Her eyes were her most outstanding feature: sable brown, and generally flashing with mischief or delight. At their corners, the skin crinkled from her almost constant smile.

Apolonya displayed the coloring of Nordic invaders of centuries earlier: braids of fine, pale yellow, the color of corn silk in late summer, crowning a narrow face with a delicately pointed chin. Skin the color of cream with pale splashes of damask rose on high cheekbones. Blue eyes that rivaled the clarity and sparkle of the water that danced in the nearby stream. Apolonya's beauty was angelic, but Jadzia's was no less charming in its earthy appeal.

But today dark circles shadowed Apolonya's eyes.

"Apolonya, did you not sleep again last night?" she asked, turning to her friend and taking both slender white hands in her own. "Did you have another dream?"

"No, it was nothing," answered Apolonya, averting her eyes from Jadzia's.

"Tell me," begged Jadzia, pulling at her friend's hands. "Perhaps together we can interpret it."

Apolonya had developed a reputation in the village for second sight. She was far from singular in that respect, as many of the women of Niedzieliska believed they could predict the future from their dreams. But Jadzia's mother had scoffed at these beliefs, calling them foolish old country superstitions.

"*Pani* Levandowska dreams of three dead crows," Jadzia's mother had said scornfully to her daughter, "and within a month *Pan* Kapusta, *Pani* Gontarska, and *Pan* Boblak are all dead. 'Ah,' says the village, '*Pani* Levandowska has second sight.' No one stops to think that they are all in their 80's and that *Pani* Gontarska and *Pan* Boblak have been sick in their beds for months. No, they wish to see it as second sight—as if anyone could really tell what will happen in the future."

But hadn't Apolonya dreamed of water flooding a coastal shore—despite the fact that she had never seen the ocean—just days before the German invasion of Poland? Hadn't she dreamed of the Przybyla family floating in the sky the very night before they had all tragically burned to death in a house fire? Jadzia looked more closely into her friend's eyes, now understanding that a sleepless night was the cause of Apolonya's peevishness.

"It's nothing. Really nothing." Apolonya turned away.

But Jadzia persisted, and finally her friend relented. "I saw a dove fly from a cave in a deep green mountain," Apolonya revealed.

"Anything else?"

"It flew into a bright red sky."

"Like a sky at sunset?"

"No. Darker. Thicker. A sky almost the color of blood."

Jadzia shivered, but continued. "But the dove? How was it flying? Did it look like it had been startled?"

Looking up, Apolonya tilted her head as if to see the dream reappearing high on the bedroom walls. Finally, she answered, "No. It flew normally, even gently, then circled twice and flew off."

Jadzia considered the dream for a few moments before offering her interpretation. "That sounds like a dream of good omens," she finally responded. "The dove is always the symbol of peace. Perhaps your dream means that the war will be over soon. Now that the Americans are in the war…"

"Yes, yes, your wonderful Americans. Honestly, Jadzia, do you really think they can help us?" Apolonya turned to the mirror to fuss with an already perfect braid.

"But in the last letter I got from Eva…"

"Of course—from your cousin," Apolonya scoffed, turning to face Jadzia. "She must have given you good counsel. I'm sure Roosevelt speaks to her at least weekly."

Jadzia began rummaging through a dresser drawer, more to hide the tears forming in the corners of her eyes than to actually search for anything. Why, she wondered, was Apolonya always so critical whenever she mentioned Eva, her cousin in Chicago, with whom she had shared a lively correspondence since they were children.

But soon a warm, comforting arm enveloped her shoulders, drawing her close. "Jadzia, forgive me. That was mean of me. I'm probably just tired. I blame that dream I had last night. It disturbed me so much. The red in the sky—it was frightening. I could not go back to sleep."

Jadzia quickly brushed nascent tears from her cheeks. There was nothing to forgive. Everyone in the village was on edge these days. Tilting her head in thought, she responded, "Perhaps the red stands for the Russians. That could be disturbing or promising. It all depends on who you talk to."

If the Germans were defeated, some villagers argued that Poland's best course would be to ally closely with the Russians, with whom they at least shared a common Slavic ancestry. Others cherished the dream of an independent Poland, although their short adventure in independence during the time between the Great War and the invasion from Germany, fewer than twenty years, had been disastrous.

"If your dream is political, Apolonya, it probably won't affect us at all," Jadzia continued. "Nothing ever happens in Niedzieliska—we're too remote. We're in the middle of a war and we hardly even feel it—at least those of us who stay here. We'll go on, farming our land, bringing children into the world, getting old, finally dying here."

"You sound as if that were a bad thing." Apolonya's raised eyebrows showed her disagreement.

"I wouldn't mind leaving this village—seeing what's out in the world."

"Two of my brothers left for America when I was just a little girl, and they never came back."

"Well, maybe that tells you something," Jadzia asserted with great conviction. "Maybe your brothers found something much better out there."

"What could be better than to be with your family and the people you grew up with?" Apolonya asked, passion creasing her forehead. "What could be better than to stay on the land your family has worked for generations? Going anywhere else, even to America, where the streets are paved with gold, is not for me. This is where I will stay. I will never leave Niedzieliska."

"Apolonya, are you forgetting? There is a war. I don't believe that all the talk about deportations to labor camps and conscriptions is only rumors. Sometimes people do not have a choice."

"Jadzia, people always have a choice."

The sound of Jadzia's mother calling the girls to church forestalled any further interpretation of dreams. "Ah, you will be the most beautiful girls at Resurrection Mass," Bronislawa exclaimed as they stepped out of *Babcia's* bedroom into the warmth of the sitting room, where new fire, blessed by Father Josef, blazed in the fireplace. Yesterday they had all attended the Holy Saturday ceremony, praying at the site of the churchyard bonfire soaring to the heavens. Then Marek and Stasiu had hurriedly brought new fire back to the house on a flaming piece of wood, replacing the old fires in the fireplace and cook stove which had been extinguished to mark the end of another church year.

Now clad in the finest apparel they owned, Jadzia's family and Apolonya stepped out into a beautiful spring day. Winter had been unusually harsh and long-lasting, dragging well into the first weeks of March, almost too cold and blustery for anyone to bear. But the celebration of the feast of St. Jozef on March 19th had brought a sudden spike of temperature into the 40's, warm enough to coax the daffodils and crocuses out of the hard ground and to bring fresh, pale green buds to the lindens and willows. The oaks would bud last, but even their branches looked supple and alive, ready to meet the spring. On this 5th day of April, nature burst with new life.

They met Apolonya's mother and brothers by the well the two families shared and began the pleasant walk to the church. Alfons, at seventeen, and Gienek, at fifteen, had grown into handsome young men, but neither was too mature to tease Apolonya about the care their sister had obviously taken in her appearance, speculating about which young man, of the few still remaining in the village, was the most likely object of her attention.

"Ach," answered Apolonya, tossing her head jauntily. "What young man in this village even deserves my attention? Clumsy Janek Jablonski? Foolish Marek Bednarz? Tadeusz Bidas, who cares more about his cows than about girls?" Jadzia laughed her agreement.

"I wouldn't be so proud if I were you, Apolonya," warned Stasiu. "Tomorrow's *smigus dyngus*, and proud girls wind up the wettest."

"That's a stupid custom," complained Jadzia, who had always found silly the Easter Monday tradition of village boys waking the girls at dawn with cold spring water dashed into their faces. "It must have been invented by foolish boys."

"But don't forget," reminded Apolonya. "We get to pay them back the same way Tuesday morning."

Soon the banter stopped as the men separated themselves into one group that walked ahead, speaking of their animals and their crops, discussing when to plow, when to plant, and the women, walking more slowly behind, caught up on village events, discussing the progress of babies newly born over the winter and reminiscing about recently departed elders. Before Jadzia could believe it possible, she saw the spire of St. Adalbert's rising above the pines and spruces that shaded the cemetery behind the church.

They entered the church respectfully, all crossing themselves with holy water from the freshly filled font in the vestibule of the church. Reaching their customary pew near the front of the church, each genuflected deeply before entering: first the girls, Jadzia and Apolonya, followed by the adults, and then finally the four boys, who took their position closest to the aisle. The heady scent of early lilacs, soon to be replaced by the more pungent scent of incense from Father Jozef's censor, filled the church.

As the priest and his attendants solemnly marched up the aisle, the congregation's song of praise and joy reverberated throughout the humble building, glorifying its stucco walls, its rough pine pews, its stone floor, its four simple glass windows, its pine altar covered in pure white cloths delicately embroidered by the women of the parish.

Father Jozef's sermon, as expected, focused on the new life promised by the Resurrection. And as also expected on a day when every parishioner who was not bedridden would attend Mass, the old priest spoke at great length, recounting familiar stories of miraculous cures and salvation from heaven. Jadzia, disappointed, had hoped he would speak of the German occupation, of what they could do to resurrect their own sense of hope for the future. She expressed her boredom by engaging Apolonya in one of the quiet finger games of their childhood, until a stern glance from her mother quickly ended that diversion.

Before long, the Mass was ended, the last "*Et cum spiritu tuo*" was sung, and Father Jozef, swinging his censor, began to lead the recessional out of church. Jadzia and Apolonya chatted amiably while awaiting their turn to leave.

But what was delaying the recessional at the door of the church? Why the raised voices, the prickling sense of alarm rolling from the church door back to the altar? Whose were those louder voices? And then why, suddenly, was the church deathly quiet?

Jadzia grasped Apolonya's hand, craning to see over the heads and backs of her family and neighbors, hoping for a glimpse of what they saw beyond the sunlight streaming into the church from the open door. Slowly the recessional resumed, but more tentatively now. Parishioners looked to each other for support, parents held their children near, as the group, acting as one unit, stepped slowly forward.

It was not until Jadzia reached the door of the church that she saw the reason for the alarm. Taking up a large area of the village square were two immense, dark green trucks, their open backs facing the church door; to the left of the trucks stood Herr Mittenberg and perhaps ten of his troops. While Mittenberg postured, gesturing wildly to direct family groups toward the ends of a long line formed perpendicular to the church, Jadzia could see immediately that another man was in charge.

This man's tightly fitted uniform was black, his iron cross and other military insignia gleaming white on his lapels and the collar of his tunic. He seemed to be speaking in confidence to Father Jozef, who looked as though he had aged twenty years in his short recessional march. The two men were surrounded by a dozen soldiers similarly attired in black, none of whom Jadzia recognized, all holding rifles or machine guns pointed at a forty-five degree angle toward the ground.

Jadzia grasped Apolonya's hand even more tightly as they stepped into the bright sunlight of the courtyard. She turned to look at her grandmother—were all these men here to take *Babcia* away? Had she been caught doing something forbidden...those missing loaves? Then, suddenly fearful of attracting attention to the older woman, Jadzia looked away, trying to focus her gaze on an empty space in the courtyard, trying to ignore the roiling of her stomach and the quivering of her knees.

Father Jozef coughed several times before speaking, first in a tight, raspy voice, then more steadily. "Everyone," he said, "you must get into your family groups immediately and form a straight line along the road. Yes, yes, like this..." he gestured, as villagers shuffled to arrange themselves as ordered. Apolonya gave Jadzia's hand one hard squeeze before dropping it to join her mother and brothers in a section of the line several family units away.

Once the villagers were arranged as ordered, the priest, looking carefully at the long line that spanned the whole west side of the courtyard, returned to the black-clad stranger. They began conversing quietly once more in German as almost the entire population of Niedzieliska stared silently at them.

Finally, Father Jozef spoke again. "Please, everyone, do exactly as these men say. Commander Mueller and one of his officers will step up to each of you. If he touches your shoulder, you must take two steps forward. If not, you are to remain standing where you are." Villagers looked at each other, and some low, quiet mumbling could be heard.

"No, no," pleaded Father Jozef. "Everyone must be quiet!" The villagers stood mute as Commander Mueller began inspecting the line from its north end, tapping the shoulders of most of the young who quietly stepped forward, but passing most of their parents and grandparents.

All commenced efficiently until Mueller tapped the shoulder of a young boy standing two family units north of Jadzia's family. Jadzia turned at the sudden cry, piercing in the dead quiet of the square, of *Pani* Oslowska, who reached out, grabbing the shoulder of her youngest son, Jan, who was obediently stepping forward.

"No, no," she cried, "he's young. Only ten. He's tall. He looks older."

Almost too quickly for anyone to see, the officer standing with Commander Mueller raised his rifle into the air, smashing *Pani* Oslowska's forearm with the heavy wooden butt of the weapon. Her scream of pain was drowned by the Commander's loud command for silence, and Jadzia looked in horror as *Pan* Oslowski, taking his wife's limp, bloody arm in one hand and placing his other hand as gently as he could over her mouth, begging her to be silent, nodded acquiescence at the Commander, who continued on.

The Commander passed Jadzia's parents, grandmother, and brother Stasiu, but tapped Marek and Jadzia, who stepped forward immediately. Jadzia could feel rather than hear the low moan leaving her mother's body, could sense her mother's heart reaching out to her own. She glanced only slightly to the right when Mueller reached Apolonya's family, who stood near the end of the long line, and hated herself almost immediately for the sense of relief she felt when she saw Apolonya and Alfons step forward. At least wherever she was going, she would not be leaving her dearest friend behind.

For one quick moment she thought of what else she would be leaving behind—her family, of course, and friends. The cottage that had been her home her whole life. The barn animals, and old Cesar who, she realized with a start, she would probably never see again. The little pine box that held Eva's letters. The box! That might yet be saved for her return to the village. She turned to tell Stasiu to hide the box, to bury it under the barn, but a stern look from the soldier standing nearest to her stopped her motion immediately. Better to do nothing that would call attention to herself and her family.

The selection completed, Father Jozef and Commander Mueller conferred for just a minute before the priest confirmed what the villagers all suspected—that those selected were to proceed in an orderly fashion into the open trucks. Starting from the north end of the line, many of the young men and women of Niedzieliska, looking back longingly but for just one second, parted from their families and friends and from the only lives they had ever known. They were separated again into two lines and jostled up the step stools behind each of the waiting trucks into the darkness within.

"Oh, please," prayed Jadzia silently, "please let Apolonya be in this truck with me. Please let her be going wherever I'm going," as one of the soldiers stationed by the nearer truck grabbed her arm to escort her into the darkness within.

Her silent prayer was cut short by a sudden shout that froze movement in the whole square. "*Halt, halt, Fraulein!*" Mueller screamed, and all eyes turned as one to see what he glared at so intently. Jadzia too looked, and to her horror, saw the slim frame of Apolonya as she walked deliberately across the square, directly toward her home. The bright sun in a cloudless blue sky threw a shimmering frame around her white/gold hair, her long graceful neck and the white muslin dress as she walked.

"No, Apolonya!" cried Jadzia, but her voice was drowned by the Commander's final order, "*Fraulein, halt!*" Apolonya continued to walk, appearing to not even hear the command.

Commander Mueller nodded to the soldier standing nearest to him, who lifted his rifle and pointed it straight at the white figure, now walking steadily just past the center of the town square. The sound of the gun's discharge, a single shot, erased any other sound, indeed any other thought, within the square.

Chapter Two

Jadzia, Niedzieliska, Poland

August, 1933

10 lipca, 1933

Moja Droga kuzynko Jadwigo!

   Wszystkiego najlepszego z okazji Imienin. Spodziewam się, że otrzymasz ten list jeszcze przed 18 sierpnia. Ty mnie nie znasz. Ja jestem Twoją kuzynką Eveliną, córką Sofi, która jest siostrą Twojej matki.

Jadzia Czarnecka burst from a small stand of white birch, waving a pale blue envelope as she ran toward the old stone well the Zadoras shared with the Czarnecki family, their nearest neighbors. "Apolonya! Apolonya! Look what I have!"

"Jadzia, you startled me! I almost dropped the bucket. What is it? Why are you so excited?"

"A letter from my cousin in America. It came today!" Jadzia suppressed her enthusiasm long enough to help her dearest friend pull the heavy wooden bucket to the top of the well. Apolonya's thin arms looked too frail for the task at hand, but her almost wraithlike form disguised strength comparable to that of her sturdier friend.

"Be careful then," Apolonya warned, sloshing water over the side of the bucket as she detached it from its iron hook. "You don't want to get your letter wet. I didn't know you had a cousin in America."

"Yes. Three cousins. Two boys and a girl. And Evelina, the girl, is almost exactly my age. Her mama, my mama's sister, moved to America years before we were born. And now Evelina has written to me!"

The girls were dressed similarly in long-sleeved, simple white smocks that stopped mid-calf over worn leather boots, but otherwise they were a study in contrast: Apolonya tall, slim, and blonde, with pale, almost translucent skin; Jadzia several inches shorter but a few pounds heavier, with a dusky complexion and dark hair and eyes her maternal grandmother attributed to some ancestor from the ancient Tartar invasions. Carefully placing the bucket at her feet and wiping her hands on the hem of her skirt, Apolonya reached for the envelope, respectfully turning it to look at either side before focusing on the writing on the front. "Your cousin has a neat hand," she complimented, "but very different from Polish writing. And such funny stamps. Shall I take it out of the envelope, Jadzia, or do you wish to read it to me?"

"Let me read it to you," responded Jadzia, relishing the pleasure of hearing the letter's words out loud as she shared them with her friend. "I only read it once before I came here. I was so excited to show you." Receiving the envelope back, she positioned herself primly on the well, then removed the letter and carefully smoothed it against the skirt of her smock before reading:

10 July 1933

My dear cousin Jadwiga!

Happy Name Day. I hope this letter comes to you before 18 August. You do not know me. I am your cousin Evelina, daughter of your mother's sister Sofia. I am nine years old like you. My mama talks of your mama all the time, and misses her very much. She says that when they were little girls, they were great friends. I thought that maybe, in letters, we could become friends as well.

First, hello from Mama to Aunt Bronislawa and all your family. Mama wants you to know she thinks of all of you and prays for you every day. Even if I never hear from you, I will from now on think of you and pray for you every day as well.

I have two brothers. Mama says that is just like you. My older brother Henryk works at a big job in the city with my Tata, and Andrzej is just a little boy, only three years old. He is a very handsome and smart little boy, and Mama trusts me to take care of him during the day when she is busy in the kitchen or on Monday when she does laundry. I also take him to the park sometimes.

In the fall I will be in the fifth grade, and my favorite subjects are reading and spelling. Half of every school day we study in English, so we can become good citizens of this country and help our parents with the government papers, and also to tell them all the news that is not in the Polish language paper. My teacher last year was Sister Athanasia, and she said that mathematics is very important, but I do not like that subject very much.

I wish you a Happy Name Day for 25 August—Mama says that is your day. How wonderful that our Name Days are only one week apart! How do you celebrate your Name Day? We always have cake and flowers on my mine. And sometimes, if I have been very good, Tata will take us on an adventure. One year he took us on the Milwaukee Avenue trolley all the way to the end of the line, to have a picnic in the beautiful forest that is there. Mama says the forest reminds her of Poland.

But this year I have a special wish—to see the Century of Progress. It is a world's fair to celebrate the 100th birthday of Chicago. I have heard of many wonderful things there—the Enchanted Island, with many rides, especially the Sky Ride way up in the air. I think that would be very exciting. There is a Belgian Village and a temple with many wonderful things from China. There are even very brave men who wrestle with ALLIGATORS (please excuse the English word. Mama does not know how it is said in Polish.) I myself have never seen an alligator. If we go, I will ask for a penny to buy you a picture from the fair.

Please write to me when you can and tell me about your life in Poland. May God be with you and your family this day and always.

Your loving cousin,

Evelina (but please call me Eva, because we are family) Bialek

Jadzia paused, looking toward Apolonya for some response. But Apolonya seemed lost in thought, the wonders of this letter obviously being too much for her to handle all at once. Finally she spoke. "What is an *alligator?*"

"I don't know. I hoped you would. Perhaps an animal?"

"Maybe a man. Who would wrestle with an animal?"

"Who knows? In America...But I shall ask her when I write back to her."

"No, you can't do that. What would she think of us? She might think we were fools." Jadzia's brow furrowed and her smile faded at her friend's criticism. Sometimes Apolonya could be so harsh—but then, thought Jadzia, she was usually right. What if Evelina began to think of her as nothing but a foolish farm girl—then they might never become friends.

"Your cousin sounds very pious," Apolonya soon added, seeming to respond to the concern she saw in her friend's downcast eyes.

"Yes," Jadzia responded, smiling shyly. "She goes to church school just like us."

"Mama says all Americans are godless," Apolonya contested.

This was too much for Jadzia. "Perhaps your mama does not know everything," she blurted out, immediately regretting her harsh words upon seeing the crestfallen look in Apolonya's eyes. Feeling contrite, she changed the subject. "My cousin wishes for me to call her Eva, so I'll ask her to call me Jadzia. That way, we'll become friends even sooner."

Apolonya didn't answer. Jadzia wondered if Apolonya was jealous of her new friend. Apolonya could be so difficult to fathom at times, so easily offended and hurt. She wore her heart on her shoulder. But Jadzia was too excited today to worry overly long about her friend's feelings.

"Think of how different Evelina's life must be," Jadzia finally said. "Taking a ride in the sky. Traveling with her family on a trolley. Having a brother and father with big jobs in the city." She looked dreamily into space, her mind suddenly several thousand miles away. "It must be wonderful to be an American and to be so rich."

"Poland has rich people too, and big cities with jobs and trolleys."

"True. But will we ever see them?"

Before Apolonya could answer, Jadzia heard her friend's name being called in the strident, impatient tone they both recognized so well.

"Oh, the water. Mama is making *ogorki*. She needed this water right away." Apolonya quickly bent to lift the heavy bucket. Folding the letter and placing it in a pocket of her smock, Jadzia grabbed the bucket along with Apolonya, and the two, waddling duck-like in their attempt to spill as little as possible while moving as quickly as they could, followed the narrow path around a patch of black currant shrubs, soon arriving at the little clearing which was the homestead of the Zadora family.

"Ach, I should have known," huffed Danuta Zadora at the sight of Jadzia. She stood in the narrow doorway of their split-board cabin, its mortar chipped and dingy, its thatched roof rising steeply above her. "Were you two gossiping while my *ogorki* are spoiling in this heat?" Jadzia and Apolonya could smell the brine—vinegar and dill—thirty feet from the cabin door. Closer, they could feel heat emanating from within.

Pani Zadora stepped back from the open door into the kitchen, sharply raising her hand as her daughter passed before her, then dropping it, either reconsidering her intended action or simply too tired to deliver the blow. Apolonya ducked from long habit, then struggled to place the bucket on the chipped wooden table next to the cast iron stove. Each grate held an immense iron pot in which dill brine bubbled furiously. "Mama, Jadzia was reading me a letter she received from her cousin, all the way from America," she offered in explanation.

"Hurry," said *Pani* Zadora, ignoring her daughter's news, "and wash that last bushel of cucumbers. Jadwiga, since you're here anyway, make yourself useful and fill those pots with water." *Pani* Zadora returned to her task of stuffing cucumbers into jars. Though not yet forty, her hair, thin and gray, dangled from the scarf she wore tied at the base of her neck, and her faded print housedress sagged over slumped shoulders. Apolonya was the sixth of her seven living children, her only daughter; five other children lay quietly in the graveyard of St. Adalbert's church, along with *Pan* Zadora, who had died in the last war. Danuta had not remarried: no bachelor or widower in the village had stepped forward to shoulder the burden of the Zadora family.

As Jadzia ladled fresh water from the bucket into the pots, she covertly glanced around the one room that comprised the Zadora household, so different from her own, meticulously kept home. Pallets, some jumbled with dingy gray linens, haphazardly lined the walls. Old battered boots lay tossed in a corner, and the litter from the morning meal had not yet been discarded. Jadzia worked in silence, following the example set by Apolonya and her mother.

As the last of the dill and the cucumbers were stuffed into jars and *Pani* Zadora began to carefully ladle the brine to cover them, Apolonya quietly, almost shyly, asked, "Mama, do you know what an *alligator* is?"

"All-i-ga-tor?" Danuta asked, carefully sounding out the word syllable by syllable.

"Yes. In Jadzia's letter from America, her cousin wrote of going to the fair to see some men who wrestled alligators."

"Ach, America." Danuta almost spit out the words. America and its wonders held little charm for her, particularly since her two oldest sons had disappeared three years earlier, leaving word with their brother that they were going to Bremen, and from there to America. No one had heard from them since.

Finally returning to her daughter's question, Danuta answered, doing nothing to hide her disgust. "An alligator...it is like a bear. Foolish Americans have nothing to do but play with bears. They are a godless people, Americans. The less we have to do with them, the better."

But as she looked at the many jars of freshly-made pickles, Danuta seemed to relax a bit, her shoulders losing their rigidity as she stuffed a loose tendril of hair back under her scarf. "Thank you for your help, *dziewczyno*," she said, a satisfied look on her face. "I would never have finished so soon without you. Would you like some *kolaczki*?"

"Yes, Mama," Apolonya answered, while Jadzia nodded her assent. "But Mama, even more than that, I would like to go swimming in the river with Jadzia this afternoon. May I?"

"I don't know. How about your chores? The chicken coop?"

"Cleaned, Mama. And the chickens are fed."

"The vegetable patch?"

"Weeded. And I picked a full bushel of onions."

"Gienek..."

"Playing in the woods with Alfons, Mama. You know that now he is six he wants nothing to do with me."

"I'll need more water."

"We'll go right to the well. Then may I go?"

"Be careful. Remember the Pokrzyk boy drowned there."

"We will, Mama. We will be very careful," Apolonya promised, turning away from her mother. Jadzia tried not to smile as she observed her friend's eyes rolling toward the ceiling. The Pokrzyk boy, who had been only three when he wandered away from his home, had died many years before she or Apolonya were born, and he had died in the spring, when their stream, a tributary of the great Vistula River, had rushed full force toward its destination. Now, in August, it lazed its way gently toward the river, pooling in shallow areas on either bank. Still, that unfortunate child yet served as an instrument of warning for every mother in Niedzieliska.

Hours later, winded from their time spent swimming in the stream and splashing each other in its pools, Jadzia and Apolonya lay on the bank of the stream, gazing at the late afternoon clouds, discerning shapes of animals in their billowing masses. "There, that one. A bear," said Apolonya, pointing to the right.

"The dark one? Next to that little bit of cloud?"

"No. To the right and below. Do you see it?"

"A bear?"

"Yes, lying on its back, with its paws up in the air. Do you see it now?"

"Well, all right, a little bit. Or maybe it's an alligator," offered Jadzia.

Apolonya's sigh suggested impatience with yet another mention of the letter from America.

"Apolonya, wouldn't you like to go to America some day?" Jadzia persisted, confused at her friend's lack of interest in a subject that had so captured her own imagination.

"Perhaps." But Apolonya's response was anything but enthusiastic.

"Think of all you could see there, and all you could do."

"I like it here. There are things to see and do here, you know."

"Silly, if you went to America, you could always come back to Niedzieliska." Immediately, Jadzia wished she could take those words back, knowing the Zadora sensitivity to talk of travel to America. "I'm sorry. I didn't mean…"

"Don't be. I hardly remember my brothers. I was only six when they left. And it's not as if I don't have more than enough brothers still here, anyway." Jadzia knew how much Apoloyna's older brother Antek teased her, and how much time she had to spend caring for her younger brothers. "So it's not that my brothers somehow disappeared there. It's just that America is so far away, and so strange. I like being here, living with everyone I know."

Jadzia could not understand her friend's reluctance to look beyond Niedzieliska. Apolonya had so little here, nothing but work and difficult brothers and harsh words and hard slaps from a mother who did not appreciate her. Then thoughts of *Pani* Zadora reminded Jadzia of the package she had sent with the girls. Swimming always made Jadzia hungry; perhaps Apolonya's mother was not always so terrible after all. "Are you hungry for some *kolaczki?*" she asked, very pleased when Apolonya pulled out the package, wrapped in paper that contained the pastry and some plums. Relenting in her internal criticism of *Pani* Zadora, she added, "Your mama makes the best *kolaczki* in Niedzieliska."

"Thank you. And your mama, what did she say about your letter?"

"Mama was not home when *Tata* brought me the letter from town. She and *Babcia* are still at *Pani* Lesniak's house," Jadzia responded, choosing an apricot pastry from the selection Apolonya offered her.

"They left two days ago. Why so long?" questioned Apolonya, delicately biting into the prune *kolaczki* she had chosen for herself.

"Sometimes it takes a long time for a baby to come into the world." Jadzia's grandmother, Stella, was the region's premiere midwife. Bronislawa often accompanied her mother-in-law on midwifery visits, particularly when the labor was expected to be difficult.

"Still, three days is too long. Poor *Pani* Lesniak," added Apolonya, who still had nightmares about the night, six years ago, when her brother Gienek had been born. Her mother had screamed for hours. "Time to go back," she said, brushing some powdered sugar from Jadzia's cheek. "I need to help Mama with dinner."

The girls got up and retrieved their smocks from the sunny hill where they had left them to dry. They loved this little alcove they had found, with its own still pool, hidden within the shade of towering pines. Here, in their hideaway, apart from other children, they could swim free as fish, lie in the sun in just their underclothing or in nothing at all, and speak of their dreams in private.

As they walked along the stream bank toward the Zadora home, they heard the ruckus before they saw what was causing it. Apolonya's brother Antek was standing in the deepest part of the stream, holding a canvas bag high above his head, laughing. Tall and sturdy for his age, with thick blonde hair tousled in the breeze and clear slate blue eyes sparkling as brilliantly as the glints of water rushing about his hips, he shook the bag, then reached his arm backwards as though to fling it forward.

Gienek, a tow-headed miniature of his older brother, stood screaming on the bank, while Alfons was making tentative forays into the water, pulling back when the current tugged at him, then pushing forward again. The girls ran to Alfons, Apoloyna grabbing him just as he, too, was about to step into the stream.

Jadzia waded in to catch Gienek by the arm, pulling him back to the bank, while Apolonya hugged Alfons close to her. "What? What's happening?" she asked, wiping her brother's tear-streaked cheeks and runny nose with the hem of her smock.

Alfons fought her, trying to get back to the stream, but finally recognizing his sister's greater strength, cried out through his tears, "Bika's kittens! Bika's kittens!" He pointed at his brother Antek.

Apoloyna looked out to the center of the stream, where Antek stood, still laughing. Looking more closely at the bag he held, she now saw that it was alive with squirming motion. "Antek," she shouted. "Come here right now. Bring those kittens here!"

Antek laughed harder, plunging the bag into the stream as his brothers shrieked, holding it low in the water, then pulling it up over his head again. "Mama said to get rid of these."

"Not like this. And I'll talk to Mama. You come here right now, you devil!"

He only laughed harder. "Come and get me!" he challenged, drawing his upraised arm back, obviously preparing to fling the kittens into the current. The cries of the younger children pierced the air. Jadzia stood immobile, mesmerized by the scene being played out before her. Her own brothers never acted this way.

"*Pan* Holicki's shed!" Apolonya suddenly shouted. Miraculously, Antek's arm stopped mid-fling.

"What are you talking about?" he screamed back. He was not laughing now.

"You know exactly what I'm talking about. *Pan* Holicki lost his best rig in that fire."

"So? What is it to me?" But Antek was now striding through the current toward them, the bag held firmly in his hand. Reaching the bank, he tossed it to the ground, and out wobbled four tiny kittens, two orange, two black and white. Alfons and Gienek, released from their captors, rushed to scoop up two kittens each, cradling them, crying and whispering soft words into their wet fur. "You should mind your own business," Antek spit out to his sister.

"This *is* my business."

"Keep sticking your nose where it doesn't belong and it'll get punched someday," he muttered, turning his back on all of them and shuffling off into the forest.

Jadzia stood, silent, staring at the sister and brother. Apolonya: how brave she was. And Antek: how handsome.

Jadzia knew, even before stepping into her family's cottage, that her mother and grandmother were home. Somehow the cottage, even from the outside, looked different—more beautiful, more serene—when Mama and *Babcia* were there. Stepping in, she found her mother busy at the stove, her grandmother carefully wrapping the midwifery instruments before placing them into the pine chest that stood on the far wall.

"Ah, you're home." Bronislawa, a tall, strong woman with a long, narrow face, the kind some would call handsome rather than beautiful, bent to receive her daughter's kiss.

Jadzia then crossed the room to kiss her grandmother, whose lean frame was bent with fatigue, her normally neat bun now straggly with errant wisps of gray hair. "*Pani* Lesniak?" Jadzia asked, turning back to her mother.

"Doing well," responded Bronislawa.

"And the baby?"

"A boy. Very small and weak, but I think he will be all right. He came turned around. That is why we were away so long." Bronislawa turned to Stella, "Some tea, Mama?"

"No, I think I'll just rest for a while before dinner." Stella turned to go into the small room that was her own.

"Your grandmother worked miracles again today," said Bronislawa as the bedroom door closed. "She is very, very tired." As was the custom, Stella had moved into the home of her eldest son upon the death of her husband. She and her daughter-in-law had reacted contrary to custom, however, in that they had not begun their new living arrangement vying for power, resenting and envying, and then finally despising, each other. Rather, they had become dearest friends. For this, Stanislaw Czarnecki was the envy of all the men in the village.

By Niedzieliska standards, the Czarnecki home was almost a palace, with one large room for cooking, eating and relaxing and two tiny bedrooms for the adults. Jadzia had moved out of her parents' bedroom just two years ago, and now set a pallet up every evening in a corner of the big room, while Marek and Stasiu slept in the storage room on the east side of the house.

The sitting room was beautifully furnished, its heavy cherry furniture crafted by Jadzia's father and buffed to shiny perfection almost daily by her mother. The focal point of the room was an immense china cabinet her father had built which elegantly displayed her mother's pride, the floral-patterned china service with its delicate pink roses on a cream-colored background. This was used only on very special occasions, when their everyday tin ware would simply not do.

The cast iron stove was new, and Jadzia's brothers kept both the stone fireplace and the stove well-stocked with hardwood logs they had dried in the woodshed. The long dining table had been painted white to match the much smaller table, set off to one corner that held the family shrine. Here an intricately carved crucifix and an old, faded picture of the Black Madonna of Czestochowa stood, and blessed candles from the village church, St. Adalbert's, flickered at meal times and during dark evenings. Every day in the summer, a cut crystal vase held flowers freshly picked from the fields or the garden. Everything was tidy and sparkling clean, a testament to the care Jadzia's mother and grandmother took of all things that mattered to them—so different, Jadzia thought with pride, than the Zadora home.

"Mama, a letter came for me today, while you were gone. From Evelina."

"From your cousin in America?"

"Yes," Jadzia trilled, reaching into the pocket of her smock to retrieve the letter.

"How wonderful! What did she have to say? Is everything all right with Sofia's family?"

"Yes. *Ciotka* Sofia sends her love."

"Read it to me while I make dinner." Bronislawa opened a cupboard door and reached for the earthenware jar that held flour. "I think we must have *babka* tonight, to celebrate two safe deliveries."

"Two deliveries?"

"Yes: of little Piotr Lesniak and of your letter."

Jadzia laughed at her mother's cleverness, then began to read, stopping at that strange English word to ask if her mother knew the meaning of *alligator*. "Is it some kind of bear?" she asked.

"No, no. It's more like...well, I think we have nothing quite like it in Poland. But you know what a lizard is."

"Yes. We see them sometimes in the woods."

"It's like that, only much, much bigger. Sometimes more than three meters long. And with a green skin that's bumpy like a toad's. And very, very large teeth."

Jadzia shivered just thinking of such a monster. Then she said, disdainfully, "*Pani* Zadora said it was like a bear."

"Well, anyone can make a mistake."

"She could have said she didn't know. She didn't have to make up a lie. And she's so mean to Apolonya sometimes."

"You must try to understand, *moya droga*. *Pani* Zadora has had a very difficult life."

"Father Jozef says all life is difficult, that life is a 'vale of tears' that we must learn to bear."

"Perhaps. But for some people, things are much more difficult. Did you know that when Danuta and I were growing up, she was the prettiest girl in the village?" Jadzia looked skeptical. It would be hard to see *Pani* Zadora as anything but faded, tired and dejected. And loyalty told her that her own mother, Bronislawa, must have been the prettiest—wasn't she now the prettiest of all the mothers in the village?

"And she was the best dancer by far," continued Bronislawa, "and her voice was the loveliest of all in the church choir." This seemed truly impossible to Jadzia, who could not reconcile this description to *Pani* Zadora's exhausted shuffle, her strident, nagging voice.

"What happened to her?"

"Many problems. You don't remember Apolonya's *tata*, Gienek, do you? He was away so much when you were young."

"No, but I've seen his picture. The one *Pani* Zadora keeps on her shrine."

"He was a very handsome man. His son Antek looks just like him." Bronislawa was too busy kneading *babka* dough to notice Jadzia's sudden blush. Jadzia could see, once again, the stream, and Antek holding the bag of kittens up high in the air. She considered telling her mother, then immediately reconsidered. Mama would only tell her to stay away from Antek.

"Anyway, Gienek was a man who could not stay in one place for very long. Unlike most men in the village, who avoided joining the Prussian army whenever they could, Gienek enlisted. Often, he was home only once a year—and soon Danuta would deliver another child. Sometimes a child would come weeks before it could live, and Danuta had to deal many times with that terrible grief. When Gienek died she was left alone with many children and no husband to help her."

"But Apolonya is so good, and yet her mother hits her and says mean things." Jadzia felt a glow of gratitude for her own mother, who never hit her, who seldom even raised her voice.

"Much falls to Apolonya, I know. It is wrong for Danuta to take out her sorrow and worry on her daughter. But it's very hard to have so many mouths to feed and only one daughter."

By this point Jadzia was kneading her own little *babka*, adding in just a few white raisins and almonds. She loved it when her mother allowed her to make her own miniature copy of whatever pastries were being baked that day. "The boys could help in the house," she suggested.

"And pears could grow on willow trees," laughed Bronislawa. "Have you ever seen boys working in the kitchen in any house in the village—even in this one? It is simply not done."

"All right," Jadzia admitted, laughing. The idea of boys peeling potatoes or rolling out *pierogi* dough was pretty funny, now that she thought of it. Boys did nothing in the kitchen but eat—their work was out in the fields and the barn.

"Why does *Pani* Zadora hate America so much? I know about her two oldest sons who left for American and never came back. But she has five others, and they don't seem to be doing her or Apolonya any good at all."

Bronislawa laughed once more. "Ah, *dziecko*, you do not yet know what it is to be a mother. But one day you will." She brushed a wayward strand of curly brown hair back from Jadzia's forehead, leaving a smudge of white flour. "Every child is a precious gift from God." Jadzia basked in the undeniable constancy of her mother's love.

But only a moment later, another question came to mind. "*Pani* Zadora says Americans are godless, but even Apoloyna noticed how pious Evelina sounds from her letter. Do you think Americans are godless?"

"No, dear. I am certain that Evelina and all her family are good Catholics, just like us. But America is not like here. In Poland we are all Catholics, but in America Catholics live among people who worship God in many different ways, or not at all."

"We have Jews here."

"Yes, you're right. In Poland there are many Jews as well." Bronislawa clarified her statement. "I meant that Slavic Poles are Catholic."

"Many of my friends don't like Jews."

"I know that. Many of their parents feel the same way. But that is wrong. The Jews live apart from us. They live their own lives their own way and cause us no trouble at all. I'm sure they are good people."

"My friends say they killed Jesus."

"Ach, do not listen to such foolishness. The Romans killed Jesus. And the Jews who wanted Him killed lived almost two thousand years ago. Would you like to be blamed for something your ancestors did? Or even for something I did, or your brothers? Of course not. Now, this *babka* is ready for the oven. *Tata* and your brothers will be back from the fields any time now. Unless you have any more questions?"

"Only one. Do you think *Tata* will play his concertina for us tonight?"

"I believe he can be persuaded. He had a short day in the fields, since he spent the morning in town. And we have much to celebrate—a beautiful new baby boy for the Lesniaks, and your very exciting letter from your cousin. You must share it with *Tata* and *Babcia* and your brothers tonight. Will you write back to Evelina soon?"

"Just as soon as I can. I know we are going to become good friends."

Chapter Three

Evie, Chicago

September, 1933

5 sierpień, 1933

Moja Droga kuzynko Evelino!

Byłam bardzo zadowolona z otrzymanego listu. Ja też bardzo dużo słyszałam o Tobie i Twojej rodzinie. Spodziewam się, że będziemy dobrymi przyjaciółkami

"A letter? For me?" Eva's hazel eyes riveted on the battered onion-skin envelope. "Is it from Jadwiga? May I open it?"

Sofia Bialek, her brow furrowed in amazement, scrutinized the envelope, turning it over and over in her work-reddened hands, now lightly dusted with flour. "Yes, *moya droga*," she answered. "It's from Jadwiga in Niedzieliska." This was unprecedented—a letter, all the way from Poland—for her nine-year-old daughter. Had she ever believed that Jadwiga would answer the letter Eva had sent weeks earlier? Wiping her floury hands on her apron, she suggested, "Open it now. Let's hear what Jadwiga has to say."

"Oh, Mama…" Eva wailed. "Can I read it myself first?" Eva felt guilty seeing the disappointment in her mother's face. Of course, Mama would want to hear news from Niedzieliska—it had been so many years since she had left, and receiving a letter from Poland was so infrequent as to make its arrival a special occasion. But this was *her* special occasion, not her mother's.

"But Eva…" Eva did not wait for her mother to finish the sentence. With a sheepish smile she gently lifted the envelope from her mother's fingers, then twirled toward the door and dashed to her escape.

She turned right toward the parlor, planning to open her letter while embraced by the comfort of the old horsehair sofa. Set into a bay which took up almost the entire front wall of the parlor, the sofa offered more than deep, soft cushions. On this September day, unseasonably warm for Chicago, the weak breeze gently fluttering the scalloped edges of the white Austrian panels that graced the open windows provided further incentive.

Besides, the parlor offered the only area of the first-floor flat that Eva could consider formal enough for the momentous occasion of opening her first letter from Europe—indeed, the first letter she had ever received in her life. Besides for the sofa, it held her *tata's* russet-colored easy chair, faded with use but still serviceable. Although Eva and her brothers fought for this chair when *Tata* was at work, they all knew to flee from it the moment they heard his key at the front door. Her mother's tattered blue easy chair was another option. *Mama* never objected to sharing it, or anything else for that matter, with her children.

The parlor was also home to the aged walnut bureau and coffee table Mama polished with lemon oil every Saturday morning. On the far end of the bureau sat the family shrine to the Blessed Mother, which featured both a plaque of the Black Madonna of Czestochowa, much beloved by the inhabitants of her mother's home village of Niedzieliska, and a small plaster statue of the American Mary, dressed in a flowing blue robe, its folds draping gently over the wrists of her outstretched arms. A large vigil candle stood guard between the picture and the statue, and behind the arrangement stood a crystal vase for fresh flowers plucked from the garden: lilacs or daffodils in the spring, daisies or marigolds in the summer, chrysanthemums in the fall, pine branches in the winter.

But the room's crowning glory was the cut glass chandelier centered high above the coffee table. Every other month Eva assisted in cleaning it: standing on the table, she would remove each pearl-shaped droplet and hand it to her mother, who would then swirl it in a basin of vinegar water and, after buffing it gently in a piece of cheesecloth, return it to be replaced. Eva often wondered why they worked so hard on the chandelier, but in the evening, when its lights flickered on each teardrop, sparking it with diamond-like brilliance, she understood.

Stepping into the parlor, Eva was disappointed to see that she was not alone. Andrzej sat on the rose-patterned carpet, playing with the paint-chipped wooden blocks that had been passed down to him first from Henryk and then from herself. "Eva, play blocks with me?" he pleaded, looking up, fixing her with eyes the blue of a jay's wing. But Eva's desire for privacy overcame the power of Andrzej's blue eyes.

"Later, Andziu," she promised, turning left toward the three bedrooms at the end of the long, narrow hallway. Her long, strong legs carried her swiftly through the narrow hallway to the relative privacy of her room. True, it was not hers alone: she had to share the tiny space, hardly larger than a closet, with her three-year-old brother. How unfair that her older brother, Henryk, had not had to make way in *his* room for Andrzej's pallet and packet of belongings when Andrzej grew too big to share *Mama* and *Tata's* bed. Closing the door, a privilege she was normally not granted but which seemed appropriate for this august occasion, Eva collapsed onto her narrow bed, the fascinating missive clutched tightly in her hand.

And yet, despite her overpowering curiosity, she could not immediately open it. Turning it over from hand to hand, much as her mother had done, she examined it carefully. The handwriting was very neat and easy to read, but also unusual in some indefinable way. The address was correct, *Panna Evelina Bialek, 1815 Haddon Avenue, Chicago, Illinois, USA*. The stamps were beautiful, two big ones the color of steamed plums, one overlaid with marching soldiers sporting strange feathery helmets that gave the appearance of wings and spears pointed straight ahead. The other big stamp depicted the round, tired face of a kind-looking older man. Smaller stamps, of many colors, carried an image with which she was very familiar: the Polish eagle, sporting pointy feathers and outstretched claws, head turned regally to its right.

Suddenly she could wait no longer. She tore into the letter, but not so carelessly as to damage the stamps or any tiny bit of the writing. Inside she found a single page of onionskin, densely covered in small, neat script, most of it in Polish but with one section in a language, not English, that was unfamiliar to her:

5 August 1933

My dear cousin Evelina!

How happy I was to receive your letter! I have heard so much about you and your family as well, and hope that we can become very good friends.

Blessings to you and your family from Mama and Tata. Isn't it very strange that we both have two brothers and no sisters? Mine, Marek and Stasiu, for brothers, are not too bad. I do not miss having a sister so much because my very best friend, Apolonya Zadora, is like a dear sister to me. Do you have a good friend too?

My babcia, who is Tata's mother, also lives with us. She is midwife for our village, and is very much respected in Niedzieliska. Mama sometimes helps her in her work, and perhaps, when I am a little bit older, I will be able to help as well.

I am starting my fourth year of school. We study mathematics (my worst subject—we are alike that way!) and history, and also Esperanto. Fari vi studi Esperanto ankaux? I am so happy you can read and write Polish, even though you were born in the USA, since no one in Niedzieliska knows English.

We live on a farm, with many chickens and two cows, not in a very big city like you. Tata has promised to someday take us to Krakow or Czestochowa, but Mama says your city is much bigger than those. I cannot even imagine what it must be like.

I hope you get to go to the World's Fair and see the alligator. Mama told me all about it, but we have no such animal in Niedzieliska, and I can hardly even imagine it. If you can send me a postcard, I would always treasure a picture of the alligator, or of the Sky Ride. Any picture would be wonderful.

I hope you will write to me again soon, and I know that we will become good friends. Tata repairs shoes during the winter months when our fields lie fallow, and he has told me that if I polish the shoes until they shine, he will reward me by posting my letters to you. So I will be able to write often. I hope you can write often as well. We know that Americans are very rich, but Tata says things are very hard all over the world right now.

I send a prayer for God's blessings to you and your family, and will watch every day for a letter from you.

> *Your loving cousin,*
> *Jadwiga Czarnecka, but please call me Jadzia,*
> *because, as you said, we are family*

Eva breathlessly read the letter through a second time, then more slowly a third. Carefully placing it back into its frail envelope and turning it over to re-examine the stamps, she was almost overwhelmed at the knowledge that this letter had come from her cousin, Jadwiga—no, Jadzia—across the ocean, all the way from Poland. Mama had told her about leaving Poland and her beloved sister many years ago—in 1912—and now, through their letters, she and her cousin Jadzia were about to connect their families once more.

"Evelina!" Eva could hear the irritation in her mother's voice, muffled though it was through the closed door. "What does the letter say? Is my sister all right? Her husband? The children?"

"Yes, Mama," Eva shouted back. "Everyone's..." But in only a moment shouting was unnecessary, for the door opened quickly, revealing an increasingly impatient Sofia.

"Then come back to the kitchen and read your letter to me. Come. I need your help with the *pierogi*. I need for you to get the boiling pot from the top shelf."

Sofia's height, just under five feet tall, was one reason she often relied on her daughter for such tasks, but there were others. Although her mother's brown eyes were as dark as in the wedding picture Eva often studied on the master bedroom dresser, the picture's youthful, hopeful glow seldom sparkled in those eyes. And although Sofia was still a young woman, only thirty-seven, her previously dark braids were now liberally sprinkled with gray, and her cheeks, formerly plump and rosy, now revealed high cheekbones over pale hollows. Eva thought her mother looked too frail for many of the heavier kitchen tasks.

By contrast Eva, taking after her 6'2" father, had surpassed her mother's height over a year before. Though tall and gangly, with skin that displayed the pallor of city life, she was a strong, sturdy girl, and looked it. "I don't know why we have to make *pierogi* on the hottest day of the year," she complained as she reached up to the highest shelf in the cupboard.

"Because your *tata* and brother will want them when they come home from work, and once they are made, you will want them too." Henryk, at 15, was already working full days with his father at the tannery. Eva knew that her mother hoped that in September, when the new semester started, Henryk would return to Wells High School for his sophomore year. But her brother was neither a talented nor a motivated student, and the money that a strong young man could make was very important to a family in such difficult financial times, particularly when so many, even the heads of households, could not find work.

In the kitchen, Eva filled the heavy pot with water and placed it on the back burner of the cast iron stove, adding a handful of salt to ensure that the dumplings would rise. Sofia turned back to the dough she'd been rolling before the postman arrived. "Now," her mother said, "read your letter to me."

"I cannot read it all. Some of it is in a funny language."

"Let me see." Eva pointed out the offending passage. "Oh, that's Esperanto. It's an invented language for all the world to learn, so we could all communicate. It is taught in many schools in Poland—maybe because it was invented by a Pole—but is not so popular in this country."

"Can you read what the Esperanto says?"

Sofia peered closely. "I know a little. Jadwiga asks if you study Esperanto—then you could write in Esperanto, and if not, then in Polish, she says. Now, read the rest of your letter to me, *dziecko*."

Eva read the letter, clearly and with the proper inflection. Her Polish was much stronger than her English, probably because she used Polish so much more than the language of her native country. In her neighborhood, Polish was the language of commerce, of gossip, of the playground. It was the only language she spoke at home: her parents' knowledge of English, despite their many years in Chicago, was very limited. English was to her almost a foreign language, one she studied half-days at St. Casimir's Elementary School, and a language she considered harsh-sounding and abrupt.

Although her parents demanded more studying and better grades in her English class than in any other, she could see little benefit to it. She much preferred the formal rhythms and polite patterns of the Polish she spoke at home. She especially loved the way Mama spoke—all those gentle sh-, ch-, sz- and cz- sounds pouring out like water lapping the stones in a stream bed. Everyone said Mama's Polish was very dignified—that she spoke like an empress.

"Ah," Sofia sighed once her daughter finished reading, expertly flipping the dough over to roll it even thinner. "Your cousin Jadwiga sounds very smart, like her mama. Bronislawa always took firsts in school when we were little girls."

"You, too, Mama, I'll bet."

"Well, sometimes." Sofia paused to wipe her brow with the cuff of her sleeve. "But the fair. Eva, I know you want to go. But things are very hard now."

"But *Tata* promised!"

"I know, *moya droga*, but we will have to wait and see."

Eva sighed. Mama's "wait and see" usually took precedence over *Tata's* promises. She wanted to complain about the unfairness of this, but a quick look at her mother's face showed that Sofia was more disappointed than she herself was.

"It must be fun to live on a farm," she offered, to ease the moment for both of them.

"Yes, in many ways it is," Sofia answered, perhaps a little too brightly. "But it is very hard work too. The farm where your cousin lives is the farm I grew up on. It's been in our family for many generations."

"Why did you leave?"

"Ah, child, I have told you this many times. Things were very hard in Poland. Always war. Never enough food." Appearing satisfied with the flatness of her dough, Sofia reached for a tin cup, which she would use to cut out flat, thin circles, then continued, "Your *tata* and I came here for a better life."

Eva considered how much better her own life would be if she could go to the fair, but responded with the safer, "Don't you miss your family, Mama?"

"Yes, every day...but some things cannot be helped. So, potato and cheese *pierogi* for *Tata*? And maybe some sauerkraut for Henryk? How does that sound?"

"Good. And what kind for you, Mama?"

"Oh, you know I like them all."

"No plum today?" Eva asked, wondering why her mother never seemed to have a preference about anything.

"I don't know. I would need someone to go down to the cellar to get a jar of plums." But Eva was already heading out the kitchen door toward the outside entrance to the cellar. She had a sweet tooth, and this teasing game was one she and her mother often played.

When Eva returned, she stood silently next to her mother as together they expertly filled and enclosed each packet of dough, forming a half-circle, then pressed the edges with a floured fork to hold them together, readying them for their saltwater bath. Sofia trusted her daughter with the tricky job of retrieving the *pierogi* as they popped to the top. Too long a time in the boiling water and they became rubbery; too short a bath and the *pierogi* would fall apart as they were placed on the cooling racks.

Finally, when all the *pierogi* were cooling and the kitchen counter and utensils had been scoured, Eva asked for permission to go to the park. "Only if you take your brother with you," came the reply, and although Eva scowled, it was the answer she expected and one she truly didn't much mind. Andrzej was a sweet child, undemanding, who could amuse himself for hours playing in the sand with a cigar box and a couple of old spoons, leaving her time to reread her letter and think of the response she'd make to her cousin.

And so, less than a half hour later, Eva deposited her brother in the big wooden sandbox at Kosciusko Park, one of the dozens of small local parks that dotted the neighborhoods of Chicago. This park sported no gushing fountains or expansive flower beds like she'd seen the time *Tata* had taken the family on the bus to Lincoln Park. But there were a sandbox and a rickety slide, as well as two rusted swing sets, one offering three canvas swings for the older children, the other two wooden box swings for the toddlers. Every spring, maintenance workers planted a few petunias and marigolds around the cement sign at the park's entrance, but the combination of hot Chicago summers and the stomping of many small feet did little to enhance any horticultural endeavors.

Eva pored over her letter while dreamily rocking and circling on the center swing of the big kids' set. What to write back to her cousin, now that they were sure to become good friends? Surely more about her family's life in the yellow brick three-flat on Haddon Avenue. She could tell her about the Tomczak family with the three little children who inhabited the third floor, or about old *Pani* Poniatowska, the tenant on the second floor, who relentlessly but uselessly complained to the landlord about the noise six children generated. She could tell her about their cellar, the home to whole colonies of rats, and how brave she felt when she stomped into its damp darkness on an errand for her mother, shouting her arrival above the sounds of their tiny feet skittering to shelter.

She could tell Jadzia about Americans—how they celebrated only the days of their births and not their Name Days, and she could certainly find many other examples of the exotic lives led by non-Poles in this country. She had learned a lot about American culture—actually a foreign study to her—in school.

She should mention St. Casimir's, of course, and that, although she and Jadzia were the same age, she herself had finished the fourth grade, having been double-promoted after first grade. While Esperanto was not part of St. Casimir's curriculum, studying English for a half day must be at least as commendable. She could tell her cousin of her success at English spelling, how she was the champion at her grade level in the school's weekly spelling bees.

But what of a best friend? She had no one to compare to Jadzia's friend Apolonya Zadora, despite her many efforts to find a good friend among the young girls in her class. Perhaps it was her height—she towered over not only the girls, but also all of the boys in her class—and her height was only intensified by her gangly awkwardness, long arms and legs shooting out everywhere when she walked or inevitably sprawling into the aisle from her too-tiny child's desk at school.

But it was most probably not her physical awkwardness, but her social awkwardness, her timidity and the blustering, stuttering way she often responded to questions, that had earned her the hated nickname of *Mysz*. That, combined with the drab brown color of her hair and the grayish pallor of her skin, had resulted in the unlikely nickname of "Mouse" for such a tall, gangling girl. But of course, Jadzia did not need to know any of this.

One comment in her cousin's letter baffled her: how would she address Jadzia's belief that she and her family were rich Americans? Her mother's comments about the Century of Progress had made her feel anything but rich. But then, her family didn't think of themselves as poor, either. They were no richer or poorer than any of their neighbors, after all. Eva knew she would not have to polish shoes to earn the money for stamps. Her mama would find the money for postage. So perhaps, compared to her extended family in Poland, she and her family were rich—certainly a novel thought.

"*Mysz! Mysz!*" The shouts jolted her out of her reverie. Looking up, she saw that ugly boy, Mikosz Sienko, leading three of his nasty sixth-grade cohorts into the sanctuary of **her** beloved park. Time to go home.

"Come, Andrzej," she exhorted, hoping that her brother's good nature would overcome his disappointment at being torn away from the mound of sand he was carefully building.

"Don't go, *Mysz*. Stay and play!" Mikosz's band of hooligans laughed uproariously at this.

"I'm going home. This park is beginning to s-s-s-smell bad."

"Oh, little *Mysz*, you don't have to be afraid of us."

"I am **not** afraid. And don't call me M-m-mysz!" But the jeering sounds of "*Mysz, Mysz, Mysz*" followed Eva and Andrzej out of the park and half way down Division Street toward the relative safety of Haddon Avenue. "*Andziu*," she pleaded, holding his small hand tightly in her own, walking at a speed that seriously challenged the ability of his pudgy legs, "don't you ever grow up and be like those mean boys."

Later that night, dinner done and cleared away and Andrzej tucked snugly into bed, Eva and her mother sat in the parlor, on the comfortable sofa covered by a pale pink chenille spread that had once been a vibrant rose. They looked more closely at the letter from Poland and talked of many things. Neither *Tata* nor Henryk had come home for dinner, and Sofia speculated that they "were working late at the tannery again." Eva had smiled and nodded. Now they were carefully examining the stamps on the letter. "Who is this man?" asked Eva, pointing to the kind-looking mustachioed gentleman on one stamp.

"That is Jan Sobieski, the famous king of Poland."

"He's the king now?"

"No, *moja droga*. From many, many years ago—in the 1600's, when the Turks were invading Europe. He stopped them and saved Poland and the rest of Europe for the Church. Otherwise you would be a little Muslim girl, wearing a turban on your head. Would you like that?"

Eva laughed, although a turban, she thought, might be a delightful thing to wear. "What of these funny soldiers, Mama? Are they King Sobieski's soldiers?" She pointed to the feathery-helmeted marchers.

"No, that stamp celebrates the revolution of 1830, and those men are the winged Polish hussars. They fixed feathers—eagle and ostrich—to frames and wore them into battle."

"Why did they wear feathers?" asked Eva, stifling a laugh. "It makes them look so funny."

"Maybe funny to you, but maybe not so funny if you were an enemy across the field. Imagine how big the hussars must have looked, charging into battle on their magnificent horses. The enemy must have thought they were giants."

"And this battle was like the American Revolution?" Eva had studied the American Revolution—Washington, Franklin, Jefferson—in history class.

"Very much like the American Revolution, but against the Tzar of Russia, Tzar Nicholas. Russia owned much of Poland then, just as England owned the American colonies before the American Revolution."

"And did Poland win?"

"No, *moya droga*, Russia won. Many Poles died in the battles, and many more were sent to camps in Siberia, where it is very cold and they, too, died. It was very bad times for Polish people. Poland was divided for many years. When your *tata* and I came to this country, his village belonged to Prussia, and *Tata* knew that if he stayed in his village, he would soon have to become a soldier for Prussia."

"*Tata* a soldier?" Eva speculated, trying to imagine her father in a soldier's uniform but not succeeding in that effort.

"Well, we were both much younger then," Sofia sighed, "although you might be surprised at how different your *tata* and I were long ago. I bet you do not know that at one time your *tata* dreamed of being a professor."

"A professor?" To Eva, imagining her father as a teacher seemed even more preposterous than imagining him in a soldier's uniform. "What happened?"

"Well, *dziecko*, sometimes things do not happen just as we wish they would. Your *tata* is a good man—he works very hard for us. It's just even when one tries his very hardest…"

Eva saw for just a moment a familiar, far-away look darken her mother's now tearful eyes. Eva had seen this look most often when her mother spoke of times long past. But soon Sofia abandoned her thought and recovered, asking as she pointed to one of the smaller stamps, "Evelina, do you know this bird?"

"Of course, Mama, the Polish eagle," she answered, having seen this eagle displayed on posters and signs in many of the shops on Division Street and on many of the products imported from Poland that were for sale there. A person could not travel far in their neighborhood without encountering the strange-looking bird.

"See how he looks to the right?"

"Yes."

"This is because Poland has always looked to the right—to the West— away from Russia, toward the countries of Western Europe, especially France." But Eva's eyelids were beginning to droop, her body beginning to relax against her mother's, signaling that this too long, too exciting day for a nine-year-old was about to come to a close.

"Eva, go to bed, *dziecko*," Sofia said softly, hugging her daughter and placing a feathery kiss on her cheek. "Enough history for one night. We will talk more in the morning."

In her bed, Eva listened to the steady whispering sound coming from her brother's cot. Despite the itchiness of her eyes and the heaviness in her limbs, she could not immediately go to sleep. She closed her eyes tightly, hoping to force sleep to come, to be dreaming of something wonderful before *Tata* came home. But thoughts of Poland and of her cousin kept intruding.

She wrote and rewrote in her mind the next letter she would compose. There was much more to tell Jadwiga—and much to not tell her. She would tell about her home, her school, her family. She would tell about what life was like in Chicago for those who had emigrated to America. Someday, when their relationship had grown and they were truly friends, she would tell Jadzia of her dreams and aspirations, about her ideas concerning what life was all about.

She would not tell Jadwiga about some of the mean children at school, especially that horrible Mikosz Sienko, or about her unsuccessful efforts to find a good friend. She would certainly not mention her nickname, *Mysz*.

Most of all, she would not tell her about those nights when *Tata* was very late coming home, and frightening sounds—low slurred shouts and rapid bursts of higher-pitched speech, sharp claps and heavy thuds—would sometimes come from the bedroom at the end of the hall. She would not tell about her mother those next mornings, about the dark circles under Mama's eyes or about how slowly she moved about the kitchen on those days. Or about sometimes finding Mama sitting alone in the kitchen, her shoulders heaving with silent tears.

Although she had never been told this, she knew that in families there were things that were not to be discussed—certainly not outside the family, but even not between its members—and that what happened behind her parents' closed bedroom door was one of those things. Screwing her eyes together even harder, she focused on her letter from Jadzia, finally finding her land of dreams.

Chapter Four

Jadzia, Niedzieliska

September, 1936

14 sierpień, 1936

Moja najdroższa Jadziu!

Przepraszam, że nie odpisałam na Twój list wcześniej. Dziękuję Ci za pamięć i modlitwy za mnie oraz całą rodzinę. Mama czuje się dużo lepiej.

Stanislaus Czarnecki tapped the dust from his boots before crossing the threshold into his home. His long walk to and from town had been fruitful; today he carried with him the letter for which his wife and daughter had been waiting so anxiously. As he stepped in, Bronislawa and Jadzia, who had been preparing the afternoon meal, turned expectantly toward him.

"Yes, a letter came at last. From Evelina," he answered, forestalling the question he could clearly see in the tilt of their heads and their raised eyebrows, his daughter's expression mirroring her mother's.

"Thank God," Bronislawa sighed. "Will you read it aloud, Jadzia? Or perhaps..."

"I'll read it now," Jadzia offered. For the past year she had read her cousin's letters privately, only later paraphrasing for her parents, and her mother seemed to understand. After all, no matter how close they were, young girls did not always want to share all things with their mothers. But Eva's last letter had told of her mother's frightening fall down the stairs, threatening not only her own health, but the health of the baby she carried. A feeling of anxiety had permeated the whole Czarnecki family since, rising in intensity every time Stanislaus arrived home from a visit to town. Jadzia did not wish to make her mother wait even one more minute to hear further news of her sister Sofia. Offering a silent prayer to the Virgin Mary, she opened the letter and began to read aloud.

August 14, 1936

My dearest Jadzia,

Forgive me for not answering your letters sooner. Thank you for your loving thoughts and your prayers, and for the prayers of all your family. I am certain they made the difference, as Mama is doing much better. Our whole family is now—very impatiently!—awaiting the arrival of my new brother or sister, which could happen any day now.

"Good news, Mama," she smiled. "*Ciotka* Sofia and the baby are doing well."

"Thank God!" Bronislaw and Stanislaus whispered in unison, crossing themselves in silent thanksgiving. "See, *moya droga*," he said, "again you worry for nothing." Already late for his morning chores, he kissed her cheek gently as he grabbed a hat and headed out to the barn.

Jadzia continued her reading.

I have left school for a little while to stay home and take care of the house and Andrzej. Tata says I can go back as soon as the baby is born and Mama is back on her feet again. I do miss school, but know I am needed here.

"Oh, no, Mama. That's unfair. She's the best speller in her class."

"Well, I'm sure your cousin is needed at home. Sofia's pregnancies were always hard, and now she is older. Eva will be able to return to school soon. Does your cousin have anything else to say?"

Quickly perusing the rest of the letter, Jadzia responded, "No, Mama. Nothing of any interest."

"Good then. I'll get back to my baking." But Jadzia could not miss noticing her mother's wink and sly smile as she turned back to her kneading. Silently this time, she read.

I'll bet Apolonya is very excited about her brother's wedding, and about being a bridesmaid. Her new sister-in-law-to-be must be a kind girl, to invite her to stand up to the wedding—some girls would not be so nice. And I'll bet you're excited about the wedding, too—a chance to dance with a certain tall, blonde young man? It seems to me, dearest cousin, that he is always on your mind—at least he has been whenever you've written letters to me lately! You must tell me all about the wedding—write to me the very next day.

Well, I must go. Forgive the shortness of this letter, but there is laundry to do and supper to begin. Know that you and your family are in my heart and thoughts every day.

Your Eva

Jadzia, sticking the letter in the pocket of her apron and joining her mother at the table, began kneading a ball of dough that would soon become a loaf of Bronislawa's acclaimed rye bread. "Eva sounds different in this letter somehow...so much older," she said.

"Eva would be different now. Responsibility ages a person quickly."

"But it isn't fair that she has to leave school."

"Life is not fair, Jadwiga. You're old enough to know that. Her *tata* and her brothers need her at home now."

"Do you miss your sister very much?" Jadzia asked, remembering how, in the last couple of weeks, her mother's uncharacteristic peevishness and small displays of temper had shown how worried she had been. Even *Tata* had steered clear of her for several days.

"Yes, very much, even though I haven't seen her for almost 25 years, and I suppose I will never again see her in this world. But it's always been a comfort to know that she is in America, doing well, raising her family. She has always been very special to me."

"So you will go to the wedding reception tomorrow night, after all?" Bronislawa had several days ago, in a moment of pique, stated that none of them should consider celebrating when their family in Chicago was in such distress. She had suggested they attend the church ceremony, but nothing else. Jadzia had fretted about her mother's words for days.

"We'll go for a little while, at least for dinner. But *Tata* and I will have to leave early. *Babcia* is getting too old to stay up so late, and I'd worry about her walking in the woods by herself late at night." Bronislawa paused in her kneading and smiled at her daughter, waiting playfully.

"Mama, uh...I wonder...do you think?" But Jadzia could not finish her sentence. It seemed to her an eternity before Bronislawa's smile broadened as she said, "I see no reason why you can't stay for the reception. You're getting older, and your brothers can watch out for you and walk you home."

Jadzia uttered a silent prayer of thanks. The upcoming celebration had been highly anticipated in the village. In a year that had seen more poverty and loss than usual, Pawel and Helena's wedding promised to be the social event of the season for the people of Niedzieliska. Jadzia was grateful that she would not have to miss it—for so many reasons.

Jadzia had never before seen the church hall look so beautiful. Normally simple and plain, this evening it was a fantasy of color and form. Long tables filled the front half of the room, each covered with its own lovely cloth of lace or linen, and a stunning centerpiece of fall flowers graced the head table. The other tables held mosaic centerpieces of colorful fall leaves, and garlands of woven leaves gracefully draped the length of each table, their colors contrasting beautifully with the ivory or pure white of the tablecloths.

Toward the back of the hall the band had already assembled and had begun playing immediately upon the arrival of the first guests. Later in the evening, the volume would escalate as the concertina, flute and fiddle combined to produce the polkas, mazurkas and waltzes that would set the whole room spinning. One table set apart from the others held the *kolaz*, the wedding breads, ring-shaped pastries filled with nuts and fruit pastes and decorated with hearts or with chickens and roosters, all shaped from dough. As if these were not enough, trays of madeleines, *kolaczki*, and butter teacakes abounded.

No more impressive than the hall were the people within it, villagers whom Jadzia saw every day, but who today were so splendidly attired that she hardly recognized them. Every man and boy was arrayed in his best suit, and every woman in her most elegant dress. Jadzia was dressed like most of the girls, in *krakowania*, full, starched gauze skirts in purest white decorated with horizontal bands of brightly colored ribbons and topped by white peasant blouses delicately embroidered at the neck and short sleeves. Over this, heavily sequined black velvet vests were laced together tightly with ribbons of red and white, and more ribbons secured the bases of braids or dangled from headpieces worn high on the crown of the head.

But Jadzia's attire was set off by one very special ornament: her grandmother's amber beads, which gently draped her neck, falling several centimeters below the neckline of her blouse. *Babcia* had handed the necklace to her, secure in its lacquered pine box, just as she had been about to leave for the wedding. Even in the box it had been beautiful: its beads sun-colored, were the sun muted by a milky cloud, with the large center bead, almost 2 ½ centimeters wide, elegantly set off by tapering pairs of perfectly matched beads that met in a tiny gold clasp. When *Babcia* had fastened it around her neck, leading her to the mirror on her bureau to see for herself how beautifully the necklace set off her dark coloring, Jadzia had blushed with pleasure.

As much as the hall was a delight of sight and sound, it offered gratification to the nose as well. Wonderful smells emanating from the kitchen set Jadzia's mouth watering. As Pawel's new bride came from a family considered rich by village standards, three meats, beef, roast chicken and *kielbasa*, would be served. Side dishes would include *pierogi*, *kapusta* (a sauerkraut casserole made with dried peas), *kluski* (egg noodles with poppy seed) and fresh cucumber salad. And there would be no stinting on the alcoholic beverages, which would include beer, wine and vodka.

Jadzia took her place at one of the long tables between her brothers Marek and Stasiu and bowed her head as Father Jozef rose from the head table to say the blessing. She prayed, as did many in the hall, that he would not take too long. Next came the traditional parents' blessing, during which *Pani* Zadora and Helena's parents offered the new couple their traditional first wedding gifts: bread, that they never go hungry; wine, that they always enjoy the sweetness of life; salt, that they be able to overcome life's bitterness; and a silver coin, that they be blessed with wealth and good health. Helena wept during this ceremony, which Jadzia knew to be a very auspicious sign. A bride who did not cry at her wedding was sure to cry many, many times during her marriage.

At last the massive trays of food were brought from the kitchen, and all dug heartily into each dish. The meal was interrupted frequently by many toasts to the bride and groom, and Jadzia participated, raising her glass of soda water laced with just the teaspoon or two of wine that her mother had permitted.

During one toast she glanced at the bride, blushing prettily, just as she had blushed in St. Adalbert's when Pawel had lifted her veil and Father Josef had joined their hands together, symbolic of the now eternal joining of their lives. Every female cheek in the church had glistened with tears at that moment; even her *babcia*, usually regally composed, had cried. But the church was quickly forgotten when Stasiu passed a tray of *pierogi*, calling her attention to the single remaining plum dumpling, swimming in butter, that he said was surely meant for her.

As soon as dinner was over and Apolonya was released temporarily from her bridesmaid's duties, she came to Jadzia's table, grabbing her hand and pulling her outside. It was a clear night, uncharacteristically warm for September. A full moon lit the forest, surrounding the old stone church with a hazy glow. "Is it fun to be a bridesmaid?" Jadzia asked. Then, not waiting for an answer, "Do you like your new sister-in-law?"

"She seems nice enough. Not at all proud and haughty like I expected. And we did have fun. I helped her to dress and to fix her hair."

"You did a wonderful job. But surely she's jealous. *You* are the most beautiful girl at the wedding."

Apolonya did look beautiful in the pale blue dress overlaid by delicate ivory lace her mother had made for her. Her blonde hair, nearly white in the moonlight, cascaded in soft braids down her back almost to her waist; two slender braids were pulled up to the crown of her head and intertwined with dusky pink chrysanthemums. Around her neck she wore a tiny amber necklace in the shape of a heart which Helena, her new sister-in-law, had graciously lent her.

"Nonsense. All brides are beautiful on their wedding day. Helena is surely the most beautiful girl here today." But Apolonya beamed.

"The wedding was lovely. Did you cry at the cemetery?" The entire wedding procession had stopped at Gienek Zadora's grave to pray for his blessing on the union.

"A little—I couldn't help thinking how different today might have been if *Tata* had lived to see it. Did you cry too?"

"Of course," answered Jadzia. The traditional visit to the cemetery to invoke the blessings of those who had passed always brought tears to the eyes of everyone celebrating a wedding. It was a reminder, even in all the day's excitement, of those who could not be there and would always be missed.

The strains of the evening's first polka quickly terminated any further talk. The music drew the girls back into the hall, where dining tables had been removed and the older guests had already gathered, sitting in small groups, to talk and drink. Boys and girls stood at opposite ends of the room, also talking in small groups but eyeing each other surreptitiously. The first to begin dancing were the young married couples and the children, whose inhibitions were diminished respectively by their status or their youth.

As the beginning notes of the second polka sounded, Apolonya's brother Tadeusz strode across the room and offered his hand to his sister, leading her out to dance, leaving Jadzia alone to sip her lemonade. She tried to look nonchalant and very interested in her drink, but was saved from desperation by her brother Marek, who kindly stepped up to lead her, as well, onto the dance floor.

Soon the floor was being crossed by many young men. In moments the room was alive with couples swinging in time to the lively tempo, young women twirling, right hands held high in the air, young men stamping hard on the solid pine floor, hooting "Aih!" whenever their exuberance reached crescendo. Around Jadzia and the other dancers children careened wildly, though amazingly no injuries occurred.

After several dances, a chorus of moans followed the concertina player's announcement that the first set was finished. The younger dancers resignedly segregated themselves into their original positions while the band members sauntered over to the bar. Jadzia found her abandoned glass of lemonade and drank greedily at first, then remembered her mother's admonition, as she, *Tata* and *Babcia* had left the hall, to "act like a lady." She began taking only tiny sips. Apolonya soon appeared beside her, looking for all the world like a delicate blue angel, fresh and composed, despite the lively dancing she had just done.

"Ach," blurted Jadzia, "I must look like a washerwoman next to you." Jadzia was acutely aware of the dampness under her arms and around the neckline of her black sequined vest, which fit more snugly in the chest than it had the previous summer when she had last worn it.

Eyeing her friend closely, Apolonya responded, "Actually, you look very nice." Jadzia did look lovely. Her skin glowed with exertion. The vivid pink in her cheeks complemented her duskiness. Curls of dark hair escaped enchantingly from the braids that tightly circled her head. "Black suits you."

"Oh, you're just saying that," answered Jadzia modestly.

"No, I mean it. And your grandmother's necklace suits your coloring very well—it would not look nearly as nice on me. But let's go back in. I think I hear the band tuning up."

By the time the next set started, Jadzia felt cool and rested, ready for whatever the evening would bring. She saw Apolonya's brother Antek, surely the most handsome young man present, striding across the room toward the area she and Apolonya had staked out for their own. Shyly taking little sips of her lemonade, certain that Antek was about to ask his sister to dance, she almost choked when, incredibly, she heard the words she had only dreamed of for days: "Jadzia, would you like to dance?"

Of course, in her dreams she had not felt so flustered upon accepting his invitation. As he took her hand to lead her to the dance floor, she prayed that he could not feel the dampness of her palms or hear the rapid beating of her heart, now threatening to burst through the bodice of her blouse.

As Antek took her into his arms for the first waltz of the set, Jadzia was mesmerized by the feel of him, the muscles of his back so hard under her outstretched hand, and by his smell, of wool and cigarette smoke and beer, and of an underlying scent of woods and fields that was surely his alone. He did not speak to her at first, but this was a blessing. She could not accomplish any semblance of poise if she had to balance her dance steps, his nearness, and intelligible speech, all at the same time. Soon they were dancing a polka, the relative distance between them giving her a chance to pull her thoughts together, the vitality of the dance providing a physical excuse for the rapid beating of her heart. The next dance was a Brahms waltz. Antek, pulling her closer for the dance, whispered into her ear, "You look very pretty tonight, Jadzia."

"Yes," she stammered. "I mean, thank you." She wondered if he was teasing her. Boldly, imagining what Apolonya might say upon receiving a compliment from a handsome man, she quickly added, "You probably tell all the girls that."

"Ah, so you too judge me by my reputation."

"Or perhaps by the fact that I've known you all my life." She looked to his expression for a clue to his thoughts: was he smiling or smirking? Had he been offended by her statement, or was he flirting with her? This type of boy-girl interaction was new to her, and so very confusing. She longed to know exactly how to respond and how to look up into his eyes in a way he would remember for days.

Antek, holding her now at a distance from which he could look more directly into her eyes, asked, "Do you really think you know me, Jadzia?"

"Why, yes. Of course." As she spoke these words, she knew they were a lie. She really did not know him at all, despite a childhood of shared experiences. But she wanted to know him, to understand what he thought and felt, who he really was.

"I don't think so," he said with a quick laugh. "Otherwise, you might not be so quick to disapprove. I'm not as bad as they say."

"I don't disapprove of you," Jadzia insisted, returning his direct look with one of her own.

"If that were so, you would be the only one in town."

"Oh," laughed Jadzia softly, "Things can't be that bad."

"Perhaps not for you, or for anyone who wants nothing more than to stay in this miserable hole of a village for the rest of his life. But that's not for me. I want to go places, see things. I want to be a part of the bigger world, away from the same people, the same houses, the same cows and chickens every day."

Jadzia struggled to find the right words—words that would help Antek understand that she shared his restlessness, his eagerness to be free. To think, another person here in Niedzieliska who felt just as she did—a person she'd known all her life—but perhaps not really known. The end of the waltz completed the set. All too soon the band members were placing their instruments aside and heading toward the bar, and Antek was silently leading her back to her place at the far wall.

Jadzia, inwardly cursing the relativity of time that had made the last forty minutes seem like forty seconds, was joined moments later by Apolonya, whose presence she had lost sight of during the last set, but who eyed her with great amusement now. "Jadzia, are you blushing?" she asked slyly.

"Just heated from the dance," Jadzia answered, immediately regretting the double meaning inherent in her response.

"Yes, I imagine. You and Antek looked very intent out there. Although I cannot imagine what you see in that nasty brother of mine. He's been nothing but a curse to me my entire life. But then, we see brothers in a different light from other boys, don't we?"

Trying to change the subject, Jadzia asked, "Did you dance the last set?"

"Oh my, your eyes certainly were filled with stars," Apolonya responded, "if you did not see me stumbling all over the floor with that clumsy Piotr Wiewiura. I think he was wearing the same boots he wore out in the fields this afternoon!"

"Would you like to step outside for a bit to get some fresh air?" Jadzia asked, hoping that a few minutes in the woods would bring her heart rate back to normal.

"No, I can't. I believe the next dance is the Money Dance and then the *Oczepiny*. I promised I would help the maid of honor. A bridesmaid's work is never done! And they're already beginning to line up. I must go."

A mere spectator to the next event, Jadzia was able to calm herself as she stood in the wide circle now surrounding Helena. A line of men stood, laughing and drinking, behind the maid of honor, whose job it was to receive the *zlotys* each man offered for his chance to waltz for a few moments with the bride. Apolonya's job as first bridesmaid was to transfer the money into the satin and lace purse that had been lovingly stitched by Helena's mother for this purpose. Helena good-naturedly took on as dance partner every man present, from Apolonya's and Jadzia's older brothers to ancient *Pan* Dombrowski, knowing that the proceeds from the Money Dance would help her and Pawel in setting up their new household.

The *Oczepiny*, which followed the Money Dance, was the most meaningful part of the whole wedding ceremony, as it marked the entrance of the bride into her new role as wife. Helena sat in a chair in the middle of the circle of celebrants who slowly walked, holding hands and singing softly. Her mother stepped behind her, and removing Helena's veil, began to undo the heavy braids pinned in a thick circle around her head. She brushed out Helena's rich chestnut waves into the long flowing hairstyle that would now identify her as having entered the world of women. Jadzia watched, entranced by the scene, so full of pride and love between mother and daughter.

Jadzia sighed softly as she watched Helena's mother take the white linen cap, embroidered and trimmed with lace, that Helena would henceforth wear to church and on holidays to signify her status as a married woman. Placing it on her daughter's head, she adjusted Helena's voluminous curls to fit most attractively around the cap. Finally, taking Helena's hand, she placed it into the hand of Pawel, who was by that time standing next to his bride.

As Helena's mother and the bridesmaids joined the circle of guests, Pawel and Helena danced their first waltz as a married couple. It was understood by all attending that they were not truly married until the ceremony of the *Oczepiny* was completed.

Soon Apolonya was required to join the other members of the wedding party in escorting Pawel and Helena to their new home. They would not return for some time, as it was absolutely necessary that the bridesmaids and groomsmen serenade the young couple with bawdy calls and love songs for an hour or so before finally leaving them in peace and returning to the reception.

The other wedding guests resumed their drinking, eating of pastries and dancing with even more gusto: a Polish wedding could last for three days, but in this case, it was understood that the reception would end at dawn. Some elderly party-goers grumbled, but most understood that in such times even villagers as well-to-do as Helena's parents could not afford such lavishness.

Jadzia distractedly danced with several boys from the village, her eyes discreetly searching the room for Antek's tall, slim body and blonde thatch of hair. Finally realizing that he, as well as both of her brothers, was not present, she waited for a break in the music to search outside. While she would no more march up to Antek and begin to speak to him than crow at the moon, she could, without appearing too bold, approach one of her brothers and speak to him. She stepped outside, contemplating various pretexts for such a conversation: to ask when they would be leaving for home, perhaps, or whether they had seen some person or other come outside.

The sound of male voices and a cloud of smoke emanating from a small clearing in the forest no more than forty steps from the church directed her in her search. She paused just outside the clearing, where she could see not only Antek and her brothers, but three or four other young men of the village, some standing, some sitting on tree stumps or resting against trees, all smoking and drinking from a bottle of vodka they passed around. Antek held the floor, his voice passionate, gesturing vividly with his hands. To Jadzia he looked powerful, in charge, and she could not stop herself from stepping behind a wide oak where she could observe him and hear what he was saying.

"I hope you got your fill of meat tonight," Antek addressed Janek, the youngest son of one of the poorest families in Niedzieliska. "You're not likely to get any more for a year."

"Don't be rude, Antek," responded Jadzia's brother Stasiu, "you know how ill Janek's parents have been over the past few years."

"I'm not blaming Janek or his parents," Antek explained. "I'm talking about all of us. Will anyone here have enough to make it through the winter all right?"

"Times are hard all over," responded Marek. "We've always survived."

"But that's just it. Times aren't hard for everyone," Antek argued, pausing for effect and appraising the questioning looks he saw on his listeners' faces. "The Jews don't have it so bad."

At this the whole party of young men laughed. Tomas, a tall, thin young man with a vivid birthmark on his cheek, was the first to speak. "What are you saying, Antek? The Jews have *less* than we do. Have you never seen one of their farms?"

"I'm not talking about *our* Jews. I'm talking about the city Jews. *They're* the rich ones."

"What do you know about city Jews?" jibed Tomas. "You've never been more than 10 kilometers outside of Niedzieliska." The men laughed once again.

"I don't have to leave this village to know what's going on in the world. To know that the Jewish bankers have all the money in Poland—they're strangling all of us. They're why our mothers spend their nights crying and our fathers spend their nights drinking, and some of our littlest brothers and sisters won't be alive come next spring." Antek spat out the words bitterly.

Ah, thought Jadzia *more politics.* Why did the men always have to talk about politics? What possible difference could politics mean to them, tucked away as they were in a little forgotten town in one of the poorest parts of Poland.

"We've heard this all before, but where's the proof?" Marek challenged. "And even if it were true, what could we do about it?"

"This new man in Germany—he's got some good ideas."

"Germany!" Now it was Marek's chance to spit out bitter words. "Germany! Are you crazy? Nothing good for Poland has ever come out of Germany!"

"Have you forgotten about the last war, Antek?" asked Stasiu. The other men murmured their agreement.

"The last war is history. I'm talking about right now, and about the future. Things are different in Germany now. Mark my words. This Hitler is going to change everything. The German Republic will be the reigning power for the rest of this century. If Poland were smart, we would ally ourselves with them right now." Antek's eyes gleamed with fervor.

"Ally with Germany!" Marek spit onto the ground. "I've always thought your brains were a bit addled, Antek. Now I know you've lost your mind!"

Antek sprang toward Marek, and, fists balled, swung at his face. But Marek was too quick: with a counter of his forearm against Antek's right hand, Marek swept his left foot against his adversary's ankles, effectively tumbling him onto the hard ground. Soon the two men were scuffling, crablike, arms and legs flailing so fiercely that Jadzia could no longer restrain the scream she'd felt rising in her throat.

For a moment, all action in the clearing stopped, as every young man seemed frozen in place. Soon Antek was restrained by the two young men standing closest to him while Marek raised himself from the ground, brusquely brushing his pant legs. The men sheepishly turned to Jadzia, whose look of horror, eyes wide as daisies, jolted them out of their contentiousness. Even Antek became subdued.

"Jadzia," asked Marek, cooling down immediately, "how long have you been standing there?"

"Just a moment," she lied. "Are you all right, Marek?"

"Yes, of course. Never better."

"And you, Antek?"

"I'm fine," he answered, using the back of his hand to wipe a small trickle of blood from his left cheek. "We're just having a little bit of fun here, Jadzia. Nothing to worry about."

"Jadzia, there's no reason to mention to *Tata*..." Marek looked beseechingly at his sister.

Jadzia considered her parents' most likely reaction to knowledge of what she had just seen. Helena's would not be the first Polish wedding reception that had ended in a fight. But Mama and *Tata* would be furious with their son for fighting, particularly when he had been entrusted with her care. And certain events in the village had already given them an unfavorable opinion of Antek.

"No. Of course not," she responded. "There's nothing to tell."

"Good," nodded Marek. "Why don't you go back inside then, Jadzia? Have another piece of cake."

Jadzia looked first at her brothers, then at Antek, feeling her loyalties torn between them. She sensed the still restless undertones in their stances and the tautness of their upper bodies and feared what would happen if she walked away. She realized that she could change the outcome of this evening. With a weak little smile and in a voice smooth as cream, she said, "I've been looking all over for you. I'm so very tired, Marek, and maybe I had just a little bit too much wine. I was wondering if you and Stasiu could take me home right now."

Chapter Five

Evie, Chicago

October, 1936

Moja Droga Evo!

Kiedy otrzymasz ten list, Twoja rodzina już będzie świętować narodziny dziecka. Myślę, że będzie to malutka siostrzyczka, której tak bardzo pragnęłaś.

Eva rushed to the door the moment she glimpsed the blue uniform of the retreating postman. She needed something, anything, to distract her from the pandemonium. Horrible screams came from the closed bedroom door: the midwife had been there for only two hours, but it felt like two days. Every scream from the bedroom evoked an accompanying scream from Andrzej, who refused to be distracted with his toys or a licorice, begging to go to his mama. But there was nothing he or Eva could do for her right now.

Tata and Henryk had retreated hastily upon the arrival of the midwife—everyone knew that in this most elemental women's business, men were better off far away. But why had *Tata* not sent Mama to the hospital, Evie wondered. More and more, women were giving birth in hospitals, not at home. Even *Pan* Tomczak, who had lost his job weeks earlier, had taken his wife to the hospital for the birth of their fourth child. But *Tata* had put his foot down. Hospitals were for rich people. He and Mama had been born at home, as had his other children. This new little *chlopiec* or *dziewczyna* would be born at home as well.

Eva scooped up the letters that had fallen through the mail slot, her heart leaping at the now very familiar handwriting she found on one envelope. A letter from Jadzia—just what she needed to lift her spirits and get her through this awful day. She took the letter into the parlor, where Andrzej sat dejectedly on the floor, sucking his thumb and sniffling. Trying to interest him in his little wooden locomotive—usually his favorite toy—she was rewarded only by another howl from him. "Fine," she said curtly, "have it your own way. Sit there and cry. There's nothing I can do for you." Sinking into the comfort of the sofa, she tore open her letter and began to read quickly, hoping to finish in the lull between screams:

20 September 1936

My dear Eva,

By the time this letter gets to you, your family will be celebrating. A new baby! I hope it will be the little sister you've always wanted. We both know too well what having brothers is like.

Love and many blessings from Mama and Tata and my whole family. We pray for a safe and quick delivery for your mama—if only my mama and babcia could be there to help! Then I know everything would go very well.

I hope you had a happy Name Day. Mine was wonderful—the best yet. I received a new dress and boots, but the best gift was from Tata. He made me the most clever wooden box, intricately carved in a beautiful floral pattern and stained dark. This box is especially for my letters from you! He put a little lock on it with my own little key, so I can keep your letters private, away from the prying eyes of my brothers. I wish you could see it. I have included a tracing of the pattern on my last page, so you can get some idea of the beautiful new home your letters will enjoy!

Hello from Apolonya. I speak of you so much, she feels that you are one of her best friends as well. But things are very sad for Apolonya. Just weeks before classes started, her mother told her she must leave school! What a blow! It's true that Pani Zadora needs Apolonya's help at home, but I think the reason is much more than that. Pani Zadora thinks in the old ways—she believes that too much education is not good for a girl. Many in our village feel the same. Have you started back to school yourself?

And now, of course, I must write to you about the wedding. It was wonderful! Good food, great music, and dancing...Yes! Antek asked me to dance. Eva, I cannot believe this, but Antek and I think so much alike. We share many of the same hopes and dreams. How two people who are so similar can find themselves in the same little town—it is hard to believe.

There was a little trouble after the reception, but nothing serious. Antek does not think like the other boys. He is much more worldly, so they do not understand. But enough of this—I hope to have much more to discuss along this line in the future!

Write to me as soon as you know whether you have a new little brother or a new little sister. Our family certainly seems destined to produce mostly boys. So often I believe boys to be a curse. But I must admit that they are not so bad once they grow up (as long as they are not your brothers!)

Love to you, your mama and tata, your brothers (and maybe a new baby sister!)

Your Jadzia

Eva had just finished reading the last paragraph when yet another scream, more piercing than any so far, burst from the bedroom, followed by a heartbreaking sob from Andrzej. Taking pity on her little brother, she shoved the letter into the pocket of her skirt and bent to pull him close. "There, there," she soothed, hugging him to her chest. "It'll be all right. It's almost over. Soon we'll have a little brother or sister. Will you like that?"

"I want my mama," he sobbed, collapsing like a rag doll, arms and legs limp, into her arms.

"I know. I know. But we must be brave for Mama."

"My tummy hurts."

Eva placed her hand firmly on his forehead. "And you're very warm, too. See, all your crying has made you sick. We can't have that, not now. Here, rest against me and try not to cry. Should I sing you a song? Your favorite—"*Siedziec na koniu*"—the one about the horsie?"

At his tearful nod, Eva began to softly croon Andrzej's (and her own) favorite nursery song, about a father's trip to the market to purchase a blue pony for his beloved daughter. She rocked him gently back and forth, stroking damp hair away from his face, concerned about the heat radiating from his slender frame. The last thing she needed now was the responsibility of a six-year-old with influenza.

As they rocked together she thought of the letter she had just received. Things seemed to be going very well for Jadzia, she thought. Now she truly had Apolonya's brother to dream about. She wished she herself had some handsome boy she could write about to Jadzia. But the only boy at school who had ever paid any attention to her was that awful Mikosz Sienko—and all his attention was the wrong kind. He would pull her braids, call her names: surely the most stupid boy who had ever been born!

How thoughtful *Wuj* Stanislaus had been to make a wooden box for the letters she had sent: Jadzia's letters to her were stored in a battered old cigar box under her bed, and even the scraps of gaily colored cloth she had glued to the box could not make it look like anything more than what it was. Perhaps she could ask *Tata* to make her a beautiful box. *Hah!* she thought. Even if he knew how to do that, it was unlikely that he would even try.

She tried to suppress her nascent envy, but it was difficult. She thought back to her own Name Day, which had hardly differed from any other day this difficult summer. Mama, exhausted with the stifling August heat and the extra weight she had to bear, had been too tired to even think of baking a cake. Because *Tata* and Henryk had been laid off from the tannery for the two weeks preceding her birthday, there had been no gifts, not even any flowers, this year. Her twelfth birthday had been an even greater disappointment than her ninth, when instead of a day at the Century of Progress, she had received a small bunch of daisies and two pairs of heavy black stockings.

No sign of any improvement had yet to touch their area despite President Roosevelt and the New Deal everyone spoke so highly of. Most men were not working, or worked infrequently. The repeal of the Volstead Act three years earlier had reinstituted the neighborhood saloons—not that anyone had actually been able to stop people from drinking during the years of prohibition. But now drinking was legal and open, and the saloons were filled every day but Sunday with men too demoralized to face their wives and children at home.

And then there was Mama's fall. Even before the fall things had been terrible. *Tata* had been laid off again from work, and for days their home had shaken with the thunder of his angry voice. He could not be appeased. Then one terrible morning Mama could not get out of bed. She said she had fallen down the stairs in the night—but Eva was not so sure. The only stairs she could have fallen down were those leading to the cellar, and what would she have been doing in that dark, scary place late at night?

In the next days *Tata* became kind and loving, but he refused to take Mama to the hospital, despite Jadzia's pleas. He said he did not trust doctors or hospitals, that they themselves could care for Mama much better at home.

The sudden creak of the bedroom door startled Eva, setting off another howl from Andrzej, who had just begun to doze off lying against his sister. Both children's eyes riveted on the entrance to the parlor as *Pani* Bodek shuffled in, looking older than her seventy-five years, even older than she had looked when she had appeared at their front door almost twelve hours earlier. The twinkle of the old midwife's eyes, hidden deep within the wrinkles of her face, and the trill of her voice, however, gave them hope. "Go to your mama," she grinned.

"Is she...Did she...?" Eva hardly knew what to ask first.

"Go to your mama. And meet your new baby sister."

"A baby sister!" Her prayers were answered! But Eva had only a moment to contemplate this miracle before she was chasing Andrzej, who had bolted away from her and was dashing toward the open bedroom door. In just a moment he would probably climb right into bed with Mama—the last thing their exhausted mother needed right now.

Grabbing him by the arm just as he reached the bed and clutching him against her skirt with her forearm, she almost gasped at how frail her mother's body looked, now missing the bulk of her pregnancy. Eva was alarmed at her mother's face as well—so pale, the skin almost translucent, the eyes dull and sunken deep into their sockets. But Sofia smiled weakly at her daughter and whispered, "Meet your new little sister Stephania." Only then did Eva notice the tiny bundle, wrapped in a soft blue blanket, cradled in the crook of her mother's arm.

Pani Bodek had shuffled, unnoticed, into the room. Lifting the bundle gently from Sofia's arm, she motioned to Eva to take the baby. Eva relaxed her hold on Andrzej's body only a little, but this gave him the opportunity to jump onto the bed, landing almost upon his mother. As he smothered her with kisses, Sofia drew him to her with the same arm that had held the baby. Eva looked down at the miracle she now cradled in her own arms.

She was first surprised by how little the baby weighed—perhaps as much as a few potatoes in a sack. But this bundle did not feel like potatoes in a sack, not with the vital force of life surging through its little form.

Shyly, Eva moved the folds of the blanket to view more of Stephania's face and was rewarded by the kind of vision that surely inspired artists to paint the faces of angels: a tiny heart-shape of purest ivory framed by thick black curls. Dark blue-black eyes set deeply beside a perfect little scallop of a nose. Rosebud lips. Cheeks the delicate pink of the peonies that bloomed in their front yard in the spring. Surely no baby had ever been born more beautiful than Stephania Bialek.

Eva had only a few minutes to revel in the beauty of this miracle child before *Pani* Bodek was reaching for the baby. "Eva, do you know where your *tata* is?"

Eva nodded. Of course she knew where he was. Where he always was these days.

"Then go get him. Bring him home now." Reluctantly, Eva handed Stephania over and headed out of the bedroom.

Despite having retrieved her father and brother many times from the dank, sour-smelling environs of the tavern just down the corner from their flat, she could not overcome her discomfort at the task. When she came to the storefront saloon, lodged in a building even more dilapidated than those surrounding it, with paint peeling from the shutters and sickly dandelions growing in the small patch of ground between the building and the sidewalk, she waited outside. Hands clasped behind her back, she nervously stepped from foot to foot, occasionally peering at the one word on the faded wooden sign, *Stasiu's,* as though she had not read it dozens of times before. Finally, a kind-looking patron approached the door.

Stopping him with a tentative hand on his forearm and a polite *"Prosze, Pana,"* and giving him the names of her father and brother, she waited only a minute before Henryk emerged from the darkness within. "Eva, has the baby come?" he asked, concern overcoming the hard demeanor he normally affected. Eva could see why all the girls admired her brother. He was tall, over six feet, and his work in the tannery had developed his chest, back and arms beyond those of the normal 18-year-old. He constantly brushed a shock of sandy hair away from smoky eyes, more for the attention this gesture received than for any other reason.

"Yes. *Pani* Bodek says to come right away."

"Boy or girl?"

"A little girl—the most beautiful little girl you've ever seen. Mama has named her Stephania."

"Ah, a sister for you! And Mama?"

"Very weak, but doing well, I think." Henryk re-entered the bar, and within a minute Eva was startled by a loud noise, but one she soon recognized as a cheer. A minute or two later Henryk again appeared, alone, explaining that they should go home and that *Tata* would follow them soon, since courtesy demanded that he stay for the round of drinks that had been ordered to celebrate the arrival of his new daughter. *Saloon courtesy indeed,* thought Eva, but her brother was already racing toward their home, and she had to rush to catch up with him.

Hours later Eva tossed in her bed, too excited by the events of the day to sleep. *Pani* Bodek had allowed her to change little Stephania, and as Eva had unwrapped the squiggly bundle from its blue swaddling, she had marveled at the perfection of every tiny pink finger, every stubby pink toe. *Tata* had arrived home much later than promised, but came bearing gifts—flowers for Sofia, hard sugar candies for the children—before leaving for a rare night shift at the tannery.

Complaining of a stomachache and sore throat, Andrzej had refused his candy, an unprecedented event, but *Pani* Bodek had explained that he was just jealous of all the attention being received by his new little sister, a common enough occurrence for a child his age. In only a few days, she assured Eva, he would get over it, but for the time being, Henryk moved

Andrzej's pallet into his parents' room, where the boy could take comfort in his mother's closeness. When Eva had checked before going to bed to see if her mother needed some water or something to eat, she was not surprised to find Andrzej snuggled up close to her. Little Stephania slept peacefully in the carved wooden cradle that had served Henryk, Eva and Andrzej so well in earlier years.

Despite her exhaustion, Eva could not sleep. She continued to worry about Andrzej, who usually was a good little soldier when it came to handling illness, and about her mother, who through the whole day had been listless and quiet. But then, she thought, Mama had worked hard that day, producing a miracle. A sister! Thoughts of the baby's angelic face replaced her worries. Eva couldn't wait to write of her great news to Jadzia the next day.

The letter would not be written the next day, or for over a month.

Pani Bodek woke Eva before the dawn. "Eva, run. Get the doctor." The anxiety in *Pani* Bodek's voice was enough to forestall any questions Eva might have had.

Dr. Raymond's diagnosis was no surprise to Eva once she saw the rough, pinkish rash on Andrzej's neck that extended down his chest and into his armpits. The boy radiated heat that could be felt half a meter away. Dr. Raymond's solemn intoning of the terrifying word, *scarletina*, and his posting of the quarantine sign on their front door were only confirmation of what she already feared.

The next three days Eva would remember, for the rest of her life, in the blurred vision of a dream. Once arrangements were made to lodge Stephania safely with a neighbor who had just that week lost her own infant, the task of caring for Andrzej fell to Eva and *Pani* Bodek, both of whom had already been exposed to the illness. Henryk stayed with a friend while their father came home only infrequently to pass out, usually inebriated, on the sofa in the parlor.

Pani Bodek and Eva spent the first day bathing Andrzej with cloths dipped in cool water to bring down his fever. To forestall dehydration, they gave him endless teaspoons of sugar water, as much as he could tolerate, and bits of chipped ice that had been brought by a kind neighbor who owned an icebox. The medicine the doctor had given them seemed to be doing a little good, and they prayed that soon his fever would break.

Their other invalid, Sofia, needed much care as well. The doctor said that she had lost too much blood during her delivery, but she was unable to eat the nourishing vegetable beef soup *Pani* Bodek had prepared to build up her strength. Most of the time she slept or dozed, and when she awoke all she took was small sips of tea. The first day she asked interminably about Stephania although she had been told many times where the baby had been placed.

But on the second day, Sofia exhibited the same pinkish rash. Her tongue, the swollen red strawberry tongue common to scarlet fever, confirmed the diagnosis. Dr. Raymond suggested to *Tata* that they move the patients to the hospital. But *Tata* had shouted at the poor old doctor: "Who's to pay for it? You? And who's to say those doctors will take any better care of them than we can here? Those bastards treat us like garbage—they don't want any immigrants dirtying up their pretty white floors."

Eva and *Pani* Bodek worked and waited and prayed. But it was to no avail. Andrzej died in his sleep the afternoon of the third day, and Sofia followed him just before dawn the following morning.

The neighbors who came to the house for the viewing that evening brought pans of fried *pierogi*, trays of fresh-baked *kolaczki*, and fresh *kielbasa* with sauerkraut, which Eva accepted and placed on the over-filled kitchen table covered with a clean white lace cloth. Eva managed to swallow the angry words that wanted to spring out of her mouth when *Pani* Poniatowska assured her that it was a blessing that her poor little brother had his dear mama to lead him through the heavenly gates. Who, she wanted to scream, would raise Stephania? Who would deal with *Tata*, with his anger, now boiling dangerously at the surface, and with Henryk's stony silences?

And who, God help her, would now lead her through this life on earth? Who would fill the hole where her heart used to be? Who would make *kolaczki* with her, and tell her stories of Poland, and celebrate her achievements at school? Who would perform the unveiling ceremony years from now at her wedding, and guide her in raising her own little children? *Tata*? Henryk? A whole lifetime without Mama—how could she bear to even think of that?

She wanted to scream, to stamp her feet, to throw the brightly colored bowl of potatoes that the stupid old woman had just handed her against the kitchen wall. Instead, she thanked her, trying to remember that *Pani*

Poniatowska had been a dear friend of her mother's, and meekly accepted a kiss on her tear-stained cheek.

The viewing was possible because Dr. Raymond had lifted the quarantine once he determined that no one else in the household showed signs of having been infected. Scarlet fever was, after all, a children's disease, not one adults normally caught. Had Sofia not been weakened by her difficult pregnancy and delivery, her body would most likely have resisted the infection.

Eva almost welcomed the mindless work she had to do before the viewing—washing all linens and surfaces in the bedroom with hot water and bleach—while the job of preparing the bodies for burial and arranging the parlor fell to *Pani* Bodek. Now the bodies lay together within one polished wooden coffin supported on a long table at the far end of the parlor. Sofia embraced Andrzej as she had so many times in life, giving the illusion that they but slept, mother comforting son. But now her hands were folded together, the beads of her pearl rosary intertwined. The soft glow of beeswax candles provided the only light in the parlor; that, and the vases of fall flowers—chrysanthemums, gladiolus and some late-blooming zinnias displayed on every available surface and on the floor surrounding the coffin—did much to conceal the shabbiness of the carpet, the worn spots on the sofa.

Eva kneeled and bowed her head deeply, along with all her assembled family and friends, when Father Tadeusz came late that night to offer requiem prayers. She chanted with the assembled mourners the Latin responses they knew by heart, words meant to comfort the living and to bring the dead swiftly into their heavenly abode. The next day at the Mass for the Dead, her words, along with those of all who had come to pay their respects, lifted with clouds of fragrant incense into the vast rise of St. Casimir's church, from there to ascend to heaven.

But as her lips formed the familiar, beautiful words of the *Pater Noster* and the *Ave Maria,* Eva felt deep within her heart that that's all they were—beautiful words—and that, beyond the confines of this building, there was no one to hear them, and no one who cared.

Chapter Six

Jadzia, Niedzieliska

April, 1941

The sound of the gun's discharge, a single shot, erased any other sound, indeed any other thought, within the square.

For one moment Apolonya stood completely still, and hope flooded Jadzia's heart. A warning shot! Apolonya would now turn around and come back to the trucks.

But soon Jadzia saw a dark circle of red, rapidly growing like an unfolding rose, at the very center of Apolonya's slender back. She stared in horror as Apolonya, never once glancing back, dropped first to her knees, then tumbled gently forward into the tender young blades of grass just beginning to break the soil in the town square.

Jadzia's scream died in her throat as she was forcibly shoved into the darkness of the truck's interior. She felt a slight tug at her neck, then a sprinkling of drops on her shoulders as her *babcia's* amber necklace caught on a latch, its sun-colored beads scattering beneath her in the dirt. Tripping on another body, perhaps that of her brother Marek scrambling to get his bearings in the darkness, her palm scraped the ridged surface of the truck floor. She felt something—something round and smooth—and quickly placed it into her mouth, hiding it in the fleshy area under her tongue.

Immediately the two heavy doors of the truck swung shut with a loud crash, and with one more grating sound, metal sliding on metal, that signified the fastening of the lock, and then two sharp thumps of a heavy hand hitting the side panel, the truck grunted into motion and began to bear its human cargo westward.

Chapter Seven

Evie, Chicago

October, 1941

15 marca, 1941

Moja najdroższa Evo!

Nie wiem czy kiedykolwiek otrzymasz ten list. Brat Apoloni, Józef obiecał wysłać ten list z Anglii, jeśli tam kiedyś dotrze. Józef planuje wstąpić do Armii Polskiej, którą zorganizowano w Anglii, ażeby walczyć przeciwko Nazistom.

Anyone who did not know them would assume they were a married couple, quite young of course, attending Sunday mass at St. Casimir's with their daughter. He stood ramrod straight in a dark brown suit, following carefully in his missal the Polish translations of the Latin prayers that Father Tadeusz solemnly intoned on the altar. She, in a short-sleeved print shirtwaist with a Peter Pan collar, a circular lace kerchief pinned over cascading curls of chestnut brown, stood beside him, head bowed, the beads of a pearl rosary dripping slowly from her fingers. The cropped raven curls of the little girl wedged between them danced with every turn of her head; obviously, it took the girl's entire stock of self-control to suppress her natural exuberance during the long, tedious incantations in a language she did not understand.

They looked like a young family as well during their four-block walk home from church, Stephania skipping between them, holding in one pudgy hand the hand of her sister and in the other the strong, callused hand of Mikosz Sienko, Eva's fiancée. Even now Eva was in awe at how the awful little boy she remembered from grade school had grown into this handsome, very desirable man.

In little less than a year they would be a real family. Eva was to finish high school in June, her graduation postponed for one year by the responsibilities she had taken on with the death of her mother. Then she would be free to marry Mikosz, whose intelligence and hard work at the valve factory had already earned him a promotion to night shift supervisor. They would take Stephania into their home to raise as their own. After all, Eva was the only mother Steffie had ever known, and the thought of her sister being raised in a house of men—particularly when those men were Wladyslaw and Henryk Bialek, who knew nothing of the needs of little girls—was unacceptable to Eva.

But for now their family of three was only an illusion: Eva and Stephania lived in the old apartment on Haddon Avenue with her father and Henryk, and Mikosz with his mother, the indomitable *Pani* Sienka, just a few blocks away. It was to Haddon Avenue they were now headed, to share Sunday dinner with Eva's father and brother, as they had every week for over a year.

"So, *kochanie*, tell me more of this letter from your cousin." Eva had had only a moment to tell Mikosz about the long-awaited letter from Jadzia as she had met him at the church door

"It's months old—from March." It was already the first week of October, and Chicago was enjoying a late Indian Summer, with temperatures in the 80's and a gentle breeze stirring the last of the autumn leaves dangling on the trees. "She gave it to Apolonya's brother Jozef. He promised that if he could escape to England, he would post it from there."

"So he must have made it. What does she say about conditions in Poland?"

Because they were already at the door of the apartment, Eva promised to read the letter to Mikosz later. She had much to do. The *golabki* were already browning in the oven of the cast iron stove and the *baba*, which she planned to serve with some of the peach preserves she had canned during the summer, had been baked the day before. Now Eva needed to peel and boil potatoes and make cucumber salad.

And after dinner, of course, as she washed dishes and cleaned the kitchen, *Tata*, Henryk and Mikosz would settle in the parlor for their Sunday afternoon tradition, a shot glass or two of vodka while they listened to the Polish station on the old wooden radio—battered but still emitting a decipherable sound through the static—and talked of men's concerns: work in their respective factories and which new orders had come in that week; politics and the effect of President Roosevelt's economic policies on the country; and now, always, of the war in Europe, whether or not the United States should become involved. It was all exceedingly boring to Eva, but she was grateful, at least, that *Tata* had accepted her engagement to Mikosz and the two men seemed to get along.

It was already past 3:00 when Eva, sitting at the kitchen table flipping through ads in the pages of the *Zgoda*, the Polish newspaper, was suddenly encircled by the powerful arms of Mikosz. Sneaking up behind her, he bent to nuzzle her neck, planting a quick kiss on her cheek. "Are you ready for our walk, *moya mala Myszko?*"

Eva loved the way those words, his special name for her, "my little mouse," rumbled from deep within his throat, especially during evenings in their parlor, when *Tata* and Stephania had gone to sleep and Henryk was out seeking his own distractions. She would sit on Mikosz's lap, accepting his kisses and allowing his hands to wander over her body, stopping him only when his heightening passion or the tingling deep within her told her they were nearing danger. She was, after all, a good girl, and Mikosz had reluctantly accepted her insistence that they wait until their wedding night to fulfill their love completely. She knew it wasn't going to be easy for either of them.

Eva called to her sister, who had already changed from her Sunday dress and shoes into a sturdier playground outfit, and the three of them made their way to the park. As Eva and Mikosz sat on a wooden bench watching Steffie play with some other children on the swing set, his arm possessively draped around her, she removed Jadzia's letter from its dirty, tattered envelope and read aloud:

March 15, 1941

My dearest Eva,

I do not know if you will ever receive this letter, which Apolonya's brother Jozef has promised to post from England if he ever arrives there. Jozef plans to enlist with the remnants of the Polish army that have assembled in England to fight the Nazis, and he's not the first of our village to attempt this. I told him it was too dangerous to carry this letter, but he assured me that, if he were caught, he would be imprisoned or shot anyway—letter or no letter—so I'm writing to tell you of our lives here.

Since the German invasion of almost two years ago, our part of Poland has been considered a colony of Germany, and our governor is a Nazi named Hans Frank. Our village commandant, Hans Mittenburg, is perhaps not as bad as many others. For all these changes, our lives in Niedzieliska have not changed very much. Tata, Marek and Stasiu are still here, working on the farm, although they must now turn all our crops over to the German officials in town who then give us a percentage for our own use. We do not receive very much food back, enough for us to live on, but just barely. Farmers are probably the most fortunate in this occupation, as the Nazis need us and what we produce for their war effort.

No one has been taken away from Niedzieliska, but we hear rumors that this is happening in villages all over Poland. I think this occupation is much worse for the people who live in the cities—we've heard of executions and deportations of many Poles and Jews. We can only hope and pray that we will remain safe—our village is so small and remote, perhaps the Nazis will not really notice us until this terrible war is over.

Apolonya's family are well, as far as we know. Her brothers Antek and Wladek disappeared one night early in 1940—most in the village believe they ran away to join the Nazis! While this is hard to understand, there are some few Poles who have believed for several years that an alliance with Germany is in our best interest. But I can hardly believe, even now, that Antek would actually do such a thing. As you know, Apolonya's two oldest brothers emigrated to America many years ago. Now with Jozef gone, only Apolonya and her youngest brothers, Alfons and Gienek, are left at home. This must be very difficult for Pani Zadora, who seems destined to suffer one loss after another.

I hope your family is well. Is Stephania still so beautiful as she was in that picture you sent? She must be almost old enough for school by now. And your tata and Henryk, are they well? Is your tata any kinder to you than he has been in the past? In the last letter I received from you (so long ago—we have not had regular mail delivery for over a year) you mentioned you were seeing Mikosz Sienko. How funny that you started seeing that same boy who used to torment you so much in grade school! Are the two of you still a couple? Any exciting news coming from that front soon?

It gives me and my whole family great comfort to know that your family is safe in America. We do not know from minute to minute what will happen here. I know you yourself are probably in no position to change matters, but we pray for the day that America will enter this war. Talk to people you know—the British alone cannot hold out forever against the Axis. And who knows, when Britain falls, perhaps the United States will be invaded next. It seems impossible, but who would have expected the Polish, and especially the French, to be defeated so soundly?

Please pray for us, and know my love and prayers come to you and your family with this letter. Mama, Tata and Babcia, as always, send their love to all of you as well, and we wish you and your family a blessed Easter. We here all look forward to the holiday, which will give us a break from our everyday work and troubles. I hope that soon hostilities will end around the world, and that you and I will be able to write freely as we did before.

Your loving cousin,
Jadzia

"Your father doesn't..." Mikosz's arm tightened protectively around Eva's shoulders, responding immediately to the reference about her father.

"No, not any more. Not for a long time."

"Because, if he did..."

"I know, Mikosz. I would tell you." Eva knew exactly what Mikosz referred to, what she, herself, had tried to think of as just a bad dream. The beatings had started only days after her mother's funeral, when she had tracked mud into the kitchen. Eva had immediately understood what she had only previously suspected—the horrible meaning behind all those frightening sounds coming from her parents' bedroom late at night for so many years. *Tata* had never hit her before her mother's death; Eva understood how much Mama had suffered to direct his rage away from her children. Now her mother's protection was gone, and Eva realized she would bear the brunt of his anger and desperation.

For four years, though she had tried her best to please him by keeping the house immaculate and preparing his favorite foods, nothing had worked. It had been only a year ago, when Stephania had spilled milk at the kitchen table and Wladislaw had grabbed the child, reaching for his belt buckle with his other hand, that Eva had been infused with the courage to challenge him.

"You touch her and you'll regret it," she had screamed, bolting from the table and grabbing his arm.

"You! What could you do?" He had pulled his arm away from Evie, raising it above his head to deliver a backhand blow.

"You don't want to know, old man," she had said, stepping deftly away, pulling Stephania to her. "If you ever touch her, or me again, you'll pay." Eva could not believe she was saying these bold words.

Wladislaw had paused. The punishing labor at the tannery, the years of vodka, and the encroaching disabilities of age and asthma had all had their effect. Still, he was the father. He looked menacing as he stood up, unfastening the heavy leather belt Eva had learned to fear. "What could you do?" he repeated, taking a step toward his daughters.

"I could tell Mikosz." At the time Eva had been seeing Mikosz for about three months, and already she considered him her protector.

"Tell Mikosz what? How disobedient and disrespectful you are? You think Mikosz will want you then?" Wladislaw had laughed. "Besides, you think he won't be the boss in your family when you marry him? Then it will be his job to keep you in line."

He took another step closer, now towering directly over Eva, the heat of his anger and the smell of stale beer almost overwhelming her. She still grasped Stephania, who stood, eyes closed and fists held tightly against her ears, almost hidden within the folds of her sister's long skirt. In desperation Eva blurted out, "Maybe I can't stop you right now, *Tata*, but you have to sleep some time!"

For one very long moment, these words seemed suspended in the air. "What are you saying? You threaten me? *You?*" he questioned, his face horribly contorted in rage and surprise.

"Not threatening, *Tata*. Promising." Eva's eyes had met her father's. For a moment the two stood inches apart, glaring at each other. Miraculously, Wladislaw was the first to look away.

"What kind of daughter is this that is so disrespectful of her father?" he had muttered, taking a step back. As he shuffled away toward the parlor, buckling his belt, Eva had heard him mutter, "What kind of country is this where children grow up to defy their parents?"

"Promise you'll tell me if he *ever…*" Mikosz insisted.

"I will. I *have* promised you." One of the things Eva loved most about Mikosz was the fact that, over time, she had learned to trust him enough to tell him things she had never spoken about before, things that had shamed her into silence. He had become a dear friend to her even before he had become her betrothed.

Of course, she had not shared with him details of her father's abuse: some things, after all, were better off not talked about. She had come to terms with her father's cruelty, had come to see it as the response of a man who, like so many others in their neighborhood, felt helpless in the face of a life over which he had lost control.

Besides, if *Tata* and Mikosz were to become family, it was better that Mikosz not know everything. The one time she had referred to *Tata's* abuse had been enough to rile Mikosz into wanting to confront the old man; Evie had had to lie to him, to assure him that her father had been only a harsh disciplinarian, not the cruel tyrant she had known him as.

"All right then," Mikosz responded. "Let's get back to your cousin's letter. It sounds like you've written a lot about me," he smiled, responding to the two sentences that referred specifically to him.

Mikosz's dark mood had lifted immediately, another quality Eva had learned to find endearing. How simple his needs were at times—how transparent his thoughts and feelings. "What did you say to her, *moja droga?*" he teased, chucking her gently on the chin. "Did you tell her how handsome I am?"

"Why, maybe. I hardly remember," Evie teased, looking slightly up and away from him, eyelids fluttering. "I think perhaps I told her you grew up far less ugly than I expected when you were in the sixth grade." Mikosz planted a quick kiss on her cheek, laughing.

"But Mikosz," she continued, are more soberly, "we shouldn't be joking. The rest of Jadzia's letter is terrible. I'm afraid they're all in danger."

"She says they're safe right now. We can only hope for the best. If the United States would get into this war, then in only a short time..."

"Do you really believe this will happen?"

"I'm surprised it hasn't happened already. The U.S. is already sending war supplies to England. I can't believe they haven't come to the support of their allies. I don't know what it'll take to change Roosevelt's mind."

Ach, thought Eva, *men and their wars. Wasn't there enough death in the world without war?* It was time to collect Stephania and head back to the apartment. As Eva looked over to the sandbox where she had last seen her sister's dark curls tumbling in the breeze, she could imagine another little head there, its blonde curls bent over a battered red truck—a vision from not so many years before that still held the power to take her breath away.

Weeks later, on the first Sunday of December, Eva was busy with the finishing touches of Mikosz's birthday cake, a massive *mazurek* of alternating layers of chocolate and almond, its glazed topping of raisins, dates and nuts gleaming. This was to follow a pot roast dinner, an American recipe she had found in a magazine. Such expense! *Tata's* eyebrows had almost hit the ceiling when she had asked him for grocery money. But after all, the 21st birthday of one's fiancée came only once in a lifetime. It was a day to celebrate.

Glancing at the clock, she realized that, according to the recipe, the roast was just about finished. She stepped to the kitchen door and called out to her sister, who was playing in the tiny back yard of the apartment with the little girl who lived next door. As Steffie tumbled into the house, Eva bent to unfasten the wooden buttons on her blue wool coat and free her tight black curls from a knitted plaid scarf that had been Eva's years before. "Ah, Steffie, your hands are so cold," Eva said, rubbing them within the warmth of her own. Winter had come to Chicago early this year; it was very cold for December 7.

"Is dinner almost ready?" asked the little girl, her nose raised in the air as she sniffed in anticipation of the coming feast.

"Yes, in just a few minutes."

"And we have a cake? And we'll sing *Sto Lat!* for Mikosz?"

"Yes and yes. Now go wash your hands—you look like you've been working in a coal mine. And I want you to set the table for me in the dining room. We're using Mama's good china, and so I'm trusting you to be very careful."

Dinner was every bit as successful as she had hoped. Even *Tata* had commented on the tenderness of the meat, the richness of the cake. Her family, at Stephania's urging, had sung three choruses of *Sto Lat!*, the traditional Polish birthday song that wished for 100 years of life for the celebrant: Stephania had asked if this meant they had wished 300 years for Mikosz.

Now the men were relaxing in the parlor, listening to the radio, as Eva finished cleaning the kitchen. She had asked them to refrain from their usual vodka shots since she was preparing a birthday toast which the whole family could enjoy: Manischevitz concord grape wine in whiskey glasses for the men, and mixed with soda water in tumblers for her and Stephania, whose tumbler of soda water contained just a half teaspoon of wine.

Eva knew the moment she turned the corner into the parlor bearing her tray of drinks that something was terribly wrong. *Tata*, Henryk and Mikosz sat immobilized, each craning toward the radio like flowers reaching to the sun. Silently, eyebrows arched and mouths open, they strained to hear every word. Even Stephania stood immobile, her favorite rag doll hanging from her hand, obviously stunned by the atmosphere in the room, so like that moment of tension between the jolt of lightening and the crack of thunder that follows.

Eva, terrified, wished to cry out, asking what was wrong, but restrained herself. She tried to concentrate on the words of the Polish announcer, which first came to her as a jumble: "Arizona"; "Japan"; "Hawaii"; "Pearl Harbor." So many places. What could it mean?

It meant war. This was the consensus of the men, who sprang into discussion immediately after the news announcement ended and the radio station switched to some somber Chopin etudes.

"The United States will have to go to war now," Henryk asserted. "Roosevelt will surely declare war on Japan."

Japan, Eva thought. *Not Germany. The other side of the world. No help for Jadzia and her family.*

"And that will surely get us into the war in Europe as well," Mikosz added.

"But why?" Eva asked shyly. "Japan is very far from Europe."

"Because they're allies," Mikosz explained gently. "If we declare war on Japan, Germany will have to declare war on us. And then we'll be in the middle of it all."

"Thank God we're here," said *Tata*, "away from all the wars in Europe. There are always wars in Europe. We'd do better to stay out of it altogether."

"Yes," agreed Eva, placing the tray of drinks on the coffee table, "that would be best."

"But it won't happen," argued Henryk. "We'll go to war. *I'll* go to war!"

"I forbid you!" *Tata's* fist slammed onto the coffee table, jolting the tray of drinks, the tinkle of glass hitting glass sounding incongruously melodious. "You'll stay right here, in Chicago. You'll work here and help support the family. I didn't leave Europe to have my own son die there years later."

"You won't be able to stop me, *Tata*. I'll enlist. And what about you, Mikosz?"

All eyes were suddenly on Mikosz. Eva's eyes, in particular, burned into his. "Well," he answered finally, "I believe I must go too. I don't think we have any choice."

"Stupid, stupid," muttered *Tata*, while Eva, shoulders drooping and mouth slightly open, tried to process this new, horrible information. Mikosz looked steadily into her eyes.

"Ach," countered Henryk, "nothing to worry about. The war will be over six months after the Americans go in. Maybe even three months."

"We'll probably not even get to Europe before the war is over," soothed Mikosz, who stepped toward the coffee table and started to pass drinks around. "Let's drink to a quick victory for the Allies."

"Think of how handsome Mikosz will be in his uniform." Henryk winked at Eva as he lifted his glass for the toast. "Why, you'll fall in love with him all over again!"

"Stupid, stupid," muttered *Tata* once more, accepting a shot glass and immediately downing it, not waiting for the toast. For once, Eva agreed wholeheartedly with her father.

"To victory!" shouted Henryk and Mikosz, raising their glasses high before bringing them to their lips. "To victory," whispered Eva prayerfully, although she truly knew not to whom she prayed.

Later that evening, when *Tata* and Stephania had gone to bed and Henryk had left for the evening, Mikosz and Eva sat on the chenille spread that covered the sofa in the parlor. She was uncharacteristically silent, distractedly fingering the fringe of the spread while he stared morosely at his hands, folded in his lap. The distance between them was as emotional as it was physical. Finally Mikosz, moving closer to her, placed a tentative arm around her, not really surprised by her failure to yield to him. *"Kochanie,"* he whispered, "I *will* come back to you. I swear it."

"Now you sound like Henryk," she spat back, finally saying the words that had been churning inside her all evening. "You can't know this. You'll leave me to go play soldier and die a thousand miles from home. I'll never see you again."

"No, no, *moja gwiadzko*—my star. This I know for a fact—I *will* come home to you. We'll marry and raise beautiful children together." She resisted his efforts to embrace her. "Eva," he pleaded, "you have to understand. It's my duty as a man to go. You wouldn't have me shirk my duty?"

"Duty! What do men know of duty? What about your duty to me?"

"My heart is here, *kochanie*, and it will always be. *Daj mi buzi*—give me a kiss—and tell me you love me. I'll carry your love with me into battle and it will save me from harm."

Chapter Eight

Jadzia, Dahlem, Germany

August, 1941

Polskie dziewczyny!!
Rub pszed sniadanie
Pszynies jajka
Nakarmi kury
Pospszontaj kurnik
Doi krowy
Biesz krowy na pastfisko

Jadzia woke to what in the Eifel was a balmy dawn, with temperatures in the upper 50's already dispersing the ever-present morning fog. Nudging the arm of Sabina, who slept soundly on the hay-filled mat they shared, she announced the morning in her most commanding voice: "Wake up, Lazy Bones. Time to start another day." She was not, under any circumstances, going to complete the morning chores by herself this day.

As she splashed water onto her face from the wash bucket, memories of the journey that had brought her here threatened to unbalance the composure she tried so mightily to maintain. Her days in Dahlem, the town where she now lived, were too filled with work to allow much thought. It was only for a few moments in the early morning and then again before she fell into an exhausted deep sleep that her thoughts inevitably strayed to the events of several months before.

The horror of those first few hours, jostling on dirt roads in a dark closed truck, reawakened pain she tried to ignore. While listening to the cries and prayers of the others, she tried to convince herself that Apolonya had been only injured. Then the terrible circle of crimson on Apolonya's back would begin to fill her mind. She knew she would never see her friend again. She herself would live—she vowed she would live! Marek echoed her thoughts—buzzing in her ear—We will live!

The truck had stopped at the train station at Krakow and Jadzia and the others were pushed into an already crowded boxcar. The train stopped frequently at small stations, sometimes for an hour or longer, and occasionally at these stops the wide doors of their boxcar slid open. Heavily armed soldiers would board the boxcar, sometimes gathering a group to remove from the train, sometimes adding a new group of terrified people into the mix. Women would wail and moan as they were separated from those they loved, but no one resisted.

It was at a much larger station, one that a more-traveled passenger identified as Prague, that Marek and all the remaining young men in the boxcar were taken. Marek had kept his eyes locked on Jadzia's as though willing her to courage until the last moment, when he was pushed out the open door and dropped from her sight. Through that long night and the next day Jadzia could hear bits of conversation among those remaining, all women, but she chose to close herself off from these strangers. Through their lamentations and fearful cries all that echoed in her mind was one unthinkable question: would she ever see Marek or any of her family again?

She was taken from the train at Wiesbaden and transferred, along with six other young women, to an oxcart. From there they took a long, meandering journey through the forested, rolling hills of southwest Germany, stopping at small villages to deposit one girl at a churchyard, two at a farmhouse. Even though their driver, an older man—obviously a farmer—was their only guard, and the villagers who met the girls were often elderly couples or single women, Jadzia had no thoughts of escape. She was numb in this foreign land.

Her own journey had ended at what, she would soon learn, was the grandest house in the town of Dahlem: the home of the mayor, Herr Heinemann, his wife and their youngest son, Wilhelm. The two-story dwelling of white clapboard with a peaked, red tiled roof was surprisingly tall, but Jadzia soon discover it typical of Eifel homes, where farm families lived in very small villages, their homes built above their barns. Twice a day cattle were driven through the narrow streets of Dahlem to pasture in triangular fields that formed a circle of ownership around the village.

Jadzia tried once more to wake Sabina, this time shaking her shoulder roughly, but then decided to handle the chickens herself. She would try again just before it was time to drive the twelve dairy cattle to pasture, a job she could not accomplish by herself. Late last night Jadzia had heard Sabina steal out of the house's attached lean-to where they slept and head toward the barn, sleeping quarters for Leo and Casimir, two workers brought from the area near Katowice. Jadzia had slept too soundly to hear Sabina return.

On her way to the chicken coop she checked the morning chores list, written in Casimir's execrable Polish:

Polish Girls!!
Do bifor brakfus
Collek eggs
Fid chiks
Klin koop
Milk kows
Tek kows to pastur

She considered her relative good fortune; she knew that many Poles were slave laborers in German factories, forced to take the place of German workers fighting for the Reich. Lives in these factories were often brutal and short. Other Poles did forced labor on large farms, endless, back-breaking days of repetitive planting or picking. Work on a small farm was at least familiar to her and involved many diverse tasks, although working from before dawn to well past dusk six days a week was beyond any experience she had ever had at home, even during harvest.

Grabbing the chicken feed she entered the pen, then released the latches, freeing her small feathered charges from their coops. Broadcasting the feed with a practiced flick of her wrist, aiming for the far reaches of the pen, she hoped to lure as many chickens as possible from their roosts to avoid receiving painful pecks from sitting hens. She hand fed a few grains to two of her favorites—a busy little red and a haughty black-spotted white—before collecting the eggs.

Returning to the lean-to, she now needed to rouse Sabina in earnest. "Get up. Get up. We have to drive the cows," she demanded, nudging the sleeping girl with one toe. "Do I have to get the water bucket?"

"No, dammit. I'm getting up." Sabina Mazurek sat up slowly, rubbing her eyes with balled fists, then running one hand through long, wavy hair the color of the hay tangled in it. At 23, sun-bleached and muscular from her work on the farm, slim but bosomy and with a large mouth, sooty grey eyes, and a sassy attitude, Sabina was much admired by the few men still living in Dahlem. She had been brought to the farm six months earlier than Jadzia.

"You shoulda' come to the barn with me last night," Sabina said as she and Jadzia released the dairy cows from their stalls and began slowly herding them down Zur Steinkaul, the main street of town. The sun had just fully emerged from behind the hill directly ahead of them. "Casimir and me stole some beer from the cellar," she boasted.

Jadzia twitched her nose in disgust. Her single sip of the bitter drink several years earlier had left her wondering why anyone drank it.

Despite receiving no response from Jadzia, Sabina continued teasingly, "I think Leo likes you."

"What wonderful news. My future is assured," Jadzia answered scornfully. Leo was six inches shorter than she was, stocky and dimwitted, and was entrusted with only the most menial jobs. He always smelled of the manure he was constantly sweeping from the barn or spreading on the fields. More seriously, Jadzia asked, "Aren't you afraid of getting caught?"

"By who? Frau Heinemann? That old bitch? She sleeps like a mule."

"Still, if she told Herr Heinemann..."

"I know how to handle that old goat. Besides, he's almost never here." In addition to mayoral duties, Herr Heinemann had other responsibilities involving conscriptions and enlistments in their region that kept him from home many nights. "And I think Frau Heinemann's too damn stupid to know much of what's going on anyway."

"I don't think she's stupid. I think she's kind of nice," Jadzia offered, smacking Gertie, a large Guernsey with a mind of her own, with the stout stick she carried. Gertie ambled back closer to the herd.

"Nice? Are you crazy? It's not bad enough she works us to death every day. You'd think she could give us Sunday off—not make us go to that damn heathen church of hers and then listen to her brat all afternoon."

"I kind of like our Sundays," admitted Jadzia. True, the small, austere Lutheran church where they listened to endless sermons in German was nothing like St. Adalbert's, but the two-hour Sunday service gave her a chance to think. And she enjoyed the afternoon violin recitals Wilhelm performed in the Heinemann's drawing room after Sunday dinner.

"Watch Helga. She's gettin' ideas," Sabina warned, alerting Jadzia to a cow that had begun to veer toward a neighbor's hedge. Sabina continued, her stern look commanding attention, "One thing you gotta remember as long as you're here. That Helga. She's a good milker, yes?"

"One of the best."

"But what would happen to her if she couldn't give any more milk?"

"Well, she'd go to the butcher. That's how it is on all farms."

"Right, Jadzia, but what you gotta remember is, to Frau Heinemann and everyone else in this cursed country, you're no different from that cow."

Jadzia's heart resisted Sabina's words. People were people, after all, some good and some not, no matter where they came from. Sometimes people just got caught in situations over which they had no control. And Frau Heinemann looked at her so tenderly at times, not at all like Herr Heinemann, who always glared at her as if she were some sort of large, ugly bug.

More than once, while dusting the heavy, ornate bureau in the dining room or polishing the massive wardrobe in the main bedroom, Jadzia had chanced upon Frau Heinemann, her graying head nodding, her clear blue eyes behind round spectacles awash in tears, reading old letters or gazing at photos of her older children. Jadzia knew that Frau Heinemann's oldest son had died in the French campaign and was buried in the pretty little cemetery high on a hill just outside town. Her middle son was currently missing in action in Russia. Frau Heinemann had a daughter as well—a beautiful girl if the wedding photos on the mantel did not lie—who lived with her husband and their small child in Koblenz. Frau Heinemann had not heard from her daughter in many months. Jadzia chose to ignore Sabina's bitter remark.

"Jadzia, help me with this latch." Sabina was struggling with the gate to the Heinemann's pasture. The girls, finally releasing the latch, herded the cows into the open area.

"You have to admit this is beautiful country," Jadzia suggested, gazing out at the valley before them. Unlike the industrialized north or the commercially agrarian south of Germany, the Eifel region, just east of Luxembourg, was composed of small tracts of cultivated land and pastures nestled among gentle hills and stands of deep coniferous forest. The area was dotted with small lakes, some of them, almost perfectly circular, the result of ancient volcano activity. An ever-present mantle of fog softened the features of the land, giving it a mythical appearance. Jadzia could easily imagine a troll, dwarf or elf emerging from a wooded patch like the ones pictured in the books of fairy tales Frau Heinemann had saved from when her children were young.

"The Eifel?" Sabina was unwilling to relent in any detail. "You mean the 'armpit of Germany,'" she laughed, referring to the insulting sobriquet they'd heard the area called. Far from the famous political, commercial and cultural areas of Germany, the Eifel was known for being backward and primitive. But to Jadzia that took nothing from its beauty.

They could not dally long at the pasture gate; there was much more to be done that day. The morning chores list was followed by the household chores list, which involved such tasks as batting linens and rugs, sweeping floors and polishing silver. Jadzia had always considered her mother an excellent housekeeper, but Frau Heinemann was much more meticulous. She could abide no stain, no bit of dust in her well-appointed home.

Before lunch, Jadzia and Sabina were also required to tend to the flower gardens, including carefully grooming the masses of red and white geraniums blooming from a dozen window boxes, and to sweep the sidewalk and the street. This last task seemed overly fastidious to Jadzia until she noticed that sidewalk and street sweeping was a daily task for every *hausfrau* in Dahlem.

After lunch the girls usually joined Casimir and Leo in the fields to plant, weed, water or harvest. Evenings were spent mending clothing or embroidering linens by candlelight. Jadzia was amazed that most nights, at least when Herr Heinemann was not home, Sabina was energetic enough to sneak from their lean-to into the barn for a rendezvous with Casimir and Leo. But then, Sabina had had almost a whole year to adjust to the work; in just a few days, on September 6th, Jadzia would mark the beginning of her fourth month in Dahlem.

"So," Sabina asked as they began their short journey back to the house, "are you joining us in the fields this afternoon?"

Jadzia knew that their Saturday routine annoyed the older girl. Jadzia worked with Frau Heinemann in the house while Sabina was in the fields. Jadzia had been in Dahlem for only six weeks when she had replaced Sabina in helping prepare the home and family meal for Sunday—much lighter work than she would have had otherwise.

"I think I'm in the house. Frau Heinemann is making sausage this afternoon." Herr Krueger, a neighbor and friend of the Heinemann's, had slaughtered the last of his pigs several days earlier and had shared some of the pork with his neighbors. He had tied the slaughtered pig to a wooden rack, its belly slit wide open from throat to tail. Jadzia thought it looked like some bizarre crucifix, then crossed herself quickly when she wondered whether the comparison might be sacrilegious. A stream of thick red blood had drained into the street, which seemed terribly wasteful to Jadzia: at home her family would have saved the fresh blood to make *kiszka*.

"I imagine you enjoy your Saturday afternoons in Frau Heinemann's kitchen. I don't blame you: it's better than being in the fields. But before you get too close to our jailers and start thinking of them as family, remember what I said," warned Sabina.

It was hard to see Frau Heinemann as a jailer that afternoon while Jadzia assisted her in making sausage: their activities too closely resembled so many afternoons spent with her mother and grandmother. The seasonings for the knackwurst and bratwurst Frau Heinemann made differed from the garlic and mustard seed her mother used for *kielbasa*, but chopping the meat into small pieces, grinding it, mixing in the seasonings, stuffing the casings, then finally boiling or smoking the sausage were familiar tasks to women whether they were German *hausfraus* or Polish *gospodyni*.

Through her Saturday afternoons with Frau Heinemann, Jadzia had picked up enough German to carry on simple conversations. Frau Heinemann, patient and understanding, spoke slowly and simply, as to a small child, and even dropped in an occasional Polish word she had learned from her workers. As the last sausage casing was stuffed and tied, Jadzia motioned to indicate that she would now return to work in the fields.

"No, no, you stay," insisted Frau Heinemann, grabbing Jadzia's hand and pointing to the canister of flour sitting on a high shelf. "Can you get?" Jadzia reached high for the canister.

"How you call in Polish?" Frau Heinemann asked.

"*Maka*."

"Today we celebrate Krueger's pig. Use *maka* to make strudel. You make apple strudel in Poland?"

"Oh, yes," Jadzia answered. "With raisins and almonds."

"No raisins or almonds any more, what with the war," Frau Heinemann sighed, wiping her hands on the apron that barely covered her ample waistline. "Only apples from the orchard."

"I'm sure it will be very good. Sometimes we had no raisins and almonds when I made strudel at home with Mama." Jadzia looked down at her hands, a familiar memory suddenly misting her eyes.

"Ah, *liebchen*," Frau Heinemann sighed more deeply this time. "You miss your mama, no?"

"Yes, very much."

"Soon the war will be over, our boys then come home, you go home to your mama, yes?" Frau Heinemann's reassuring hug almost convinced Jadzia that those words would come true.

Just as Jadzia was carefully placing the strudel into the heavy, cast iron oven, Wilhelm entered the kitchen, giving his mother a quick peck on the cheek and nodding companionably to Jadzia.

"Strudel, Mama?" he asked, "what's the occasion?" He brushed long bangs of thin brown hair from his eyes. At fifteen, Wilhelm was tall and very thin, with clear white skin and blue eyes pale like the shells of robin's eggs. He was a young man of many passions—art, literature, philosophy, music—which made him unlike any boy Jadzia had ever known in Poland. Once, as Jadzia had scrubbed linens on a laundry board in the kitchen, she had heard Herr Heinemann in the sitting room accuse his wife of spoiling their youngest son by keeping him inside too much and shielding him unnecessarily.

Frau Heinemann's excuse, that Wilhelm's asthma and his artistic personality made him more fragile than their other sons and, indeed, even their daughter, soon silenced her husband's complaints. Jadzia wondered if Wilhelm was Frau Heinemann's favorite, or if she coddled him because deep inside she feared he was her only surviving child.

"We are celebrating Herr Krueger's generosity," smiled Frau Heinemann. "Tomorrow we shall feast. Are you going back to the library?"

"No, Mama, enough Kant for one day. I'm going to practice my music for tomorrow."

"And what will you be playing for us?" Her eyes shone in what looked to Jadzia like pure adoration.

"I thought I'd work on some Liszt or Haydn for tomorrow, Mama. Or perhaps something from Tchaikovsky's *Concerto in D Major*? Do you have a request?"

"Oh, I love whatever you play, Son."

"Then what about you?" asked Wilhelm, turning suddenly toward Jadzia, who with one hand was brushing tiny scraps of dough and a dusting of flour into the apron she held out with the other.

"Me?" she replied, looking steadily into the scraps in her apron, hoping he would not see the color rising in her cheeks. "Herr Wilhelm, I know nothing about violin music." Her answer was true enough. While she had heard fiddles at weddings and holiday celebrations her whole life that music did not compare to the sweet, delicate tones or the lively, full-bodied melodies that emanated from Wilhelm's violin.

"Perhaps. But you've heard me play many times," he insisted. "Is there anything you remember hearing that you'd like me to play?"

Jadzia cursed her shyness and her ignorance. Why was such a simple request throwing her into such confusion? She looked away for a moment, hoping Wilhelm would return to his conversation with his mother, but the silence began to become uncomfortable.

"Ach, Wilhelm, leave the girl alone," suggested Frau Heinemann. "She doesn't know classical music."

"But Mama, I play every Sunday. She has ears, doesn't she? Besides, I'm just trying to be considerate," he responded, a touch of petulance sharpening his voice.

Finally a thought entered Jadzia's mind. "I liked that song," she offered, "the one you played three Sundays ago. The one that reminded me of hummingbirds."

"Hummingbirds? I don't know..." Wilhelm tilted his head as though the name would soon appear near the ceiling to his right. Perhaps it did, because suddenly, his eyes brightening and his lips forming a broad smile, he asked, "The Rossini? *Flight of the Bumblebee?*"

"Yes, that's it, I believe. A bee—not a bird."

"Very well, then. Rossini it shall be," he asserted, turning briskly toward the door, leaving Jadzia confused and more than slightly discomfited.

The spring of 1942 marked Jadzia's first full year in Germany: a whole calendar year of seasonal farm tasks, of course, but more poignantly, a whole year that saw her name day, All Souls Day, Wigilia and Christmas, Palm Sunday, Easter, all spent away from her family. In truth, she did not know whether her parents, grandmother, or brothers were alive or dead. Thinking she might sense a death, might feel something special when a family member was hurt or lay dying, she constantly examined her emotional state for some special insight. But none ever came. Finally she gave up, recognizing that though second sight seemed to have been bestowed upon practically every young woman in Niedzieliska, she herself had not been so blessed.

Thoughts of second sight always reminded her of Apolonya. She tried to remember their lives together in Niedzieliska—the long, lazy afternoons in their secluded alcove by the stream, the excitement of Helena's wedding— but her thoughts inevitably returned to the vision of a slender white back and its growing blemish of red. Then she would pray—for the repose of the soul of Apolonya and for the lives and well-being of her family members, extending her prayers to include friends and neighbors and eventually all Poles. In this way she hoped to keep alive some connection with her former life.

The first time she found herself including the Heinemanns in her prayers she had abruptly stopped praying. Sabina's constant reminders—that all Germans were enemies—intruded. But on further reflection, she realized she could not see the Heinemanns, at least not Frau Heinemann and Wilhelm, as enemies.

She wondered how God saw them. Every Sunday the Heinemann's prayed reverently in their plain Lutheran church. They believed that God heard them, that He was on their side, that He supported them in what they thought was a just cause. They believed that Germany's success in the war proved the righteousness of their country's actions. They certainly did not see themselves as evil people purposely pursuing evil goals.

Sharing these insights with Sabina had been a mistake, she realized too late one afternoon as they cleaned the chicken coop together. "What? Are you a fool?" Sabina had looked at her incredulously. "Have you forgotten your friend, the one who died with a Nazi bullet in her back?"

"No. I wish I *could* forget—that sight is burned in my mind forever. And the dreams I have!" Jadzia had responded. "That soldier and what he did was evil: I know it."

"Well then?"

Jadzia paused to collect her thoughts. How could she explain her feelings to Sabina? Finally, she answered as simply as she could. "What that soldier did doesn't make Frau Heinemann evil."

"She don't carry a gun or wear a uniform, but that don't mean she's our friend. All Germans are enemies to all Poles." Sabina had practically spit the words into her face. "It's them or us."

Jadzia was still not convinced. "Frau Heinemann has been good to me," she had argued.

"Frau Heinemann!" Sabina spit on the ground. "Why should that bitch live, when my own mama lies dead in the ground, dead from a German bullet!"

"I'm sorry, Sabina. I didn't know."

"My mama, my little sisters—my whole family! Dead! And you dare to defend that German bitch—or any German?"

"I…I don't know what to say." Jadzia could feel Sabina's pain emanating like a hot blast from a fireplace. "It's just that Frau Heinemann and Wilhelm…"

Sabina looked intently into Jadzia's eyes. "Wilhelm? Is that it? That boy? Has he turned your head? Is he the reason you wanna be with enemies instead of with Casimir and Leo and me—your countrymen?"

"No, it's not like that," Jadzia insisted, turning away from eyes that seemed to bore straight into her brain.

"Well, I'm not surprised. Since you came here you been acting like you think you're too good for us. You act like some kind of saint—Saint Jadwiga. Too holy to drink beer. Too holy to have some fun with us in the barn at night. But maybe that's only because you've got something else going on. Is that it?"

Jadzia turned to walk away, but Sabina, grabbing her arm and looking reproachfully into her eyes, shouted, "It's true, ain't it? You're seeing that boy." Sabina spit on the ground once more in disgust. "You're no saint. You're nothing but a collaborator, a traitor to your country! "

With these words Sabina had released her hold and turned her back on Jadzia, and since then they had had no conversation beyond what was absolutely necessary to do their work. Jadzia was sure she was no traitor. She loved her family, her village, her country. The very thought that Sabina could so misjudge her filled her with indignation.

But there was truth in Sabina's accusations concerning Wilhelm—some truth at least—only not in the evil way Sabina had made them.

Wilhelm had assured her that the things she had done with him had nothing to do with the foulness of the barnyard, but with art and beauty. What did Sabina know of art? Of beauty? The first Sunday afternoon when she and Wilhelm had walked together, taking a secluded trail that led to the ruins of ancient Roman fortifications high upon a hill, she had not realized that the sketchpad he had brought with him was to be used to draw her. He had asked her in his beautiful German, a language she now understood quite well, to pose reclining against a large oval opening in the stone wall overlooking Dahlem. Once he had finished the sketch her initial embarrassment had been transformed into surprised pleasure. Was that beautiful creature depicted on the sketchpad—with flashing eyes and winning smile—what Wilhelm truly saw when he looked at her?

Several times since, they had returned to their hilltop retreat after Wilhelm's recitals, but only when Herr Heinemann was out of town and Frau Heinemann, occupied with some social engagement in town or abed with one of her frequent headaches, had dismissed Jadzia for the rest of the day. It was on their third visit to the ruins that he had asked her to remove the blouse she wore under her dirndl. She had objected at first, but was persuaded when he reminded her of the paintings he had shown her an earlier day in one of his art books: paintings of women in various stages of undress, lounging beautifully on velvet sofas or posed gracefully against trees in woodland settings.

"These paintings are art, Jadzia, not sin," he had insisted, turning a page to another picture of a partially undressed, voluptuous woman reclining on a deep blue sofa. "Some of them even hang in the Vatican, the holiest shrine of your religion," he had added.

"No, that can't be. What would the Pope say if he saw them?"

Wilhelm had laughed. "The Pope, your blessed Pius XII, passes pictures like these every day. He probably bought some of them himself!"

Jadzia crossed herself twice to counter this sacrilege. "Wilhelm, I cannot believe that..."

"Oh, Jadzia," he had said, smiling indulgently. "You just don't understand art. Nothing in these books is bad or dirty. It only depicts God's creation, and all of His creation is good."

Jadzia reconsidered. She told herself that in serving as Wilhelm's model she was helping him improve his art.

But spring in the Eifel, just as elsewhere, was potent. The very air, gently warmed by a sun recalling its powers, refreshed by gentle breezes, perfumed by heady scents of budding trees and bushes, seemed to encourage intimacy. And they were young: Wilhelm only recently turned sixteen, Jadzia, nineteen. She knew that had there been no war, she would surely have married by now, perhaps become a mother caring for a son with Antek's handsome features. She might have had a second or even a third child already on the way. There was no sense wishing the past had been different—she needed to live now, in the present.

On their fourth trip to the hilltop they had become lovers. Their lovemaking was tender, tentative, exploratory. To Jadzia, every touch, every kiss was new and intoxicating. She was awestruck by the wonders of Wilhelm's body: by the beauty of his long, slender limbs; by the sinuous curve of his back tapering into a slender waist as he turned away from her; by his hands, their long, slim fingers tracing patterns gently over her body.

If occasionally, while they lay together, she imagined her arms embracing a taller, sturdier body or her fingers stroking a thicker mass of blonde hair, Wilhelm seemed not to notice. The look of awe and wonder she saw in his eyes as he studied her naked body lying beside him was almost enough to banish her thoughts of another, even if only for the time they spent at their hideaway.

This Sunday Frau Heinemann had been invited to dinner at the home of her sister, who lived in a village just two kilometers west of Dahlem. Herr Heinemann, who was working on conscription rolls in Wiesbaden, had not returned as expected the previous evening. Jadzia was concerned when Wilhelm, complaining to his mother of a headache, had concluded his recital after only two songs. But a furtive wink from Wilhelm once his mother's back was turned had assured Jadzia that his headache was just a ruse, that he was as eager to commence their Sunday afternoon activities as was she.

Like young goats they scampered up the last half kilometer of path leading to the top of the hill. Holding her hand, expressing affection now that heavy woods concealed them from the village below, he drew her through the wild blackberry bushes marking the entrance to their hideaway. Stooping to reach under a particularly full bush, he removed the old wool blanket he had taken from the bottom drawer of his bedroom dresser weeks earlier and spread it evenly on a level section of grass. When he begged her to remove her clothing, she eagerly complied.

Their first coupling, as always, was quick but very satisfying, quenching for a time their pent-up longing from having been separated for two weeks. Wilhelm, looking drained of passion but full of emotion, leaned against the trunk of a fallen tree and pulled her to him, cradling her in one arm. In this position they rested for some time, she gazing at the village far below, he gazing at her firm young flesh. She idly fingered the bodice of the dirndl lying balled at her side, feeling for the smooth bead she had carefully sewn into a seam, becoming, as always, more composed when her fingers found its familiar round shape. Soon Wilhelm began to trace gentle circles around her left breast.

"Again, Wilhelm?" she asked. "Already?"

"No, not yet, *liebchen*," he responded lazily. Her nipple hardened as he rubbed it gently between his fingers. "I just want to look at you and touch you for a while. You don't mind, do you?"

"No, I like when you touch me," she responded. She loved nothing more than these voluptuous moments lying nestled in Wilhelm's arms, gazing down at the peaceful village, its cottages laid out in a symmetrical grid, while the sun and the hilltop breezes took turns, first cooling her skin, damp from exertion, then gently warming it.

"Jadzia," Wilhelm said, his voice low with emotion, "I don't believe you know how beautiful you are. I know you don't believe this can ever happen, but I truly want to marry you."

"Ach, Wilhelm," Jadzia sighed. They had had this conversation before. "Your papa would never allow it."

"My papa will not be able to tell me what to do forever, Jadzia. After all, I will soon be a man, allowed to make my own decisions."

"It's not that easy," she responded. She knew that here, on this hilltop, Wilhelm's love was sincere. She also knew, however, that away from this setting, the rest of the world, with all its rules and expectations, would make him see the futility of hoping for a shared future.

"Maybe not now. But later, after the war," he insisted. "And maybe not here in Dahlem. But in Munich, or Paris, or even in the United States. Once the Reich is victorious, the whole world will be open to us. I'm not cut out to be a farmer anyway. I've never wanted this life. We'll live in a city somewhere, I'll become a famous musician, maybe even a composer, and you and I..."

Pulling his head toward her, she cut off his words with a kiss, knowing this would rekindle his passion. She did not even want to think of a Nazi-controlled world. And besides, she knew that their lovemaking this next time would be slower, would build up to crescendo, thus being more satisfying for her. It was as he bent to encircle her breast with his hungry lips, an embellishment to their lovemaking they'd both found intoxicating, that she heard the out-of-place snapping of a twig.

Looking up over Wilhelm's shoulder she saw Herr Heinemann's heavy walking stick poised in the air, about to land with force on Wilhelm's bare back. But her scream of warning was lost in the crack of wood hitting skin, in the angry guttural roar of Herr Heinemann and the terrified screech of his wife.

Jadzia heard two more blows before Wilhelm was able to pull away from her, revealing in full a furious Herr Heinemann, his arm raised high ready to strike again but impeded by Frau Heinemann, who clasped his raised arm tightly in her own two. The difference in their heights lifted her into the air, her toes scrambling to brush the ground.

"Stop!" Frau Heinemann screamed. "Stop! Stop!" In the moments Herr Heinemann took to pry loose his wife's arms and place her firmly back on the ground, Wilhelm quickly rolled away to slip on his trousers. Jadzia, wrapping herself as modestly as she could in the wool blanket, looked frantically toward the bushes. But her only possible escape route was blocked by Sabina, Casimir and Leo, who stood watching the scene dispassionately.

"Stop," Frau Heinemann begged, "you'll kill him! You'll kill my boy!"

"Maybe that's what he deserves!" her husband responded, pushing her away from him.

"They're only children! It's only natural that they'd…"

"That they'd what?" he screamed into her face. "That they'd make more Polack bastards? Aren't there enough of those already?"

"Papa, it's not like that," Wilhelm pleaded. "Jadzia and I, we love each other."

"Love!" Herr Heinemann screamed, brandishing the walking stick again and moving menacingly toward his son. "You are as stupid as your mother! Such 'love' is an abomination to the Fuhrer and all he stands for! Germans can have no congress with inferior races!"

"Ulrich, please. The boy just…" Frau Heinemann interjected.

"Yes, he is a boy, and he'll never become a man if it's up to you! You baby him, Trudie, you always have. He's going into the army! He'll learn what his duties to his country are there—not bringing more bastard Polack mongrels into this world."

"No," Frau Heinemann cried, falling to her knees, grabbing the belt of her husband's trousers. "Not to the army! Please, Ulrich!"

"Papa, I'll go into the army if that's what you want," Wilhelm pleaded. "Just please, don't hurt Jadzia."

"You have nothing more to say here." Herr Heinemann spat the angry words at his son. "Casimir, Leo, take him back to the house."

Jadzia, terrified, watched the short scuffle as Wilhelm tried to pull away from Casimir and Leo, but he was no match for the older, bigger men. Soon Wilhelm was being pushed forcibly through the blackberry bushes, his cries of protest becoming fainter every moment as he disappeared from view. He was followed by Sabina, who tossed a derisive glance over her shoulder. Jadzia suddenly knew by whom she had been betrayed.

"You too, go back to the house," Herr Heinemann commanded his wife who still knelt before him.

"Ulrich, please, I beg you. Don't send Wilhelm away. He's all I have left!" Frau Heinemann begged through her tears.

"Trudie, there are some things a woman doesn't understand." His voice was now less commanding, more persuading.

"But some things a woman does understand, better than a man! It's not Wilhelm's fault," she cried, her piercing eyes now trained on Jadzia. Jadzia looked in vain for some glimmer of compassion in those eyes.

"Trudie, you're distraught. You saw him…"

"I know! But still, it's not my boy's fault! It's...it's all *her* fault!" Herr Heinemann's eyes followed his wife's finger pointed directly at Jadzia, who stood very still, eyes downcast, shivering uncontrollably despite the blanket she held tightly around her. "Look at her. Look. She's guilty. She seduced him!"

"Perhaps, Trudie, but..."

"Look how dark she is. She must be part gypsy. You know how they are—how they corrupt young men. Send *her* away!"

"Trudie, I will send her away. She will never see Wilhelm again. But still, Wilhelm should not have..."

"Or maybe she's even a Jew, plotting against us! Look at her eyes—how dark they are! You cannot blame Wilhelm—not my boy—*our* boy. He's too young to understand. Please, Ulrich!"

"All right, all right. We'll talk of this later. Now go—go back to the house. I'll take care of things here."

Frau Heinemann, her shoulders stooped and shaking violently, did not look back at Jadzia as she stumbled toward the break in the bushes. Even at that moment Jadzia could not blame her, knowing deep within her heart that her own mother would have done the same thing, would have betrayed anyone to save one of her own.

But now Jadzia was alone with Herr Heinemann, and one look into his cold blue eyes told her that his rage had not cooled, that he was not through with the walking stick for this day. She loathed him and everything he stood for, despised him, a pathetic old man, ugly and coarse, for thinking himself superior.

For one fleeting moment she thought of Apolonya walking away from the Nazis, defying them. Apolonya was a martyr—probably now a saint. But she and Marek had vowed to survive. Not for her Apolonya's fate: a senseless death in a new and horrible, God-forsaken world where no one cared about principle and life was cheap. She refused to die on this beautiful day at the hands of the hideous monster before her.

Dropping the blanket, she paused, then slowly, silently counted to three before taking a step toward him. "Herr Heinemann?" she whispered.

"You She-devil," he snarled, beginning to raise the stick.

But Jadzia saw his clear blue eyes begin to film and the firm set of his jaw slacken. She became more confident. Forcing a smile, she stepped even closer to him.

"Yes?" she responded to the name he had called her. "What do you wish of me...Ulrich?"

Chapter Nine

Evie, Chicago

November, 1942

October 8, 1942

My dearest Eva,

Received 2 V mails from you yesterday, and am happy to hear that you and your family are doing well. Seems that mail is finally beginning to catch up—the last letter took only 2 weeks to get here. Also received the package. Thank you very much. The cookies were very good, hardly stale at all. And the sweater fits like it was made for me—oh, that's right, it was! Thank you so much for all your work on it. I'll really need it here, since England has a very cool and damp climate with not much sunshine.

Did you get the pictures I sent you? Those tin huts are what we sleep in—more comfortable than you would think. Spent a weekend in London last month—it's only about 60 miles away from Winchester, which is the closest town to us. Stayed in a Red Cross club in London and had a swell time. Had hoped to pick up some good Christmas presents, but everything is rationed here, and we don't get ration cards. Still, I did find a little something for you and for Steffie—hope it gets to you before December 25.

Next week some friends and I are going to XXXXXX for a couple of days. Seems like a lot more action is about to happen. I hope so. For now we've been very busy XXXXXX. It will be good to just get this war over and come home, maybe some time XXXXXXXXXX.

Don't ever worry about me because if there's anyone who takes care of himself, it's your Mikosz. I think of you all the time, and of the life we'll share once I get home. I hope you'll want to get married just as soon as I get back. Being so far from home has made a lot of things clearer—being in a war really helps a fellow see what's important in life.

Say hello to your family for me, and write back soon. You can't imagine how much receiving your letters means to me. I'll write to you again as soon as I can.

Love,
Mikosz

"Sweetie, get me some matches from the kitchen, would you?" Eva requested.

Stephania tore herself away from the bedroom she still shared with her older sister and from the fascinating toilette she had been observing. Eva sat perched on the edge of her bed. One long, bare, shapely leg supported her, and the other, visible through the split in her wrapper all the way up to the lace on her satin bloomers, was bent at the knee, its heel pressing the edge of the bed. She had just finished varnishing—Ruby Red—the pinkie toenail of her right foot and was about to tackle the left foot, first weaving a twisted strand of tissue paper carefully around each toe. She'd be wearing open-toed pumps tonight, and it was imperative that her toenails, which would match the Ruby Red on her lips and fingernails, be perfect.

"Here, Eva." Stephania offered the box of kitchen matches to her sister with all the pride of a vassal offering a jewel to a princess.

"Thanks, honeybunch," Eva responded, delaying her toenails long enough to light a cigarette from her almost empty pack of Pall Malls, taking one deep draw and then expertly flicking an errant tobacco flake from her tongue as she placed the cigarette in the ashtray tilted on the bed.

"Are you going out again after work tonight?" Steffie asked.

"Mm hmm." Eva concentrated on spreading the nail varnish smoothly on the big toe of her left foot. Then, looking into her sister's adoring eyes, she continued. "Big USO dance tonight."

"You're going to dance with soldiers?"

"And sailors, airmen and Marines, too, if I'm lucky." She looked critically at her toenails, finally satisfied with her job. Tossing her auburn curls, now beautifully hennaed and cut in the style they called "pageboy," she took another deep drag on her cigarette while waiting for the varnish to dry. "It's all part of the war effort, Steffie. We need to keep up the morale of the troops," she smiled. "And you remember we can't talk to *Tata* about the dances and all, right?"

Steffie nodded solemnly.

Eva wondered for just one moment how much her father actually knew. Surely he must have suspected something by now. He'd had no complaints about the money she gave him every week—exactly the amount she would have been making had she gotten a job at the dress factory—enough to make up for the loss they had suffered once Henryk had enlisted and they could no longer count on his salary. *Tata* was working overtime at his factory job now: the war effort had provided plenty of work for everyone who wanted it. Because Eva's schedule was so different from her father's, he had never been home to see her leave for work or come home in her new clothing—the long flirty gored skirts and satiny white and pastel blouses, the big floppy hats and the cute shoes—or the make-up she now wore every day. But he had to know something.

The morning after her high school graduation, Eva had taken the Division Avenue bus west, telling her father she was going to apply for a job at Blomberg's Dress Factory. He had at first complained, asserting that "a woman's place is in the home." But even he had observed the changes in their neighborhood—women, even wives, going to work—now that so many men were overseas. And after all, his wife Sofia had worked as a seamstress early in their marriage; sewing had always been considered acceptable employment for a woman. Eva was just following her mother's example. *Tata* had finally consented, informing Eva that she would still be responsible for making the family's meals and cleaning their apartment and that her wages were to be turned over to him every week.

But Eva had not gotten off the bus at Blomberg's. Instead she had transferred onto the Western Avenue bus going south and exited at the Doall Valve Company, which had been converted into a defense factory early in the war and where not shirtwaists and ball gowns, but electronic components for trucks and tanks, were manufactured. Friends at school had assured her that she could make almost twice as much money doing defense work as she could sewing. She found that to be nearly true.

She had been hired on the spot and was told to start that very day on the swing shift, working from 4:00 p.m. to midnight six nights a week. Fortunately it was early enough for her to return home and put together a dinner of cold chicken, potato salad and sliced vegetables and to arrange for Steffie to spend the afternoon with *Pani* Poniatowska before rushing back to the personnel office. There she was introduced to Mel Skinner, who was to be her shift supervisor.

Mel took her through a series of long, mustard-colored hallways, finally opening a heavy, studded metal door into what, had Eva read Dante, might have reminded her of one of the lower levels of hell. From a metal landing at third floor height she gazed at a hub of activity: hundreds of men and women, some seated, some standing, some pushing carts or dollies of materials, all enclosed in one huge gray room filled with enormous gray machines. From the machines rose a wall of heat so intensely alive that it seemed capable of flattening her against the wall. And the noise! Clanking, rumbling, buzzing, thumping. How could anyone survive even minutes in this underworld?

But she gamely followed Mel down two flights of open metal stairs to a supply area where, after appraising her carefully and finally mouthing "Small," he sorted through a pile of blue fabric, finally pulling out a pair of denim coveralls and a long canvas apron, which he handed to her. He pointed to a small door at the right of the room, saying, "You can change in there. Bring your clothes out with you and I'll show you your locker."

Eva had never before worn trousers, much less coveralls, and was disconcerted at the almost sensual feeling of dense, heavy fabric brushing against and between her legs. Apprehensively, she had stepped out of the changing room back into the factory's din. Only the sight of the dozens of similarly attired workers she passed on her way to her "station"—mostly men but with a smattering of women—helped to ease her embarrassment.

Finally Mel stopped at a group of workers seated at heavy metal tables circling a small open flame. Motioning toward an empty space at one of the tables, he introduced her co-workers. "Eva, meet Candy and Lou. They'll show you the ropes around here." Eva had nodded and managed a wry smile for the two thin women whose similar pale skin, clear blue eyes and straw-colored hair made them look like sisters. Then he was gone, leaving her lost and confused.

"Don't worry, honey," the woman called Candy said. "This ain't so hard, once you get usta' it."

"They usta' give new folks a trainin' session," Lou added, "but they don't do that no more, seein' as how there's so many orders to fill. But solderin' ain't so hard—not when it's little wires like this. See here?" Evie looked closely at the gadget Lou held in her hand.

"This here's an ignition switch for a truck," she explained. "What we're doin' is solderin' four wires—see, like these here—onto the switch. It's easy work, not like weldin' big parts for ships or airplanes. Ya just gotta' be real careful and precise."

Eva was mesmerized by the slow roll of English on their tongues, the "ah's" appearing where she expected "i's." But she was most impressed by the air of friendly informality they shared.

"You got a bandanner?" asked Candy.

"A what?"

"A bandanner," repeated Candy, "for your hair. You gotta' wear a bandanner so's your hair don't get all caught up in the machinery. Here, I got a extra one I can lend you for today. You can warsh it up an' give it back to me tomorrah'." Candy pulled a square of cotton, blue with large white polka-dots, from her pocket.

"Oh, a *babushka*," Eva said, then, embarrassed, looked away. But Candy and Lou were already folding Eva's long brown braids into the bandanna, tying it snugly on top of her head.

There," huffed Lou, looking satisfied at her work, "that oughta do ya. Now, ready to learn how to solder?"

Candy pointed to two wood-handled soldering irons lying on the table, saying, "Them are yours. Keep one heatin' up in the fire and use t'other one." Handing Eva her own heated iron, she maneuvered Eva's right hand around the handle into a position that felt extremely awkward.

Lou placed an ignition switch and a wire into Eva's left hand. "Now," she advised, "take it slow and easy. Just a little bit. No—ya gotta' have a light touch. Too much. There, that's right. Now you're gettin' it."

Eva was pleased to find that within just a few tries she was able to control the thin stream of liquid metal. It was delicate work, well suited to women's small hands and her own familiarity with intricate activities such as needlepoint and hand stitching. By the time a shrill bell, loud enough to be heard above the din of the factory, announced the dinner break for their area, Eva was on her way to becoming a solderer.

She learned during that first dinner that Candy and Lou were cousins, not sisters, who had traveled north to take advantage of opportunities unavailable to them in the hills and hollows of their native Arkansas. She also observed their kindness when, upon noticing that Eva had brought nothing to eat, Candy offered her half a ham sandwich and Lou pushed an apple to her across the table. "Oh, I couldn't. I'm not really hungry," Eva had told them. But they insisted, and with her first bite of the sandwich Eva realized she was famished.

After their meal Lou pulled a small bag and a packet of thin tissues out of a pocket in her coveralls and proceeded to expertly roll cigarettes for herself and Candy. "You smoke, Evie?" she asked.

Smoke? Women smoked? This was yet another revelation for Eva. Men smoked, of course, and drank too much, and swore, and stayed out all night, too. But certainly no woman of her acquaintance had ever done any of these things—they were all part of the lives of men. Of course, no woman of her acquaintance had ever worn coveralls or soldered ignition switches, either.

"I...I," she stammered.

"They say it ain't good for ya," Candy added, "but most folks here at Doall smoke. If you're a smoker, ya get two fifteen-minute breaks besides for lunch. It's almost worth pickin' up the habit. Wanna try one, Evie?"

It was all so strange, working in the bowels of hell, wearing stiff denim clothing, being called by a nickname that was not her own. Eva considered correcting Candy on the pronunciation of her name, but reconsidered. "Eva" would never have smoked a cigarette. But how about "Evie"? Evie might.

"Roll one for her," Candy suggested.

That first inhalation dizzied her and then made her cough, but by the end of the cigarette she was beginning to enjoy the feeling of light-headedness, the relaxation in her shoulders and neck. It somehow made the thought of returning to her station for four more hours of pounding noise and heat more palatable, the thought of the long bus ride home in the dark less menacing. In some strange way, it made her feel tough, like a woman who could take care of herself.

Every morning that first week working at Doall she had awakened to aching shoulders and arms, a pain deep in her lower back and a dizzy humming in her ears. Early each morning her aches and pains convinced her to quit Doall Valve and apply to Blomberg's after all. But by 3:00, with dinner prepared and laid out for later consumption by her father and sister, she would find herself walking to the bus stop with an unfamiliar spring in her step. And on Friday, when she received her first paycheck, she knew her name would never appear on Blomberg's employee roster.

One Saturday during their second cigarette break Lou had asked companionably, "Ya like Katharine Hepburn?"

"I don't believe I know her," Evie answered. "Does she work swing shift?"

"Yeah," Candy laughed, "Katharine Hepburn at Doall Valve. That'll be the day!"

"Katharine Hepburn, the movie star," Lou persisted. "Do you like her?"

"I don't believe I have ever seen her in a movie," Evie answered, too embarrassed to admit she had never seen any movie at all.

"*The Philadelphia Story* is playin' at the Bijou tonight. Me 'n Candy's goin'. Wanna come?"

"Tonight? After work? So late?" Evie was incredulous at the thought that theaters would be open after midnight. She'd noticed lights on in restaurants and bars every night on her long bus ride home, but hadn't thought much about it.

"Sure—everything's open late since the war—movie houses, bowlin' alleys, saloons, restaurants," Candy assured her. "With so many people workin' swing and graveyard, you could see a movie twenty-four hours a day if ya wanted to. Ya wanna come?"

Evie at first demurred, but the following hours of routine soldering gave her the opportunity to rethink her decision. Between working double shifts and his fondness for vodka, *Tata* had been sleeping like a hibernating bear lately. Stephania too was a good sleeper. Neither of them would even notice if she got home a couple of hours late.

And besides, the next day was Sunday when she could rest, although she had to admit that after those first two or three hard days of adjusting, her work at the factory did not leave her exhausted. The previous night she had felt so energized and alive at 1:00 a.m. that it had been difficult to sleep.

So it was with a light heart and few reservations that Evie accompanied Candy and Lou under the bright lights of the marquee and into the cool, dark recesses of the Bijou Theater. Such wonders she encountered there. The Bijou was an enormous baroque palace of entertainment, with massive pillars and fancy cream and blue-colored wood trim setting off larger-than-life-sized reproductions of Renaissance masterpieces. While its earlier glory had faded through time and hard use, Evie was too awed by its opulence to notice the chips on the scrolled banisters or the worn spots on the crimson-colored plush velvet seats.

First came the newsreel, which focused on the brave exploits of handsome American soldiers jumping out of tanks or filing onto great ships. This gave her confidence. How could the Americans lose the war with so many handsome, eager young men, Mikosz and Henryk among them, fighting? The cartoon that followed was Evie's first introduction to the charming antics of Mickey Mouse. How clever these cartoonists were! But many exciting new experiences were yet to come: the sight of enormous figures of actors coming to life on the screen; the taste of popcorn, salty and rich; the sound of the musical score, so different from the polkas and waltzes she heard at home. Perhaps the most striking experience for Evie was the sight of young people in the theater, dozens of them, many coupled up, some kissing and hugging unashamedly.

But it was the movie itself that opened her eyes to a much larger world. *The Philadelphia Story* gave her a peek at lives she could never have imagined, lives of privilege and wealth and charm. Katharine Hepburn was a revelation: Evie had never known women who were not only beautiful, but smart and witty as well, and who could hold their own against the men, even a man so dashing, so debonair (how she loved the sound of that word!) as Cary Grant. She vowed to become more like Katharine Hepburn in every way: to speak in a lower, more clipped voice; to toss her head and laugh gaily; to float down a flight of stairs as though she were dancing, although not, perhaps, when she was descending the hideous gray metal stairways at work.

Ah, the lessons of moving pictures! There were many to come...

Mrs. Miniver turned her vaguely pacifist complacency into active support for the war. And *Sergeant York*, starring Gary Cooper as a pacifist who later became a war hero, made her long for Mikosz. She imagined him a hero, killing Nazis, taking prisoners, and rescuing innocent civilians. She vowed to find the time to volunteer with the Red Cross.

With *How Green Was My Valley* Evie was introduced to a poor Welsh family who had had to change their lives just to survive. Wales, in some strange way, seemed much like Chicago, with all the changes happening now in her family and her neighborhood. And Maureen O'Hara—what a beautiful, noble woman, with her masses of auburn hair. Evie wondered whether auburn would complement her own coloring, whether it would bring out the flecks of green in her eyes. But dying her hair? What would *Tata* say? Perhaps, she had thought, if she did it gradually—a little less mousy brown and a little more auburn every few weeks...

"Eva, are you going to wear Mama's amber cross tonight?" Steffie had removed a necklace, one that had belonged to the mother she had never known, from Eva's jewelry box, and was stroking it gently with a pudgy thumb.

"Steffie, how many times have I told you not to touch my things." But the quick tears that came to the child's eyes and the sudden quivering of her rosebud lips caused Eva to capitulate.

"I'm not wearing that tonight, honeybunch," she added sweetly, gently brushing an errant strand of hair out of her sister's eyes. She planned instead to wear her new set of pearls and matching earrings—only paste, of course, but who could tell the difference?

Eva removed her pearls from the little pine jewelry box with the decoupage of pink roses that she had purchased with her first paycheck. She had bought the box to duplicate one Jadzia had described in a letter, so it always reminded her of her cousin, who she hadn't heard from in over a year. The newsreels showed terrible fighting all over Europe, with many people displaced from their homes. Jadzia could be anywhere, or, God forbid, even...no—Eva refused to think of that. As she did whenever thoughts of Jadzia came to mind, she whispered a quick prayer to St. Jude that her cousin and her family were safe.

"What? Did you say something?" asked Steffie, still sniffling.

"No, darling—not to you."

"It's not fair," Steffie whined. "You always get to wear such pretty things."

"And you will, too, when you're older. But for now, would you like to wear Mama's cross for a little bit before you go to *Pani* Poniatowska's for the afternoon?"

Stephania nodded, all signs of tears quickly retreating. Turning to have the cross fastened to her neck, lower lip jutting out provokingly, she whined, "Do I have to go? I hate *Pani* Poniatowska. She always smells like cabbage."

Eva wondered whether she herself had been this difficult as a seven-year-old. She didn't believe so. But then, she'd grown up with her mother always at her side; Steffie had had to settle for much less. Reaching for her sister, holding her close and brushing her cheek with a quick kiss, she said, "Now sweetie, don't pout. Do you think I want to go to work every day? Be a good girl. We all have to do what we can to support our soldiers and the war effort."

By 1:00 a.m. Evie was supporting the war effort with every ounce of energy in her body. How she loved to dance! She adored swing with its dips and twirls that sent her gored skirts flying up mid-thigh, exposing her legs. She could think of nothing on this earth that rivaled the intoxicating beat of Glenn Miller's "Pennsylvania 6500" or the wild ecstasy of the Andrews Sisters' "Boogie Woogie Bugle Boy of Company B."

At the USO dances she now regularly attended she was seldom at a loss for a partner. She liked how the music made her feel. Some songs, like Spike Jones' or Cab Calloway's, made her laugh. Others, like the smooth melodies of the Tommy Dorsey Band or Guy Lombardo's Royal Canadians, made her thoughtful and dreamy. No music in her earlier experience—not the polkas or the mazurkas of her youth, or even the majesty of Chopin—had ever affected her the way this music did.

She knew she looked particularly stunning in her sapphire-colored fitted dress with padded shoulders and a shirred top. Its tapered neckline showcased her long, slim neck, now draped in pearls, its décolletage displaying a degree of cleavage that would have been unthinkable only a few weeks earlier. The dress's diamond-shaped inset accentuated the slenderness of her waist. It was designed for dancing, with a flared skirt that swirled wildly during the fast dances while slithering provocatively around her legs during the slow ones. Obviously, it had been worth its exorbitant price: Evie had had young men lined up to dance with her all evening.

As lights dimming in the vast hall signaled only two dances yet to come, Evie recognized the first notes of a song that, while her favorite, always brought a catch to her throat and tears to her eyes. Hoagy Carmichael's "Stardust," particularly the first four lines, evoked loving remembrance of Mikosz, of his deep gray eyes and the warmth of his smile. She invented a hasty excuse for the handsome young sailor with whom she had been dancing and hurried toward the chair she had abandoned at the beginning of this last set, quietly intoning the first lines of the song: "Sometimes I wonder why I spend/The lonely night dreaming of a song;/The melody haunts my reverie/And I am once again with you." If only those words could come true!

A quick tap on her shoulder halted her progress away from the dance floor. "Hey, Toots," she heard, "You saving this one for me?" She turned to deny, as gently as possible, whichever soldier or sailor was requesting the next few minutes of her time. But the sight of a grey pin-striped suit, so out-of-place in this room of gowns and military uniforms, caught her eye. As she looked up into the face of the man wearing this anomalous attire, she saw an attractive thatch of tousled, sandy hair, so different from the sea of military crew cuts that surrounded them, and limpid green eyes, the color of a mossy bank.

Before she could refuse, the handsome stranger had encircled her waist with his arm and was decisively leading her back onto the dance floor. Soon she was enveloped in his arms, discovering the pleasure of being the partner of a man who truly knew how to dance. So unlike the shy stumblings of her other partners, his moves were deft and sure. Her body instinctively melded into his as he led her into moves executed with an expertise she did not know she had.

Midway into the song he asked her name. "Evie," she whispered into his pause before the next step. "And yours?"

"I'm Charley," he answered, expertly shifting her body to reverse position for a backward motion. "I haven't seen you here before."

"I...I just started coming here."

"You here by yourself?"

Evie was taken aback by his forwardness, but not so much that she considered for one moment not answering his question. "No, I'm here with my friends. Candy Nivens and Lou Gentry." She glanced around quickly as though looking for proof of her statement in the swirl of dancers.

"Candy and Lou. I know them. They work at Doall Valve, don't they?" Charley was dipping her now, just slightly.

"Yes. That's where I met them. I work there too."

"Well then, that makes it unanimous." Evie was about to ask him which shift he worked, but he forestalled her question with another of his own. "You havin' a good time this evening?"

"Yeah," she responded, "it's been swell."

As the song ended, she waited a moment for him to escort her away from the dance floor. It was customary for girls to dance just one dance with each partner—after all, there were always many more young, lonely servicemen at these dances than there were women to dance with them. She was not disappointed, however, when Charley stood his ground. "One more?" he asked.

The heavenly sounds of Glenn Miller's "Moonlight Serenade" filled the room. Not waiting for an answer, Charley, looking directly into her eyes, pulled her to him, almost indiscernibly closer than he had held her before. "You know, Evie," he said midway into the dance, "I hope you don't mind my saying this, but I haven't been able to keep my eyes off you all evening. You certainly are the loveliest woman here." Now his forwardness had turned to brass, and Evie stiffened in his arms.

"You do mind," he said, seemingly hurt by her response. "I certainly didn't mean to offend you. I'm only speaking the truth."

"No, no, I'm not offended," Evie stammered. She considered telling him about Mikosz, but then, grateful to hear the concluding melody of the song, she quickly added, "I, I have to find my friends."

"Of course," he responded, leading her back to her table. "But Evie, the night is still young. Would you like to stop somewhere for a cuppa' joe? Or maybe something else?"

"No, no...I need to go home now."

"Can I offer you a ride?"

"No...I need to go home with my friends."

"Okay then. I hope to see you again soon. Will you be here next week? They're having a name band—Stan Kenton, I believe. It's gonna be the cat's pajamas."

"I, yes, I will. I p-p-probably will," she answered, discomfited by the tilt of his head and the knowing sparkle in his eye. Was he making fun of her in some way?

"I hope so. Thank you for the dance, lovely Evie." His broad shoulders melted into the crowd just as she heard a familiar squeal.

"Oooh," swooned Candy, rushing up to her with Lou only steps behind. "We saw ya dancin' with Mr. Dreamboat."

"Just now? With Charley?" Evie answered, looking at her friends' smiles.

"*Charley*, is it?" hooted Lou, peering narrowly at Evie. "Imagine that! Our Evie's on a first-name basis with the high 'n mighty!"

"High and mighty?" laughed Evie. "I don't think so. He works at Doall Valve too." At this Candy and Lou broke out into screeching laughter.

"I guess ya could say that," Candy finally coughed out between laughs. "Evie, dincha' know you was dancin' with Mr. Charles Honeycutt III— known as Mr. Dreamboat to all the gals at Doall?"

"Then you know him too. Does he work swing shift?"

"He don't exactly *work* for Doall, an' if he did, it wouldn't likely be swing shift," Candy answered knowingly. "Honey, you was dancing' with Doall Valve royalty. I guess ya ain't heard of his daddy neither—Mr. Charles Honeycutt II—owner of our company and a few others besides."

"Dincha' wonder why a strappin' young man like that wasn't in uniform?" Lou asked. Evie thought back to the grey pin-striped suit that had fit her dance partner as though made for him. She reflected now that it probably had been.

"Yep," added Candy, nodding her head firmly. "No war for the likes 'a him. His daddy's kep' him out of the service."

"But that's not fair." Evie bristled at the injustice, thinking of Mikosz. Why could Charley stay in Chicago while Mikosz was far away, risking his life? Why did being rich give a man all the advantages?

"Some say it's 'cause he's needed at home for the war effort," Lou said, "seein' as how Doall is workin' on military contracts. And some folks say he's got flat feet or somethin'."

"They kin say anythin' they want. He sure didn't look 4F to me while he was out there dancin'. He oughta' be outa' them fancy suits and into a uniform, just like the rest of the boys," asserted Lou.

"But he's still a dreamboat," laughed Candy.

"No denyin' that!" Lou relented.

On the long bus ride back to Haddon Avenue from Navy Pier, Evie responded good-naturedly to her friends' ribbing, to their references to her "hobnobbing with the muckety-mucks" and her "new, fancy-pants friends." But inside she smoldered with resentment. How dare Mr. Charles Honeycutt III tease her so blatantly. How dare he make fun of her. Why, he was probably laughing himself silly right now, thinking of how he pulled the wool over the eyes of a naïve young girl, one of his employees, no less.

She considered applying at Blomberg's after all but quickly reconsidered. Why should the arrogant Mr. Honeycutt deprive her of the extra income she was making at Doall Valve? Why should she have to abandon her new, exciting life and the opportunities it provided, just because he had the poor breeding to get some paltry enjoyment out of toying with her? She would keep her job, she finally decided, and if he ever dared looking for her there, if he walked up to her and spoke her name, the chill he'd feel would lower the temperature in that whole sweat box of a factory his daddy owned.

Chapter Ten

Jadzia, German/Polish border

June, 1943

Do Oswiecimia

She caught its twinkle for just a moment as the train rumbled east: a star, the third she had seen through the tiny crack in the boxcar's ceiling. Only seven more and they would all be safe. The game Jadzia had devised for the long trip home sustained her now.

Home. But not really. The train was heading east, back to Poland. But not to any Poland she remembered—this she knew. The card the soldier in Wroclaw had pinned to her chest as she had been transferred into this boxcar was printed with her name and the words *do Oswiecimia*—to Oswieciem—a small town very near her own village of Niedzieliska. The Germans called the town Auschwitz. Jadzia had heard only horrible things about the camp there.

She had tried to make conversation with some of the shadows in the boxcar: that was the only word that could describe her fellow travelers. She had sought out some Polish-appearing strangers in the boxcar, hoping to numb the hours with some bit of conversation, but if any one of her companions was Polish, he or she would not speak. Instead the shadows huddled in small quiet groups or lay tumbled on the floor, like heaps of rags barely visible in the dimness. When a bit of light slipped through one of the slats and illuminated a face, that face would be gaunt and still and gray, ghostlike.

They looked like what they would soon be—and she as well—thought Jadzia in her most desperate moments. Even the children's faces were the faces of ghosts: living ghosts created by starvation and the other deprivations of their short lives.

Because her situation was too horrible to contemplate, Jadzia had invented a game. If she could glimpse ten stars tonight through the crack in the ceiling of the boxcar, everything would be all right. All in this boxcar would survive. When her rational mind rebelled at the foolishness of this game, she forced herself to believe. After all, anything was possible in this world the Nazis had created. She had seen that with her own eyes. Her game was no more irrational than the philosophy that had brought her and all those with her to this boxcar rumbling its way to Poland.

There, a fourth star. Almost halfway to salvation. They still had a few more kilometers to go, so her goal was attainable. And then, only moments later, a fifth star appeared twinkling unimaginably far away. The elation!

Ah, she thought, *don't be a fool.* As it had been this whole journey, whenever moments of faint hope would gladden her heart, the other part of her mind took over—the part that damned her for her childishness and reminded her of who she was and where she was going.

Nor did she want to think of where she had most recently been, of those three days with Herr Heinemann. Being locked in an old storage shed, beaten—well, anyone could survive a beating. It took only the unflinching belief that a battering of the body did not necessarily bruise the soul.

No, it was the other things she wished and prayed she could forget. She thought of Wilhelm, in whose arms she had felt worthy and safe and alive. She tried not to think of his father, of the brutality of his calloused hands, of how debased she had felt when he had torn into her. How different were the father and the son. She fought her own guilt, knowing she had done what she needed to do to survive. The worst memory of all, the vision of Herr Heinemann's eyes—icy blue orbs looking right through her as though she did not exist—that was the hardest to erase.

She wondered where Wilhelm was now, whether Frau Heinemann had managed to save him from the military...Then she cursed herself for caring. After all, what was he but another German who would probably grow to be just like his father. And even if that were not the case, if the boy retained his sensitivity in this mad world, what did it matter? So many others were far more worthy of her concern.

Did she even have a family? Were her parents, her grandmother, her brother Stasiu still in Niedzieliska, perhaps thinking of her right this minute, praying for her? She imagined them seated in their customary places at the heavy dining table *Tata* had made, Mama serving *pierogi* from a large, rose-patterned serving plate or ladling out *zupa grzybowa* from the matching tureen. She visualized this scene over and over, as if thinking it would make it so.

And Marek. Was he safe in Germany, working on a farm? Or had he escaped, made his way to England, perhaps joined the Polish army there?

She thought of Eva and hoped the war had not extended to the United States. And of Apolonya—she knew too well where Apolonya was. Perhaps Apolonya had been the most fortunate of them all.

Thoughts of Apolonya inevitably led her mind to Antek. Could he have had any idea of what changes his beloved Nazi ideology would bring to his family and his country? Was he the enemy, even now? She could not reconcile this thought with the handsome, fearless boy she remembered.

Another star appeared, then another. This must be a sign. Seven was a lucky number. Fixing her eyes on the tiny peephole, she desperately sought those last three stars. But the sky was less dark now. Was morning approaching? Feeling the train begin to decelerate, she cursed the grinding, jolting stop that signaled the end of her game.

Or perhaps not. She had one last chance—she might see three stars in the night sky when the soldiers slid open the wide doors of the boxcar. That would count, wouldn't it? Her game, her rules. But the train had stopped in Katowice, a mining town so filled with coal dust that for years its residents had not seen stars, nor even the Carpathian Mountain range lying not many kilometers away. The passengers were unloaded from the boxcars and herded into a large open enclosure, its eight-foot fences topped with barbed wire. A Polish voice over a loudspeaker, a voice that quickened her heart, explained that the prisoners would be processed to their new destination in the morning. She was confused—why had the voice affected her so? It carried the cadences of her home region, but still, there seemed to be much more than that.

No food was offered, but many drank deeply from a large, galvanized tub of scummy water placed in one corner of the enclosure. Jadzia could smell the lavatory functions being carried out in the corner of the enclosure diagonally across from the water tub.

Too dejected to attempt conversation, she found an empty spot and sat, determined to spend the night in wakefulness and prayer. So it was with some surprise that the next thing she perceived was the sound of truck engines awakening her to dawn breaking over a pale blue sky. How could she have slept through the night in this place?

Already soldiers were rousing those who could be roused—ignoring the heaps that would never rise again—and hustling them into long lines. Silence was demanded, but based on her experience in the boxcar, Jadzia knew that the soldiers could process the silent husks of human beings even without having to give specific orders.

For hours, heavily armed guards moved the lines of people slowly, inexorably, toward three long tables in the distance, stations for checking identification before prisoners would be loaded onto trucks. At each table sat two German officers who matched nametags against stacked pages of typed rosters. *So many people*, thought Jadzia as she shuffled up a half step in her line. *So many people to be processed, and probably the same yesterday, and again tomorrow.*

It was almost noon when Jadzia reached the table that marked the end of her line. "*Namen?*" demanded the officer, who was, Jadzia noticed, really only a boy, perhaps even younger than Wilhelm. His partner looked to be in his late teens.

"Jadwiga Czarnecka," she answered, her years in Dahlem having given her a good working knowledge of the German language. The older officer checked her spoken name against the name written on her tag while the younger shuffled through the alphabetized lists.

"Czarnecka, Czarnecka," the younger muttered, running his finger down a list of names that started with "C." Then he stopped. "What does this mean, Helmut?" He pointed to initials marked next to her name. Jadzia wondered what could be different about her. Why was she being singled out?

"Yes," answered the older officer, bending to make out the initials. "I knew I remembered something about that name." From the desk he removed another, shorter stack of papers from under the rock serving as a paperweight. "Something...wait, here. What are those initials again?"

"AZ."

"Yes, this is it," he said, selecting two sheets and removing them from the stack, then quickly scanning them. "Special processing. On orders of the Pole."

The younger officer looked confused. "Which Pole?"

"You know. Zadora. The tall one."

Jadzia's heart skipped a beat. The name "Zadora." The letters "AZ." She longed to look around her, to search the faces of the uniformed men milling around, but feared making any movement that might call further attention to herself.

"Damn," cursed the younger officer, "I know the one you're talking about. What I don't know is why the Reich is still using Polacks?"

"To process Polacks, just like we need French to process French and Jews to process Jews. Don't worry," Helmut laughed. "We won't need them much longer."

"So," the younger man sighed, looking for the first time at Jadzia, then back to his partner. Jadzia wondered what he saw when he looked at her—

whether he saw a person or just a problem. "What the hell does Zadora want us to do with this one?"

"It says send her back to Germany—to Frankfurt." He handed the paperwork to his partner.

Jadzia scarcely dared to believe that she would be saved. How had this happened? Had her salvation truly been in the stars?

The boy officer reached into a satchel for a stamper and inkpad, muttering "Damned Poles" as he stamped the papers. Returning one sheet to the stack, he handed the other to Jadzia, then pointed her toward an open box car on a train facing west.

Now, two years later, Jadzia was taking another train back to Poland, but this time the ride was very different. She looked at her companion snoring gently beside her. Roman's head bobbed on what had once been the first class compartment's plush, deep rose velvet upholstery, its nap now worn flat, its color faded to pinkish grey. Though he was thirty-six, only fifteen years older than she, hard work and sorrow had aged him, making him look more like a man of fifty. She had promised to wake him before they entered Poland, but hesitated.

Did she want to share this time with him, conflicted as she was? How fearful she had been in the camp at Katowice, and then how grateful for her delivery. Now she was returning to Poland, but what would this return bring her?

Pushing aside the tattered gray curtain as far as she could, she rubbed the window with the sleeve of her sweater, trying to remove some of the grime accumulated over years of neglect. The conductor had told her they were just a few kilometers from Gorlitz, the train's entry point into Poland, and she did not want to miss the first possible glimpse of her homeland.

Roman Kaminski was a good man, she knew. In the two years she had worked side by side with him, cutting and sorting hog bristles for the brushes produced by the factory where they had both been sent to work, she had never known him to say or do a cruel thing. His was the first face she had noticed when she entered Frankfurter Brushworks for the first time. His smile, sad but somehow encouraging, had given her the strength to face whatever her next challenge would be.

Despite her fears, she soon found Frankfurter Brushworks to be a haven, one Antek had chosen well. True, the work was hard and monotonous, but the factory, situated as it was in the Bavarian forest, was far from the military and industrial targets destroyed by Allied bombers. It had been a place to survive at a time when so many others were dying. Unlike German factories that, by the end of the war, were nothing more than death camps, the Brushworks actually manufactured a usable product. Most of its supervisors treated their labor force more like employees than prisoners.

Though their twelve-hour work days allowed little time for socializing, she and Roman had snatched first a few subtle glances, then a few shared words, during mealtimes or as they left the factory for their separate dormitories. Then, with no advance warning, had come that wonderful and horrible day when allied troops had stormed the factory, lining all the German supervisors and clerical workers against one long wall in the storage room. "Here," the soldiers had said, handing rifles to some of the Poles, Czechs and Russians who made up the labor force. "Kill whoever deserves it."

Some had eagerly complied. But Roman had not. Handing the rifle back to the young, fresh-faced soldier who had given it to him, he had turned to Jadzia, softly saying, "Enough have died."

His action had given her hope. Often, in the past few years, she had wondered whether those who had lived in complete degradation of spirit—the fear, the casual savagery, the imminent specter of death endured by those caught in the Nazi trap—could retain any little shred of humanity. This man had.

In the months between their liberation and this train ride home, they had become close friends. As she looked fondly at his face, normally careworn but now peaceful in sleep, she smoothed a lock of thin, graying hair back toward his already receding hairline. *Sleep well*, she thought. *You deserve a time of rest.*

Soon she and Roman would change trains at the border, and in just a few more hours they would arrive in Katowice, Roman's home town and the place where her fate had changed two years earlier. Roman had descended from generations of coal miners, but his hard work and initiative before the war had elevated him to the rank of small shopholders. The dry goods store he and his wife, his childhood sweetheart, had established was successful, and they had looked forward to the birth of their first child.

But his wife, his child and his store were gone, lost in the rubble of a German bomb. Roman had no reason to leave the train at Katowice. Instead, he had offered to remain on the train with Jadzia through Krakow, and then to accompany her to Niedzieliska, wishing, he said, to protect her from the bands of starving refugees and soldiers roaming the Polish countryside. Jadzia had accepted gratefully, but now feared what she would find once she arrived home. Only the kind steadfastness of her traveling companion gave her the courage to continue her journey.

"Papers." The conductor's voice relieved Jadzia of her responsibility of waking Roman: the authoritative voice jolted him from his sleep. "I must have slept for over an hour," he said, rubbing the bridge of his nose with one hand and reaching for the satchel carrying his traveling papers with the other. "We're almost to the border, yes?"

"Yes," Jadzia answered, pointing out the window toward the east. "That way. Poland must be over there." His eyes followed the direction to which she pointed. "I often wondered if this day would ever come."

"It has. We made it, Jadzia. We're home." He paused for the shuffle of handing over papers, his and Jadzia's, to the conductor and then, following the conductor's curt nod, to collect their few belongings. They would need to change trains at the border.

When Roman turned back to her, the mist in her eyes had turned to a stream of tears glistening down her cheeks. "Jadzia." He took both her hands in his.

"I'm so afraid, Roman. I'm afraid of what I'll find there."

"Prepare yourself for the worst, Jadzia," he advised, his sad eyes reflecting her pain. Surely he understood how she felt. "Imagine no stick standing of your home, no one left in your whole village. Then everything and everyone you find will be a blessing."

It wasn't hard for her to imagine the worst as they traveled through the devastation of southwestern Poland, first by train to Krakow, then little by little, sometimes walking, sometimes catching a ride on a truck or an oxcart: churches in ruins, entire villages destroyed, bridges gone or dangerously fragmented. Most fields, which should have shone green in the August sunlight with crops almost ready for harvest, lay fallow.

They spent the night in the ruin of a barn on an abandoned farm, still a full day's walk from Niedzieliska. So Jadzia's first glimpse of her village came through the filter of twilight, as she and Roman stood on the crest of a hill less than a kilometer from the village. He suggested they continue their journey through the marketplace: perhaps they would find some shop open where they could purchase bread and cheese. But Jadzia, unwilling to speak to her neighbors of many years before, fearful of what she might hear, insisted they take the footpath through the woods that, skirting town, led directly to her home.

Emerging from a familiar stand of white birch, Jadzia and Roman came upon the old stone well that marked the junction of the Czarnecki and Zadora properties. Here time seemed to have stood still: the clearing, the well, the birches all looked to Jadzia exactly as they had four years earlier, as they had looked in her dreams since then. With her knees buckling and her whole body trembling, Jadzia felt unable to take even one step forward.

"Jadzia, are you all right? Are we almost there?"

"Just through those trees," she answered, pointing.

"Do you want to sit by the well for a moment before we go on?" Roman asked, taking her trembling hand and looking into her eyes, now wide with fearful anticipation.

"Yes, I think I must." He lifted her up, placing her gently on the smooth old stones, then leaned toward her, cradling her firmly in one strong arm. Jadzia breathed deeply, hoping to slow the rapid palpitation of her heart. But she could not free her mind of the image evoked by her first sight of the well: a slim frame bending gracefully over the well, brushing with one delicate stroke of long fingers at strands of white-gold hair, laughing. That laugh, high and tinkling like altar bells, seemed to drift through the trees, enveloping her in swirls of sound.

"Jadzia?" Roman's voice broke the spell. "Are you ready? We should go, *moja droga*. It's almost dark."

Nodding slowly, Jadzia slipped off the well and, taking Roman's hand, stepped onto the short path leading to her home. As they reached the clearing, she hoped she was not dreaming: before them stood her house, the old barn, and even the family outhouse, all weathered and badly in need of repair, but still standing. The fields she could see from this vantage point were barren, and weeds had overtaken the garden her mother and grandmother had worked so hard to maintain. What struck Jadzia most at this time was the silence: no barking of dogs or lowing of cattle, no skittering chickens cackling a busy welcome.

They walked up to the house and knocked on the closed door; then, with much difficulty due to missing hinges, Roman pushed it open. In the dim light Jadzia saw mostly emptiness, bare spaces where her mother's furniture had stood, pale shadows where pictures had hung. But there were signs of habitation: two milking stools brought in from the barn, a pile of tattered rags in a corner that still carried the indention of a recent sleeper, a rusty knife lying on the kitchen counter beside a heel of rye bread.

"Anyone here?" Roman called as he advanced further into the house, but his voice was drowned by the low howl of a wraithlike figure, clad in tattered rags, flying through the open front door. Jadzia watched, terrified, as the figure, holding a stout stick high in the air, advanced on Roman. But even in her terror she saw something familiar in the movements of the wraith.

"Stasiu?" she cried, halting the figure, which turned to look at her through dirty grayish locks of hair that almost covered his eyes.

The figure stood immobile for a moment. Then a voice deep with emotion cried "Jadzia? Can it be?" Dropping the stick, he rushed to her and grabbing her in a fierce embrace, rocked her back and forth. "This is a miracle. Thank God," he said over and over, kissing her hair and the salty wetness of her cheeks.

When he finally broke his embrace, Jadzia called Roman to them, introducing the two men who, shaking hands formally, bowed slightly in the old way.

"He is...?" asked Stasiu, ever the older brother, turning toward his sister.

"A friend," replied Jadzia. "A good friend who wanted to make sure I got home safely."

"Forgive me for before," Stasiu bowed once more to Roman. "There are so many thieves and murderers in the countryside now—returning soldiers, villagers with no place to go. I thought you were one of them, here to rob me. Not that there's much here to rob."

"It is nothing," responded Roman. "I understand."

"But have you eaten? I have some bread and potatoes. The potatoes aren't too bad."

Jadzia knew her brother well enough to understand his intent. He was stalling, trying to put off answering the questions she needed to ask. Still, she had to know. "Stasiu, are you...are you alone here?"

Shaking his lowered head slowly in a gesture that reminded Jadzia of their father, Stasiu pulled one of the milking stools forward, softly saying, "Sit down, *kochana*. Yes, I am alone here. There is much you need to know."

She asked first of their parents. "Gone," he said, "in the winter of 1942. Pneumonia. It was such a cold winter, and there was no food and of course no medicine. Many in the village perished."

Jadzia, leaning back from the milking stool, slumped against Roman, who stood behind her, his hands gripping her shoulders, offering what little support he could. Jadzia told herself that this was no worse than she had expected, that in her heart she had known that she would find sorrow here. Growing pressure in her chest threatened to overtake her efforts at finding out what she needed to know, but taking a deep breath, she asked, "And Marek?"

"I've heard nothing, not since the Nazis took him that day with you. But he could be alive." Stasiu hurried to comfort her. "He could come back any day. God knows there were times I did not believe I would ever see you again."

Jadzia took another deep breath. "*Babcia?*" she asked through a strange hollowness that was beginning to overtake her. What she was hearing was too painful to bear, but she needed, after all her days and nights of wondering and worrying, to know everything that had happened.

"Shot dead by the Nazis in the summer of 1942." Stasiu once again shook his head in that familiar gesture.

"But why?" asked Jadzia, trying to make sense out of senselessness. "She was just an old woman. She never did anyone any harm."

"She and *Pani* Zadora and some of the other women were hiding some of the Jewish children from the settlement—trying to smuggle them to France. They got caught. The Nazis lined them up—five of them there were—against the church wall. They made us watch." Stasiu hung his head in shame. "There was nothing we could do, Jadzia. Even *Tata.* Watching his mother die that way. He was never the same after that."

Jadzia nodded slowly, feeling as though she was tumbling down slowly into the darkness of a well shaft. For a time the three were silent.

Roman finally breached the silence. "Your grandmother must have been very brave."

"Yes," Stasiu nodded, obviously grateful for Roman's efforts. "She was always the stubborn one. No one ever told her what to do."

"I, too, had a *babcia* much like that," Roman added.

"They're a dying breed. But we were more surprised about *Pani* Zadora. That one had never in anyone's memory done anything for anyone else in her whole life."

"I'm not surprised," said Jadzia softly. Thinking of all the children that Apolonya's mother had lost in various ways, she understood why *Pani* Zadora would give her life to save someone else's child. Jadzia finally asked "And the Zadoras? Are any of them alive?"

"Gienek was taken to Germany during the last year of the war, but he returned a month ago. And Pawel and Helena—Gienek received a letter from them. They're safe in England. They have two children now." Jadzia thought back to their wedding. Had it really happened only eight years earlier?

"No one else?" she asked. "Nothing of...?"

"No. Gienek hasn't heard from..." Stasiu quickly glanced at Roman, then at Jadzia, "...from any of his other brothers. But Jadzia, will you eat something?" He now looked closely at her face, deathly pale beneath the tracks of dried tears, her eyes lifeless like the glass eyes of a doll. Then, turning to Roman, he added, "I have some vodka hidden in the barn. Shall I get it?"

"Yes, please," answered Roman. "Perhaps Jadzia will eat and also have some vodka. And then, I think she needs to sleep for a very long time."

"Ah, Stasiu thought you would be here." Roman joined Jadzia on the low stone bench that graced the Czarnecki family plot in St. Adalbert's cemetery, carefully placing a box wrapped in dirty oilcloth at his feet. "This is a beautiful place."

The cemetery had changed little through the last tumultuous years. In the light of a new dawn, willows waved gently in the wind, some singly, some in small groups, one rising majestically behind the bench on which they sat. The rolling hills were dotted with statuary—the Angel Gabriel, the Holy Mother, and countless cherubs, some dating back a hundred years or more—standing their gray watch over the tombstones.

On the ground at Jadzia's feet were three relatively fresh graves, each marked for now with only a rough wooden cross and a name. On each grave lay a small bunch of wildflowers—lilies, violets, wild roses—that Jadzia had picked in the forest earlier that morning.

"Did you sleep?" he asked.

"A little," she answered with a weak smile as she looked thoughtfully at her hands, clasped loosely in her lap, the fingers of her left hand gently rolling something round and yellow.

"Did you find something?" he asked, pointing to her hands at a flash of yellow caught in an early sunbeam filtering through the willows.

"Oh, this...no. This is nothing," she smiled, dropping the bead into the pocket of her full skirt.

"Are you feeling any better?"

"I feel strange." Now she shook her head slightly. She had only vague memories of the previous evening, after her first glass of vodka. "I feel empty somehow. I can't cry. I wish I could—but I can't."

"Your tears will come later," Roman told her. "Don't try to force them." After a moment he added, taking her hand in his, " It's very peaceful here."

"This whole village was, not so long ago," she answered, looking down at the graves before her. "It used to be so peaceful, I could hardly stand it. All I ever wanted to do was to get away." He smiled with her. "And now I sit here, Roman, and wonder 'Why?' Was it something we did...some terrible punishment from God?"

"Not from any God who we call our Father," Roman assured her. "Jadzia, of course you want to think that way—that there was some cause, something that would help make some sense out of the past few years. But we can't do that. Thinking that way will destroy us. What we have to do is go on from here, never forgetting, but not letting it stop us from living our lives."

Jadzia looked down at her hands folded in her lap. She knew he was right, but words were all he offered. To put those words into action seemed an insurmountable undertaking.

They sat quietly for several minutes, gazing at the graves, at the beauty of the surrounding area, and rarely, at each other. Finally Jadzia asked, pointing to the ground at Roman's feet. "That box. What is it?"

"Oh," he replied, picking it up and trying to brush off loose dirt. "Something of yours. Stasiu said he buried it behind the barn the day the Nazis took you away."

"I can't imagine..." But immediately upon taking the box from him, Jadzia knew what it was. Her fingers shaking, she peeled away the layers of oilcloth, finally revealing a wooden box, stained dark, intricately carved in a floral design. A tiny brass lock, its key dangling from a little piece of twine, protected the box's contents. Jadzia sighed deeply, holding the box close to her bosom. "God bless you, Stasiu," she whispered.

"Ah, some memento from your childhood?" asked Roman.

"Yes. This was made for me by my *tata*, to hold letters from my cousin Eva in America. We wrote to each other for many years." Jadzia felt a first warm tear trickle down her cheek.

"Does Eva know you have survived the war?"

"No. I haven't written," Jadzia responded. "It all seems so very long ago." She wiped tears from her cheeks with one hand, still clutching the box closely to her with the other. "But I'll write to her again—soon."

"Do you wish to go back to the house now? Or would you wish me to go back alone?" he asked solicitously.

"No. No. I'm all right. Please stay," she said, gaining composure as she placed a hand on his forearm. There would be time to weep a sea of tears later, when she was alone. Loosely rewrapping the wooden box, she placed it tenderly on her lap. Again they sat, silently, companionably, for several minutes.

"Jadzia," he finally asked, "what will you do now?"

"I don't know. Stay here, I suppose. Try to help Stasiu get the farm back in order. And you?"

"I'll go back to Katowice."

"And open another store?"

"No, *moya droga*," he answered sadly, "that would not be possible. I have no capital, nothing to begin a business with. I'll go to the mines. There will be work there."

"But Roman," she said, "you worked so hard to get out of the mines."

"It doesn't matter. The mines were good enough for my grandfather and my father. They will be good enough for me."

They sat quietly once again for several moments, each looking at the peaceful beauty before them, each lost in thought. Then, suddenly, Roman broke the silence.

"Jadzia," he said, his voice cracking just a bit. "Look at me." She did, and saw in his eyes something other than his customary sadness, something more lively, more determined.

"Jadzia, there is nothing for you here," he continued, his voice becoming stronger. "It will be years before Stasiu makes the farm workable again—what with no animals, no seed."

She tried to respond, but he stopped her with a finger placed gently on her lips. "No, Jadzia, let me finish. Please." He waited until her soft smile told him to continue.

"Jadzia, I know I have very little to offer a young, beautiful girl like you. In a different time, I wouldn't even think to ask this. But Jadzia, *kochana*, I want you to come back to Katowice with me. If you will have me, if you will be my wife, I promise to make a good life for us and to be a loving, faithful husband to you, through all the days of my life."

Jadzia looked down at her hands, now clasped firmly in Roman's, then to the graves at her feet. She had not expected this. She knew she could trust Roman's promises. Still, this was not the proposal she had dreamed about, had whispered about to Apolonya so long ago. Looking up, for one long moment she glanced through the forest in the direction of the Zadora homestead.

She needed more time. She did not know everything she needed to know to respond to him right now. But would Roman wait for an answer? Would it be fair of her to ask him to do so? Was she deceiving herself in imagining a future that, most likely, would never exist?

At last her eyes returned to Roman's, her gaze focusing as though searching for something deep within them. Roman was a genuinely good man. And she was so weary, so confused about what direction she should take in this sad new world.

Finally, she answered, in a voice both steady and fond, "Roman Kaminski, I would be honored to become your wife."

Chapter Eleven

Evie, Chicago

September, 1945

June 8, 1945

My dearest Eva,

Just received your letter of the 20th of last month. I'm still in France and getting along pretty well. Getting used to the French now. Still don't know what they're talking about, but I can buy what I want in the local stores. I just use the few French words I know and wave my arms around a lot. Can't buy very much, plenty of perfume around though, lot of wine too. Never really drank much wine before—you know I'm more of a beer man. But the stuff's pretty good.

I'm healthy as ever. Climate here is a lot better than in England. We don't work too hard, most of our hard work is done by German prisoners. All our boys do is supervise. We don't get too much time off, but I finally did get a weekend pass and made it to Paris. Beautiful city, what's left of it. Saw the Arch de Triomphe and Notre Dame—really pretty church. Took some pictures and will send them soon—plenty of film here. Maybe someday we'll be able to come back here together and I can show you the sights.

Glad to hear Henryk made it back all right. How's he readjusting to civilian life? I thought I'd be back by now, what with the war being over. But there's still things we have to do here. One of the fellows said that he heard our unit's being sent back early next month.

I look at that picture you sent me about a hundred times a day—the one in the bathing suit. Honey, you look prettier in that picture than Betty Grable. One thing that worries me, though—you said in your last letter that maybe we should wait a while before we get married. Eva, one thing I know is that I want to get married just as soon as we can. I'm almost 25 already, and if it wasn't for this war, we would have been married already, maybe even had a kid or two by now. I've learned in the last couple of years that life is unpredictable—there's no sense putting off what you want to do. And I know I want to be with you forever. You feel the same way, don't you, darling?

Give my regards to your family, and give Steffie a big kiss for me.

Love,
Mikosz

Evie, lost in thought, almost dropped the wine glass she was polishing when she heard the doorbell ring. She was here! The indomitable *Pani* Hanka Sienka, Mikosz's mother, was here to formalize wedding plans with her father. Evie took one more quick glance around the kitchen to assure herself that nothing was in disarray, that every surface spoke of cleanliness. She had spent two whole days cleaning the apartment and preparing the refreshments—*kolaczki*, of course, and her most successful recipe for poppy seed coffee cake. She had agonized over whether or not to offer wine, then finally decided on a very weak wine punch.

She waited long enough to give her father time to welcome their guests and settle them into the sitting room. Then, straightening her shoulders and holding her head high, she lifted the tray with the wine glasses and strode forward.

"Ah, here's Evelina," Wladyslaw said upon the entrance of his daughter. Evie noticed that he sat on the sofa with Mikosz; *Pani* Sienka had appropriated his easy chair, occupying it like a throne. *How different* tata *is*, thought Evie, *now that he's old. He's nothing but a toothless old lion.* She wished that her mother had lived to see this remarkable transformation. Perhaps *Pani* Sienka's forceful character was moving mountains.

Pani Sienka, despite her regal bearing, was a short woman, under five feet tall, and almost as round as she was tall. Her hair was still dark brown, almost black, the cause of much speculation in the neighborhood. She was dressed, as always, in severe black crepe trimmed in even blacker lace on the neckline and the three-quarter length sleeves. Today she wore a short, double strand of pearls partially hidden within the folds of skin at her neck; she complemented the necklace with large pearl-toned earrings and a gold pin trimmed with dangling strings of tiny pearls. On her dark head was a flat, round hat, also black, with a black net veil covering her forehead and dipping over her eyes. Evie had known *Pani* Sienka all her life and could never remember her ever having looked any different, nor even any younger.

Mikosz rose to take the tray from his betrothed's hands, depositing a chaste kiss on her cheek as he did so. Then, taking her hand, he walked her the three steps to the easy chair where his mother sat. Evie bent, hoping to deposit only a quick kiss on the heavily rouged and powdered cheek, but was grabbed by two remarkably strong arms and pulled into a suffocating hug.

"Ah, *moja corka!*" *Pani* Sienka cooed, squeezing Evie against her firm bosom.

Moja corka? thought Evie for just one moment. *My daughter? Not moja synowa, my daughter-in-law?* Dutifully accepting a kiss on each cheek, she pulled away, saying with all the sincerity she could muster, "Welcome, Mother Sienka."

"Ah, Evelina, I hope someday you will call me Mama—though I could never hope to take the place of your dear, departed mama. I knew her well."

Yes, thought Evie, *and she knew you too. She knew you enough to stay away from you!* And how, thought Evie, could anyone, particularly this woman, believe she could take the place of her own dear mother. Never!

Mikosz placed his arm around Evie and drew her to the sofa, Evie's father squeezing tightly against the sofa's arm to give them room. Wladyslaw opened his mouth to speak, but was drowned out by the voice emanating from the easy chair.

"Such a beautiful girl, Mikosz. You have chosen well."

While Mikosz nodded, smiling, Evie replied, almost choking on the words, "Thank you, Mother Sienka." Only yesterday Steffie had repeated to her a conversation she had overheard in the butcher shop. Hidden behind an aisle, Steffie had heard Mother Sienka discussing Evie with her old friend *Pani* Johaniewicz, complaining about the tall, skinny, cigarette-smoking girl with the dyed hair who had somehow bedazzled her darling Mikosz.

What a hypocrite she is!, Evie thought, biting back words that wanted to explode out of her mouth. Instead, "Some pastry, Mother Sienka?" she offered. *Pani* Sienka chose a selection of *kolaczki*: prune, cheese and apricot.

Biting into one and brushing powdered sugar from her lip, she nodded. "Excellent, Evelina, but next time, *kochana*, use only egg yolks. It will give you a dough that's more firm, not as crumbly."

Only egg yolks indeed, fumed Evie. Hadn't she made *kolaczki* with her mother a hundred times? Her mother had never separated the eggs.

She was glad when they got down to the serious business of wedding plans. It was easy to decide the location of the wedding and reception: every wedding Evie had ever attended had been at St. Casimir's Church, every reception in the church hall. Evie had at first resisted *Pani* Sienka's suggested dressmaker, but realizing that she knew no dressmakers herself, deferred to her future mother-in-law's recommendation. *Pani* Sienka's offer to pay the bar bill was presented with great magnanimity and accepted with many thanks, even though everyone present knew that, by tradition, the bar was always the groom's family's responsibility. Mikosz's recommendation of his cousin's band was welcomed by all: the Polka Knights were neighborhood favorites, and the family connection would assure a good discount.

"Three meats?" asked *Pani* Sienka, although her question sounded much more like a statement.

"Yes," replied Evie's father, "we can do that: beef, chicken, *kielbasa*."

"Good. Then here's my list." *Pani* Sienka reached deep into her large woven straw purse gaily trimmed with multi-colored cloth daisies, pulling out several sheets of paper covered in her small, neat script.

Wladyslaw sighed deeply as he glanced over the list. "*Prosze, Pani*, so many?" he asked in awe. "There must be one hundred names here." His face paled noticeably and tiny droplets of sweat suddenly sprang just beneath the hairline on his forehead.

"One hundred seventeen."

"And they are all for the reception? None for church only?" *Pani* Sienka nodded solemnly. "But *Pani*, the expense. We were thinking of something smaller—just close family and friends." Their own list of guests numbered fewer than twenty. He looked to Mikosz and Evie for support, but Mikosz seemed to be engrossed in studying the knuckles of his left hand. Evie, busily rearranging *kolaczki* on the plate, wondered at the transformation of her father. Why had she feared him so as a child? Today, bowing to the force of this tiny woman, he was folding like a bad poker hand.

"Those *are* my dearest family and friends. All will want to be there for the wedding of my only child. You would deny me this?" *Pani* Sienka's hand dipped back into the straw purse, withdrawing a delicate, heavily scented handkerchief embroidered in pink roses and trimmed in Austrian lace. With this she dabbed at her eyes.

"No, no," Wladyslaw replied. "But...I don't know quite how to put this. Could you...*Pani*...the expense." Evie thought the strain in his voice was painful to hear.

Pani Sienka, clutching the handkerchief to her bosom, suddenly sat upright, her four feet ten inches looking remarkably formidable. "*Pan* Bialek, you would not be suggesting...you know that the wedding feast is the responsibility of the bride's father."

"Yes, but..." Wladyslaw looked like something was twisting his inner organs.

"Mama, I have some money. I could..." Mikosz interjected helpfully.

"Shush, *Syn*. This does not concern you."

Evie looked toward Mikosz, thinking he might challenge his mother. Not concern him? Wasn't it his wedding too? But all he did was pour himself another glass of punch.

"*Pan* Bialek," continued *Pani* Sienka, "I understand your concern, but there is little I can do. After all, a poor widow must watch every penny."

Lord, no, thought Evie, *now she's really gone too far. Pani* Sienka had been a widow for as long as Evie had known her. *Pan* Sienko had left her three apartment buildings, from which she collected the rent of eight tenants. For years before the war she had complained, along with everyone else, of financial strain. When neighbors' looks would signal their doubt, she would respond, "Ach, you think I am wealthy because of my buildings. But you can't eat bricks." Still, *Pani* Sienka's standing order at the butcher shop had not changed, and her black crepe dresses never took on the familiar sheen of too much wear.

Wladyslaw looked to his daughter, then to his future son-in-law, and finally down at his folded hands. With a sigh and a lowering of his shoulders, he capitulated. "Of course, *Pani*, you are right. We will manage."

"Ah." *Pani* Sienka visibly brightened. "Then we are agreed." She indicated the mantel clock. "But look at the time. Mikosz and I must be going soon—there is much to do. Evelina, let me help you take these things back to the kitchen."

"No, no, Mother Sienka. I can do it."

"I insist." With this she picked up one glass and marched toward the kitchen. All Evie could do was follow. Placing her tray on the kitchen counter, Evie turned back toward the sitting room but was stopped by a firm hand, sparkling with opal and amber rings in intricate silver settings, grasping her arm.

"Evelina, before we go back, I must speak to you."

"Why of course, Mother Sienka."

"As much as this pains me, I must tell you. I have heard things, Evelina."

"Heard things?" Evie tried to keep the panic out of her voice.

"Yes," *Pani* Sienka continued. "I have heard things about you that concern me very much."

Evie shook her head as if confused. But she had plenty of reason to fear what *Pani* Sienka had heard.

It had been very warm all day. The resort town of Lake Geneva, snugly nestled in the woody lakes region of northern Illinois, was crowded for the holiday—full of families and couples eager to celebrate their first post-war Independence Day. Of course the war against Japan continued in Asia, but everyone knew that would be wrapping up pretty soon and the rest of the soldiers would be coming home. Evie had much to think about.

But Evie didn't want to think. The cottage was the perfect place to get away from the heat and din of the city. It was located on the quiet side of the lake, away from town, away from tourists. It was a small cottage—just two little bedrooms, a kitchen and sitting room—built of local pine painted white with black trim and shutters, a twin to most of the other privately owned vacation cottages in the area. The property had been in the Honeycutt family for generations: it was here the family spent summer vacations and long weekends. Had Mr. and Mrs. Honeycutt not been called away for a family emergency—something involving one of Mrs. Honeycutt's brothers—the Honeycutts would have been here right now. And Evie would most certainly have been somewhere else.

Languidly rolling over from her stomach to her back, she brushed from her thighs some sand that had worked its way through the loosely woven blanket. She wondered why she was still waiting for her beer. The cottage, after all, was only a stone's throw away. What was taking Charley so long?

She glanced at the Chris Craft powerboat docked at the end of the short pier, its dark teak hull gleaming in the sunlight. Maybe they would have time for one more ride before heading home. Evie had been terrified her first time out in the boat, unfamiliar as she was with the noise and surge of a powerful inboard motor and the jolt of wave riding. But once she had adjusted to the rhythm of the ride she found everything to her liking: the breeze blowing against her face, the tiny doll houses across the lake quickly looming to full size cottages, the brisk spray tickling her nose after a quick turn into another boat's wake.

The irregularity of the shoreline and its densely wooded acres afforded the property a great deal of privacy; from some vantage points, only water and forest could be seen. This attracted Evie more than anything else. Here she could believe that she was alone in the world.

Well, not completely alone. She jumped, yelping, as she felt a sudden wet iciness in the crease between her shoulders. "Charley, you dope!" she cried, scooping a handful of sand and flinging it behind her toward her tormenter.

"Hey, cut it out, kiddo! Behave or you won't get your beer." The summer sun had tanned Charley to a deep amber and had streaked his sandy thatch of hair, now tousled by lake breezes, with luminous golds and coppers. His misty green eyes radiated mischief. Sitting up, elbows on bent knees and arms folded, she turned to glare at him. "Nope, that's not the face I want to see," he complained.

Responding to her purposely fake smile, he started laughing. "That's a little bit better. But you're still gonna have to pay for this, Toots."

Now pouting, she gazed back over the lake. Half a minute passed before the sun's heat reminded her how thirsty she was. Besides, how could she resist him? He looked as elegant and dashing in swim trunks as he had looked that first evening at the USO dance...perhaps even more so. "Okay," she capitulated, "what do you want?"

"A kiss."

"Just a kiss?"

"Well, for now, anyway."

One kiss led to another, but before too long Evie extricated herself from his embrace and was sipping her reward, again looking out over the lake. Charley had planted himself next to her, his arm around her shoulder. In just a few minutes his fingers were stroking the iridescent green sharkskin fabric of her bathing suit just above her breast. Soon they traveled under the strap of the suit, then dipped into the cup of the suit's reinforced bra, searching for the nipple hidden behind the wire and intricate cotton padding.

"I thought you said just a kiss," Evie complained, though she did nothing to stop his fingers.

"I lied." Now Charley was tugging at the strap, pulling it down her arm, exposing her breast.

"Stop it, Charley. Not here in broad daylight," she fussed, snapping the strap back up to her shoulder.

"Aw, nuts, don't be such a prude. No one can see us." Pushing her shoulders down to the blanket he bent over her for another kiss. She turned her face away.

"What's the matter now?" he complained, sitting up again. "You've been funny this whole trip."

"I've just got a lot on my mind," Evie answered, resuming her previous posture.

"Aw, what's troubling that pretty little head of yours?" he asked, tracing a finger gently down her arm. "C'mon baby, you can tell Charley."

"I just..." Evie began, but the words caught in her throat. How could she explain her feelings without appearing too bold, too needy. She had determined to talk to him before they returned to the city, and she would, if only he'd keep his hands to himself. Now his finger was tracing patterns above her bent knee, slowly advancing up her thigh. Grabbing his hand and holding it firmly in her own, she continued. "I just sometimes wonder about us, Charley."

"What about us?"

"Well, about where this is going. Where we're headed."

Turning away from her, Charley looked out across the lake. He took a deep swallow of his beer before answering. "Honey, it's like I told you before. I'm not really free to make my own decisions."

She waited for him to continue, then realizing he wouldn't, placed a hand on his shoulder. As he turned toward her she looked directly into his eyes, searching for answers she feared she'd not find there. "You said you were going to tell your parents about us. Have you?"

"It's not so easy. You know they expect certain things from me—to take over the family business, for one."

"But why is that a problem?" Evie had hoped to keep her question light and upbeat, but she could hear an annoying, whiny tone creeping into her voice.

"Honey, you just wouldn't understand. Dad's so old-fashioned, and Mom's worse. If they knew I was going out with someone from the factory..."

"So that's it. I. . I. . I'm not good enough for you."

"You know that's not true." Charley turned back to her, gently lifting her chin to face him once more. "You're plenty good enough for me. I love you, Evie. I want to be with you. It's just going to take time."

Unfortunately, time wasn't a commodity Evie felt she had. She'd received Mikosz's letter over a week ago—soon he would be home. Charley knew nothing about Mikosz—and obviously, Mikosz knew nothing about Charley. Mikosz had made his feelings for her perfectly clear. But as for Charley, well, he could be as slippery as those trout they had caught in the lake yesterday. She never really knew where she stood with him.

"Aren't things good the way they've been going? Hasn't it been fun?" Charley asked.

Pushing his hand away, Evie began drawing circles in the sand. Fun was the problem. She enjoyed being with Charley too much. It had started innocently enough—running into him at a few more USO dances, going bowling a couple of times, then to a couple of movies. He was a welcome distraction, a cure for her loneliness.

But soon their evenings together had become the most important part of her life. Her time with Charley was so different from what she had previously known, so much more pleasant: riding in a car instead of waiting for the bus, eating out at beautiful restaurants instead of cooking at home, sunbathing privately at Lake Geneva instead of among the mobs at North Avenue Beach.

And Charley himself was uncomplicated, unlike all the other men she knew. He was never depressed, never dark or moody. He never groused about money or work or politics. He drank but never got drunk, so unlike her father or Henryk. Charley was fun, and Evie realized that one thing that had been missing from most of her life was fun.

She felt his finger again tracing a soft pattern on her upper thigh. When they had first become lovers, Charley had treated her gently, initiating her into lovemaking with sweet words and tender caresses. She had responded completely. Over the past few weeks he had become more passionate and demanding, and she had responded in kind. He knew how to give her what she wanted and needed. Finally she answered him. "Fun," she sighed. "Yeah, Charley, it's been fun."

Smiling, he pressed her shoulders back down onto the blanket, more forcefully this time. "I love you in that bathing suit, baby," he purred into her ear, and Evie, for one quick moment, thought back to the day when he had taken her picture in this suit, the same picture she had later sent to Mikosz. Mikosz. Sometimes she felt she hardly remembered him. It had been so long—four long years. Still, he was her fiancé—she'd made a vow.

"I don't think..." She pressed her hand against his shoulder.

"But I'd love you better out of it."

She had tried to protest. "It's getting late. Maybe we should go..." But her body was already surrendering, seeking him, betraying her with its longing for him.

Much later that night, when Charley had dropped her off in front of her home, she had hoped to sneak up silently to her bedroom as she had so many nights before. Noticing a light on in the sitting room and thinking that Steffie had once again been careless about the electricity, she entered the room and was startled to find Henryk sitting on the sofa, fingering a glass of beer resting precariously on his knee.

"Henryk." She smiled sheepishly at her brother. "You're up late."

"You, too," he had answered.

"Well, I was just checking on the light," she had said, turning back toward the hallway. "I thought Stephania left it on again, and you know the old man has fits when that happens. Good night then."

"Not so fast," he had answered, the tone of his voice raising goosebumps in the space between her shoulders. "Come, Eva. Sit."

"It's late. I have to go to work tomorrow and…"

"Dammit, Eva," his voice exploded in the small room. "I know where you been and who you been with."

"I don't know what you're…" Evie didn't have time to finish her sentence. Springing from the sofa, sending his beer crashing to the floor, in just two steps Henryk towered over her, grasping her shoulders roughly in his hands.

"*Curwa!*" he had shouted into her face, his fingers digging deep into her flesh. "Whore! Slut!"

"Henryk, please, stop it. What are you talking about?" She was crying, knowing all too well why he cursed her in both English and Polish, demanding to know how she could even think of cheating on her fiancée, a serviceman fighting for his country. What kind of woman would do such a thing? She was a disgrace to the family.

"Stop. You're hurting me," she cried, more in shame than in pain.

"And who are you hurting? Did you ever stop to think about that?" He grasped her in a close embrace and led her to the sofa, pulling her down with both hands to sit next to him. "It's all his fault—that bastard Honeycutt," he said, traces of tears forming in his eyes. "He took advantage when I wasn't here to watch out for you. You're just a kid—you didn't know what you were doing." Evie felt that she had known very well what she was doing, but sensed that this would be a poor time to contradict her brother. "I could kill the son of a bitch."

"Henryk, no!"

"Don't worry, Sis. I wouldn't hurt the bastard. It wouldn't do any good anyway. And besides, I've seen enough death for one lifetime. But think about what you're doing, if not for Mikosz, at least for yourself." He paused, then, firmly but gently, "Honeycutt will never marry you, Eva."

"You can't know that." Eva's tears flowed freely now—she had given up any attempt to stop them. "Henryk, you don't even know Charley."

"Honey, I know a lot of men just like him. He's using you. He'll have his fun and toss you aside for the next girl. You're throwing your life away. And Mikosz is a good man." Henryk took his sister's hands into his own, pressing them firmly as he looked directly into her eyes. "He'll make a good life for you."

"I know that Mikosz is a wonderful man. That's what's killing me. I love Mikosz, I think I've loved him all my life, and I can't stand the thought of hurting him. It's just that..."

"No excuses, Eva. You wouldn't just hurt him. You'd kill him."

"No," she cried. "Don't say that." But the horror in her eyes seemed to only encourage her brother to continue.

"You can't know what it was like over there, during the war. Hell, I wouldn't want you to know. The only thing that kept men like Mikosz alive was knowing that they had a gal at home, waiting for them—that they'd be together soon. Take that away from him and you'll destroy him."

Evie had never meant to hurt Mikosz. She knew her brother was right—Mikosz's last letter had assured her of his love. And yet..."I don't know what to do," she cried. "I thought that all I wanted was Mikosz. But then Charley..."

"Think about it!" Henryk interrupted, the anger returning to his voice. "Think about what you're saying. Even if things are different—if Mikosz doesn't come back, say, or if *he* changes his mind—it still wouldn't be right, you and that guy. He's not like us. You'd never fit in with his family. You'd be miserable."

From the start, she'd tried to resist Henryk's words, but a nagging voice deep inside her echoed his concerns. Did she really love Charley, or only the image of a life with him? Could she trust him? Wasn't what Henryk was saying exactly what she had been feeling at the cottage?

Did Charley really love her? Or was Henryk right? Had she been the biggest dope of all time?

If only she had more time. But time, she knew, was the one thing she had run short of.

"Mother Sienka, I really don't know what you're talking about." Evie swallowed hard, trying to ease the nausea that was overtaking her. She considered her foolishness in having thought that in this neighborhood, where every old *pani* spent most of her time looking out the window searching for new gossip, she could ever have kept Charley a secret.

"I think you do know. And yet," the older woman continued with a deep sigh, "my son seems to be smitten by you. There is only so much a mother can do. And it is time he marry—'better to marry than to burn,' as God's word says. But I just want you to know, *dziecho*, I will be watching you." As if to demonstrate, she glared deeply into Evie's eyes, reminding Evie of the defiant glares she would sometimes get from the dark eyes of the rats in the cellar.

"Now, we must go back," *Pani* Sienka demanded. "The boys are waiting."

"*Prosze*, Mother Sienka," Evie pleaded, "just a minute. I need to rinse these dishes."

"All right then. Don't be long."

As Evie watched the black crepe-draped bulk of Hanka Sienka's back disappear into the hallway, disparate emotions swirled in her mind. Had she made a terrible mistake? Was it too late to change her mind, change the course of her life? She did love Mikosz, had loved him since they were children. But she was a different person now. And so was he. And while she knew he loved her, there was a new look in his eyes, a desperate, haunted look she hadn't seen before the war. Sometimes he became quiet for hours, lost in his own thoughts.

Besides, if he ever found out...and he could find out. There was a wedding night in their future. She'd been haunted for weeks by the refrain of a popular song, one that had had plenty of radio play through the war years: "Don't sit under the apple tree with anyone else but me...'til I come marching home." She'd sat under the apple tree, and then some. Would Mikosz know? And if he did, could he forgive her? She didn't think so.

And what of Charley? She'd never had more fun in her life than when she was with him. But was Henryk right? A future with Charley, she realized in her more rational moments, was unlikely to happen.

Was there a third alternative? If so, she couldn't imagine what it was.

One thing was certain—hiding in the kitchen any longer wouldn't do. Stepping back into the sitting room, she saw Mikosz and her father laughing awkwardly over glasses of punch. She had hoped that *Pani* Sienka would by now be showing some evidence of leave-taking, but the vile woman had settled once more into the easy chair. On seeing Evie, she reached deep into her straw purse and extracted a tissue-wrapped package. Beaming, she handed it to Evie, saying, "Here, *moja kochana,* something I made for the wedding. I know this is something your dear mother would have done for you. I hope you do not mind my taking her place in this little matter."

Evie took the package as gingerly as if she expected serpents to spring from it. Slowly unwrapping the tissue paper, she found a heart-shaped pillow of white satin trimmed in lace and crystal beadwork. Sounds of "Ah, how beautiful," and "Did you make it yourself?" came from the men.

"For the Money Dance," suggested *Pani* Sienka, smiling broadly at her future daughter-in-law.

So, thought Evie, *this is how it's going to be.* Nascent anger began to churn deep within her. *Her* Money Dance. *Her Oczepiny.* These were things she was supposed to share with her mother, not with this wicked, manipulative woman. How dare *Pani* Sienka think, even for one moment, that anyone—particularly she—could take her own mother's place?

This wasn't a situation that called for the easy grace and charm of Katharine Hepburn, but for the iron determination and cunning of Greer Garson. She knew that if she did not assert herself now, at least in this one little thing, she probably never would. "Mother Sienka," she responded, a sweet smile beginning to light her face. "I'm afraid there won't be any Money Dance."

"No Money Dance?"

"No Money Dance. And no *Oczepiny.*"

"But...it is tradition," countered *Pani* Sienka. "What are you thinking? *Every* wedding has a Money Dance and *Oczepiny.*"

"In Poland, perhaps." Evie smiled broadly, directly at her future mother-in-law, daring her to pull out the old handkerchief, to reference her widowhood. "But this is America." Yes, she thought, *at least I've learned something from being with Charley. Even Milwaukee Avenue is America—not Poland.*

Evie could sense wheels spinning frantically in that hat and veil-bedecked head, could almost feel *Pani* Sienka being torn between her desire to dominate and her fear of waging a battle she might not win. *Pani* Sienka turned toward her son, opening her mouth to speak, and for one terrible moment Evie feared the woman would denounce her before Mikosz and her father. But Mikosz did not look up from the smudge he was busy rubbing off his left thumbnail, while her father had seemingly become engrossed with examining the few remaining *kolachki* crumbs left on his plate.

But at last, though Evie could scarcely believe it, a miracle occurred: she observed *Pani* Sienka shrinking, perhaps just a millimeter or two, but shrinking nonetheless. "Well, we'll see about this," *Pani* Sienka finally muttered, pulling herself clumsily out of the easy chair. "Come, Mikosz, we must go."

Mikosz dutifully followed his mother out the door but returned just a moment later, ostensibly to retrieve a jacket he had left behind. Placing his arm around Evie and kissing her cheek, he smiled broadly, saying, "See, *moja droga*, it's just like I told you. You had nothing to worry about. Mama loves you!"

Chapter Twelve

Jadzia, Katowice

November, 1956

Moja najdroższa Jadziu!

Przepraszam Cię, że nie odpisywałam tak długo. Ja i Mikosz byliśmy bardzo zajęci. On był na urlopie pracowniczym. Remontowaliśmy trzecią sypialnię dla Peggy.

"Jadzia, Jadzia, is that you?"

Jadzia slowed her purposeful stride long enough to look up. Deep in thought, she had not noticed the long line of women, dressed in the same dark coats and fur hats against the biting November wind, patiently waiting outside the greengrocers. Quickly examining the faces nearest her in line, she soon determined the source of the call.

"Ah, Marysia." Past the navy and white fringe of the scarf that partially obscured her was the face of her good friend, Marysia Yamnik. Marysia lived across the corridor from Jadzia in one of the many complexes of sprawling cement prefabs erected by the Soviet government to house the burgeoning Polish postwar population. "What are you lined up for today?"

"Who knows?" answered Marysia, eliciting knowing smiles from the women standing nearest to her. "And who cares? Whatever it is, I'm sure I don't have it at home." Motioning Jadzia to join her in line, she bestowed on the elderly woman standing immediately behind her one of her radiant smiles. "*Prosze, pani?*" she asked.

"*Tak,*" answered the older woman, stepping back a half pace to allow room for Jadzia. No one could resist Marysia. Her cherubic cheeks and twinkling blue eyes radiated good humor and a pleasant nature, charming even strangers who had spent no more than moments in her presence.

"*Prosze Pani,*" Marysia asked the elderly woman in her most gracious tone, "do you know what we're standing in line for?"

"I think bananas," the old woman suggested.

"I think coffee," came a voice from farther ahead in the line.

"I hope chocolate," came a third. "But not that waxy stuff. Some of that good Wedel, like they had a couple of weeks ago. Or Wawel is good, too."

Several women in the line murmured their agreement: some good Polish chocolate, of the little that was not exported, would be best.

"I'm not sure I can stand in this line very long," Jadzia said. "I have to get the children from kindergarten before it closes. Is the line moving fast?"

"Like molasses on a Siberian plain in January," confided Marysia. "But stay for a few minutes, anyway. I haven't seen you since last week."

This was true. Jadzia had been very busy at work, taking on additional shifts at the hospital whenever they were offered to add a little more to her special fund. She hoped to have enough by the end of March to arrange an early April trip to the Yugoslavian seashore for Roman and herself. He would object, of course, suggesting many more practical uses for the extra money.

The trick would be to convince him that it was *she* who needed some time in a warmer climate. If he knew the motivation behind her planned trip was her own constant worry about him—about the pallor of his skin, the dark circles under his eyes, the coughing that kept them both awake at night—he would refuse straight out. He was certainly the most stubborn man ever born of woman.

"So how are those beautiful children of yours?" asked Marysia.

"Doing very well." Jadzia beamed a grateful smile. For such a long time she and Roman had doubted they would ever have children. The two miscarriages she had suffered early in their marriage had been devastating, though not unusual. Many young women who had faced the war's deprivations had such difficulties. When seven years into her marriage she had finally delivered Marek, a healthy son, both she and Roman had felt blessed. The arrival of little Magdalena two years later had made their world complete.

"How is the kindergarten?" Their housing complex included a state-sponsored kindergarten, which cared for children from three to seven years old, as well as a nursery for younger children. Unlike most children, Marysia's four were watched by her mother, a kindly old *babcia* who was spoiling them to be as plump-faced and sweet-tempered as their mother.

"*Pani* Levandowska can be a real witch, but for the most part I think it's one of the nicer kindergartens in Katowice," responded Jadzia.

"Katowice? Ach, Jadzia, don't let any *Ruseks* hear you. Wouldn't want anyone to think you were unpatriotic. Remember we live in Stalinograd now!" Marysia's scornful laugh was echoed by every woman within hearing distance. When the Soviet government had renamed cities to honor Communist heroes—as was done in Russia—they encountered only resistance and derision from the Poles. Katowice had officially become Stalinograd in 1953, but no one in town, other than the few Russian officials in residence there, took the name change seriously. "Katowice" it had always been, and "Katowice" it would forever be.

In the first years of Soviet rule, Jadzia and her friends had feared their Russian occupiers. Now they saw Russia as an inept giant, full of bunglers who could not produce quality materials, promote useful agriculture, or even keep store shelves adequately stocked. They hated the government: its corruption and ineptitude, its petty bureaucracy. They resented the shortages of goods, the poorly made and inelegantly designed apartment complexes now filling their once-gracious cities, the Russian language courses their children were required to take in school, the Soviet intolerance of Catholicism. Yet, for the most part, they lived in much the same way they always had.

Looking at the wristwatch, her tenth anniversary present from Roman, Jadzia shook her head. "I must go, Marysia. I can't stand another one of *Pani* Levandowska's evil looks if I come late again. I'll have to miss out on whatever treasure you're waiting for in line. You and Tadek are still stopping by tonight, yes?"

"Only if you have some of that cherry cordial left," Marysia teased.

"I do, but you need to bring up what we talked about. Remember? "

"Of course."

"And Tadek too? He knows what he has to say?"

"Don't worry," laughed Marysia. "We won't let you down."

Breaking from the line, Jadzia hurried the six blocks to the elegant old villa that housed the kindergarten her children attended. Located near the center of her apartment complex, before the war it had been the home of a rich mine owner who had hosted many magnificent dinner parties and formal balls. Less fortunate city dwellers had made a game of observing gleaming carriages with their teams of powerful stallions parked in the circular drive and speculating about which wealthy manufacturer or member of the royalty was stepping out into the stately gardens.

Remodeled as a child care center, the villa's front gardens, fenced in for safety's sake, now sported not lilac and rose bushes, statuary and crystal clear fountains, but a rope and tire swing hanging from an ancient oak and a sandbox fashioned from an old packing box. Jadzia was not surprised to see Marek, even on this cold November afternoon, swinging high into the air, his sturdy little four-year-old's legs pumping powerfully with every forward thrust, his thatch of wheat-colored hair waving wildly with each cycle of forward and backward motion.

"Marek, Marek," she called. "Time to go inside. Mama's here."

Jadzia stepped into the vestibule of the building, its high vaulted ceiling and last remaining chandelier the final vestiges of its former elegance. Turning into the pale yellow room in which the youngest children stayed, she saw little Magda, her mass of dark curls framing a face taut with purpose, hunched over a drawing board. Her pudgy hand clutched a fat green crayon with which she shaded in the grassy section of a playground scene.

"Mama! Mama!" On first sight of her mother, Magda dropped her crayon and flew across the room to her mother's arms.

"Magda, clean up your station," warned the stern voice of *Pani* Levandowska, who signaled her disapproval of both mother and child with first a critical look at the drawing board, then another at the large clock on the wall clearly displaying the time: 4:05.

"Sorry, *Pani*." Jadzia rushed to get Magda's coat, scarf and mittens from her wall hook and her sturdy little boots from the mat immediately below. "Magda, where's the bag for your slippers?" she asked, then turning toward the scowling face and folded arms of *Pani* Levandowska, "*Pani*, if you could just call Marek inside, we'll be out of your way in just a moment."

Soon, released into the freedom of a brisk afternoon, mother and children walked through the community park to their building, Magda clutching her mother's hand, Marek darting around his mother and sister, sometimes walking backward to share with them tales of his exciting day. Their apartment was in one of four identical buildings, all five stories of cement block with a yellow stucco finish. The front of each building was nondescript; children were occasionally found wandering in the halls looking for their apartments in the wrong buildings.

The back of each building, however, displayed more character, as each back apartment boasted its own narrow balcony. Balcony apartments like Jadzia's were coveted for many reasons, but particularly as areas for drying clothes.

Jadzia, stopping in the lobby of their building long enough to check her mail slot, found a letter there from Eva, the first she had received in months. Hurrying the children up the three flights of stairs to their apartment, she settled them into the room they shared, rummaging through a pine chest for Magda's favorite story book and Marek's toy trucks, then returned to the living room to sink gratefully into her overstuffed sofa. She opened her letter.

November 3, 1956

My dearest Jadzia,

Forgive me for taking so long to write. Mikosz and I have been very busy. He took some time off from work and we remodeled the third bedroom for Peggy—it used to be Mikosz's den, and believe me, he wasn't too happy to give it up. But the girls are just getting too big to share a bedroom.

Jadzia looked at the cramped apartment she called her own. Ah, to have the luxury of the home Eva had so often written about in earlier letters: three bedrooms, a big living room and dining room and a backyard in which to grow some vegetables and flowers, and perhaps a fruit tree or two. Eva's descriptions of her home always made Jadzia a little melancholy—not that she had anything to be ashamed of in her own dwelling.

Though small, the apartment was always immaculate. Jadzia loved her living room, with its pale green walls beautifully stenciled with a tiny floral pattern in bright gold. The sofa and two massive chairs of brown and gold-patterned horsehair were comfortable as well as attractive, and the dark cherry finish of her end tables and bureau contrasted beautifully with the creams and ivories of the delicate lace cloths that covered them.

Fresh flowers always graced the dining table and the bureau, which held her shrine, the centerpiece of the room. The crucifix was new—one blessed by the Pope himself—but the icon of the Black Madonna of Czestochowa was her greatest treasure, as it had been her mother's. Stasiu had found the old, faded picture in a junk pile behind Jadzia's family home, and knowing how much recovery of this item from their childhood would mean to her, he had cleaned it up as much as possible and given it to her as a wedding present.

Jadzia's long, narrow kitchen was small but efficient, its pure white porcelain sink, modern gas stove and tiny electric refrigerator seeming to her incredibly modern, especially when compared to the kitchen of her family home at Niedzieliska. Still, especially since Magda was born, she often dreamed of a third bedroom, a larger dining area and more storage space. New apartment assignments were due any day now; perhaps Roman's name would be on the list.

But if not, this apartment would do. Compared with other accommodations she'd dealt with in her life—well, some things were better off forgotten. She returned to her letter.

We are so looking forward to Christmas. Mikosz's company is throwing a very elegant party at the country club the week before Christmas—I know we'll have a swell time. I hope Mikosz "surprises" me on Christmas morning with a pearl necklace I saw at the jeweler's in town—I sure hinted strongly enough last week when we passed the jeweler's window on our way to the hardware store.

Mother Sienka is planning to stay with us for a full week at Christmas—you can imagine how pleased I am. That woman will never forgive me for the mortal sin of taking her baby boy away from her! Still, marry a man and you marry his family, so there is nothing I can do about it but just smile and try to hold my temper.

Cousin Katarina will be in Poland the first week of January and has promised to stop in Katowice to see you. Your mama probably talked to you about her—she's our mothers' cousin on their dad's side—Hanka's daughter. She'll be bringing a little something—you know what I mean.

Good, Jadzia thought. The money would arrive in plenty of time to add to her special fund. She appreciated Eva's generosity—she and Roman could certainly use the money. Even with both of them working there was never enough. While they were no worse off than any of their friends, she often wished she were in a position to politely refuse Eva's donations. Eva had her own family, her own responsibilities, after all.

The girls are growing like weeds. Penny is doing very well in school—Sister Athanasius says she is at the top of her class in both spelling and reading. Peggy starts kindergarten next year. We are getting her a new tricycle for Christmas. I bet she'll be riding it all the way around the block by the first week of spring.

How is your work? I can't imagine how you manage both a family and a full-time job. It must be very difficult. Although I must admit, I don't quite know what it will be like when Peggy starts school next year, and especially the year after when she'll be gone all day. The house keeps me busy, but there's only so much you can clean in one day. I talked to Mikosz about maybe getting a little part-time job in town, but he won't hear of it. It's different here than in Poland—a wife having a job kind of suggests that her husband can't support his family. And I'm sure he's right. He knows so much more about these things than I do.

Still, there are times I actually miss Doall Valve—can you believe it? It was hard work, but we had fun there too. Well, those days are gone for sure.

How strange that Eva's beautiful home did not seem to make her happy, thought Jadzia, and that her cousin did not anticipate with pleasure the leisure time she would soon have. Jadzia herself would give almost anything right now for some free time, despite the satisfaction her work provided. Helping to bring new life into the world was one of the finest occupations a person could have. But she could certainly find plenty to do with even one free afternoon every week. Katowice had a remarkable library and several fine movie houses, and often the ballet company or opera house would offer a matinee. How wonderful it would be to have the time to take advantage of all these city amenities.

Is Roman feeling any better? The last time you wrote you said he had a bad cold. Have you been able to talk him into seeing the doctor? Men must be the same all over the world. I know when my Mikosz is sick, he won't see the doctor for anything. All he wants to do is sit around the house, moaning and making my life miserable with his "Honey, can you get me this?" and "Honey, can you get me that?" Men! Still, what would we do without them?

Please give our love to Roman and a great big kiss to each of your darlings from us. Keep an eye out for something coming in the mail. Please give your children a Christmas kiss for me, and know that I wish you and yours the happiest, most blessed Christmas of all time.

Your loving cousin,

Eva

Folding the letter, Jadzia carefully placed it into the rosewood box her *tata* had made so many years before. For a moment, her fingers traced its intricate carving—on some days, this simple act could bring her thoughts back for an hour or more to her life in Niedzieliska. But not this afternoon. Roman would soon be home and would want his dinner. The house could certainly use a quick dusting before the Yamniks arrived. Dry laundry on the balcony needed folding. And it would be nice to prepare some little treat, perhaps a fruit compote, for their company tonight. What to do first?

"So, Marysia, what treasure did you finally purchase at the market?" asked Jadzia later that evening, pouring cherry cordial into the intricately etched liqueur glass her friend held out. "Was it chocolate?" Jadzia smiled at her company; despite the trouble and expense of entertaining, she always enjoyed the role of hostess. The apartment looked lovely and Marysia and Tadek had enjoyed the apricot compote, each taking a second helping. Roman was in good spirits despite the pallor of his skin and the exhaustion she saw in the slump of his shoulders.

"No," Marysia answered, her face pitiably drawn in exaggerated mock tragedy. "It was..." she paused for effect "...only...," one more sad pause, "toilet paper!" Laughter bounced off the walls of the small apartment.

"Still," said Tadek, a stout, handsome man with a wild profusion of red-tinged chestnut hair and a full matching beard, "a useful acquisition. You are to be commended, *moya droga*, for your enterprise!"

"Yes," agreed Roman, "one thing about toilet paper. When you need it, it's nice to have around." He smiled companionably.

"Not that the newspaper doesn't come in handy sometimes," suggested Marysia, smiling mischievously. "Good for that and for wrapping up kitchen garbage."

"True," added her husband, giving her a wink. "That propaganda piece isn't good for much else." Tadek was a particularly harsh critic of all things Soviet.

"Still, once in a while there's good news." Jadzia attempted to bring the conversation to a topic more elevated than toilet paper. "Cardinal Wyszynski's reinstatement is good news, yes?"

"It's about time," added Roman indignantly. "Imagine, expecting a cardinal to take a loyalty oath. Those idiots should have known better than to stick their dirty fingers into church business."

"Maybe his reinstatement will mean they're going to loosen their grip a little," suggested Marysia. "That would be better."

"Probably for a while," agreed Roman, "but then they'll get rough again, then loosen up a bit. Nothing ever changes with those fools."

"Damned *Ruseks!*" Tadek's face took on the florid hue that arose every time he discussed politics. "And damn the *sukinsyni* who sold us out to them at Yalta!"

"Ach, my husband," complained Marysia. "Forgets my name day three years in a row, but it's been eleven years and he remembers Yalta as if it happened yesterday." Marysia handed her empty liqueur glass to Jadzia for a refill.

"How can I forget? Damned Churchill and Roosevelt, handing over Poland to the Russians as if we were theirs to give! Betraying us to our worst enemy!"

"Worse than the Germans?" asked Jadzia, incredulously.

"Well, maybe second worst. But Poland fought against Germany, too! You don't treat an ally that way." Tadek accepted another vodka from Roman.

"I don't blame Roosevelt," Roman offered. "He was an old, sick man. He only wanted to end the war."

"Yes, I know," responded Tadek. " God forbid I should say anything bad about your hero Roosevelt. But I think the Americans are just as bad as the English and the *Ruseks*."

"No comparison," argued Roman, leaning forward in his seat, obviously ready to give reasons to support his point.

Marysia, raising her hands high in the air, complained, "Enough, enough of this. The past is past. There's no going back." She and Jadzia shared a knowing smile. Men and their politics! Hadn't the last fifteen years, or even the last five hundred, taught them anything? "Can't we talk about something else?"

"All right," agreed Tadek, "I'm willing to talk about something else. Let's talk about plumbing. I wouldn't mind the damned *Ruseks* so much if they just knew what they were doing."

Marysia rolled her eyes to the ceiling. Jadzia sympathized. She knew that once Tadek began complaining about the Russians, it was difficult to derail him. And yet despite his complaints about bureaucratic inefficiency and corruption, as a postal worker, he was seen as a contributor to the problem. He bragged about his disdain for the "*Rusek* dogs" who were his superiors and, through his own inefficient work habits, attempted to sabotage their success. Of course, this led mostly to inconvenience for his customers, most of whom were Poles like himself. Still he saw no contradiction in his behavior.

"Everything the government touches turns to crap," Tadek continued. "Like this damned government housing. Try getting something done. I waited two months to get someone to look at that drip in my faucet."

"Did the plumber finally come?" asked Jadzia.

"Yes," answered Tadek, "three times in six weeks. Every time he came it got worse. I finally fixed it myself yesterday."

"Good work. I didn't know you knew anything about plumbing," said Roman, raising his shotglass in salute. "*Na zdrowie.*" He quickly downed his drink.

"I don't, but then neither did the asshole from the housing office, so what did it matter?" He quickly followed suit, downing his drink with an answering "*Na zdrowie.*"

"Enough talk about politics," demanded Marysia, this time stamping her tiny booted foot on the floor. "I mean it. This is a party, not a wake for the old days, which really were not so good either, when you think of it." She stole a quick look at Jadzia. "Roman, let's talk about something more pleasant. What are your vacation plans for this year?" Marysia asked this as if the thought of vacation had just that moment entered her mind.

"Like always," responded Roman. "A week in August at the company resort." The Katowice mining company that employed Roman owned a resort on the Baltic.

"Don't you go there every year?" asked Marysia.

"Yes, but it's nice. Not too fancy, but it's all that we need. The children like the beach."

"But even in August," continued Marysia, "the weather can be bad that far north."

"So we stay inside and play cards," responded Roman. "It's still better than working. And it's cheap."

"You know," Tadek offered in his role as co-conspirator, "it's getting easier to go to one of the Mediterranean resorts in Bulgaria or Yugoslavia. Go through ORBIS—they're the best."

"We could visit my father's cousin in Dubrovnik," offered Jadzia, acting as though this was the first time the thought had crossed her mind. "You remember Jan Bodek, don't you?" She looked innocently at Roman. "I'm sure he would show us around when we got there."

"Ach, we don't need such luxury," huffed Roman. "Those trips are too expensive." He spoke as a man whose mind was set.

"Yes, of course you're right." Jadzia smiled her acquiescence. Standing, she asked if anyone would like cheese and fruit.

"Sounds good," responded Tadek with great gusto.

"Let me help you in the kitchen," offered Marysia. She and Jadzia took the few steps into the kitchen, out of sight but definitely within hearing distance of the sitting room. Clattering dishes and opening and closing cabinet doors in an attempt to disguise their interest in their husbands' conversation, they still managed an occasional, surreptitious peek into the other room.

Tadek launched into his part as soon as the women were out of the room. "You know," he said, leaning conspiratorially toward Roman, "Marysia says Jadzia has been very tired lately."

"Jadzia?" asked Roman. "She's been busy at work and with the children, but she's always been healthy as an ox. Does Marysia think something is wrong?" Further concern creased his already creased brow.

"No, but she could probably use a little time away from Katowice. August is a long time away."

"You mean the resort in Yugoslavia?" Roman asked. "It's too expensive, especially with the children."

"So don't take the children," suggested Tadek.

"What would we do with them?" asked Roman. "We couldn't just leave them here, could we?" He asked this quizzically, as though actually considering for a moment that leaving a two- and a four-year-old in an apartment for a week might be a possibility.

"Of course not," responded Tadek. "But I'm sure Marysia's mother would watch them. Now that our three oldest are in school she's not so busy."

"Thank you, Tadek, but we couldn't impose in such a way," countered Roman, shaking his head.

"So offer her a few *zlotys*. She'd be happy for it." Tadek chose a cigarette from the silver filigree holder, a pawn shop find that was one of Jadzia's greatest shopping successes, that graced the coffee table.

"I don't know." Roman was unconvinced.

"You know, Roman, that week Marysia and I spent in Bulgaria a couple of years ago? The time we left the children with her mother?" Lighting his cigarette, he leaned even closer toward Roman, lowering his voice conspiratorially. "It was like being with my Marysia when she was a bride. Remember those days early in your marriage?"

Roman still looked unconvinced, but decidedly less so. "I don't know..."

"Come on." Tadek lightly cuffed his friend's shoulder. "You're not too old to remember life before children. Think of the possibilities. Hot beaches during the day. Even hotter nights..."

Jadzia and Marysia reentered the room, each bearing a plate of sliced cheese and fruit. "Ah," smiled Tadek, "here come our beauties. Marysia, *moja perelko*, sit here, close to me." Patting the sofa cushion invitingly, he pulled her close as she sat down, then nuzzled her neck, planting a quick kiss behind her ear.

"Behave, you bad boy," scolded Marysia, her smile negating her words.

"Jadzia, thank you," Roman said, beaming at his wife as he accepted a plate of cheese and pears. Jadzia could sense a difference in the way he looked at her. "You, too," he continued, "sit here beside me, *moja droga*."

Jadzia smiled, her mind racing as she sat close to her husband, feigning interest in his renewed conversation with Tadek. She needed to get in touch with her father's cousin Jan. She wondered whether she could afford a new swimsuit for the trip to Yugoslavia. And she would definitely insist that Marysia take the rest of the bottle of cherry cordial home with her tonight.

Chapter Thirteen

Evie, Winston Estates

December, 1956

2 grudnia, 1956

Moja Droga Evo!

Witam Ciebie i Twojego drogiego męża oraz Twoje słodkie córki Penny i Peggy. Dziękuję Ci bardzo za list, który podałaś ostatniego miesiąca przez kuzynkę Reginę, a szczególnie za wspaniały prezent.

"**M**ickey, is that you?" Evie wiped her hands on her apron as she walked from the tiny kitchen through the dining room and into the six-foot square area which she euphemistically called, using the French pronunciation, "the *foyer*." "Hard day at work?" She leaned toward her husband to receive her customary "Honey, I'm home" peck on the cheek.

"Yeah. I worked my ass off today." Stamping snow from his shoes, he removed his dark gray trench coat and matching felt fedora, handing them to Evie. She twirled in place to the coat closet directly behind her, her voluminous skirt cascading mid-calf.

"Can I get you a drink?" Evie continued their evening ritual, trying to suppress the excitement she felt.

"No, I'll wait until after dinner. What are we having?"

"Pot roast. It'll be ready in about twenty minutes. But sit down in the living room for a minute. I have something to show you." She ducked into the adjacent dining room to retrieve a small stack of mail from the buffet.

"Did the electric bill come?"

"Not yet. But look," she chirped, handing the mail to her husband.

"Oh," he said, shuffling through the envelopes, "a letter from your cousin." He sat on one firm cushion, encased in heavy plastic, of the stylish, green and gold print sectional sofa.

"Yes, that came today too. You can read it later." Evie sounded just slightly impatient. "But look at the other letter—the one on top, in the ivory-colored envelope," she said, sitting on the sofa section diagonally across from him. On the wall above her hung an inexpensive print of Van Gogh's *Sunflowers*, and the glass coffee table before them held a vase of yellow plastic roses and two ceramic ashtrays painted with palm trees, souvenirs of last winter's vacation in Miami.

Mickey obediently opened the specified envelope and, taking out an embossed card gaily printed in red and green, read silently. "An invitation to the Chapmans' Christmas party," he said, finally looking up.

"Yes," Evie practically squealed with delight. "Can you believe it? An invitation to Todd and Susan's party—at the country club!"

"Well, I wouldn't exactly call it a country club," he responded, referring to the squat, one-story building, reminiscent of an airplane hangar, that served as the bar and meeting place for the patrons of the Winston Estates Golf and Racquet Club.

"Honestly, you're always so critical," Evie complained, screwing her mouth into a pout. "But what's important is the invitation. Aren't you thrilled?"

"Well, sure. I didn't know you were so crazy about the Chapmans, is all. I thought you thought they were kind of stuck up."

"It's not that I'm so crazy about them, Mickey," she said, irritation creasing her brow. "It's just that Todd can do so much for you at Pearson, especially now that he's a vice president."

"Honey, it's not like that at work," he explained with some exasperation in his voice, having had this discussion with his wife at least three times before. "What really matters is how many valve and cylinder and brake kits I sell." Mickey had been a salesman for Pearson Auto Parts for almost five years.

"Oh, Mickey." Evie was unable to hide her annoyance. "Remember what they always say, 'It's not *what* you know; it's *who* you know.'" Reaching deep into the pocket of her skirt she pulled out a pack of Pall Mall cigarettes, then leaned toward the glass end table beside her for the lighter. "It's not enough to just do your job these days. You've got to get in with management. Socialize." Lighting the cigarette, she inhaled deeply.

"Yeah, yeah, I know. It's just that's not me—I don't really like hanging around with the guys from work. Why don't we ever see Bruno and Angie or Tadek and Helena anymore?" he asked, brightening. "They haven't even seen the new place. Why don't we have them over for the holidays?"

"Maybe," Evie responded.

"Or even Lou and Candy, the gals from Doall. They were sure a lot of fun. Remember the last time we went bowling in that place on Milwaukee Avenue?"

"Yeah, sure. Maybe after the holidays." But Evie had no intention of inviting their friends from the old neighborhood to visit the yellow brick Cape Cod in the spanking new suburb of Winston Estates. It wasn't that she looked down on their old friends, but that she and Mickey now had so little in common with them. Her friends in Winston Estates golfed and played tennis and drank screwdrivers—they didn't spend time in bowling alleys or go out for a shot and a beer at a local tavern. None of them had ever worked in factories; stories about her work and her colleagues at Doall Valve would have been completely incomprehensible to them.

"Oh, wait," Mickey suddenly responded, taking another look at the invitation he still held in his hand. "We can't go to the party anyway."

"Why not?"

"It's on Christmas Eve."

"So?"

"We'd miss Mama's *Wigilia* dinner."

"Wigilia dinner?" she responded in a huff. "Couldn't we miss your mother's Wigilia just this once?" The thought of missing a party at the country club to partake once more of her mother-in-law's weak borscht and overcooked carp was unthinkable.

Mother Sienka still lived in her ancient apartment on Ashland Avenue, complete with musty overstuffed chairs, a shrine to the Infant of Prague, and dozens of doilies. Evie had resented the bi-weekly trips into the city: bundling up the girls and driving for an hour just to listen to endless complaints and advice and to eat a meal prepared by a woman whom she had soon discovered was a truly horrible cook.

She had spoken of her resentment once, more than two years ago. Mickey, acting in his habitually dense manner (Or perhaps not? Sometimes she wondered...) had suggested that, if she didn't like having to go into the city every other weekend, they could invite his mother to live with them. After all, there was plenty of room in the Cape Cod: the girls could double up in one bedroom; his mother could help in the kitchen.... Evie had never complained about their trips into Chicago again.

"Mama would be so disappointed if we missed Wigilia," Mickey countered. "And the girls too."

Evie hated to admit that the girls, especially Peggy, their younger daughter, loved their grandmother and thoroughly enjoyed holidays in the overheated, cramped apartment on Ashland Avenue. This attraction thoroughly astounded her. But she had no time right now to ponder this mystifying situation, as she needed to convince Mickey of the foolishness of placing his mother's desires over his own advancement and her desire for a rare night on the town.

Opening her mouth to speak, she was drowned out by the sounds of the front door opening and her daughters squealing as they tumbled into her freshly vacuumed and polished living room, their boots, coats, scarves and mittens laden with snow.

"Daddy! Daddy's home," they chanted in unison, running to the sofa and jumping simultaneously into their father's lap. Penny at seven was the quieter of the two, fond of books and dolls, while Peggy, the five-year-old, was the more active, finding her greatest joy in riding her tricycle and playing hopscotch with the neighborhood children. Tugging off their wool tartan-plaid scarves, they snuggled like seals against their father's chest while he tousled the identical dark, springy curls and long bangs that made them look almost like twins.

"Girls, your boots!" Evie shouted above the din.

"Aw, it's just snow. It'll melt," said Mickey. Evie prayed silently in thanksgiving for the invention of plastic slipcovers. Unbuttoning Peggy's bright red wool coat, Mickey asked, "And what did you girls do today?"

"We went sledding!" squealed Peggy, her dark brown, almost black eyes glittering over apple cheeks reddened by the cold.

"In Petersons' back yard," added Penny unbuttoning her own navy blue jacket, as befit her status as the older sister. "Joey Peterson gots a new sled for his birthday."

"Got, Penny," reminded Evie, a touch of frustration in her voice. Joey *got* a new sled for..."

But her voice was drowned out by her husband's. "Good for Joey. Maybe if you're a very good girl, Santa will bring you your very own sled." Then, turning toward his wife, he asked, "Time to eat?"

"Sure," she responded, smashing out her cigarette and rising to return to the kitchen. "But we're not through talking about Christmas eve, you know."

"Oh, I think we are," he said, raising his eyebrows and looking at her sharply.

"No, I think we're not."

The discussion tabled, Mickey and the girls moved to the dining room where he busied himself getting them seated. Opening Jadzia's letter, he called out to the kitchen, "Okay to read your cousin's letter out loud?" He heard Evie's "Yeah" amidst the sounds of pots and pans banging, perhaps just a little louder than usual.

"Girls, listen to Daddy. Here's a letter from your *Ciotka* Jadzia."

"English, Mickey," Evie reminded, bringing a large platter of beef to the table. "Remember what Penny's teacher said. Besides, Jadzia's their second cousin—once removed or something like that—not their aunt."

"Well, I'm not gonna call her Second Cousin Once Removed Jadzia. And besides, I think Penny's teacher is full of..."

"Mickey..." Evie's tone was warning enough.

"Okay, okay. Girls, this letter came all the way from Poland. Now listen up." Mickey unfolded the onionskin, spreading the pages carefully against the white cotton tablecloth, pausing just a moment to translate the first few lines into English as Evie returned to the kitchen:

December 2, 1956

My dear Eva,

Hello to you, your dear husband, and your sweet darlings Penny and Peggy.

"Do we know her?" asked Penny, reaching for the pitcher of milk that sat on the table.

"No," answered Mickey, "but *Ciotka* Jadzia and Mommy have been writing to each other almost since Mommy was as young as you. She knows all about you from Mommy's letters. Now let Daddy read."

Thank you so much for the letter that you sent last month with Cousin Regina, and especially for your kind gift. I sometimes do not know how Roman and I would manage without your generosity.

"How much did we send her this time?" Mickey called toward the kitchen. But Evie was already in the doorway, holding steaming bowls of mashed potatoes and carrots in either hand.

"Twenty."

"Whew, that much?"

"You know how bad things are over there," Evie responded, placing the mashed potatoes on the table and spooning carrots onto the girls' plates. "And with Christmas coming..."

"Oooh, Mommy, I don' like carrots!" Peggy interrupted, her nose wrinkled in protest.

"Just eat a little bit, baby," Evie coaxed. "Pretend you're a bunny. Bunnies like carrots."

"Yeah, honey, eat 'em up," Mickey urged. "They're good for your eyes." He turned back to the letter as Evie took the pitcher of milk from Peggy's outstretched hand.

"No, no, sweetie, Mommy pours."

"But Penny poured her own!"

"And when you're seven you can pour your own milk too. Now listen to Daddy."

I am happy to tell you that we are all very well. We celebrated Marek's fourth name day last month—he is such a big, strong boy, and very smart too. He is already learning his letters. I am sure my brother would have been very proud to know about his namesake.

"They never heard anything...?" Mickey asked, glancing up over the letter at Evie.

"No, not since he got out of that boxcar in Germany," she responded. "Jadzia hasn't given up, though. A lot of people are still in camps in Russia—sometimes they get released. She thinks he might be there."

"Rough," he added, shaking his head, then returned to his reading.

Little Magdalena is really beginning to talk, and she keeps me very busy running after her. She is a happy child, smiling and cooing all the time. With her head full of dark curls she reminds me so much of the picture you sent last Christmas of your own little angels.

"Who are Marek and Ma...Maga...?" asked Penny, her voice muffled by a mouthful of mashed potatoes.

"You remember, honey," responded Evie, "Magadalina—my cousin Jadzia's little boy and girl. Your second cousins. And chew with your mouth closed."

I have been very busy at the hospital. Many, many babies are being born these days in Poland. This is good, because it means that people want to get back to normal life. But often I get home very late, many times after dark.

Roman, too, has been very busy, sometimes spending twelve hours in the mines at one time. Sometimes we do not see each other, except to look at each other sleeping in bed, for several days at a time.

"Why is she in the 'ospil? Is she sick?" asked Peggy, suspiciously eying the carrot she held between her pudgy thumb and forefinger.

"No, she's not sick," answered Mickey. "She works at the hospital. She takes care of babies, just like her own Mommy and Grandma did."

"Our mommy doesn't work," asserted Penny.

"Right, sweetie. Mommy doesn't work," Mickey responded solemnly, smiling past Evie's frozen look and tight mouth. "Let's see what else *Ciotka* Jadzia has to say."

We are hoping to hear word soon about our application for a new apartment.

Now that we have two children, we are eligible for an apartment with one more bedroom, but the waiting list is very long. We hope to be able to move within the next six months.

Magdalena's christening was very beautiful. I thank you for the present that came for her with Cousin Regina as well. I will put it away for now and when she is older, tell her of you and of your love for us.

"A present too?"

"A silver baby spoon," responded Evie, pouring another half glass of milk for Peggy. "It wasn't that much—I got it from the Sears catalog."

"Holy smokes, Evie. Who do you think we are, the Rockefellers?" But his objection was only half-hearted. Evie had often spoken of her affection for her cousin, whom she regarded as her best friend. She had almost lost hope that Jadzia had survived the war until a letter had arrived in 1945—the first Evie had received in almost four years. Changing the topic, he added, "Your Cousin Reggie is becoming quite the smuggler."

"It's that honest face of hers," Evie responded, "and a good thing, too. They'd never get anything if we sent it through the mail, what with the post office being what it is over there. Finish the letter."

Mickey continued.

Our new pastor, Father Tadeusz, christened our little darling, and she behaved like an angel through the whole service. We are so grateful that it was possible to save St. Chrysostym after the bombing, and that we are still able in Poland to worship God, even though the Russians are so strongly against religion.

"I don't like religion either," Penny asserted. "Sister Mary Jerome is so mean!"

"Oh, now, Penny, don't say that," Mickey responded. "Sister is just trying to help you. You need to be a good girl and do everything she says."

Evie smirked at him across the table. It was ridiculous to send the girls to parochial school when there was a perfectly good public school, a school that offered foreign languages and gym classes, just a block away. But he and his mother had insisted that St. Bonaventure it must be. Still they weren't the ones getting Penny up a half hour earlier in the morning to catch her bus or devoting extra hours every week to helping her memorize pages from the *Baltimore Catechism*.

What was the point of learning all that stuff in the catechism, anyway? Evie wasn't sure she believed in God—he hadn't been around when she'd needed him most. And she wasn't so sure people needed religion to be good. She thought about her mother-in-law—the way she used religion as a club.

Mickey ignored the smirk directed his way. Returning to the letter, he read:

May the blessings of Our Lord be with you and your whole family this Christmas season and through all of 1956.
Your loving cousin,
Jadzia

Folding the letter, Mickey placed it on the table. "Well, it seems like they're doing better," he said, then, to his daughters, "Looks like both of you cleaned your plates. Mommy, what did you make us for dessert tonight?"

"Jell-o," Evie responded. Shouts of "Jell-o! Jell-o!" echoed from both girls.

"Aren't you ever going to make *kolaczki* again?" he complained. "We haven't had them in months."

"The girls like Jell-o, Mickey," Evie said, collecting plates to take back to the kitchen. "And it's good for their bones. But speaking of *kolaczki*..."

"We can talk about Christmas Eve later, Evie, after the girls are in bed," he answered. "No Jell-o for me, but could you get me a beer? And honey," he added with a wicked wink, "why don't you bring everything out to the living room so the girls and I don't miss the beginning of *Father Knows Best*."

Mother Sienka's voice boomed over the din from the television as Evie stepped into the living room, "Ah, Evelina, how beautiful you look." Hugging her granddaughters sitting on either side of her, Mother Sienka pointed to Evie, adding, "Look, Pennucia, Peggucia, look at you Mommy. She is like movie star."

Evie cringed once again at the hated nicknames, remembering her mother-in-law's objection seven years earlier to the name she had chosen for her firstborn: "What kind of name is Penelope? I never hear of such a name." Mother Sienka had requested that her first grandchild be named after "her own dear sister" whom she hadn't seen in forty years, but Evie refused to consider for even one moment naming her daughter Czeslawa.

Mickey simply did not see why she should care what his mother called their daughters. "Because," she had explained to him, "those nicknames make them sound like DPs." He had been offended by that term, but everyone used expressions like that for newly arrived immigrants—DPs, for displaced persons—those who had "just got off the boat." Still, she had dropped her complaints about the ear-grating "Pennucia" and "Peggucia," especially since the girls giggled with pleasure whenever Mickey or his mother called them by those silly names.

Evie responded to her mother-in-law's compliment with a weak "Thank you, Mother Sienka," but then, looking at her younger daughter, asked, "Peggy, what's that all over your face?"

Mother Sienka, pulling a heavily embroidered handkerchief from one of the deep pockets of her duster and touching one of its corners to her tongue, wiped the white powdery outline of Peggy's mouth. "There. Is all gone."

"But what was it?" Evie asked, restraining herself from commenting about how saliva spreads germs.

"Cookies, Mommy," Peggy admitted, eyes downcast.

"Peggy, I told you no more of grandma's *chrusciki*." Peggy loved the little bow-tie shaped almond cookies that were Mother Sienka's specialty and perhaps the only truly edible recipe the woman could prepare. "You're going to get sick," Evie warned. "And you hardly touched your dinner. Besides, it's almost bedtime. Both of you girls—upstairs now and into your jammies."

"But Grandma said..."

"Is *Wigilia*, Evelina. You should let them stay up late tonight." Mother Sienka interposed, hugging the girls even more tightly to her, neither of whom was making any movement toward the staircase.

Evie felt her cheeks redden and heard the tone of her voice rise. "I know what day it is, Mother Sienka, but ..."

Walking in from another room, Mickey pulled Evie's coat from the crook of his arm and held it open for her. "Here, let me help you with this. Come on, Good Lookin'," he said. "We're already late for the party."

"Mikosz, Evelina," Mother Sienka smiled smoothly, "you go, have good time. You don't worry about nothing. The girls and me will have good time too, right?" Penny and Peggy nodded their assent.

"See ya later, alligators," Mickey called to the girls as he led Evie toward the door.

"After while, crocodile!" they giggled back as Mickey ushered Evie out the door. Unfortunately, he was not quick enough to prevent her from catching a glimpse of her mother-in-law's triumphant smile.

Evie swayed gently to the strains of "Someone to Watch over Me" wafting from the juke box in the far corner of the dark bar. She loved Frank Sinatra—Frankie, her Frankie. And Mickey, of course. She loved Mickey too. Such a good man. And so handsome, certainly the most handsome man at this party. Even now, her darling Mickey was at the bar getting her another martini—her third? Maybe her fourth.

She loved the country club too, its large dance hall beautifully decorated for this party with glittering Christmas trees on the bandstand and cute Santa centerpieces on each table. Even the bar, where she and Mickey had retreated from the heat and noise of the dance floor, was bedecked for Christmas, with gaily-colored lights framing the large mirror behind it and shiny *Noel* banners gracing every window and doorway.

She had loved the *hors d'oeuvres*—tiny wieners in cute little packets of dough, crackers stacked with cheese and topped with everything imaginable—olives, onions, meat paste, clever little carrot curls. And the martinis. The first one had smelled and tasted like turpentine, making her wonder why anyone would want to drink something so foul, but the second was much better. She had actually enjoyed the third—maybe too much. Everything in the bar looked a bit out of focus, and her head was spinning, but in a very pleasant way. Was she drunk? Maybe just a little tipsy. But it didn't matter—it was Christmas Eve, and she was with the most handsome man at the party. Life was good.

And now the jukebox was swinging into "I Get a Kick Out of You," her second favorite song, after "Someone To Watch over Me," of course, or no, maybe her favorite. Hard to pick a favorite when it was Sinatra. "I get no kick from champagne," Frankie crooned. *Maybe you should try a martini,* she thought, giggling just a little.

It had been an almost perfect evening. She had found an amazing dress. The strapless satin gown of iridescent emerald, a color that brought out the auburn in her hair, hugged her slim waist, then billowed into a graceful half-hourglass. Of course, what the dress needed was a pearl necklace to set it off. But when she had hinted that she'd like to receive her Christmas present before leaving for the party, Mickey, looking confused, had pulled a big box out of the closet. "Honey—the rug looks fine," he had said, and her quick look at the tag, on which he'd written "To the girl who swept me off my feet" had sealed her fate. Tomorrow morning she'd be "oohing" and "ahing" over the vacuum cleaner she'd pointed out at the hardware store and trying to look grateful. "You're right," she'd responded, forcing a smile. Well, there was always her birthday...

But she couldn't complain about the party. She and Mickey had danced until her feet ached. They had swayed to the music, the full circle of the skirt cascading gently six inches above her ankles. Now at the bar she wore the matching short jacket that reached just to the middle of her ribcage, exposing bare arms beneath its capped sleeves.

Besides, she had won the battle of the country club, although her victory had come at a price. The invitation she had had to make to her mother-in-law to spend "a few days over Christmas" with them still rankled. She'd hardly been able to force down a bite of Mother Sienka's modified Wigilia at their home—only seven courses as opposed to her standard nine. And she could hardly look forward to the next day, when her father, Henryk and Steffie would join them all for dinner.

Early in her marriage Evie had established a holiday compromise acceptable to both families: Christmas Eve with Mother Sienka, Christmas Day with her family. This suited her father and Henryk, who avoided contact with Mother Sienka as much as possible. No one was really pleased with this year's holiday plans, except perhaps for Mickey, who always seemed blissfully oblivious to the ongoing Bialek/Sienko Wars.

She decided to put aside worries about tomorrow: this evening had been an unqualified success. She had done everything the *Ladies Home Journal* and *Good Housekeeping* suggested to support her husband and reflect well upon him. Looking beautiful was important, of course, but much more was involved: being graceful in all things, knowing when to speak and when to listen intently. Even when that obnoxious Marv Greenwood, his breath spewing alcohol fumes just inches from her face, had bored her for a half hour with tales of his sales exploits, she had reacted graciously. She was sure she had succeeded in her most important job—helping Mickey succeed.

Often she wondered why so much fell to her, if she were somehow more ambitious than Mickey, more willing to do whatever it took to get ahead. Not that she wished to work outside the home; that would be ridiculous. She had given up her job at Doall Valve—all the women had—when the men came back from war. It was the patriotic thing to do.

And she knew she was fortunate. Her suburban home, with its new appliances and modern furniture, its back yard more than three times the size of any she had ever seen in the city, was so much more than her own mother had ever owned. Most of all, she loved being a mother. But sometimes the days were very long; next year, when Peggy started school, they would be even longer.

Still, she told herself, she loved Mickey with all her heart and was happy to be his wife, despite all his flaws. When three years earlier she had chanced upon the wedding announcement in the *Tribune*—Charley Honeycutt had married some New York heiress—she hadn't had even one twinge of envy or regret. Henryk had been right: Mickey was a good man, and he had made a good home for her and her daughters. She had made the right decision.

At the band's announcement of a short break, she and Mickey had retreated to the bar for a few relatively quiet moments together. But now Marv was leading his wife Trixie toward their table. Evie realized that she needed to overcome her pleasant wooziness: her evening's work was not yet complete.

"Mind if we join you, pretty lady?" Marv asked, already pulling out a chair. "Where's your old man?"

"Over at the bar, getting me a drink." Evie smiled, focusing through her martini haze.

"Are you enjoying the party?" asked Trixie companionably. She was a tall woman, easily twenty years older than Evie, with masses of platinum-colored hair piled high atop her head and a face heavily plastered in make-up. Evie knew her from several other Pearson Auto Parts occasions and had always liked her.

"Yes, it's been swell," Evie nodded as the other couple joined her at the table.

"And how are those darling little girls of yours?" asked Trixie. "Marv, you remember seeing Evie's girls at the Pearson picnic last summer, don't you? They were just as cute as a button, both of them. Like peas in a pod. How old are they now, Evie?"

"Penny's seven and Peggy's five."

"Bet they keep you busy," Trixie commented. "Who's watching them tonight?"

"My mother-in-law," Evie responded.

"That's swell. Baby-sitters are so darned expensive today, and it's hard to find a good one. Most of them would rather spend the night on the phone yakking with their friends than watch your kids. You're so lucky."

"Yes, I am. I'm very lucky." Evie smiled weakly, thinking back to several hours earlier.

"Here's the man of the hour," crowed Marv as Mickey returned to the table with Evie's drink. "If I didn't say so before, old man, congratulations."

"Congratulations?" Evie questioned, smiling prettily at her husband as she accepted the martini he handed her over the table. "Mickey, have you done something special?"

"Not really," he answered, sitting in the chair next to her.

"Hey, don't be so modest, buddy. Makin' top sales the last three quarters in a row is nothin' to sneeze at," objected Marv. "Say, you wouldn't be bucking to replace Simmons when he retires next year as regional manager, would you?" he added, eying Mickey closely.

"Naw," Mickey answered, taking a sip of the beer he had brought himself from the bar. "Besides Marv, you know you've got that promotion pretty much sewed up." Mickey smiled broadly across the table at Marv, who was slowly stirring his gin and tonic.

"I thought I did, but now I'm not so sure. Sales have been slow in my region, especially after Trenton's Chevrolet closed down. I was hopin' Pearson would assign a little slice of McGiven's old territory to me. "You got pretty much all of that territory, didn't you?"

"Well, a little better than half—Burgess got the rest. I guess Pearson figured I could use some expansion."

"Hey, fellas, enough shop talk," Trixie piped in. "This is a party, right? Evie, do you want to listen to any more talk about auto parts?"

"No!"

"Besides, we get enough of that at home," Trixie added. Evie smiled, but wondered why she was just now hearing of Mickey's accomplishments at work.

"So let's get this party back on track. I know a good joke," offered Trixie. "What's black and white and red all over?"

"A newspaper?" asked Evie, thinking that even her mother-in-law probably knew that old saw.

"Wrong!" Trixie countered. "A nun that fell out of a 10-story building!"

"Pretty good, honey," Marv responded after the group stopped laughing. "You ever hear that one before, Evie?"

"No," she responded, reaching into her small beaded evening bag for her cigarettes and lighter. "That's a new one on me." Evie thought her girls, especially Peggy, might like this joke, but then reconsidered ever telling them: they were probably too young.

"I got a good one," said Marv, grinning. "Why did the Polack submarine sink?"

"Oh," said Trixie, drumming the table with her fingers. "I heard this one before. What was that punch line?" A look of deep concentration wrinkled her brow.

Marv waited a few seconds to build suspense. "Anyone?" he asked, looking directly at Mickey. "Okay—'cause they put in screens and someone opened the window!" Marv accentuated his loud guffaw by pounding on the table.

After the laughter subsided, Trixie jumped in. "That reminds me of another good one. Why do Polack neighborhoods have such a low suicide rate?" Looking individually at every face around the table, she waited for a response. When none came, she blurted out, " 'Cause you can't kill yourself jumping out of a basement window!"

Evie almost choked with laughter, but another sip of her martini remedied that. When Marv asked Mickey, "So, buddy, you got any good Polack jokes?" she turned, laughing, toward her husband who, she was surprised to see, wasn't laughing.

"No, Marv," he said evenly. Evie recognized something she did not like in his tone. "I don't know any."

"Well I got another good one," Marv offered. "Why did the Polack elevator operator lose his job?"

Trixie appeared to be studiously considering a possible answer, but Evie was looking carefully at Mickey. "Any guesses?" Marv asked. "Mickey, you know the answer to this one?"

"No, Marv, I'm afraid not." Mickey pushed his beer bottle away and started to get up. "Evie, it's getting late. Time to go."

"So early?" Trixie asked. "The party's just beginning. Evie, tell your husband you're not ready to go home yet," she suggested, embracing Evie's arm as if to hold her there.

"Yeah, Mickey. We can stay a little bit longer, right?" But one look at her husband's face told her it was time to put out her cigarette and reach for her purse.

"Don't anyone want to hear the punch line to my joke?" asked Marv, his hurt tone betrayed by the mischief in his eyes.

"Yeah, baby, we want to hear." Trixie mouthed a kiss across the table to her husband, her evening's consumption of alcohol beginning to show. "Why'd that poor Polack lose his job?"

" 'Cause he forgot the route!" Marv brayed like a donkey, this time slapping the table hard with his open hand. "Hey, Sienko, where you goin'?"

But Mickey was already half way to the door, leaving Evie to collect her things. "Is something wrong?" asked Trixie.

"No, no," Evie tried to assure her. "Everything's fine. Mickey just remembered something we have to do yet tonight. Good night, everyone. Merry Christmas."

Despite her haste at the coat check, she didn't catch up to Mickey until they were in the parking lot. Indignation and anger seethed within her—all her work this evening undone by some snit of his. What could have gotten into him? Once they were both seated in the car she exploded, "What the hell was that all about?"

"You really don't know, *Mysz*?" he asked quietly.

For a moment, Evie was taken aback by his use of her old nickname. *Mysz*—Mouse. He hadn't called her that in years. But soon she was back on the offensive. "No, Mickey. I don't know what's going on. We go out for a nice evening, everything's going fine, and then you march off like some madman."

"Evie, don't you know when someone is making fun of you?"

This stalled her for a moment, but soon she understood. "You mean the Polack jokes? That's what upset you?" He didn't respond, but starting the car, backed out only slightly more rapidly than was normal. "Mickey, honestly, that's nothing to get upset about. People don't mean anything by those. There you go again, making a mountain out of a molehill."

"Really. Is that what you think?"

"Well, sure. They're just jokes. You need to be a good sport about stuff like that, for cryin' out loud. You can't get upset over dumb Polack jokes. Everyone tells them."

"Fine then. Don't get upset about them. Pretend like everything's fine. Let our girls grow up hearing those jokes and thinking they're stupid and low class and that other people are better than them."

"Mickey, our girls aren't Polish. They're American."

"Polish-American then. And they ought to be proud of that."

What's to be proud of? thought Evie, thinking back to her days on Haddon Avenue. She wanted to forget those days—the poverty, the loss, the despair. Dealing with a drunken father every night, having to be a mother to a baby when she was only a child herself. If only she could make Mickey understand.

But looking closely at her husband's profile, his jaw taut, his eyes glaring straight ahead through the windshield, she knew she'd get nowhere tonight. Lowering her eyes and clasping her hands in her lap, she softly countered, "Mickey, you're making too much of this."

"Am I?"

Chapter Fourteen

Jadzia, Katowice

August, 1968

12 lipca, 1968

Moja najdroższa Jadziu!

Przede wszystkim nie martw się o nas. Ja wiem, że słyszałaś o rozbojach w Chicago pomiędzy buntownikami. Moja droga kuzynko i przjaciółko było to jednak daleko od nas.

"Stop right there!" The slight figure, swathed in a black wool coat that just covered the tops of shiny black boots, halted at the partially opened door. "Don't you say 'hello' to your *Ciotka* Marysia anymore?"

Shrugging, Magda closed the door, then, with a smile that looked only slightly forced, turned toward the two women sitting at the kitchen table. "*Ciotka* Marysia, how are you? How are the girls?"

"Doing very well. Irena is expecting her baby any day now."

"How exciting for you," Magda replied, this time with a smile so wide it crinkled the corners of her dark brown eyes and brightened every bit of her lovely, heart-shaped face. "You're going to be a *babcia*."

"Ah, don't say that so loud, child. I am too young to be a *babcia!*" But the contented look on Marysia's face belied any discontent in her words.

"Magda, are you going out?" Jadzia asked. "Don't you have time to join us for tea?"

"No, Mama. I'm meeting Halina at the coffee shop. We're going to study our Russian for the test on Monday."

"You girls could study here," offered Jadzia. "I don't know why you choose to study in a busy coffee shop, where there's so much distraction." Magda's furtive smile suggested that distraction was exactly what she sought.

"And anyway,' continued Jadzia, "why are you wearing that heavy coat? It's August. You'll die of heat stroke out there."

Pale blue skies, just visible through creamy lace curtains, were the last remnants of a gentle shower that had produced warm, muggy air. Far below on the pavement could be seen pedestrians strolling about their business. The park across the street and seven stories below was filled with activity: children playing on swings and slides, old women sitting on park benches, old men gathered around a group of tables where other men, Roman and Tadek among them, played chess.

"No, Mama, I'll be fine."

Jadzia, considering the eccentricities of fourteen-year-old girls, let this pass until she considered, as well, the deviousness of fourteen-year-old girls. "Magda, darling, come here. Show me what you're wearing under that coat."

"Oh, Mama, it's all right. Everyone today wears..."

But it was too late. As Magda turned to face her mother, her heavy coat opened enough to show dark blue fabric ballooning from the tops of her boots.

"What are you wearing? Farmers' pants?"

"*Jeans*, Mama. You know that's what they call them. Everyone wears jeans now." Magda's words dripped aggravation and just a touch of defiance.

"And if everyone jumped off the steeple of St. Ursula's Church, would you do that too? Where did you get those pants? They're very expensive!"

"They're Halina's, Mama. She let me borrow them."

"Then give them back to Halina when you see her at the coffee shop. Go back to your room and change. Nice girls don't wear jeans in town. Why don't you wear your blue banana skirt? It looks beautiful on you."

Magda's expression clouded perceptibly. Her blue skirt, with banana-shaped panels cut partially on the bias, producing a swirl of fabric at the hem, now hung, almost forgotten, in the back of her closet. It was, after all, last year's fashion. With tears just beginning to form at the corners of her eyes, she looked beseechingly toward Marysia, who now appeared to have found something that needed careful scrutiny deep within her cup of tea. "*Ciotka* Marysia, I bet you let your girls wear jeans!"

"Ah, child, don't get me mixed up in this!" Marysia answered with a small chuckle. "Anyway, my girls are older. They do what they please now."

"But you would let them, when they were younger? Right?"

"Enough!" interrupted Jadzia. "Quit arguing, Magda. Either go into your room now and change clothes or stay home."

"But..."

"That's it. Those are your choices."

With a swirl of black wool Magda stamped back to her room, the heels of her boots punishing the pine floor. The next noise Jadzia and Marysia heard was the angry slam of a door. Jadzia's first thought was to follow her daughter and reprimand her, but she reconsidered. Instead she turned to Marysia, shrugging in the hopeless manner of mothers of teen-aged daughters the world over.

"More tea?" she asked wearily, lifting the teapot, its stylized floral pattern, cobalt on white, shimmering in the rays of a sun that had just emerged, triumphant, out of the gray haze.

"Yes, please," answered Marysia. "You know, it does get better. Children do, finally, grow up."

"I know," answered Jadzia, craning her neck, trying once again, unsuccessfully, to ease the crick that had settled into it. "It's just that everything seems so hard right now. I don't have the patience for Magda's tantrums and dramatics. Would you like some sugar for your tea?"

"No, not today," Marysia answered.

"No sugar? I thought you liked sugar."

"Yes, I used to. But, you know, too many calories. We have to watch our weight," Marysia replied with a small laugh.

"You? Watch your weight? Why, you have a beautiful shape. And I'm sure Tadek loves you just the way you are."

"Still, we have to be careful."

Jadzia wondered if a new-found wish to be slim was really the cause behind Marysia's refusal. Both women knew how expensive sugar was, and how hard to find. None of the stores in Katowice currently had any in stock. Still, Jadzia always tried to be a good hostess. "So, any advice on how to handle my daughter?" she finally asked, dropping the subject of sugar altogether.

"I'm sure she's a very good girl, Jadzia, just a little rebellious right now."

"I like to think that. But she's been coming home smelling of smoke." Jadzia stopped for a moment, drawn by the sound of the door to the hallway opening quietly. One quick peek assured her that her daughter was now wearing a short red skirt and a light jacket. Jadzia considered stopping her to say good-bye and perhaps to add a few kind words to smooth over their argument, then decided against it. No sense stirring up more trouble. She waited until she heard the door close to resume her conversation. "Magda says the smoke is from others in the coffee house, but I don't know. And last week I saw her trying to leave the house wearing green eye shadow."

"Oh, such horrible crimes!" laughed Marysia. "Report her to the authorities!"

"You laugh, but she's only fourteen! What will happen when she's sixteen, eighteen? Girls grow up too fast today."

"True," answered Marysia, "but that's probably what our own mothers said about us. Anyway, growing up in the city isn't the same as growing up on a farm. There's so much more to do here—both good and bad."

"Yes, but why do they always have to look for the bad?"

"Again, probably what our mothers said about us," Marysia laughed. Then, changing the subject, she continued. "Before we saw Magda weren't you saying that you got home very late last night? Was the Panek baby all right?"

"Yes. Small, but I think she'll be fine." Jadzia had left her onsite hospital position two years earlier, when Roman's declining health had required more attention than she could give him with a full-time job. She now worked on call as a midwife, traveling to some of the smaller towns and rural areas surrounding Katowice when her services were needed, which was happening less and less frequently. Even rural women were choosing the type of obstetric services they could get at Katowice Central Hospital.

"Did they have to take her to the hospital?"

"No. Thank God." Many babies, it seemed to Jadzia, were born small and weak these days. But taking them to hospitals did little good: often the hospitals, where shortages and inefficiency were as much the rule as they were in all other sectors of society, were the last places one would want to take someone ill or weak. Better the newborns should take their chances at home, Jadzia believed, where they would at least receive the loving attention they needed.

Hospitals weren't the only problem. Poles had long been discontented with their lives under Soviet rule, but 1968 had been a particularly difficult year. The student protests in March, which the government had cleverly blamed, as always, on the Jews, had led to even more repression, with the reforms of the late 1950's being repealed at every turn. Even worse to Jadzia were rumors that the Soviets would soon invade Czechoslovakia, and that Polish troops would be part of the invasion, a situation Jadzia had found intolerable, particularly in its possible effect on her son.

In a conversation they had had just two days ago, Marek had hotly supported the prospect of an invasion, arguing that it was necessary to keep the rebellious Czechs in line. To Jadzia's horror, he bewailed the fact that, at sixteen, he was unable to join the invading forces, informing her that he planned to enlist in the military once he got his diploma from the polytechnic instead of entering college for his engineering degree. This had led to another argument, another slammed door.

When Roman had returned from the park where he had gone to play chess with some old friends from work, he had found his wife weeping uncontrollably. Once she told him of her concerns, she was devastated to receive a far different response than she had expected.

"Don't blame the boy," he had said, folding her into arms that had once been solid and strong but were now increasingly feeble. "He's only sixteen. War is romantic to him."

"Romantic! What's romantic about death and pain and starvation!"

"Yes, *moya droga*, we know that. But how can he?"

"He should know. He's heard us talk. And what makes it even worse—he would be fighting for the Soviets!" Jadzia shuddered at that thought.

"His whole life, Jadzia, that is all he has known," answered Roman gently. "He went to Soviet schools, and learned Russian. His summer camp was government-run, and all his clubs."

"Yes, his clubs. We should never have let him join the SZSP." Last year Jadzia had argued, unsuccessfully, against Marek's joining the *Socjalistyczny Zwizek Studentow Polskich*, the Polish Students' Socialist Club, believing, as did most people in Katowice, that it was not a legitimate political organization but only an arm of the Russian government.

"But all his friends were there," responded Roman. "It was expected."

"Then he should have found other friends."

"Jadzia, Marek needs to make his way in *this* society, even if it is not what we wish for him. He has no other choice."

Jadzia had pulled away from her husband, disgusted. The thought of her handsome, bright boy joining the military and dying on some forsaken field haunted her daily thoughts and her nightly dreams. Hadn't she seen war, in all its horror, the young, dead before their time, their bodies mangled beyond identification? Hadn't she seen how war changed people, scarring the hearts and souls of everyone it touched and making true monsters out of some? Hadn't Roman seen the same?

Why did no one ever learn?

Marysia asked, "Did you say you got a letter from your cousin in America?" wondering, perhaps, why her best friend, who had always been so focused and energetic, was lately almost incapable of keeping up her end of a conversation.

"Yes. Eva wrote."

"And how are they? You said you were worried about all the violence in Chicago, with that terrible assassination and the riots."

"No, Eva's family lives far from the city, where all the commotion was going on. I have her letter right here," Jadzia responded, riffling through some papers on the table. "Should I read it to you?"

"Of course."

"*12 July 1968,*" Jadzia began.

"And you just got this letter?"

"Yes, yesterday."

"Ah, our Soviet postal service is improving! Less than a month now to get a letter from America."

"Now, Marysia, you don't have to always be so critical. Should we complain about the Russkis, or do you want me to read?"

"Read."

First of all, do not worry about us. I know you have heard about all the violence in Chicago with the summer riots, but, my dearest cousin and friend, that is all very far from us. We are not affected at all. So, lose no more sleep worrying about us. I promise we are all fine.

"Thank God for that," responded Marysia.

"Yes, I had been worried." Jadzia continued reading.

How are you and your family? Is Roman feeling any better?

The girls are enjoying their summer. Penny is very excited to be starting her junior year in college, and Peggy, who has been a bit down on school for a while, is now excited again—senior year is always the most exciting year of high school: the prom, graduation, visiting colleges. She has all that to look forward to.

For me, things are quiet. Bridge group and book club will start up in the fall again. Mikosz thinks I should take up golf, but I'd rather do volunteer work at St. Bonaventure's. He's doing very well, as always, at work, but lately it seems that all he can talk about is the day he can finally retire. Heavens, what would I do with him home all day—it would be a nightmare. I love the man, but a little bit of separation is a good thing.

Well, this is all for now. Please write soon—it always seems like you have so much more to say than I do!

> *As always, my love and prayers to you and your family,*
> *Eva*

Both women sat in silence for a moment, staring into their now tepid cups of tea. "Short letter," said Marysia.

"Yes, I thought so too. She used to write more."

"Well, Americans are busy people."

"I suppose. You know, when I was a little girl, I often wished our family had emigrated to America."

"Now Jadzia, I imagine they have their own problems there."

"Do you really think so, when you hear Eva's letter? Wouldn't you rather deal with book club and bridge group than standing in line for sugar and worrying about war in Czechoslovakia?"

"Things cannot be rosy for everyone there. After all, they're at war too—in Viet Nam. And they have riots too, just like us."

"I know you're right. And don't get me wrong. I'm happy that Eva and her family have things so good—that they don't have to deal with the kinds of problems we do. It's just that..."

"It looks like someone is having problems here right now," Marysia interrupted. The sound of a siren had drawn her to the window, where she could see the flashing lights of an ambulance turning into the driveway that led to the park's amenities.

"Probably another child fell off the slide," she continued. I'm sure the men will tell us all about it when they come back. So, do you still wish your family had gone to America?"

"Sometimes. Life would certainly have been different." Jadzia often considered how different her life would have been. Her parents might still be alive, and her brother Marek would not have disappeared, never to be heard from again. Who knew what Stasiu's life would have been—definitely very different from his existence as a near-hermit in Niedzieliska. And there were so many others, lost to her forever. Of course, if she had emigrated, she would never have met Roman, but then...

Her thoughts were shattered by a sudden hard knocking at the door. By the time she reached it, frantic shouting accompanied the pounding— "Jadzia, open up! Hurry!"

She had no sooner turned the knob when Tadek rushed in, almost knocking her over in the process. "Tadek, what...?"

"Hurry, Jadzia. It's Roman. We were playing chess in the park when he just suddenly slumped over onto the board. It happened so fast. He was talking to me, and then..."

"Where is he?"

"A patrol officer called the hospital."

"The ambulance we just saw?"

"Yes. They took him to Katowice Central. Hurry! I grabbed a cab—it's waiting for us downstairs."

Just one step in front of the other. That's all I need to think of right now. But Jadzia's mind would not obey: it flew in many directions as she trod slowly up the winding path that led to Niedzieliska's ancient cemetery, high on the hill behind St. Adalbert's.

Why are cemeteries always at the highest point of any village? she thought as she followed the stately black hearse, pulled by two bay mares, up the graveled path. *To save the very best property for those who have passed? To place them as close as possible to God? To give struggling mourners time to think about life, and time for a bit of self-reflection, and self-chastisement, as well?* She was certainly chastising herself, both for things she had done and for things she had failed to do, just as she had prayed at the Act of Contrition during the funeral mass.

As the road veered sharply to the left, she could see before her the altar boy struggling under the weight of the heavy gold cross he bore, followed by the parish priest, old now and bent, so shriveled that his purple vestments floated about his body in the wind. Then came the hearse, looking like a black version of Cinderella's carriage but for the colorful masses of wreaths attached to its sides and the array of matching floral arrangements visible through its large windows.

Then, of course, followed the widow—herself—and the children, whose faces reminded her of shell-shocked soldiers she had seen wandering the countryside after the war. Behind them marched many more than Jadzia would have expected: her brother Stasiu, Marysia and Tadek, friends of Roman's from work, several members of the Zadora family, and most of the town of Niedzieliska who did not know Roman but must have come to pay respects to her family.

What had brought her here? Were it not for the young doctor at Katowice Central, would she be holding this ceremony elsewhere? The doctor had seemed so compassionate, so professional, when he had first approached Jadzia, Tadek and Marysia in the hospital waiting room.

"*Pani* Kaminski?"

"Yes?" she had asked hopefully despite the somber expression on the doctor's face.

"I am so sorry, *Pani*, but your husband suffered a massive heart attack. We could do nothing to save him. I am sure he did not suffer."

Without the support of Tadek and Marysia at either side, she would surely have tumbled to the floor. Leaning completely into them, she was folded into their love and concern. But within moments she felt a slight tug at the sleeve of her blouse.

"*Pani?*"

"Yes, Doctor?"

"I am sorry to have to ask you this now, but we need to know...where do you wish us to take the body?"

The body? For a moment she was confused. The body. *He means Roman,* she suddenly realized. Already, her husband was not Roman but something else.

"Could I see him now?" she managed to ask.

"Of course. We will take you to him immediately. But afterwards, we need to know where you wish to dispose of the body. May I recommend Lewandowski's Funeral Home, a fine place not far from here, with excellent service and a reasonable price?"

Already? Roman dead only minutes, and already someone wished to make money from him? Jadzia glared at the open, appealing face of the doctor, wondering how many *zlotys* he would realize from this referral.

Suddenly, she was sick of it all: the graft, the corruption of the city. Sick of waiting in lines, of constant shortages of the most basic needs. Sick of her apartment on the seventh floor of a nondescript building that looked exactly like dozens of others in Katowice. Sick of her job as a midwife working for this very hospital, where her life's work was undermined daily by young upstarts just like the man she faced now. And mostly, sick of worrying every day about her children and the directions their lives were taking: Magda with her coffee house, Marek with the SZSP and his fascination with war.

"I want his body shipped to Niedzieliska. He'll be buried there."

That sudden, unexpected statement had brought them all here, to this windy hillside behind St. Adalbert's Church. "But *Mama*," Magda had cried, when told of the burial plans. "How will we be able to decorate *Tata's* grave every All Saints Day?"

"Don't worry," she had consoled her daughter at the time. It would be better to wait until days after the funeral to explain to her children why they'd be leaving Katowice and moving to Niedzieliska. Neither would like giving up their relatively luxurious home in the city for a primitive cottage in the country. Neither would understand, but they would have no choice.

And Niedzieliska itself was much more modern than when she had left it. There were more stores; the schools were better. Her children might even find country life more enjoyable than they would expect. Before long, they would be adults who could live wherever they chose. In the end, they would forgive her. They would have to.

Jadzia could see the statue of the Angel Gabriel, gleaming white, guarding the section just to the left where the Czarnecki family plot was situated. This was where Roman's body would lie forever. But what of his spirit? He was with God now—of that she was sure. But had he forgiven her? Did he understand?

He had been such a good husband, a good father, a good man. What would she have done without him after the war? Would she have been able to survive then on her own, a young girl with no family, no home? He had saved her from some fate too horrid to even imagine.

And in the years they were married, how had she repaid him? How many times had he told her he loved her and received only her same response? A smile. Sometimes a kiss. Had she ever actually told him that she loved him? She couldn't remember.

She *had* loved him, of course. How could she not? But the truth was that she had never loved him as he had loved her. He must have known that his passion for her was matched only by her great respect for him. Had that been enough for him?

The carriage stopped before the deep, open pit that would forever hold what was left of this kind, gentle, courageous man. Into that pit, knew Jadzia, would go so much of herself as well. For twenty years she had identified herself as Roman's wife; for almost as many, she had thought of herself as the mother of her children and as a midwife, the practitioner of a noble profession. All that would change. The children would grow and leave her. She would resign her position at Katowice Central. And Roman—well she wasn't leaving him. She would be here, with him, in Niedzieliska.

The priest began the final requiem prayers. "*Dominus vobiscum,*" he chanted amidst a cloud of smoke emanating from the gold censor the altar boy swung slowly.

"*Et cum spiritu tuo,*" responded the gathering as one.

Jadzia glanced through her black veil at all those assembled, dressed in their finest, darkest clothing, their heads bowed solemnly in prayer. Looking beyond the crowd of mourners she could see the outlines of the village, the spire of St. Adalbert's dominating the center square. So much history had occurred in that square, but now its rugged cobbled stones were peaceful, devoid of traffic.

"May God have mercy on his soul," the priest intoned. "And may perpetual light shine upon him," came the response. Jadzia recognized many of the mourners, of course, but she had only faint memories of her life with some of them so many years earlier. Dozens of the town's children were complete strangers to her, but she'd have time in the future to sort them all out, to determine which little towheads were *Pani* Witnik's grandchildren, which were *Pan* Zdunek's.

Jadzia glanced in the direction of her family home, where she could see the roofs of cottages, some shingled, some thatched, all partially hidden among ancient oaks and weathered pines. In the distance she could see small cleared areas, with brown splotches that she knew were cows and small white dots she knew were sheep. To one side crystal blue and white glints marked the river, its rushing sound just barely audible beneath the soft voices of prayer.

The pallbearers repositioned themselves to lower the body slowly into the grave. This was the moment she had dreaded—the moment of final parting. Yet, as she watched the pallbearers expertly maneuver the ropes that would allow the pine coffin to descend, she was surprised to feel her heart and mind becoming as peaceful and quiet as the area that surrounded her. She suddenly knew, deep within her heart, that her decision was the right one.

She wasn't escaping her life in Katowice. Rather, she was moving toward something, she knew not what, but something that had drawn her here, to this place, this time. As she heard the soft thud of the coffin touching the ground, she knew that this was exactly where she needed to be.

Chapter Fifteen

Evie, Winston Estates

August, 1968

10 lipca, 1968

Moja najdroższa Ewo!

Miło było otrzymać Twój ostatni list i dowiedzieć się, że wszystko u Was jest w porządku. Proszę pogratuluj Twojej córce sukcesów na studiach - dobrze mieć wspaniałą studentkę!

"Look at those idiots. Damned Yippie draft dodgers! They oughta' toss 'em all in jail." Mickey pulled the tab from another can of beer, placing it among the empties and one crushed potato chip bag that littered the end table next to his recliner. "Damned candy asses. Their parents work their butts off to give them everything they want, then these ungrateful brats turn around and riot in the streets." Mickey emptied half the can in two deep gulps.

"Don't get started now. You'll only get upset." Evie wondered why she even responded. She knew her request would go unheeded. Once Mickey began railing about war protesters, there was no stopping him.

"Upset! Damned right I'm upset. Every time I see these long-haired little punks I want to cut their hair and slam them against a wall. Look at that one!" He pointed disgustedly toward the television screen, where a slim young man, wearing ragged jeans and a tie-dyed tee shirt, jubilantly waved an American flag in circles around his head. "Jesus! Look at that! Where are the cops? That kid oughta' get his teeth knocked out!"

"He probably will," worried Evie. "A lot of kids are getting hurt." When the first anti-war protestors had assembled in the early days of the Democratic National Convention, Evie hadn't been too concerned. Protests against the war were becoming so common that news releases and *Tribune* photos of mobs of angry young people were almost routine.

But the protests had become more and more violent as the convention wore on, and today's disturbance at the bandshell in Grant Park, where a young man had torn down and desecrated the American flag, had occasioned a response from the police and the National Guard that was truly frightening.

215

Chicago was still reeling from the riots that had occurred earlier that summer when Martin Luther King, Jr., had been shot. The burned-out businesses and homes along Madison and Crawford Avenues no longer smoldered, but the city and its surrounding suburbs still seemed to. Evie could not believe that, in 1968, riots could happen in Chicago, that people—Negroes, college kids—were so angry they wanted to destroy what many had spent so much time and effort trying to build. Where was all the anger coming from?

The whole fabric of society seemed to be tearing apart, going back almost five years, Evie thought, to the assassination. The pain of those days, the images—of Jackie's bloody pink dress, of the riderless horse in the funeral cortege, of little John John's heart-breaking salute—were still with her. She thought they would always be. And then this year's assassinations—King, Robert Kennedy—felt like just two more nails in the coffin of the life she knew. Could this really be the United States? Assassinations? Riots in the streets? How, in just five short years, could things have changed so horribly?

And now the convention, more proof that she lived in a country divided—just as her own family was divided. Mickey's beliefs were almost too clear, and the girls...well, even a year ago they had occasionally expressed at the dinner table concerns about the war and their disdain for President Johnson. But Mickey's bombastic responses had eventually stifled all political conversation. Now, on the rare occasions when they were all together for a meal, there was hardly any conversation at all. Evie had no idea what her girls were thinking—about the war, or almost anything else, for that matter.

But it was more than the war. Evie looked closely at her husband slumped in his recliner—she could hardly recognize him as the man she had married so long ago. Sure, he looked older—they both did. But it was more than that.

He'd had so much ambition, so much energy, when he'd started working at Pearson. Where had that gone? She still hadn't forgiven him for turning down the promotion he'd been offered thirteen years earlier, saying he wasn't up to the responsibilities of a regional manager.

That promotion could have made a difference. They could have moved to Barrington years ago, like their neighbors the Miltons and the Freiburgs had done. Not that there was anything really wrong with Winston Estates, but it hadn't lived up to its promise. The far western suburbs were far more elegant, the homes more beautiful and spacious—more what she'd hoped to have some day.

And Mickey's drinking. She wouldn't exactly call him an alcoholic, but he did get pretty hammered almost every night after work. Weekends were worse. And it looked like tonight wasn't going to be any different.

"Damn! Will you look at that!" Mickey's words directed Evie's attention to the screen, where club-wielding police chased hundreds of demonstrators down Lake Shore Drive toward one of the bridges leading to the downtown area.

"Are those...are those tanks on the bridge?" Evie asked, incredulously. "And guns?"

"Yeah—machine guns."

"You don't think they'd use them?"

"It's a mob, Evie," Mickey answered. "You do what you have to do to control a mob."

"But, Mickey. They're just kids." *Kids just like our own*, she thought. Couldn't he see that?

Mickey glared at her with a look that could freeze lava. "So were a couple of million krauts that were trying to kill me and the rest of my buddies in Germany not so many years ago. Just kids, right?"

Evie paused for a moment before responding, "That was different. They were enemy soldiers. That was a war."

"And this isn't? Dammit, Evie, these protests are at war against everything we believe in. A war against America. Can't you see that?"

"I don't think those kids think of it like that." She turned back to the screen, now showing someone being lifted into an ambulance. Hoping the young man or woman wasn't hurt badly, she silently prayed to St. Jude—a habit that thirty years' distance from the nuns of St. Casimir's School had not eradicated.

"I don't think they think at all." Mickey shook his head in disgust. "Evie, they're dragging down everything we fought for. They're trashing what a couple hundred thousand American GI's died for. Can you forget that?"

"I'll never forget the war," she responded heatedly, thoughts of the fear, the lost friends, the shortages of many necessities, the ration cards flooding her mind. But the war hadn't been all bad, at least not for her. She often thought fondly of Doall Valve, of Candy and Lou, of the USO dances. And of Lake Geneva—too fondly, too often.

She glanced furtively at Mickey, as though she believed he could read her mind. In all the years of their marriage he had never once even hinted at any doubts of her faithfulness during their engagement. But she frequently wondered if he had suspected anything. The man she had married was not the man she had sent off to war—had he doubted her, perhaps even known, but had chosen not to speak? No, that couldn't be the case: many men came back changed by the war. And now there was another war, more men coming home damaged in so many ways.

"Viet Nam isn't World War II," she added, regretting this comment almost as soon as she had said it. What was the point? It would only egg him on.

"Now you sound like one of them," Mickey thundered, finishing the rest of his beer and slamming the can on the end table. For long minutes, the room vibrated an uncomfortable silence, which Mickey finally broke.

"Honey," he said, now more gently, "it's not your fault," sighing in the patronizing way Evie had grown to hate. "Women just don't understand." Ignoring his wife's murmured objection, he continued. "No. Let me finish. It's a man's duty to serve his country. When your country calls, you stand and deliver. Whether you agree or not. How could we ever fight a war if everyone got to decide for themselves whether to go or not?"

And maybe that would be a good thing—no more wars because people refused to fight. Evie had nearly said the words out loud. Better to just let it drop.

Shrugging at his wife's silence, Mickey finally changed the subject. "Where did you say the girls are?"

After a few moments of hesitation, deciding that ending the bickering was more important than having the last word, she answered, "At the movies."

"What did they go to see?"

She had to think—what had Penny muttered as she walked out the door? "That science fiction one," she finally remembered.

"The *Space Odyssey* one?"

"No. The other one," she responded, her brow furrowed in thought. "You know. The one with the monkeys."

"*Planet of the Apes?*"

"Yeah. I think that's what Penny said. *Planet of the Apes.*"

"I thought she already saw that." Mickey looked away from the screen, which now showed dancing sunflowers advertising margarine.

"I think so too. She said she wanted Peggy to see it. And she's crazy about Charlton Heston. She'll see anything he's in over and over."

"Strange," Mickey muttered, pulling himself out of the recliner to change the channel.

The news, thankfully for Evie, was over, but it was followed by yet another baseball game. How Evie hated baseball...and football...and basketball.

"What's strange?"

"That the girls are hanging around together so much. For a while there, Penny wouldn't have anything to do with Peggy."

Evie, too, had thought it strange at first. Not that her daughters hadn't gotten along well as children—each had been the other's best friend. But when Penny had entered the new University of Illinois Circle Campus, she had left her sister behind, languishing miserably at Winston Estates High. Evie had spent a lot of nights consoling her morose younger daughter, reminding her that soon she'd be in college too. *Why did they want to grow up so quickly*, she had wondered, not for the first time. *Why can't they just be happy being kids?*

Evie thought back to the firestorm that had followed Penny's announcement at the dinner table, more than three years earlier, that she planned to attend college. Mickey had smiled benevolently at his daughter, saying, "Honey, you're a smart girl. You always were, even when you were little. But you're not thinking this one through. You don't have to go to college to marry a college man."

Mickey had seemed oblivious to the horrified look on his daughter's face as he continued. "Honey, all you need to do is get a job at a place near Loyola or DePaul—in one of the little restaurants, or maybe even on campus, at the bookstore or in the library. You'll meet plenty of nice Catholic college boys."

Penny had been too upset to respond, but her actions, pushing herself away from the table, practically running toward her room muttering something about pterodactyls, had been sufficient to make her point.

"Now what?" Mickey had asked, shrugging, both palms upraised. "What did I say?" He seemed genuinely dumbfounded by his daughter's reaction.

"Daddy, you don't understand," answered Peggy, shaking her head in what looked to Evie like complete disgust. "Penny *wants* to go to college—you know, to learn stuff. Not just to find a husband."

"What does a girl need with a college degree?" Mickey had huffed, attacking his roast beef with gusto. "She's just going to get married anyway.

Your mom never went to college, and look how happy she is." At that point Peggy, looking pointedly at her mother, had left the table as well.

Maybe that had been the turning point, the point where the girls formed their alliance. Busy as Penny was with summer classes, she had very little free time, but what she had, she spent with her sister—going to movies, seeing friends, bowling. Bowling. Who would ever have thought her girls would have enjoyed bowling? They'd stopped going to the bowling alley with her and Mickey several years earlier, saying they hated the sport and that it was for old people.

Evie wearily dragged herself from the sofa and began collecting detritus from the end table beside her husband, who had never, she grumbled to herself, learned to pick up after himself. Earlier in her marriage she hadn't minded the socks on the bedroom floor, the sports pages left on the coffee table. After all, he worked hard at Pearson every day—the least she could do was take care of the house. But now...

"You're not staying up for Carson?" he asked.

"No, honey, I've got a headache." Bending to share a quick, meaningless kiss, she turned toward the kitchen.

"You're not waiting up for the girls?"

"They said they were stopping for something to eat after the movie. They should be home in an hour or so." Evie knew she would only doze lightly until she heard the sound of her daughters' footsteps on the stairway.

But upstairs in their bedroom, away from Mickey, she realized she was not really tired—only tired of their conversation. It seemed all she and her husband did lately was bicker—except, of course, when she decided to back off into a fuming silence or on those rare occasions when their bickering escalated into full-scale argument. She considered a hot bath, but the lurid cover of the romance novel lying on her nightstand called to her. Maybe reading a few pages would be more relaxing.

Opening the book to where she had left off, finding the folded onionskin pages there, she remembered using Jadzia's latest letter as her bookmark. She'd only had time to read it once, so opening it again, she read

10 July 1968

Dearest Eva!

How good to get your last letter, and to hear that you are all well. Please congratulate your daughter on her success in college—how wonderful to have a scholar! And she wants to be a teacher—that is surely a blessing to any mother.

My children, too, are doing well. Marek is having a difficult time with physics, but I am sure he will prevail. He must do very well at the polytechnic if he is going to go on into engineering, which is his dream. Even as a little boy, he was constantly building—bridges of twigs and stones, tall buildings of canned vegetables, and forts of snow! So like his uncle and namesake— such a pity they never got to know each other. He is also involved in many clubs and sports—soccer is his favorite.

Magda, too, works hard at her studies. She wishes to go into medicine, like her mama and grandma before her, but not as just a midwife—as a doctor—a surgeon, no less! I tell her she must pay less attention to the boys and more to her studies to do well on her exams, if the life of a doctor is what she really wants.

Do you get much news of what's happening in Poland? The March student protests were very disturbing, even though they did not really affect Katowice. I was happy we do not live in Warsaw. And now there is much talk of Czechoslovakia, and rumors of a possible invasion of that country. I pray this does not happen.

Roman is doing a little better, although he spends much of his time in bed. Even a short walk to pick up the newspaper at the corner is often enough to set him coughing for hours. He has been to the doctor several times, but there seems to be little they can do. All those years in the mines are very difficult on the body.

Speaking of the man, I hear him calling me. Off I go to be the dutiful wife! Write to me when you can, and may God's blessings be on you and your family.

Your loving cousin,

Jadzia

Their letters must have crossed in the mail. Over the last couple of years, Jadzia had become a more faithful correspondent than Evie, sometimes writing two or three letters to Evie's one. But then, thought Evie, that was probably because Jadzia always seemed to have more to say. Jadzia and her family seemed to be doing so well, despite the fact that things were still very tough in Poland. What did she, herself, have to write about? she thought, placing the letter on the nightstand. She was interrupted in mid-sigh by the ringing of the phone. Picking the receiver up before the first ring was completed, her heart already beating faster, she croaked a weak "Hello." A call this late could be nothing but bad news.

"Mama?"

Evie could hardly recognize the watery voice. "Penny?" she asked. "What's wrong?" Could there have been an accident? Was one of her daughters hurt?

Evie could pick out only individual words at first, but finally the message became all too clear. "Oh, Penny," Evie sighed. "Oh, God, no...I'll have to go get your father...Of course I have to tell him...Baby, there's no other way...Where? ...Oh, Penny..."

Evie, grabbing a robe and shoving her feet into waiting slippers, almost stumbled down the stairs in her haste. In the living room, the television's flickering light showed Mickey, as she had expected, spread out in the recliner's fullest extension, snoring softly. He looked so peaceful there: she dreaded the change that was about to occur.

"Mickey, wake up," she said, roughly shaking his shoulder. "We have to go to the city."

"What? What?" he sputtered, jolting to full wakefulness. "What's wrong? The girls?"

"Yes, honey. They're okay. But we have to go to Summerdale Police Station. They've gone and gotten themselves arrested."

Evie sat on a hard wooden bench in the institutional green lobby of the police station, thinking how hideous the vomit colored wall looked. She had spent the last hour methodically picking away at the poppy red nail polish on the fingernails of her left hand, starting first with the chips at the tips of her nails, finally managing to pick two fingernails and her thumbnail completely clear. Though what she really needed was a cigarette, the station did not seem like a good place to ignore "No Smoking" signs. If she stepped outside, she would not only lose her seat, but might miss Mickey.

Engrossed in the further destruction of her manicure, she heard her husband before she saw him. "Here," he said, thrusting some paperwork under her nose and pointing toward another vomit green hallway, "Go to Room 116, down that hall, and give these to Officer Kelly. I'll meet you out front with the car so we can get the hell out of here."

"Are they...are the girls..."

"Just do it, Evie," he said wearily. "It's gonna be all right. They're releasing all the kids who don't have previous records. Officer Kelly."

"What?"

"Don't forget. Ask for Officer Kelly."

"Thank God," she breathed. Bracing for the shock of seeing her daughters behind bars, she headed toward the specified hallway, stopping at a set of double doors marked "116." Pushing the door open, she was surprised to enter not a cell block, but a large hall containing two rows of perhaps ten benches each, all now occupied by an assortment of young people—black, white and brown-skinned, hair in long chestnut braids or flowing blond tresses secured by headbands, or large, stiff Afro haloes—all of them in jeans, but sporting every color of tie-dyed and peace-signed and lettered tee shirt imaginable.

"Name," demanded a matronly woman in a dark blue police uniform.

"Kelly?" Evie tentatively answered.

"First name?"

"I don't know. Officer—Officer Kelly?" At that point Evie noticed the prominent name badge on the woman's chest.

"Lady, not *my* name. The name of the person you're here for."

"Oh—my daughters. Penny and Peggy." The look of disgust on the officer's face brought back reminiscences of fifth grade, when Sister Mary Felix's sneers could reduce her to weak-kneed protoplasm. "I mean, Sienko. S-I-E-N-K-O. Penelope and Margaret Sienko. Here's the paperwork," she finally remembered, thrusting the stapled pages toward the bulldog in blue.

Running a nicotine-stained finger down a list of names attached to a clipboard, Officer Kelly finally found what she was looking for, then pointed toward the back benches near the right wall. "There," she said. "Stop back here before you leave."

Walking quickly down the aisle at the right side of the hall, Evie saw her daughters before they noticed her. *Anyone would know they are sisters,* she thought as she approached them. At first glance Penny and Peggy still looked remarkably alike, although further inspection would reveal subtle differences. Penny was slightly taller and slimmer, Peggy sturdier and more athletic. Penny's eyes, though dark brown like her sister's, contained dancing flecks of gold, and Peggy's hair was slightly curlier. Both were dressed in what Evie thought of as the uniform of the times: tight jeans, brightly dyed dashikis—Penny's red-striped, Peggy's blue—fringed buckskin moccasins—Peggy's reaching all the way up to her knees—beaded headbands crossing their foreheads Indian-style, and silver pendants displaying the ubiquitous three-spoked peace sign they dared not wear in front of their father.

Evie did not recognize the young man sitting between them, who awkwardly rose in unison with the girls as they saw their mother approaching.

Damn, Evie thought, *how do I act?* Indeed, what *was* the proper protocol for picking one's daughters up at the police station? A stern glare? A lecture, here on the spot? A release of the tears that had been fighting to be let free over the past two hours? Finally, the protocol was decided for her. As her daughters tentatively reached out to embrace her, she did the natural thing—she embraced them back, pulling them tightly to her as though she would never let go.

"Mama," cried Peggy. The familiar title, but one that had been replaced by "Mom" or an exasperated-sounding "Mother" years earlier, tugged at Evie's heart. "We weren't sure you'd come."

"Of course I'm here," Evie answered, finally breaking from the embrace to reach into her purse for a Kleenex. "Did you think your dad and I would leave you here?"

"We didn't know," answered Penny, then, with obviously great concern, "Daddy...is he mad?"

Evie almost wanted to laugh. "What do you think? You think he's happy about all this? You know what he thinks about war protestors!" It wasn't as if her husband had kept his opinions to himself.

"I know, but..." began Peggy.

"It's been awful, watching the news on TV," she continued, "worrying about all those kids in Grant Park—and then finding out that my own girls were in the middle of it! How do you think we feel?" Her relief at finding her daughters safe began to morph into a rising anger at the reasons that had brought them here. "You lied to us—and it's probably not the first time. You went someplace you didn't have any business going. And you, Penny, it's not bad enough that you're here, but to bring your little sister—who's only in high school. What were you thinking?"

"Mrs. Sienko," said the young man, stepping forward. "Your daughters are here today for a cause they believe in."

Evie examined him. He was tall—easily over six feet—and slim, his narrow, pale face framed by long, tangled black hair. His jeans were tighter than most, more belled than most, and his tee shirt, black with a dancing skeleton that Evie thought she had seen elsewhere but could not place, stretched tightly over a chest, shoulders and upper arms more developed than one would expect in someone so slim.

"And you are?" she asked archly.

"Mom, this is Scott," Penny intervened, "Scott Tyler. We...we're in kind of a club together."

"SDS," he offered, either ignoring or not seeing Penny's gestured hushing signal, forefinger crossing pursed lips. "Students for a Democratic Society. We meet three nights a week."

"The Democratic Party? You go to Democratic Party meetings?" Evie breathed a sigh of relief. That wasn't so bad. Evie had little interest in politics, but Mickey, although he seldom voted, thought of himself as a lifelong Democrat. He wouldn't object to his daughters becoming Democrats.

"No, no, Mom," Peggy answered, "it's different. It's a protest group."

"What? Oh no, you don't mean—not that group that's been on the news every night! And Peggy—you go to these meetings too?" Her girls had been keeping a great deal from her. Bowling indeed!

"Mrs. Bialek, your daughters are both involved in a very important cause. Someday we'll change the world. Even now..."

"Well, Scott, thank you for your comments," Evie cut him off, ice glazing every syllable. "But I don't think this is the time or the place to discuss this." Leading her girls toward the front of the hall, where more paperwork and eventually the dreaded meeting with their father awaited them, she had only a moment to consider the electricity apparent in the quick look shared between Penny and the slim young man as they parted.

Mickey, having retrieved their Chevy from the parking lot, pulled up to the front of the police station to pick them up. "Get in the damn car," he had commanded his daughters through a rolled-down window. Once they were settled in the back seat, a bitterly muttered "You two look like bums" was the only comment he, or anyone else in the car, made on the long trip back home.

Once there, with the girls safely in their rooms, Mickey's anger had unleashed itself upon his wife. "It's your fault, you know—you and that damned college."

"Mickey, sending Penny to college was a good idea."

"The hell it was! College is no place for a young girl. Do you honestly think we would have spent the night at Summerdale if she wasn't at that school?"

"I don't know. But what would you do? Have her quit?"

"That wouldn't be a bad idea," he stormed. "Dammit, Evie. Can't you see? You've spoiled those girls—let them have their own way too much.

You let them forget who's in charge here. Boy, if we would have stayed in the old neighborhood..."

"What difference would that have made?"

"They wouldn't have grown up to be like all these other suburban hippie brats. They would have grown up with some respect, some common sense."

"Mickey, they're good kids." What was Mickey thinking? True, their girls had gotten arrested, and it had been a terrible thing. But it wasn't like their neighbor Rose Nielander's son, who had gotten caught stealing a car, or like the Olson girl who was in some drug rehab program. And little Timmy Harding from down the block had been getting into trouble for taking things since he'd been six—the only thing that kept him out of jail was the fact that his dad was a lawyer. Their girls, compared to most, were better behaved—more respectful, more hard-working than their peers.

What did Mickey expect from their daughters? To behave the way she had as a girl—quiet, passive, afraid of her own shadow? Did he want them to be afraid of him, the way she had feared her own father? She shuddered at that thought—of her father's violent outbursts after her mother's death, and of how defenseless she had felt. Were these the Old World values Mickey admired so much?

"Yeah, good kids!" Mickey's laugh was a bitter one. "You just keep telling yourself that and someday we'll be picking them up at some hippie commune—or at the morgue!" With that he turned from her and headed toward the front door.

"Mickey, where are you going?"

"Out."

"It's after midnight."

"I can read the damned clock!" With a slam that shook the whole room, he was out the door. Evie didn't know whether to be worried or relieved.

What had gone wrong? Things had been so much simpler when Penny and Peggy were young. She grabbed a cigarette and, with shaking hands, finally got it lit. Mickey couldn't really believe what he said. The morgue! She dragged desperately at her smoke, thinking that what she really needed was a drink.

Maybe it was the girls' ages—maybe it was the time, the place. Evie thought again of Jadzia's letter, of her pride in her children, both of them doing well. Marek was studying to be an engineer, and Magda a doctor. Evie could hardly imagine a girl becoming a doctor, and in a Communist country, no less. Of course Magda had had her mother's example of midwifery to follow. What example had her own girls had? Evie's days were spent as a typical suburban wife and mother: bridge dates, household chores, occasional volunteer work for the church and school. How different her life was from her cousin's.

But then, she was only doing what was expected of her. From the time Evie had been a little girl, she had dreamed of her wedding—of what she would wear, how she would look. And then babies, of course. Babies would follow soon after—it was every girl's dream.

And then came the war. That had changed everything. God, she'd been something in those days. Smart, beautiful, sexy. She'd known all the right things to say, all the right moves to make. She could have had any boy she wanted at Doall Valve, at the USO dances. And the one she did want... well, no sense thinking about that. She'd made her decision.

She had to admit her life was good—a lot of women would envy her. So why did she often feel such a nagging discontent deep within her heart? Why did she sometimes envy Jadzia, who had suffered so much in the war and now lived in the worst possible circumstance, in a Communist country? Evie felt shame at her own feelings, believing she really had no right to be unhappy.

Maybe Mickey was right. They were living in strange, dangerous times. Anyone would be confused and unsettled. Opening the liquor cabinet, she removed a nearly empty bottle of Mickey's Jim Beam and filled a whiskey glass to the brim. She wasn't much of a drinker, but the events of this evening seemed to demand some uncharacteristic response from her. Flipping on the radio, she turned the dial toward her favorite station, one that played big band late at night. While tuning in, she caught a fragment of an earlier interview—Mayor Daley responding to a reporter's questioning of the police department's handling of the demonstrators.

"Gentlemen," he had responded in his distinctive south Chicago accent, "get the thing straight once and for all. The policeman isn't there to create disorder. The policeman is there to preserve disorder."

After a moment of silence, head cocked and brow furrowed, she asked out loud, "Did he just say what I think he said? The policeman is there to *preserve* disorder? Well, I guess that explains everything."

Evie was laughing so hard she almost spilled her drink. Or was she crying. She really couldn't tell.

Chapter Sixteen

Evie and Jadzia, Chicago

October, 1970

Moja najdroższa Ewo!

Niesamowite, moje wszystkie dokumenty przyjęto! Przylatuję do Chicago 8 października lotem 82 United Airlines. W NewYork przesiadam się na samolot Polskich Linii Lotniczych Lot"

"Flight 82 from New York arriving Gate G5."

The announcement abruptly halted Evie's mad dash through the terminal in search of the proper concourse amid crowds of pushing, bustling travelers negotiating suitcases and travel bags. A typical O'Hare afternoon.

"That's her flight, isn't it?" Evie asked Steffie, who immediately began rummaging through the fringed suede bag she toted on her left shoulder. Evie, pleading intimidation by the Chicago expressway system, had asked her sister to serve as her driver. On the long ride to the airport Evie had finally confessed that, more than a driver, what she had actually needed was moral support. Although she and Jadzia had been correspondents for thirty-five years, the prospect of actually meeting her cousin, now that the meeting was imminent, had left her curiously flustered and at odds. What if, after all this time, they had nothing to say to each other? What if they didn't hit it off?

The stress of the previous two months had been unrelenting, and it wasn't over yet: still two more very busy days to survive before the wedding. Steffie had been happy to serve as chauffeur: she, too, was looking forward to meeting the cousin Evie had spoken of for so many years.

Steffie stopped to search her bag more thoroughly. At thirty-five she still turned heads, and today was no exception. Her snug blue jeans and tight red sweater showed off a figure trim from the activities attendant on being a high school physical education teacher, and her nearly black hair, worn long and curly today, framed a heart-shaped face still young and fresh even without make-up. Evie, in her flared slate-gray skirt and white pleated blouse, looked a full generation older: often, she and her sister were mistaken for mother and daughter.

"Here it is." Steffie produced the crumpled sheet of onionskin with a flourish, scanning it quickly in the glare from the bright terminal lights. "Flight 82 from New York," she read, then looking up, "Thank God she went through customs there or we'd be here forever." Perceiving the intensity of worry in her sister's expression, she added, "Don't worry. We have plenty of time to find her. It'll take forever for the plane to unload."

Her words proved true. Arriving at Gate G5, they discovered no one yet emerging from the jetport. Finding two adjacent seats contoured in the aqua plastic ubiquitous to airport terminals the world over, the sisters sat among a crowd of people waiting to greet friends and loved ones.

"Let me see that letter again," Evie demanded.

Steffie sighed, knowing her sister had already read the short letter enough times to have memorized it, but handed it over without complaint.

September 6, 1970

My dearest Eva,

Incredibly, the paper work has all gone through! I will be arriving in Chicago on October 8 on United Airlines flight 82, changing planes from Lot Airlines in New York. I cannot believe that this is really happening—that I will finally get to see you face-to-face, to meet your family, and especially to have the wonderful opportunity to attend your darling Penny's wedding. It all seems like a dream to me.

Once again, I thank you for your generosity. To think that you and Mikosz, with all the expense and extra work of a daughter's wedding, would be kind enough to bring me to the United States to be a part of the celebration! Alfons again thanks you for inviting him as well, but it is still much easier for a husband or wife to obtain a visa than it would be for both to do so. His thoughts and prayers will be with us on October 10 when your little girl becomes a bride.

You must be so excited. And like me, you must also wonder where the time goes. Thank you for the mass card you sent last month for the anniversary of Roman's death—it is hard to believe he has been gone two years, and your tata almost as long. I think of Roman every day. And last month marked my first wedding anniversary with Alfons. I will never stop being amazed at the strange twists and turns life takes.

Give my love and many kisses to all your family. Soon I will actually see your face, will be able to embrace you as I have held you in my heart for all these years. God bless you, and I will see you October 8.

Your loving cousin,
Jadzia

"Too bad her husband couldn't come." Steffie's voice broke through Evie's thoughts.

"Yeah." Evie would have loved to have met Alfons, Apolonya's younger brother, who had obviously swept Jadzia off her feet. How else to explain her marriage to him, just six months after the death of her husband? "But with all the unrest in Eastern Europe, Jadzia almost didn't make it out either. The Russians are really clamping down on visits to the States."

"Where did you say her new husband was all those years?"

"Argentina. He emigrated there directly from a labor camp in Hamburg, Germany." Jadzia had written to Evie of her surprise when Alfons, whom she had assumed dead, had appeared at Roman's funeral, of how they had quickly fallen in love. Evie had worried that her cousin had married impulsively, perhaps through the vulnerability that grief often brings. She knew that, although Jadzia and Roman's marriage had begun as more of a necessity than a love match—a way to survive the traumatic post-war years—through their years together Jadzia had grown to dearly love Roman, a kind and gentle man. In the past year, however, Evie had sensed an energy, a more lively spirit, in Jadzia's letters.

"And he never tried to get in touch with his family in Niedzieliska in all that time," continued Steffie. "That seems strange."

"I guess a lot of strange things happen during a war," responded Evie, now craning her neck toward the jetport. "People disappear, then reappear years later." Fumbling in her bag, she found her compact and began fitfully powdering her cheeks. "How do I look?" she finally asked.

"You look great," Steffie replied, looking fondly at her older sister. "You know, Jadzia's going to love you, no matter how you look."

"I know. It's just...well, what if I can't even speak to her? It's been years since I really spoke Polish."

"You write to her in Polish. And sometimes you and your mother-in-law speak Polish."

Evie shook her head. "Writing isn't the same. And Mother Sienka—well, we never really *speak*, if you know what I mean."

"Yep," answered Steffie, a veteran of countless Bialek-Sienko gatherings throughout the years.

Evie was hoping this visit would include long, soulful conversations with her cousin, sharing intimacies, becoming close in ways that even the hundreds of letters they had shared over the years could not effect. Steffie, seeming to sense her sister's high expectations, assured her, "You and Jadzia have been best friends since you were kids. You'll see—it'll be great." Then, changing the topic, more perhaps to distract her sister than out of any real interest in the subject of every conversation they had had in the past few months, she added, "Everything set for the wedding?"

"I think so," answered Evie. "The rehearsal dinner's all set for tomorrow night at the club. That should be easy. And then Saturday—well, no matter what, it'll all be over then!"

"And Mickey? Is he behaving?"

"As well as can be expected, I guess." Mickey had never overcome his first negative opinion of Scott. He had plenty of complaints about the boy, beginning with Scott's being neither Polish nor Catholic. But what really set Mickey's teeth grinding was Scott's continued involvement in the anti-war movement and the effect it was having on their daughters.

Evie felt that Mickey also blamed her for what he saw as his daughters' slip into the abyss of liberal thought. "That's what you get for sending them to college!" had become his standard refrain every time one of the girls did something he didn't like. But all the young girls in Winston Estates went to college; not one of them followed the pattern of Evie's old neighborhood in Chicago, where every girl's dream was to marry within a month of high school graduation. And Penny and Peggy were smart: denying them the kind of education all their friends were receiving would have been unthinkable.

Still, Evie often wondered why she was the one who always became involved in everyone else's squabbles. She wore herself out trying to maintain peace between Mickey and her daughters and future son-in-law, not to mention her own difficult relationship with Mother Sienka. She often felt that she had been walking on eggs her whole life, trying to please everyone but never pleasing a soul. Did any of them ever wonder what would please her? Did any of them care?

"Here they come!" Steffie's excited announcement shattered Evie's thoughts. The first few travelers emerging into the waiting room set off frenzies of welcoming shouts and cries among the little groups of people scattered there, who rushed to claim their own. Soon the room was so filled with the cacophony of joyous reunion that it was impossible to distinguish any particular sounds. Evie fervently hoped that she would recognize Jadzia. She had pictures of her cousin, of course, but photographs were often deceiving.

She soon found she had nothing to worry about. She recognized Jadzia— her cousin, her pen pal, her best friend—the moment she appeared, still deep within the jetport, surrounded by other travelers, all pressing forward slowly. "Is that her?" Steffie asked, pointing to the correct person, but Evie had to swallow hard before she answered, "Yes, that's Jadzia. Steffie, that's Jadzia!"

Jadzia recognized Evie immediately as well. The crush of disembarking passengers slowed her progress, making the minutes it took for Jadzia, her eyes fixed on Evie's, to emerge into the waiting room and into her cousin's arms, feel painfully long for both. But soon they were together, holding each other closely, crying onto each other's shoulders, thirty-five years of shared hope and pain and love finding its expression.

The cousins finally broke their embrace, separating only as far as hands on each other's shoulders would allow, to actually look face to face for the first time. Evie saw a woman whose every movement and expression exuded energy and a vibrancy that belied her age. Much shorter than Evie had expected, Jadzia had a trim, firm body and a smile that set her dark eyes twinkling in a round, almost dusky face. Jadzia's hair was short and curly, touches of gray at her temples only accentuating its sable lushness. "She's so beautiful," thought Evie.

Jadzia saw a slim woman, taller than she had expected, with long auburn hair just touching her shoulders in gentle waves. Evie's pale eyes, the color of dark amber, were set deep in a long, squarish face with high cheekbones that gave her a patrician look. But Jadzia caught a tinge of sadness, or perhaps, she hoped, just a little tiredness in those eyes. Echoing her cousin, she thought, "She is so beautiful."

Evie introduced Steffie who, after welcoming their cousin with hugs and kisses, led them to the luggage carousel, then volunteered to retrieve the car, leaving them to wait for Jadzia's luggage. Both cousins had much to say, but the crowded terminal was not conducive to the kind of conversation they desired. Their amiable chatter was the universal dialogue of airports.

"I can hardly believe you're here! How was your flight?"

"Very good—my first time flying, you know. It was a little bit frightening at first, but so exciting and so beautiful once I was up in the air, in the clouds. And landing—first in New York, then here—seeing all the tall buildings coming closer and closer. It took my breath away! But my American geography is maybe not so good—I did not realize Chicago was on the ocean."

"Oh, no, it's not. You must have circled in from the west and gone over Lake Michigan."

"A lake? So large?"

"Yes. We'll take you for a ride along Lake Shore Drive before you leave and you can see how beautiful the skyline is. Did you have any problems transferring planes in New York?"

"Customs was so crowded—we waited in line for such a long time, I felt like I was back home!" Jadzia's smile was infectious. "Oh, there! That one." She pointed to an old black cloth suitcase, much battered and worn. "That one is mine."

Evie had no sooner wrestled Jadzia's suitcase from the pile of luggage slowly snaking its oval path along the carousel when she caught sight of Steffie, beckoning them, pointing toward the exit beyond which she had double parked. Soon the cousins were together in the back seat, chatting so easily about the weather and the wedding and other small matters that in what seemed like only minutes, Steffie was pulling up to Evie's yellow brick Cape Cod in Winston Estates.

As Evie and Jadzia stepped out of the car into a bright, crisp October day set off by a delft blue sky and clouds of cotton candy cumulus, Evie basked in Jadzia's unabashed praise of her home: "It is so beautiful. And so large! Even larger than I had imagined! And this is all your property? Show me where your property ends."

But before any tour could begin, the front door opened, expelling an excited Penny and Peggy who rushed into Jadzia's arms with cries of "Aunt Jadzia!" "You're finally here!" "I can't believe it!" and "Mom's been a basket case waiting for you to come!" Jadzia looked flustered—she spoke little English and the girls knew little Polish—but she understood the sentiment beneath their joyful chatter.

Entering the house the girls, with Steffie as interpreter, took Jadzia upstairs to settle her into Peggy's room, which was to be Jadzia's for her week-long stay in the United States. Mickey would be home soon, bringing with him Mother Sienka, who had insisted on immediately meeting Evie's cousin from Poland, never once considering that she might be imposing. Henryk and his wife would not arrive from California until the day of the wedding.

Evie would have loved to stretch out on the sofa for just half an hour, but that, of course, was impossible. Opening cupboards and the refrigerator door, she started to assemble the ingredients she would need to prepare the all-American feast—steak, home fries, corn on the cob, apple pie—that would welcome her cousin to her home.

Already midnight? This was the latest she and Mickey had stayed up for years. But with so much to say now that Jadzia was actually sitting here in her dining room, Evie was willing to forego sleep altogether this evening.

Dinner had been a great success, with even Mother Sienka praising Evie's homemade apple pie. While Mickey had driven his mother home, Jadzia had declared the woman a "good, proper Polish lady," thereby dampening any desire Evie had of ever visiting Poland. Steffie had gone home early, pleading quizzes to grade for the next day. Penny had not yet returned from her evening out with Scott, and Peggy had headed up to bed half an hour earlier, thereby eliminating any further need of English/Polish translation. Now just Mickey, Evie and Jadzia sat at the dining room table, long cleared of dinner clutter.

"Another highball, ladies?" Mickey seemed to be enjoying his role as host. His prematurely steel gray hair had distinguished, rather than aged, him. Combined with his still-slim, erect build and the steel-rimmed glasses he had begun wearing several years earlier, his penchant for slightly formal attire—dress pants and short-sleeved cotton shirts—gave him the air of an Old World professor.

"No more for me," answered Evie.

"Perhaps just one more," answered Jadzia, "but maybe this time not so strong."

They had been discussing Poland under Soviet rule, focusing on the freedoms Americans enjoyed that were only a dream to Poles. Mickey had been very interested in hearing Jadzia's opinions on the Czech student uprising, which had lasted only five glorious days but seemed to have awakened old yearnings all over Eastern Europe.

"You know," Mickey predicted, "once people get a taste of freedom, they want more. Czechoslovakia was first, but Poland won't be far behind."

"I see changes ahead, too," responded Jadzia, "but it won't be easy. The Russkies aren't going to give up without a fight."

"Another war?" asked Evie uneasily, thinking of the stories Jadzia had written of war experiences almost too horrible to be true.

"I hope it will not come to that," answered Jadzia. "But there seems to be unrest everywhere. We hear that even in this country you have unrest—many students protesting."

"Yeah," spat Mickey, reaching into a plastic bowl for a handful of potato chips. "Draft dodgers! They oughta' toss them all in jail."

"But they protest the war in Viet Nam, no?" asked Jadzia innocently. "Isn't that their issue?"

"They have no issue," grumbled Mickey. "Damned candy asses!"

"Mickey!" Evie's eyebrows arched all the way up into her bangs.

"Sorry, ladies—excuse my French." Mickey nodded penitently at the women. "But, honestly, it's hard not to get mad. They're living in the best damned country in the world, but it's not good enough for them. They gotta riot in the streets!" Mickey emptied half a bottle of beer in one deep gulp. "I hate to say it, Jadzia," he confided, "but Penny's Scott is one of them."

"Mickey," warned Evie, "don't get started now. You'll only get more upset." Evie knew her request would go unheeded. Once Mickey began railing against war protesters, there was no stopping him.

"Upset! Who wouldn't be upset?" He turned toward Jadzia. "You can't even have a decent conversation with the kid—all he wants to do is whine about the war. It's un-American! And every time I look at him I want to tell him to cut his hair and get some decent clothes. Instead I'm handing over my daughter to him!" He finished his beer in another long swig. "Strange world."

Evie wished Mickey would quit drinking and go up to bed. She cringed when she heard Jadzia's next words: she knew how Mickey would react.

"But they're like the Czech students, no? Just protesting about what they believe is right?"

"No comparison!" assured Mickey, shaking his head forcefully. "No comparison at all! The Czech students are fighting for freedom. Our hippies are just a bunch of cowards. Do you think I wanted to go to war in 1942?" He paused, but only for effect. "Hell, no. But I went. When your country calls, you go. Period."

"Perhaps you are right," deferred Jadzia, but Evie knew her cousin had acquiesced out of courtesy, not conviction. She herself had certainly done the same thing with Mickey many times.

"Boy, 12:30 already," Evie hinted, yawning broadly. "What time are you getting up for work, honey?"

"Early. Tomorrow's gonna be another long day. I'd better head up to bed. Unless, Evie, you think they really won't need me..." He looked at his wife wistfully.

"Yes," she countered, "we do need you at the rehearsal dinner." They had had this discussion several times. "Penny would be so disappointed if you didn't come."

"All right, then. Good night." With familial kisses for both women Mickey negotiated his way to the stairwell.

Evie sighed with relief once Mickey had reached the upstairs landing. Now she would finally get to really talk to her cousin. To speak heart-to-heart.

"Excuse all the political talk," she began. "Once Mickey gets started..."

"Ah, it's the same everywhere. Roman and his best friend Tadek used to speak of nothing else when we all got together. It used to drive Marysia and me almost to drink! It's sad Mikosz—or Meekee—is that how you call him?"

"Mickey—but you're close enough," Evie laughed.

"Mickey disapproves so much of his son-in-law. Is that why he does not wish to go to the rehearsal dinner?"

"Mostly," Evie said with a small shrug. "He really doesn't like most of Scott's family. They're, well, just different from us."

"How are they different?"

"Oh, I don't know. They're pretty well-off, and their family has been in this country for generations. It's hard to explain."

"Do you, too, not like your future son-in-law?"

"No, I like Scott. I think he'll be a good husband for Penny. I just wish everyone in this country would stop arguing about the darned war—it's not like we can do anything about it. But don't worry about Mickey—that was mostly the beer talking. He's not happy about Penny marrying Scott, but he'll be all right."

"Good," said Jadzia, sipping her drink.

"The truth is, Mickey wouldn't be nearly so upset if it weren't for..." Evie caught herself. She had never spoken to anyone of what had happened at the convention two years earlier, wanting to keep it a secret from their neighbors. And yet she was dying to talk about it, if only to come to terms with her own feelings. Jadzia might be the perfect sounding board. But what would her cousin think?

Jadzia looked quizzically at her cousin, but gave her time to decide whether or not to discuss whatever was causing her brow to furrow and her eyes to mist. Taking a deep breath, Evie made her decision. "Mickey's still

mad because two summers ago the girls got arrested. And he blames Scott."
There. It was out.

"Your darling girls? How can that be?"

"Did you hear about the protests at the Democratic Convention?"

Jadzia nodded. "Of course. It was in all our papers. One more sign to
prove that the evil capitalist United States was falling apart." Jadzia's wry
laugh encouraged Evie to continue.

"Well, the girls were protesting with a group of anti-war demonstrators.
Mickey almost had a stroke when they called from the police station asking
him to post bail." Evie looked for signs of censure on her cousin's face.

"Arrested at a protest?" asked Jadzia with a smile. "In Poland, no one
would think of them as criminals for protesting against the government.
They would be heroes."

"It's different here," asserted Evie. "You live in an occupied country. We
live in a democracy."

"And so no one should ever protest anything if they live in a democracy?
Then what's the point of having all this freedom? Tell me, does Penny love
this boy?"

"Yes, I know she does."

"And is she truly opposed to this war, or is it just to please him?"

"She was against the war before she even met Scott."

"Then don't be ashamed. Be proud of her for standing up for what she
believes in."

How wonderful to hear someone else state what she had been thinking;
surely, few of Evie's friends in Winston Estates would have defended Penny.
But within days of that awful night when she and Mickey had driven into
the city to post their bail, Evie had begun to believe that what her daughters
had done was not really a crime. As they kept telling her, they had the
right to protest—it said so in the Constitution. And while Evie had never
considered herself very political, she often thought that, had she had sons
who could be drafted instead of daughters, she too might have been arrested
by now for protesting the war in Viet Nam. If she were a young man, why,
she would have probably burned her draft card just like Scott had—yet
another thing Mickey must never learn about.

"Anyway, even if I disagreed with her, there's not much you can do with
kids today," Evie continued with a grateful smile. "They pretty much do
what they want—at least in this country. Not like in the old days. Is that
true in Poland, too?"

"Yes, in Poland too, I think," agreed Jadzia. "Like Marek. I begged him not to join the SZSP."

"The SZSP?"

"Yes, of course, you would not know—the Polish Students' Socialist Club. It is a Communist group."

"Marek's a Communist?" Evie, aghast, thought of Khrushchev banging his shoe on a table at the United Nations and of all the Duck for Cover school drills she'd endured as a child.

"Evie, you know Poland is a Communist country—or at least the government is," Jadzia said. How could she explain Polish life to her cousin, who was so Polish, yet so not Polish. It would be like trying to explain color to a person who could see only black and white. "Still," she continued, "this club was not what I wanted for him."

"But you never mentioned it," Evie began. "You never said anything about having problems with Marek."

"True," Jadzia replied. "Just as you said your family was not affected by the convention..."

The confused, wary look on Evie's face matched almost exactly the confused, wary look on Jadzia's. Both women were troubled by the direction this conversation was taking. But soon, the look on her cousin's face made Evie smile. Jadzia laughed. A moment later, they were in each other's arms, both laughing.

"I always envied your life in the States," confessed Jadzia, wiping a laugh tear from the corner of her eye. "From your letters, I thought everything was perfect here."

"Well, I knew things weren't perfect in Poland—but I sure thought you and your family were the Cleavers."

"The Cleavers?"

"Oh," laughed Evie, "you wouldn't know about them. They were the perfect television family."

"My family is definitely *not* perfect," corrected Jadzia, laughing even harder. "For instance, Marek. All we do is fight. At eighteen, he thinks he is a man who can make his own decisions."

"Eighteen is a terrible age." Evie thought back to her girls' passage through the teen years—to the battles, the sullen pouts, the tears. "I wouldn't ever want to go back to those days."

"And I think it is especially hard on Marek. Perhaps if his father had lived...he and Roman were always very close."

"Oh, of course. Does Marek get along with Alfons?"

"At first they did, but now...Alfons is very different from Roman. Roman was such a gentle man, so soft-spoken, even with the children."

"It's hard to believe he's been gone for over two years."

"Yes, and even today I miss his wisdom and his kindness. He was the perfect *tata* in so many ways."

And husband? Evie wondered. *Was he the perfect husband as well?* Evie had often thought that in Jadzia's letters, Roman seemed more of a father figure than a husband.

"And Alfons," continued Jadzia, pausing just a moment to consider how to best express her thought. "Alfons, well, he is a man who speaks his mind."

"So Marek resents his step-father?" Evie questioned. "I think that's not so uncommon." Evie had read Ann Landers' column long enough to realize how difficult step-parent, step-child relationships could be. "What about Magda? Does she resent Alfons too?"

"Oh, Magda. She is like Alfons' little princess. He spends hours with her, helping her with homework, especially math and science, her favorites."

Evie considered it strange for a girl to love math and science, which were certainly male subjects. Her own girls had despised those courses, much as she had while in elementary and high school.

"And she is so spoiled, she can say anything to him," continued Jadzia. "He never gets angry with her."

"She sounds like daddy's little girl—my two were much the same," sympathized Evie. "Well, until two years ago, anyway. Mickey's only now starting to get over that arrest."

"Daddy's little girl," Jadzia mused, hearing that expression for the first time. "Yes, that is how he sees Magda exactly. But she is not a little girl anymore, and she sometimes tries to act so much older than she really is. I do not know how to make her understand." Evie nodded, understanding exactly.

"It is so different from when I grew up on the farm. Mama and *Tata* were like a queen and king. And we knew to obey every adult in the village." Jadzia continued, shaking her head slowly.

"We lived in the city when I was growing up," responded Evie, "but it was the same on Haddon Avenue. You never talked back to any adult. And Dad was a tyrant. His word was law, at least when we were younger."

"Do you miss your *tata?*" Jadzia asked, remembering disturbing hints she had gotten from Evie's childhood letters.

"Yes. Often I do, more than I would have expected," responded Evie. "He was pretty bullheaded, but at least you knew where you stood with him. I guess sometimes I miss his confidence. He was always sure he knew what was right and wrong."

"Hard to think like that today," responded Jadzia. "What is right? What is wrong? It seems to change every day."

"Here too." Both cousins shook their heads in an eerily identical manner. "I often think, if my mom had lived, maybe things would have been different for me, "continued Evie. "I might have...oh, I don't know...maybe known what to do more of the time."

"Of course. Your mama died when you were so very young."

"It's been so long I hardly even remember what she looked like. But I sometimes think maybe if she would have been around when I was in high school, and later, and even now that the girls are getting older, maybe she could have helped."

"I understand," said Jadzia. "I too miss my mama every day. But I think she's still with me. I think often 'What would mama do?' and it helps sometimes. And then I think of her in heaven, watching over me."

Evie, her head tilted up and to the left in a thoughtful pose, considered how to respond. Jadzia's words were so genuine, but to Evie, they seemed sadly naïve. She herself never felt her own mother's guidance from above. Thinking of her mother usually just left her feeling empty and cheated in some way—she tried to avoid such thoughts.

"And the wedding," continued Jadzia. "That must make you think of your mama, and of how she would be here to help you. Can I help? What still needs to be done?"

"I think we're pretty well set. Just having you here is a help." It was true. Somehow, being with Jadzia calmed Evie, helped her put all the distressing details of her own life into perspective. What was it about Jadzia that seemed to smooth everyone's ruffled feathers?

"Are many coming?"

"Almost three hundred," sighed Evie, to Jadzia's amazement. "What with the kids' friends, the Tylers and all their guests, our family and friends, and some of the gang from Mickey's work. Even Mother Sienka gave us a list of over one hundred—and was pretty upset when we made her pare it down to thirty."

"*Pani* Sienka? She seems like such a reasonable woman."

Evie's suddenly tilted head and furrowed brow elicited a laugh from Jadzia. "It must be true everywhere," she offered. "Mothers-in-law and daughters-in-law are like cats and dogs. Perhaps I am very lucky to have never had to deal with one. But how about the food for the wedding? Can I help with the food? You must have a great deal that needs to be prepared."

"All catered. We don't bring a thing."

"What a grand idea." But Jadzia found this surprising. The expense must be enormous. And what mother could trust another woman to cook for her daughter's wedding? "Then the *Oczepiny*. Let me help with the *Oczepiny*. Or maybe Americans do not do this?" she asked, catching the displeasure on Evie's face.

"It's not an American custom. We don't have anything like an *Oczepiny* here. I refused to have one. But Penny wants to do it. Her grandmother talked her into it."

"Ah, *Pani* Sienka," Jadzia said, more than a little hurt by her cousin's dismissal of a custom that she herself found extremely touching. "I can see that she could be very persuasive. But you do not approve?"

"It's not my decision. I think a lot of our guests will be confused, but..."

"Then good. Let me help with the *Oczepiny* and you won't have to."

"Thank you," Evie said, smiling, "that would be perfect." Evie was grateful that her cousin would be relieving her of a task she had dreaded. "But we've already talked too much about me. How about your life? Tell me more about Alfons—about your courtship," she said, leaning toward Jadzia with an intimate smile. "Were you attracted to him when you were younger? Did you ever think you might marry him?"

"Well, no, but..." Jadzia's face reddened as she began fiddling with a teaspoon that had been left on the table. "It was not until he came back to Poland—he thought it would be just for a short visit—and then we started to notice each other as something more than childhood friends." Now Jadzia was studying her own hands, twisting her plain gold wedding band around her finger.

Evie sensed a change in her cousin's mood, but could not imagine what might have caused it. "Has Alfons ever heard from his brother Antek?" she asked.

Jadzia's immediate reaction—a quick draining of color from her face—startled Evie, who wished she could eradicate those words, now suddenly hanging like a dark cloud in the air. Evie remembered how deeply Jadzia had cared for Antek, Alfons' older brother, when she was a girl. How, she thought, could she have been so insensitive as to bring up what must have been a painful subject for Jadzia—the loss of a childhood sweetheart?

"I'm so sorry," Evie said. "I didn't mean to pry."

"No, there is nothing to be sorry for," insisted Jadzia. "It has just been a very long day for me, and I think this last highball was even stronger than the one before. Would you mind if I went up to bed now?"

"Of course not. I should get some sleep, too. Tomorrow will be another busy day. But really, if I offended you..." Evie was sick with remorse.

"You? Never could you offend me," said Jadzia, grasping her cousin's hands across the table and looking steadily into her eyes. "Darling Eva, we are family, and you have been my dearest friend for almost my whole life. Nothing you say or do could ever be offensive to me."

One little "ping" would start it all. One knife, perhaps, lightly tapping a crystal champagne flute. Then another ping from the same table, and perhaps another. A second table would join in, then a third and a fourth, knives, forks and spoons striking water glasses, china coffee cups, and cocktail glasses. Soon every table, every guest armed with a utensil, would add to the staccato beat.

On the dais, mock resignation rolling their eyes and shrugging their shoulders, the bride and groom would finally comply with a kiss, followed by riotous clapping and hooting from the revelers. The first kiss had been short and modest, but subsequent kisses, fueled by champagne and the rising excitement in the room, had become longer, more romantic, until the last few were almost X-rated in style and duration.

Wiping away laugh tears with a lace-bordered handkerchief, Jadzia replaced her fork, her weapon of choice, back onto the crisp linen tablecloth. Despite all Evie's misgivings, she needn't have worried. Dinner had been a great success, the prime rib succulent and tender, the potatoes au gratin and green beans almandine cooked to perfection. Mickey and Evie had had time only to pick at the delicious food; now the two of them, Evie lovely in a beaded beige sheath, Mickey striking in his black tuxedo, were making their hosts' rounds from table to table, leaving Jadzia to become further acquainted with her extended family at the Sienko/Bialek table.

Pani Sienka, resplendent in a new gown designed in, instead of her customary black crepe, a more festive navy blue overlaid with an even darker blue lace, looked the picture of the beloved grandma—serene, loving, kind. Jadzia, of course, knew better, based on twenty years' worth of comments from Evie's letters. In the few minutes between the removal of the salad plates and the serving of the entrée, *Pani* Sienka had confided to Jadzia, in whispered Polish, her reservations about this marriage.

"This boy, this Scott," she had begun, "did you know, not only is he not Polish, he is not even Catholic!"

"But *Pani* Sienka, you don't have to be Polish or Catholic to be a good person."

Pani Sienka's eyebrows arched high enough to disappear under the black netting of the flowered-bedecked hat perched high on her crown of tight, still black pincurls. "Well, this is true, *Pani*, but surely you do not believe..."

"Some more *pierogi*, *Pani* Sienka?" Henryk interrupted what promised to be a scathing retort, passing to the older woman a heavy platter—a peace offering. "They're mostly cheese, but there are a couple of potato left, if you'd prefer. The potato are exceptionally good." A heavy, ruddy-faced man with fringes of gray hair beneath a monkish tonsure, he had arrived just last night from California with his wife, who smiled blankly and shrugged her shoulders, her confusion about the last interchange appearing to be only partially caused by its having been carried on in a language she did not understand.

"There's still champagne. Anyone?" Steffie held up the heavy green bottle, her smile embracing the whole table. Jadzia considered how very young Steffie looked at thirty-five, so unlike many of the women in Niedzieleska. Steffie's choice for today's festivities, a long, scoop-necked sheath in an electric blue, flattered her trim figure, and her nearly black hair, worn piled in curls atop her head, framed a heart-shaped face still young and fresh even without make-up.

"I'll have some more champagne," responded Henryk, obviously choosing to ignore the narrow-eyed glare emanating from his wife's eyes. Looking up to see Evie approaching their table, he added, "Ah, the mother of the bride. Sit down, Sis. Relax. Have some wine. Where's your better half?"

"I lost him somewhere between the Dombrowskis and the Johaniewiczes," she laughed, but soon returned to hostess mode. "Did everyone have enough to eat? Was everything all right? Wasn't the beef a little tough?"

Everything was perfect, Sis," assured Steffie, to the accompaniment of nods and murmurs from everyone at the table. "The beef was great. Now, sit. Enjoy yourself a little."

Evie sank heavily into the empty chair next to Jadzia, but still looked anxiously around her at the wait staff that scurried about, removing plates and dismantling several tables closest to the dance floor. The band, dressed in dark blue sharkskin suits with lapel-less jackets buttoned up to their stiff mandarin collars, tuned their instruments as a line formed at the just-opened bar.

"Almost time for the first dance," fretted Evie. "I hope the kids chose something appropriate. I'm not sure Penny even knows how to slow dance," Evie worried as the first notes sounded.

But Penny obviously did know how. Her train gathered over one arm, her head held straight and high by a neck that looked too willowy to support the dark curls piled under yards of stiff netting, she stepped into Scott's waiting arms as gracefully as a preening swan. Scott, resplendent tonight in a dark blue tuxedo and with his hair brushed back into a neat pony tail, more than held his own in the dance.

"Peter, Paul and Mary," identified Steffie, smiling. "'The Wedding Song.' A perfect choice."

As the entire table turned to watch the dancers, surrounded by the wedding party and those guests who were not in the drinks line, Jadzia turned to Evie. "They are a beautiful couple, Eva. They look all grown up out there."

"Yes," Evie admitted, almost grudgingly. "How did that happen?"

"It happens to all our children." Jadzia thought of her own two children back in Poland, living lives she did not completely understand. "Time is strange for a mother. The days are so long, but the years go by too fast."

Evie smiled. "That's true. Look at my Penny—she really is an adult. In my heart I know she's an adult. But sometimes when I look at her, all I can see is a chubby-cheeked, curly-haired little girl dragging her rag doll across the kitchen floor. What happened to that little girl? I could swear she was just here yesterday."

As the evening progressed, Evie became increasingly concerned about the coming *Oczepiny*, fearing the Tylers and some of their other guests would consider the ceremony quaint or silly. But soon she had no more time to worry. She could see Jadzia and Mother Sienka speaking to the bandleader, most likely requesting appropriate music. Evie wondered if anyone in this band actually knew any music appropriate to an *Oczepiny*.

They had played a polka or two along with such favorites as the hokey-pokey and the twist—but a polka would make the traditional wedding ceremony seem even more ridiculous.

Jadzia was busy arranging two chairs side by side, each facing the opposite direction, in the center of the dance floor. Peggy, looking in her deep-rose colored bridesmaids' gown not at all like the tomboy she was, assembled the guests into a circle, persuading even the most reluctant to participate. The band began playing "I Love You Truly." *Thank heavens*, thought Evie. She had feared it might be "Roll Out the Barrel." Peggy demonstrated to the guests that they needed to hold hands, and soon the circle was moving slowly to the tempo of the music. Jadzia and Mother Sienka broke through the circle, leading Penny and Scott to the chairs and seating them there.

Then Jadzia took Evie's hand and nodded toward the center where Penny and Scott sat waiting. Evie had not wanted to be a part of this ceremony, had resisted all attempts to draw her in, had dreaded the very thought of it. Yet at this moment, she knew where she belonged.

Mother Sienka rejoined the circle as Evie, giving her cousin a quick kiss on the cheek, joined her daughter and son-in-law. She unpinned Penny's veil and, folding it carefully, placed it on the back of the chair. Glancing at Scott, Evie was amazed at how mature he suddenly looked and at the naked pride that filled his eyes as he beheld his bride.

Evie helped Peggy fasten the apron, which for Polish-Americans had replaced the traditional church hat, around Penny's slim waist, then held Penny in a tight embrace that neither seemed willing to break. But break this embrace Evie must. Suddenly, the significance of the ancient ceremony became clear: Penny had committed to a marriage, not just a wedding. She needed to understand that. And as Evie pulled away from her daughter and joined Penny's hand to Scott's, she knew from the look the couple shared that both did understand.

Turning to rejoin the circle Evie saw not a disparate group of wedding guests but a union of friends, all fervently wishing the best for the young bride and groom who now danced, slowly and sweetly, in the center of the circle. Evie saw glistening eyes everywhere she looked—many guests were crying unabashedly. Every voice was singing, "I love you truly."

When she rejoined the circle, breaking between Mickey and Jadzia, both pressed her hands firmly. Mickey, looking remarkably handsome in his tux despite the tears streaming down his cheeks, bent to kiss her and, suddenly and completely unforeseen, the memory of why she had married him so many years earlier infused Evie with a warmth she had not felt for a very long time.

"Oh, look at that one! What a little devil!" With one hand, Jadzia pointed excitedly at a tiny monkey tweaking the tail of an older, wizened monkey complacently sunning himself on the very top of an immense boulder. Jadzia's other hand was busy lifting what was left of a hot dog—overflowing with tomatoes, onions and the garish green relish that signified "Chicago-style"—toward her mouth. "Mmm, good. Maybe not as good as *kielbasa*, but..."

Evie laughed at the sight of her cousin's twinkling eyes and flushed cheeks. Jadzia's laugh was infectious—and Evie was sure she herself had laughed more this week than she had in the last three years. She marveled at Jadzia's enjoyment of everything she had seen: the standard wonders of the city, of course, like the Art Institute, Buckingham Fountain, the top of the Sears Tower, and the Field Museum. But Jadzia seemed thrilled at far lesser wonders as well: the local supermarket, a hula hoop, Saran wrap. Spending this week with her cousin had, in some strange way, caused Evie to see her own world from a different perspective.

Today, the last full day of Jadzia's visit, Evie had taken her to see Brookfield Zoo. On this unseasonably mild mid-October day, the inhabitants of Baboon Island seemed to be enjoying the sunshine as much as the throngs of zoo visitors delighting in their antics. Sharing a picnic table with her cousin, Evie watched Jadzia rearrange the menagerie of plastic animals—a white polar bear, a blue penguin, a yellow lion, a gray dolphin—that she had collected as souvenirs on this visit. Jadzia had been enchanted by the machines, located throughout the park, that produced them right before the buyer's eyes.

What was it about Jadzia, Evie wondered, that caused her optimistic, almost childlike, enjoyment of life? When she laughed and clapped her hands, she seemed to be expressing the careless happiness of a child. Jadzia had lived through a war, had been recently widowed, was raising teenaged children, and lived an impoverished life in a small town in Communist Europe. The stories she told about waiting in lines and dealing with larcenous, petty officials seemed enough to depress anyone. Evie couldn't resist asking, "Jadzia, how do you do it?"

"Do what?"

"Keep smiling."

"Why not keep smiling?" answered Jadzia, illustrating with a sweep of her arm that seemed to encompass the whole zoo in all its splendor. "There is so much in life to smile about."

"But Jadzia, you lived through a war..."

"Yes, Eva, I *lived*. So many did not. How can I not be grateful for that?"

"But now you live among Communists..." Evie paused, hating the critical tone even she could hear in her voice.

"Yes" Jadzia said, smiling reassuringly at her cousin, "of course, Poland has a Communist government. There would be Communists there."

"But it just sounds so horrible." Evie shuddered at the thought that her cousin lived among people she feared, people who she believed threatened her own way of life.

"To Americans, perhaps. But Eva, Communists are just people, like anyone else—some good, some bad. Many incompetent!" She laughed.

Evie wondered how her cousin could joke about such a thing. "Jadzia, you amaze me. The next thing you'll be saying is that there were good Nazis!"

Jadzia looked closely into her cousin's eyes before answering. How to explain? "Eva," she finally said softly, "not everything is so black or white as you see it. Sometimes people get pulled into things they do not understand. Often people start with only good intentions, but find themselves caught up in situations that are unbearable. They find themselves doing things they would never have thought they could do."

As Evie shook her head in disapproval, Jadzia struggled to think of the words that would make her cousin understand. "I am sorry," she added a bit wearily, "but here, in this wonderful country, it must be hard to understand. I don't quite know how to explain what I mean. You haven't experienced war..."

Evie was not about to accept that statement. Her own war experiences were as vivid to her today as they had been twenty-five years earlier. "Of course we have, Jadzia. Mickey spent years overseas in the army. I worked in a defense factory. We had rationing..."

"Yes, I know," Jadzia interrupted. "But you have never experienced war on your homeland. You never saw your whole village, your whole life, torn apart before your eyes. In a situation like that, sometimes people do not have any choice."

"Jadzia, you always have a choice."

Jadzia's eyes were still on Evie, but she was hearing the echo of an earlier voice saying those exact words many years ago. She envisioned a slim girl in an old white dress, walking away, white-blonde hair streaming down her back. Then a red spot in the very center of her back, vivid against the white, growing like an unfolding rose. Apolonya had chosen death; Jadzia had chosen life. It was a choice Jadzia had never regretted. But how to explain this to Eva, who sat across from her, sincerity shining in her sable eyes. Jadzia feared she never could. And yet that thought pleased her. Her love for Eva made her hope that her cousin would never need to understand.

"Jadzia, I'm sorry. I've gone and put my foot in my mouth again. I don't know what got me going on this subject. Of course I can't begin to understand." Evie blamed herself for putting a pall on this, their last full day together. But all she truly wanted was to comprehend more fully what made her cousin who she was.

"No, no. It is all right. There is nothing to be sorry about."

"But you're crying."

Jadzia pulled a heavily embroidered handkerchief from a pocket in her sweater and, smiling, dabbed at her eyes. "Just for a moment—a sad memory. But I am fine now."

"Are you sure? Can I get you something?"

"No, no. But you said there were alligators in this zoo. Do you remember the first letter you ever wrote to me—when you talked about wanting to see alligators?"

Evie's tilted head signified her effort to remember. And then suddenly, "Oh—I know. I wanted to go to the Century of Progress. Funny that you remembered that!"

"Well, only because of Apolonya. You see, we didn't know about alligators in Poland way back then, and so Apolonya asked her mother...did I ever tell you about Danuta Zadora?" Arm in arm, Jadzia shared yet another story with her cousin as they walked toward the zoo's reptile house.

Charley. Wilhelm. Who would have thought the conversation would have veered so far into the depths of their personal Dark Ages?

It had to be the Sobieski. Jadzia was the one who had suggested stopping at a liquor store on the way back from the zoo, insisting that they needed to share a toast on this, their last night together.

"I have some Chablis at home," suggested Evie.

"No, that will not do. We need Sobieski, or maybe some Lubrowka—some good Polish vodka."

"Vodka, Jadzia? I don't think I ever tasted vodka."

"Then it is about time."

Dinner had been a quick affair, and Mickey, perhaps understanding their wish to be alone this last night of Jadzia's visit, had gone up to bed early. Quite suddenly, amid some rather general comments the women had been sharing about their wartime experiences, Wilhelm's name had entered the conversation. Almost before she knew it, the tale of Jadzia's German romance had slipped through her lips.

"I never knew," said Evie. "You never said anything about him in your letters. Did you love him?"

"I thought I did at the time. He was so beautiful, almost like a young German god—maybe a teenaged Thor. And so unlike many of the men in Niedzieliska—so cultured, so refined."

"What happened? How did it end?"

Jadzia considered telling of the horror of Herr Heinemann's discovery of the two of them together and its aftermath, but quickly decided against that. Some things she would keep close to her heart—never to be shared with anyone. "Oh, I was sent to work in a factory, and Wilhelm probably was sent to war."

"Did he survive the war?"

"I don't know, but I like to think that he did. That he's now the master of that beautiful farm in the Eifel, with a wife and some fat German children."

"Jadzia...again...I'm overwhelmed." Evie paused for a moment to collect her thoughts while Jadzia waited patiently. "You're—you're just so forgiving. I would think you would hate Germans for..."

Jadzia interrupted her. "Not Germans, Eva. Nazis. Not all Germans supported the Nazis."

"I suppose," responded Evie, who had considered something quite remarkable . "You know, Jadzia, as strange as it seems, in a lot of ways we've led the same lives, even though we were so far apart." Evie's bemused smile was caused only partly by the vodka.

"We are like doppelgangers?" Jadzia asked.

"Doppel...what's?"

"Doppelgangers," Jadzia laughed. "Two people who are alike—but not twins—almost like one is the ghost of the other."

Evie considered this concept for a moment before asking, "So who of us is the ghost and who's the real person?"

Jadzia's eyes opened widely. She suddenly understood the implication of Evie's earlier comment. "You say we have led the same lives," she ventured. "There was a Wilhelm in your life too?" she asked. "Tell me, Eva," she pleaded, fearing that Evie's quick shake of the head signaled reluctance.

Evie poured herself another shotglass of the Sobieski, and downed it. Shaking her head and squinting to relieve the stinging brought to her eyes by the drink, she prepared to tell her story: "Yes—but his name was Charley." And another character became part of their shared knowledge.

"And this Charley, did you love him?" Jadzia asked once Evie had finished telling her story.

"It felt like it at the time. Now I don't think so."

"Why did you break apart?"

Evie considered telling her cousin about that awful scene with Henryk, but reconsidered. No reason to bring up unpleasantness that had happened so many years before. "Well," she responded, "Mickey came home, and I made my choice. But I still wonder how different things would have been if we'd gotten together."

"If you had married Charley instead of Mickey?"

"Yes, and then I get so ashamed." Evie, her eyes downcast, slowly shook her head.

"Ashamed of what?"

"Of what I did. Jadzia, I was engaged to Mickey at the time." With a bent knuckle, Evie dabbed at the beginnings of tears forming in the corners of her eyes.

"Oh, Eva," Jadzia replied, reaching out to stroke her cousin's cheek. "It was war time. And Mickey was far away for many years. Maybe never coming home. You were young—almost a child."

"That doesn't make it right."

"No, of course not. But what makes it right is all these years since. Does Mickey know?"

"He's never said anything. But sometimes I've wondered. There are a lot of things we don't really talk about."

"Have you been a good wife to him?"

"Well, I've tried. It hasn't been easy sometimes. Those first few months after the girls got arrested," Evie sighed heavily. "Jadzia, I almost left him. He was drinking so much then. All we ever did was fight."

"But you didn't leave him."

"No. No. I stayed ...for the girls, and, I guess, for something else."

"For what else?" probed Jadzia.

"I...I don't know."

Jadzia paused, hoping that Eva herself would find an answer to her question. Then she suggested, "Maybe for love?"

Evie looked directly into her cousin's eyes. "Jadzia, of course I..."

"No, not 'of course'," Jadzia interrupted. "Mickey loves you—truly loves you. I can see it in everything he does and says." Evie tried to respond, but Jadzia, cutting her off, continued. "And what I saw between you two at the wedding. I cannot believe that you do not love him—really and truly love him."

Evie again attempted a response, but this time she cut herself off, not really knowing what to say. Was their love really so strong that others could sense it?

"Eva," Jadzia pressed on, "you need to forgive Mickey."

"Well, I always do...I have to forgive him for something or other almost every day. That's what marriage is all about."

"No, not for arguing or for leaving a glass on the table or socks on the floor." Jadzia paused, hoping to find a way to explain that would not offend her cousin. "Forgive me if I intrude too much. But you need to forgive Mickey for not being Charley—or really, for not being your memory of Charley, which is not really the man you remember. In your mind Charley is young—someone you knew during a very exciting and frightening time—and a new lover, not a husband of many years. The Charley of your dreams does not exist. Maybe, Eva, he never did."

Evie wanted to respond, but could not find the words to do so.

"And you need to forgive yourself. Have you been a faithful wife to Mickey?"

"Yes, of course."

"You say 'of course' as though it were the only possibility. But all these years together. You are a beautiful woman, a woman who, I know, would have had opportunities to be unfaithful. But your faithfulness to your husband, this must mean something. Forgive him. Forgive yourself."

Evie spent several minutes in silence, gently twisting her wedding band around her finger. Jadzia, wisely, was silent as well.

Could Jadzia be right? Truly, Jadzia was only telling her what she already knew—what she had, for some inexplicable reason, resisted for so long. Was it the emotion of the wedding that had begun to make it clear? Or Jadzia's visit? She knew she loved Mickey. True, they'd had their bad times. But he was her soul mate—had always been. She had made the right decision so many years earlier. Finally, she answered. "I will, Jadzia," she whispered, perhaps more to herself than to her cousin. "I will."

And forgive me, Jadzia thought, fervently wishing for the courage to explain why on this night of revelations she too needed forgiveness, but was unable to summon that courage.

"Oh God, I wish you didn't have to go." Evie held Jadzia's hands so tightly that both women felt their wedding rings pressing painfully between their fingers. Neither cared.

"United Flight 47 now loading at Gate F5." The pert young woman speaking into a microphone at the counter was merciless.

"I know. I know," sobbed Jadzia. "But I *must* go now." She attempted a weak smile. "They won't hold the plane for me, you know."

"I feel like I have so much more to say to you—one week wasn't nearly enough," cried Evie.

"And I...I too...have things to tell you. I wish...I wish we had more time... There are things, Eva, things ..."

"All those with tickets on United Flight 47 please board immediately."

Evie glared for one quick moment at the attendant who was pointing toward a steward already preparing to close the door to the jetport. "What things?" she asked. But Jadzia was already pulling away. With one last squeeze of her cousin's hand, Evie pleaded, "Write to me!"

"Of course I will," Jadzia answered over her shoulder as she hurried toward the jetport leading to her plane. "Thank you for everything, Eva. I love you!"

"Thank *you*, Jadzia. I love you too. So much!"

Jadzia stepped into the jetport entrance but stopped once more, turning to her cousin one last time. She knew she shouldn't leave like this. There were things Eva deserved to know. But how could she explain—here, in this amazing country. Here Eva would never understand...but in Poland, perhaps...

"Come visit me," Jadzia called. "Promise you will come visit me in Poland."

"I will. I promise. I will."

Chapter Seventeen

Evie, Niedzieliska

October, 1985

Regret. A gritty emotion, overpowering and useless. One that leaves a sour taste in the mouth.

Regret hammered Evie's head, made sore, salty wells of her eyes. It stooped her shoulders, stuck like a fishbone in her throat, rendering the simplest phrase unutterable. Most of all, it gripped her heart mercilessly. *Why* had she waited?

Evie thought back to that day in the airport fifteen years earlier. She had told Jadzia—no, *promised* her—that she would visit her in Poland. She had repeated that promise many times over the years—Jadzia had so wanted her to come. Now that she was finally on a plane bound for Warsaw, it was too late. Jadzia was gone, dead from lung cancer at fifty-eight. Her promise no longer possible to keep.

She berated herself for not arranging a flight immediately upon hearing of Jadzia's diagnosis. But who would have known the combination of a particularly deadly cancer and the inadequacies of the Polish medical system would so rapidly accelerate Jadzia's decline. By the time Evie realized the extent of Jadzia's illness, nothing—not daily trips to the city passport office to plead her case for priority, not the endless repetition of prayers she only vaguely remembered from her youth—could get her there on time.

"Go anyway," Mickey had urged on the horrible day they had received the call from Poland, the peculiarity of such a call itself a warning of dire tidings. "You already have your ticket. You've wanted to do this for years."

Alfons too had urged her not to cancel her trip. "Please come," he had pleaded on the phone. "You are welcome here. You can meet some of your Polish family and see the home where your mama grew up." Evie knew, from her letters, that Jadzia had loved the farm, and that her last years there had been among her happiest.

But what good would it do for Evie to see the old homestead now? The person she most wanted to see was no longer there. Still, the plans had already been made, and it wasn't as if anyone really needed her at home.

Mickey certainly didn't need her. When he had retired the year before, they had for a short time fallen into a pattern of constant bickering and sniping at each other. She knew he was bored and restless, but why should that become *her* problem? Couldn't he find some better use of his time than suggesting more "efficient" housekeeping methods to her—as though she needed his advice after over forty years of managing the house herself—or clipping new recipes from magazines, leaving them on the kitchen counter for her to find? Some days she cursed Social Security. But they had adjusted, as they always did. That was their pattern.

And the girls—they were involved in their own lives. Penny and their three children lived in Los Angeles with Scott, now a successful patent attorney. Evie saw them only on holidays. Peggy, divorced for the second time, lived in Chicago, but between her job managing an art gallery and her pantheon of interests—yoga and aerobics classes, travel to exotic places like Egypt and India, dabbling in oils—her visits to Winston Estates weren't nearly frequent enough to suit Evie.

Steffie had found love late in life, marrying a retired doctor and living almost nine months every year in his home in Sarasota. Evie saw them only during their long summer vacations up north. She saw Henryk, who was now living with his second wife in California, even less frequently.

Evie still enjoyed bridge with a few friends from the country club. But too many of her days were filled with TV game shows and soap operas, interrupted only by the mundane chores of cleaning and cooking for a household of two. A pointless life. And yet when someone—Jadzia—had truly needed her, she had failed. Guilt pressed her like a skin that had suddenly become too tight.

The plane landed in a gray mist that almost obscured the granite building that was the Warsaw airport terminal. While fairly modern, the terminal was small and did not bustle with the activity of O'Hare. Evie's fears of not finding Marysia and Alfons, who had promised to meet her flight, had been unfounded. Other than a few soldiers in drab brown uniforms lackadaisically strolling the corridors and the passengers who had accompanied her on the flight, very few were waiting within the terminal's dreary, mustard colored walls. Evie was able to recognize Marysia and Alfons immediately.

Marysia, much as Jadzia had described her in letters, was still a round-cheeked, bosomy bundle of energy, whose sparkling blue eyes radiated a youthfulness that belied the predominance of gray in her hair. Standing behind the partition that separated passengers from greeters, she took turns blotting her eyes with a starched white handkerchief and waving it in the air to attract Evie's attention.

Alfons, standing quietly beside her, was much more handsome than Evie had expected. At well over six feet tall and with a slim, athletic build, he stood out among the other men in the airport. His face, weathered and ruggedly handsome, with chiseled lines and a square jaw, was crowned by a thick mass of unruly brown hair streaked with copper and gold. Indigo eyes, set deep amidst tiny wrinkles that suggested pensiveness over laughter, appraised her.

"You are here," cried Marysia, pulling Evie into a hug the moment she passed through the narrow exit gate. "I am so sorry for your loss." But Evie knew that Jadzia's death had been a great loss to Marysia as well, who had remained a close friend and frequent visitor, even after Jadzia and Alfons had moved to the farm. Marysia had rushed to Jadzia's bedside two weeks earlier, when Jadzia's condition had become critical. Both she and Alfons had been with Jadzia in her last moments.

From Alfons, Evie received a formal bow and a firm but warm handshake. It took just minutes to locate Evie's one suitcase and a very short time to pass through the almost deserted corridors and out into the airport parking lot.

Later, Evie would remember very little of the first three hours of the drive to Niedzieliska, crushed with Marysia into the tiny back seat of Alfons' Fiat. They traveled on a two-lane country road through flat, grassy plains and marshland in a land empty of billboards, the only diversion being an occasional farmhouse set well away from the road, occasionally nestled in a small cluster of trees.

Alfons drove silently. Marysia tried valiantly to initiate conversation, pointing out landmarks and small towns far in the distance, and once a pelican, its swooping flight seeming to Evie out of place so far from the sea. Evie tried to respond, but the combination of sorrow, guilt, and exhaustion finally defeated her efforts, leaving both women staring morosely out their respective windows. Evie cursed herself for having come.

Eventually the landscape was transformed into the low hills and pine forests about which Jadzia had written so often. Marysia, perhaps sensing new interest arising in Evie, began acting once again as travel guide. Some of the names of towns, rivers and churches sounded familiar to Evie, and now she examined the places to which Marysia pointed, occasionally asking a question: "Didn't Jadzia have a friend who lived in that town?" "Didn't Jadzia once go to a wedding there?" "Wasn't that the stream where she swam as a child?"

Finally Alfons pulled onto a dirt path, stopping before a stone cottage with a red tile roof. Evie looked around her. There was the ancient stone barn, looking just as Jadzia had described it, and the chicken coop. There the outhouse, probably kept today only as a memento of earlier times. Off to the right stood a cluster of birches, surely the location of the well that had been the backdrop of so many of the major events of Jadzia's life.

Alfons helped both women out of the cramped back seat, then stayed behind to collect Evie's suitcase from the front seat while Marysia led her, one arm firmly around her waist, to the cottage. "Anyone home?" Marysia called at the door, knocking, then pushing it open.

"Stasiu must already be with Gienek," she offered, ushering Evie in with a broad wave of her arm. "You can use Stasiu's bedroom while you're here."

"Oh no, I didn't mean to put anyone out."

"Not at all. Those two old bachelors will have a grand time together, drinking vodka and bragging about romantic conquests that never happened," Marysia laughed. "They were always friends, even as boys, but once Jadzia married Alfons and they became brothers-in-law, they were inseparable. You'll meet them at dinner tonight."

Evie examined the room where Jadzia had played as a child, where her own and Jadzia's mothers had done the same. It was large for a room, but small for a house, perhaps twenty feet by twenty feet: she knew the only other rooms were two tiny bedrooms and a storage area. Painted white, the room now boasted new wainscoting in a dark cherry.

But for the most part, stepping into the room was like stepping into history. Everything Jadzia had ever written of, from rich-colored cherry furniture to rose-patterned china, was here, arranged in much the same way Jadzia had described. Evie noticed only two innovations: a few bare light bulbs strung in the corners of the room and a shrine holding not only a crucifix and a picture of the Black Madonna, but also pictures of Pope John Paul II and, perhaps not so strange as it first seemed, John Kennedy.

"Is this..." Evie stammered, "this can't be the original furniture, can it?"

"Oh, no. But very similar, according to Jadzia," answered Marysia. "When she and Alfons moved back here, it was not much more than a den. Your cousin Stasiu—a good man, but really never the same after the war—lived here almost like a bear, with just a couple of chairs and a mat on the floor. Jadzia wanted it to look much like it had when she was a girl."

Evie followed Marysia to a room just large enough for a full bed, a miniature dresser and a nightstand. A blue *pierzyna*, a goose down comforter that must have been four inches deep, reminded her of the one that had graced her parents' bed in the old apartment on Haddon Avenue.

"Would you like to freshen up?" offered Marysia, pointing to a basin and pitcher, heavily patterned in a rose design similar to the china in the other room.

"Yes, thank you" answered Evie, not completely understanding the significance of the pitcher. "The bathroom is...?"

"Outside."

Evie shuddered. Apparently the outhouse had not been kept just for sentimental reasons, after all.

"If you need to," continued Marysia, "well, later on tonight, you'll want this." Opening the top drawer of the dresser, Marysia produced an old-fashioned flashlight, really just a bulb set in housing, similar to what miners used many years earlier. "Can I get you anything? Perhaps you are hungry?"

"No," said Evie. "I'm just so tired. The flight..."

"Of course. Why don't you take a nap. Dinner won't be ready for hours." With that Marysia slipped out the door, quietly closing it behind her.

Left to herself in a tiny room in a little cottage near a small town almost half way around the world, Evie wondered why she had ever consented to come. Still, she could feel the presence of Jadzia in this place. But what small compensation was that for all she had lost? Overcome with exhaustion and sorrow, she collapsed onto the *pierzyna*, its thickness enveloping her body in smooth softness. Soon she was crying into the pillow, long, deep sobs, and soon after that she fell into a deep, dreamless sleep.

Evie woke to homey smells, pungent and savory. Rousing herself, she realized from the room's darkness that she must have slept for hours. Sheepishly, she opened the bedroom door.

"Ah, Eva, you are awake," said Marysia, turning from the cast iron stove where she had been stirring the contents of a massive pot. "Are you hungry?"

Evie was surprised to find that she was ravenous.

"Please, let me introduce your cousin Stasiu and Alfons' brother Gienek." Evie only then noticed the men sitting at the heavy table, who were similarly tall, stooped and wiry, with thinning yellow hair and broad, nearly toothless smiles. The slightly shorter one, she learned, was her cousin Stasiu, and both men stood, bowing and kissing her hand in the old way, upon being introduced.

"Something smells wonderful," complimented Evie.

"*Bigos,*" explained Marysia, "Hunter's Stew. Didn't your mama ever make *bigos?*"

The smell was certainly familiar, but Evie's mother's kitchen had ceased operations over forty-five years earlier. "I don't remember. What's in it?"

"Everything," laughed Stasiu.

"He's right," affirmed Marysia. "It's pretty much whatever you have left in the house. Always sauerkraut, but beef, lamb, venison—whatever meat you have—*kielbasa,* onion."

"Mushrooms, bacon," continued Gienek. "And a glass or two of wine. That makes a good sauce." Obviously Gienek's bachelorhood had necessitated his learning to cook.

"Some people like apples and sugar," continued Marysia. Stasiu's and Gienek's grimaces indicated that they were not among that group. "It's a traditional campfire meal, but people make it in the kitchen, too."

"Can I help?" asked Evie.

"You can slice the bread." Marysia handed her a large knife and a heavy loaf of dark rye encrusted with caraway seeds, then reached for a tray of small glass bowls of appetizers—pickled mushrooms, cucumbers, some meat in aspic—to place on the table.

"*Bigos* and rye bread—now that's a meal," asserted Gienek. "And my favorite—pigs' feet. You like them, Eva?"

Evie smiled weakly.

Sitting down to eat, Marysia explained that Alfons had some business in town and would not be back until much later.

"And your husband?" Evie asked, taking a moment to remember his name. "Tadek. Is Tadek here?"

"Back home in Katowice," Marysia responded. "I'm sure the old man is more than delighted to have me out of his way for a few days. But he'll be here a couple of days after All Saints Day, when it's time to take you back to Warsaw."

"You are too kind."

"Nonsense. Jadzia and I were like sisters. You and Jadzia were like sisters. So what does that make us, eh?"

Dinner was wonderful—everything fresh and wholesome—and Evie's three companions entertained her with humorous tales of farm life and small town goings-on. Apparently Niedzieliska was a hotbed of scandal, with rumors of mild flirtations and petty crimes abounding. When Evie, carrying dirty plates to the kitchen counter, looked out the window, she saw a night sky filled with stars, many more than she'd ever seen back home.

Retrieving her flashlight, she excused herself and tramped out to the outhouse, a truly medieval structure she vowed to visit as seldom and for as short a time as possible. Exiting the structure she turned toward the house, but the beam of the flashlight picked up the outline of a path leading to the cluster of birches she had noticed on first arriving.

She felt drawn to the path. Despite the darkness and the unfamiliarity of her surroundings she followed it, coming soon to a circular clearing. In its center stood the stone well that had figured so prominently in Jadzia's and Apolonya's childhoods. Smaller than she had expected, its flat surface, smoothed with time, beckoned her. Turning off the flashlight, she sat on the hard stone surface of the lip of the well, hearing only a gentle wind rustling the uppermost branches of the birches. Slowly, she felt herself pulling together. She knew she was in a place sacred to her family: those she had never met, those she knew and had lost, and even in some strange way those who were yet to come.

In the first three days of Evie's visit, Alfons and Marysia took her on a few short trips into the countryside in Alfons' Fiat, but most of their time was spent in and near Niedzieliska, visiting distant relatives or friends of Jadzia's over coffee and pastry during the day, or at the farmhouse, entertaining neighbors over vodka and creamed herring in the evening.

Often conversations turned to the Solidarity movement. *Solidarnosc* excited everyone in Niedzieliska, rekindling national pride and making their independence from the Soviet Union more than just a far-off dream. Everyone wanted to know what Evie had heard about their movement— what did the Americans think? Was *Solidarnosc* prominent in the newspapers and television? Did the Americans support the Poles?

Did the Americans admire Lech Walesa, leader of the shipyard strike in Gdansk and winner two years earlier of the Nobel Peace Prize? Were Polish-American Catholics thrilled when Karol Wojtyla, Pope John Paul II, was elected, becoming the spiritual leader of a billion people? Could Evie champion their cause in the free world—talk to people, write editorials of support?

Caught up in their enthusiasm, she agreed to do what she could, but later, on reflection, she doubted that was very much. She had heard about Solidarity and Pope John Paul II, of course, but those issues were of very little interest in her world. Winston Estates seemed almost a universe away from Poland. No one there spoke of such things—the newspapers and television concentrated on American events—and besides, Evie herself wasn't what one would call political.

It seemed every villager in town wanted the opportunity to meet Jadzia's cousin from faraway America, and Evie found that she was related, if only distantly, to a good many of them. The words "Eva, I have heard so much about you!" followed nearly every introduction.

"Of course they know about you," asserted Marysia. "Jadzia spoke of you often. She shared parts of your wonderful letters with all her friends."

"She spoke often of me? I can't imagine why."

"Surely you know how proud she was of you."

Evie was silent. What could Jadzia have possibly seen in her to occasion pride? After all, it was Jadzia who had survived both the Nazis and the Communists, Jadzia who had spent years bringing new life into the world. What had she, Evie, ever done?

"Jadzia spoke of your beauty and intelligence," Marysia continued, seeming to read her thoughts. "She believed you were the best wife and mother she had ever known. She told us so many stories of her trip to America, and especially about your daughter's wedding—how beautiful it was. That trip was one of the most wonderful times of her life. Mostly she spoke of the kindness of your heart, of how she could always depend on your love."

A lot of good that did, thought Evie bitterly, once again berating herself for coming to Poland days, no, *years* too late.

On her third day in Poland, Alfons took them to Czestochowa to see the icon of the Black Madonna at the Jasna Gora Monastery. Jadzia had spoken often in her letters of the beauty of the medieval town and the majesty of its famous shrine. Passing through the immense red brick wall built hundreds of years earlier to protect the monastery, Evie considered, for perhaps the tenth time during this trip, the antiquity of Poland, where not only monasteries but even barns could be hundreds of years old.

The basilica itself, with its tall, square spire and copper roofs, was impressive, the onion domes of the chapel reminding Evie of Greek Orthodox churches she had seen in Chicago. The courtyard, its buff-colored stone arches opening into the surrounding covered patio, looked to Evie like something that would not have been out of place in Morocco.

The icon itself, the Madonna, intricately gowned and crowned in gold, carried in a highly formal and unrealistic pose an infant whose tiny face held the look of a young man much older and wiser. Though an image Evie had seen hundreds of times throughout her life, here the Madonna moved her deeply and unexpectedly. In fact, Poland itself was not what she had expected. There was a depth here—something she could sense, but not truly describe. A depth that she felt, in some strange way, could envelop her and, perhaps, make her whole.

Back in Niedzieliska, everyone seemed very excited about the coming holiday, All Saints Day. "Let me get this right," said Evie to Marysia. "You celebrate this holiday in the cemetery?"

"Yes, of course," Marysia answered. "You do not do this in America?"

"No. Some people go to cemeteries on Memorial Day, especially if they have family who died in the war." But Evie had never been one of them, considering visiting cemeteries depressing, even a little ghoulish.

These Poles certainly had some strange customs, but Evie's desire to be a good guest and her longing to learn more about Jadzia's life assured her participation in the holiday. She had not yet summoned the nerve to visit Jadzia's grave—today would be the day.

"You will see," said Marysia. "It will be beautiful."

October 31 dawned clear and crisp, a hint of winter freshening already pristine air. Waking early, Evie found Marysia and Alfons already up, assembling various materials in the ubiquitous canvas and net bags she had seen everyone carrying. After a quick breakfast of *kasza* and coffee, they stepped outside into an almost balmy day, with a pale blue sky devoid of clouds.

They had not walked more than two minutes when they were joined by a family from a neighboring farm. The next ten minutes brought four more families to their group, and by the time they reached the outskirts of Niedzieliska, Evie could see dozens converging from every path toward town.

Evie's first sight of the town square two days earlier had been painful, reminding her of tragedies which had occurred on the stones of its granite courtyard. She wondered how the people of Niedzieliska could live, having to pass every day the site of so many painful memories. She wondered where, exactly, Apolonya had died—and where her own grandmother's life had ended. No physical signs of those horrors appeared, but the visions of those days must be etched into the minds and hearts of many in the town.

But now the square was transformed, miraculously filled with stalls of flower vendors. Evie, Marysia and Alfons wandered among stands of potted chrysanthemums ranging from the palest yellows to the boldest bronzes and oranges. Buckets of lilies, their pure white a stark contrast to the vibrancy surrounding them, were everywhere, and many counters displayed roses ranging from the tiniest pink tea varieties to fist-sized scarlet beauties. Pine wreaths were stacked against walls and tables, their tangy smells making the fragrance of the roses that much sweeter. Most stalls also held counters of glass votives of all sizes and colors, more candles, Evie was certain, than she had ever seen in her entire life.

"It smells like heaven," said Evie to no one in particular, having gotten separated from Marysia and Alfons at some juncture of mums and lilies. But soon she saw them, their arms filled with fragrant, colorful purchases, waving her over to flow with them into the stream of people heading toward the open cemetery gate.

Once inside, Evie found it a place of beauty. Bare branches of birches, oaks and willows, some of the trees hundreds of years old, stood guard over gray stone monuments and gravestones. Rolling hills, colored in their hollows by the oranges and yellows and bronzes of fallen leaves, had become canvases of brilliant color wherever floral offerings had been placed. Many people, some sitting on low benches, some standing in couples or small groups, prayed or spoke softly to their neighbors.

Evie followed Alfons and Marysia up a slight rise to an area dominated by an ancient marble statue of the Angel Gabriel—its finish eroded to a soft milky white—finally stopping at the low stone bench and wrought iron lantern that marked the Czarnecki plot. One particular grave was a mound of floral wreaths, each decorated with a wide purple or white ribbon printed with Polish words.

"Yes," whispered Marysia, leaning toward her. "This is Jadzia's."

Evie read some of the sentiments: "The last good-bye." "To a dear, dear friend." "I shall never forget you." All of these sentiments expressed her feelings as well.

Marysia and Alfons began busily arranging floral garlands and pine wreaths on every grave in the family plot and spacing dozens of vigil lights neatly on the ground, reserving some for the mounted lantern. Soon Alfons said quietly, "We need to go to the Zadora plot. Would you prefer to stay here?"

Evie nodded gratefully, appreciating their offer of solitude. She tried to pray but found the old requiems of her childhood hollow and inappropriate. For a long while she studied the tombstones, finding her whole family's history carved here in cement.

She found, side by side, the simple gravestones of her aunt and uncle, Bronislawa and Stanislaus, and next to them a more elaborate marker for her grandmother, Stella, whose defiance of the Nazis had cost her life. She found no grave but a small marker for her cousin Marek, who had been last seen jumping out of a boxcar decades earlier. Czarnecki graves, many of children, two of women who had lived to be octogenarians, dated back over a century.

She was joined after some time by a tiny sprite of a woman, a former classmate of Jadzia's, who shared stories of their time together as rambunctious nine-year-olds. An elderly man spoke to Evie of his regard for her grandmother, who had brought three of his children into the world. Friends of Marek and Magda, who had been in Niedzieliska just the previous week for their mother's funeral, stopped by to meet the *Ciotka* Eva they had heard so much about. Evie realized that she had had deep, living connections to this village her whole life.

"It's time to return to the house," said Marysia when she and Alfons returned, now empty-handed.

"Already?" she sighed, trying to hide her disappointment.

"And you thought a cemetery was a strange place for a holiday," smiled Marysia. "Don't worry. We'll be back tomorrow."

Early the evening of November 1st, Evie walked with Marysia back to the cemetery, their journey mirroring the previous day's trip, but in the deepening darkness those who joined them were quieter, more solemn. Evie had declined Marysia's invitation to attend All Souls' Day mass, pleading a headache. But in truth, her own doubts and lack of faith made her uncomfortable attending religious services with such obviously devout Catholics.

By the time they reached the cemetery the sky was already dark, but the ground twinkled with thousands of flickering vigil lights, making Evie feel as though she were stepping into an enchanted place. Arriving at the Czarnecki plot they found Alfons seated on the stone bench, his elbows on his knees, his face in his hands.

"You miss her so much," said Marysia, sitting beside him.

"She was my world," he answered simply. For a few minutes Marysia and Alfons sat together on the bench, Evie quietly standing beside them. Soon others came to visit and to pray and sing with them, singly or in small groups.

Evie had begun to believe that she must have, by now, met every last person in Niedzieliska, but she was mistaken. Many came with yet more stories to tell: a distant cousin who remembered Evie's mother's skill at milking, an old man who confessed to having been an ardent but unsuccessful suitor of Evie's Aunt Bronislawa many years previously. As night progressed, a full moon in a cloudless sky lit every tree and monument, starkly defining their outlines.

Marysia said she wished to visit some friends, nodding to Alfons, who nodded back. Several more people stopped by, but soon very few were left in the cemetery. The murmur of voices stilled, leaving only occasional rustling from the leafless trees. Evie quietly joined Alfons on the stone bench.

Finally Alfons, turning to her, cleared his throat, the sound piercing the absolute silence of the cemetery. "Jadzia spoke of you the day she died," Alfons said. "She was concerned about you."

How like Jadzia to think of her at such a time, Evie thought. "Jadzia was truly a saint," she said to Alfons, looking sadly at the lilies on Jadzia's grave, their white glowing in the moonlight.

"No, Eva. She was not a saint. She was a woman."

Evie now looked at Alfons, confused. "Well, of course. I just meant..."

"She would not wish to be canonized, Eva," he insisted. "There is something she wanted to tell you fifteen years ago, when she visited you in America. She couldn't then, afraid you would not understand. And at the time she feared for me as well. And so she left you this."

With these words he handed her a letter, which Evie took with trembling hands. She recognized the writing immediately—one last letter from Jadzia—one last treasure from her dearest friend. Yet Alfons' words disturbed her. What could this letter contain? What was it that Jadzia believed she would not understand?

Their silent walk back did nothing to satisfy her curiosity or alleviate her sense of misgiving. Arriving at the cottage, Alfons immediately got into the Fiat, telling her, but without explanation, that he would spend the night in town. As she entered the cottage, she noticed all the bare bulbs lit brightly, an unusual extravagance, and Marysia nowhere in sight. The table was set with a tea service and a small china plate of *chrusciki* and *kolaczki*, but Evie was anything but hungry. Sitting down, she opened her letter:

My dearest cousin Eva,

If you are reading this, then I know you have arrived safely in Poland to find me no longer here. How I wished to see your beautiful face one last time! But, dear cousin and dearer friend, I am sustained by the knowledge that we shall meet again in a better place, and so I do not fear death.

I am very weak, so this letter must be much shorter than I had wished. I cannot fully express how much our friendship has meant to me. Your love and constant devotion, your generosity and kindness in all things, have helped me in ways you cannot imagine. They have given me strength to go on, even at times when I had little hope.

Evie wiped a rush of tears from her cheeks. How could Jadzia have felt this way? Jadzia was the strong one, the woman of fierce determination and spirit. Evie was humbled by the thought that she, in some way, had helped sustain her cousin.

And so, it is this kindness and generosity that leads me to ask one last favor of you. Please, be kind to my husband. Help him through his sorrow. Try to understand what I am about to tell you.

I truly loved Roman. He was a man of compassion and character, and without him, I could not have survived the sorrow and devastation of the war. We made a very good life together, and our children have been the greatest joy of my life.

At his funeral, I was crushed with grief, but heartened by the people of Niedzieliska, who welcomed me back so lovingly and did all they could to ease my pain. I knew this was the place to bring my children and continue my life. I was told that Alfons, Apolonya's brother, had returned to Niedzieliska, and wished to pay his respects. Of course, I welcomed the chance to see someone from my childhood, someone who I had believed dead and who I never expected to see again. But at the moment he entered the room, I saw immediately that it was not Alfons, but Antek, who stood at the doorway.

Yes, I was shocked, and in some ways, horrified. Before me stood a Nazi, a man in some way responsible for so much grief and suffering. But before me also stood the young boy I had played with as a child, the young man I had danced with at a wedding, the man who, I realized, I had loved every day of my life from the moment I first saw him. My horror was soon overcome by joy.

It may be very hard for you to understand the decision I made—to welcome Antek back into my life, to become his wife—but I beg you to open your eyes and your heart to him, and to our lives in Poland. Only then will you understand and forgive me for not telling you sooner.

I leave you now, for the last time. Kiss your family—your darling Mickey, your beautiful girls, your sweet grandchildren, your dear sister—for me. Tell them I love them all. But most of all, know that I will always carry with me the special blessings of the love that has been ours to share.

Your

Jadzia

Evie's understanding grew slowly. Once Jadzia's meaning became clear to her, the letter dropped from her fingers, its delicate pages fluttering to the floor. She did not hear the bedroom door open, and became aware of Marysia standing before her only on hearing her strained voice.

"Jadzia made him promise to give you the letter."

"It would have better for me not to know," Evie replied quietly, pouring tea into a delicate rose-patterned cup and taking a sip. It was hot: it burned her lips. She hardly noticed. "You've known of course—for a long time?"

"From the very beginning."

"And Gienek knows...and Stasiu?"

"Yes, of course. And a few others in the town."

"And..." Evie could not really be hearing this. "And no one told?"

"No, Eva, no one," Marysia said, smiling sadly. "If anyone had known, Alfons would not be here now."

"You mean Antek."

"Very well—Antek. We don't call him that anymore." Marysia fiddled with some lace at the collar of her robe.

"What I don't understand is," said Evie, her voice now rising, "how could Jadzia, how could any of you live with him, knowing for all these years? The man's a murderer—a monster."

"You've been in this house with him for four days now," answered Marysia, shaking her head slowly. "Did you think he was a monster?"

"If I had known, I wouldn't have spent even five minutes with him! And Jadzia—after everything she suffered with the Nazis—I just don't understand."

"It's easy to call someone a name," Marysia said slowly, "a Nazi, a Communist. But you have to look beyond that to the man, to the whole person. It's..." Marysia paused, obviously seeking inspiration. "Well, it's somewhat like the *bigos*." Marysia paused for a moment, then seemed to find a way to explain. "The *bigos*, it has everything in it—sauerkraut, mushrooms, meat, maybe wine—and it's different every time. But every *bigos* has its own flavor, and it wouldn't be the same without every ingredient that went into it."

What? Evie thought. Was this supposed to explain why her cousin, why a whole family and the good part of a village, for God's sake, had hidden a criminal who should have been spending the past forty years in prison? Or even why her cousin, her best friend, had kept such an important part of her life secret from her for so many years? Evie glared at Marysia, unable to hide her anger.

"He was a boy," continued Marysia. "He didn't understand until it was too late."

Marysia continued speaking into Evie's silence. "Eva," she pleaded, "you cannot know how much he mourned his sister and the others who died here. He never killed anyone who wasn't trying to kill him. And Jadzia loved him so. They were very happy together."

"And that makes everything all right? That she loved him?" Evie asked bitterly. Marysia sighed deeply before answering. "Eva, forgive me for saying this, but it is wrong for you to judge in this matter. You were not here. Americans have never experienced what it is like to be in an occupied country. Everyone in Niedzieliska who is old enough to have been in the war has done something he is ashamed of—some act of cowardice or foolishness or desperation he wishes had never happened. We still have to live our lives."

No, Evie hadn't experienced war, at least not in the way the people of this village had. Was this why Jadzia had not trusted her with this greatest of secrets? But was that any excuse? Surely there were actions that could never be justified. And just as surely, Antek's actions during the war were among them.

"Jadzia made him promise to tell you all this for a reason," continued Marysia. "She said to me, before she died, that you needed to understand that sometimes we have to accept things we cannot change."

Evie glared at the other woman. "Oh, well, thank you for that counsel," she muttered. Marysia had truly gone too far. How dare she, or anyone in this village, cast stones her way. "I didn't realize that Jadzia was able to find time to get her degree in psychology along with all her other accomplishments."

"Eva,…"

"Not now, please. I can't talk about this anymore tonight." With that Evie strode to her bedroom door, closing it firmly behind her, finding refuge in the dark, womb-like warmth of the *pierzyna*.

While the previous day had held the warmth of late autumn, the following day forecast winter. Yesterday's gentle breeze had become a biting blast that swirled the fallen leaves into whirlpools of color. Evie desperately wished to leave Niedzieliska immediately, to get at least as far away as Warsaw. Perhaps she could find an earlier flight, or if not, a hotel for the night in Warsaw where nobody knew her.

She needed to call the airport, but the only telephone she had seen was in the town hall. She believed she could find her way to town in the light, but then changed her mind. The last thing she wanted was to run into some of the local denizens who would doubtless try to entertain her with more rural folklore that she had no desire, now, to hear.

She thought she might go for a walk in the countryside, but decided that course of action would surely lead to her getting lost. Being a city girl, every hillside, every stand of trees looked the same.

She found herself once again drawn to the well. There, with the birches cutting off some of the wind's force, she could sit in solitude and decide what to do. She listened for sounds that would warn her of someone following her. But no one came.

On reaching the well, she first stared into the woods, noticing trees other than birches, wondering what they were. There were shrubs as well, some obviously fruit-bearing varieties, perhaps the currants Jadzia had so often written about. Becoming restless, she picked up a handful of stones and began dropping them into the well, soon learning to differentiate between the faraway ping of the smaller stones and the substantial splash of the larger. After the sound of the last stone echoed away in the well, Evie stood staring into the black opening.

She wondered how Antek had managed his subterfuge. Many Nazis had escaped to Argentina after the war: that part of his story was probably true. Returning to Poland would have involved false papers, perhaps bribes. Maybe he had had help from inside—Jadzia? Perhaps Jadzia had been in on it from the very start.

And what had possessed her cousin? Was it because Jadzia had loved him as a young girl? That kind of attraction, Evie knew, lasted; she had found herself, even after all these years, occasionally thinking of Charley Honeycutt, of how different her life might have been. Besides, Antek was an attractive man even now; years ago, he must have been truly handsome. Would physical attraction have been enough? Still, she could never understand how Jadzia could have betrayed...

She could never understand... The words echoed with a hollow ring. Evie told herself those words were only an expression: they didn't really mean anything, certainly not that she was the rigid, unaccepting person Marysia seemed to think she was. Besides, no one in her life needed her understanding or acceptance.

Well, perhaps her daughters. She had to admit she was disappointed that, despite the closeness she had shared with them as children, they had chosen to grow apart from her, to close her out of their adult lives. Penny lived in California, of course. Even Peggy who lived just thirty miles away visited almost as infrequently as her sister.

And Charley. What a disappointment he had been! But then, would she have been any happier married to Charley than she had been with Mickey? And hadn't she, after all, shared a good life with Mickey? He was a good man, faithful and loving, but he wasn't Charley.

She shook her head. Why had she even thought such a thing? Surely she wasn't the kind of person who would blame a man simply for not being another man. No, she could not possibly have been that unfair to her husband of almost forty years.

The real villain of her childhood had been her father. And despite his failure as a father, hadn't she been a good daughter, taking care of him in his old age, never reviling him, as he'd certainly deserved, for hurting her? She had resented this, of course. Who wouldn't? But she had come to realize that he had been a widower with no clear understanding of how to raise his three surviving children. She had forgiven him, hadn't she?

If only her mother had survived! Then things would have been completely different. Her mother would have been a buffer against her sordid childhood, a protector, a model of wifehood and motherhood, a loving grandmother for her children. Why had her mother deserted her, a helpless child, leaving her with an abusive father and a baby to raise? What kind of woman would do such a thing to the daughter who had loved her so much? It was Sofia's fault—all of it—and she would never forgive...

Forgive? What was she thinking? Her mother certainly had not chosen to die. Why, so many years later, was she blaming that blameless woman?

The guttural, racking sobs breaking the stillness of the forest startled her, until she realized that they were her own.

By the looks of the sun overhead, Evie had probably spent at least two hours at the well: lost time, but time during which she must have drawn some measure of peace from its depths. Her heart had calmed, as had the wind, now just slightly rustling the upper branches of the birches.

She decided to walk to town after all. She stopped at the cottage just long enough to borrow a heavy sweater. Marysia was cordial, offering to accompany her. But needing some time to herself, Evie declined the offer, assuring Marysia that she would be fine, that she knew the way into town very well by now, that the weather had improved and was in fact now clear and brisk—perfect for a walk.

In Niedzieliska she paused before the town hall, which reminded her vaguely that she had planned some errand there, but she could not fully recall what it was. She knew where she needed to be—at the cemetery. Finding it quiet now that the holiday was over, she wandered in solitude, studying gravestones, finding familiar names reaching back over many generations. At the Czarnecki plot, she sat on the stone bench, now warmed by the midday sun.

The flowers had begun to fade on Jadzia's grave, the lilies turning to a pale saffron with veins now streaked with gray, no longer contrasting as dramatically with the chrysanthemums and carnations. Soon, Evie knew, this ground would be covered by snow, obliterating the last visible signs of the All Saints Day celebration.

She saw the tips of his boots, buffed to a high shine, before anything else.

"May I?" he asked politely, gesturing toward the space beside her on the stone bench. Upon her nod he sat, carefully placing a woven bag on the ground beside his feet.

Neither spoke for several long minutes, but finally, realizing that he would not initiate a conversation, Evie said, "I truly cannot believe that, in all this time, no one told."

Antek smiled sadly. "If anyone had, I would not be here now."

"But why? With all the suffering—everything you people did. Why didn't anyone tell the authorities?"

"I don't know, Eva. Perhaps they were sick of death, ready to move on with life. Perhaps it was their love of Jadzia, their wish that she be happy. Or maybe some of them saw the darkness in their own hearts and were willing to forgive."

Evie nodded her head slowly. The one thing she could understand was the village's regard for Jadzia, their joy at seeing some happiness come into her life.

"Eva," he said sighing. And for the first time she saw a broken man. "I have one more thing to ask of you."

Evie looked up at him in surprise. What could he possibly want from her?

"Eva, hate me if you wish. Notify the authorities—it really does not matter now. But please, Eva, forgive Jadzia. Do not let this come between the love you shared. Do not let it harden your heart against her—not even the slightest bit. She kept my secret out of love. She was a woman capable of so much love."

Evie broke away from the intensity of his eyes and bent to pick a fading rose from Jadzia's grave, rubbing one velvet petal between her fingers. Maybe the visible signs of All Saints' Day—fading as they were—were least important. Next year the villagers would gather again in this place, to pray, to talk, to sing, as villagers had gathered here for hundreds of years. This would be repeated for as long as the village existed.

For as long as Evie lived as well, she too would remember this place and all she had learned here: that her grandmother was revered as a war hero; that her Cousin Marek, though he had not been seen in decades, would never be forgotten; that her own mother, as a child, could milk a cow with the best of them. That Jadzia was not quite the person—had not been as honest and forthcoming—as Evie had believed her to be.

But then, who was? Whose inner self, in all humanity, was not far more complex than the persona she shared with the world? Who did not harbor, deep within her heart, hopes and fears, motivations and disappointments which were never given voice? Who could ever fully know the heart of another? Or even the heart beating within her own breast?

Of course, she would forgive Jadzia. True, Jadzia had kept secrets. But Evie, too, had kept secrets—some of them even from herself.

Turning once again to Antek, she found him holding on his lap the package he had brought. "*Prosce*, Eva, accept this as a gift from Jadzia."

Evie knew immediately what it would contain. Reaching into the woven bag, she pulled out the intricately carved wooden box, crafted by her Uncle Stanislaus so many years before. She traced her fingers on the floral pattern, thinking back to Jadzia's pencil tracing of so many years ago.

The key to the box dangled from a bit of twine attached to its tiny brass lock. Opening it, she found several envelopes addressed in her own childish hand.

"There are more letters at the cottage," Antek assured her. "We believe all your letters have been preserved. You may take them back with you."

"Thank you. But wouldn't Marek and Magda wish to have them?"

"We've made copies, and would very much appreciate copies of any letters of Jadzia's you might still have."

"I have them all—and of course, will send copies as soon as I get back home."

"There is something else in the box," he added, reaching into it. As he lifted the letters, she saw a tiny velvet pouch, royal blue, tied with a gold-braided, tasseled string. "This too is yours from Jadzia," he assured her. "Please, open it."

At first, upon loosening the string and tipping the velvet pouch into her hand she saw nothing, but a slight shake of the pouch revealed its contents. A small amber bead rolled into her palm, settling into its very center.

"Ah," Antek said, looking at the tears streaking her cheeks. "I do not have to tell you the significance of that bead."

The significance of the bead. She held it up to the sun. Its rays illuminated the bead, making it appear as radiant as a tiny sun itself. It had been Jadzia's last remembrance of her grandmother. It had sustained her through captivity and through many other challenges during her life. She had kept it safe for all this time.

"Surely Marek and Magda would want this memento," she said, tears rising. Despite her longing to keep it for herself, she added, "Do they know what it meant to their mother?"

"They do. And they also know what *you* meant to their mother. They want you to have it."

Looking into Antek's eyes, Evie saw for the first time the kindness and gentleness Jadzia had found there. She felt uplifted, as though some long-lasting burden had been taken from her. The sky looked brighter. The air felt crisp—invigorating. She knew what she needed to do.

"Antek," she asked, "is it too late to go to Krakow?"

"Why, no. It is not far. I have my car here. Are you...your flight isn't until late tomorrow. Do you wish to leave now?" he asked. Jadzia could see the disappointment on his face. "I can take you back to the cottage for your things."

"No, I don't wish to leave. I wonder if you could take me shopping."

"Shopping? Why, of course. What are you looking for?"

"For Polish souvenirs, but nice ones," said Evie.

"Ah," said Antek. "I know just the place—'*Polska Wspomnienie*'."

"Memories of Poland," Evie translated quietly. "That sounds like just what I'm looking for."

They drove through a blustery countryside to Krakow, negotiating the narrow streets of an older section of the city, stopping finally at a large building with a subdued façade. Entering it, Evie knew she would find what she sought.

She chose for her granddaughters dolls—Polish dancers, men and women, all dressed in the colorful costumes of Krakow, and for her grandson a wooden train, hand carved and painted a bright red, with a tiny wooden engineer and conductor and six miniature passengers. She anticipated the looks she would see in her grandchildren's eyes when she presented these gifts, having decided to book a flight to Los Angeles just as soon as she got home. Penny had often asked her to visit—Evie wondered why she had waited so long to do so. She'd stay a week—longer, if Penny seemed to enjoy having her there—and get to really know her grandchildren. And they'd get to know her.

For Henryk and Scott she selected stout, handsome shepherd's walking sticks, intricately carved on the handles with the wise old visages of mountain goats. Mother Sienka's gift was a beautiful reproduction of the Black Madonna which the older woman would surely appreciate. Perhaps she'd offer to take her mother-in-law to a meeting at Club Niedzieliska when she got back.

She chose a heavily leaded glass vase, intricately faceted in a repeated floral design, for Steffie and her husband. She'd convince Mickey to visit Sarasota after the holidays; it was past time for them to get to know Steffie's husband better.

She carefully examined tiers of amber jewelry laid out on black velvet, the colors of the pieces ranging from palest yellow to honey-color to a deep chestnut, the settings intricate masterpieces of silver or gold. She was surprised at an unexpected warmth emanating from deep within the stones. This was amber—the gift of Poland's ancient pine forests—preserving its history, evoking its mystery.

She finally selected a beautifully etched cross for Penny and a starburst patterned pendant for Peggy, then chose several smaller pieces for her granddaughters, her mother-in-law and her sister. She'd call Peggy immediately upon arriving home, inviting her to dinner, perhaps to stay for the weekend. Evie had always wondered why Peggy had so many diversions in her life. They'd talk. She'd find out.

For Marysia and Antek she selected silver filigreed picture frames for the copies of a photograph of Jadzia she had brought for them. It had been taken at Penny's wedding and was Evie's favorite, the photographer having caught Jadzia in an uncharacteristically pensive pose, the candlelight from the table picking out the deep intensity of her eyes, the warm, inviting expression of her mouth.

She had no idea what to get for Mickey, what would be most meaningful to him. Funny she had never considered how difficult retirement must be for a man who had devoted so much energy to his work. He still had plenty of energy, but no outlet for it. She wandered the aisles, picking up carved figurines, pipes, shepherd's vests and caps. Nothing seemed right.

Finally she came to a small table at the back of the shop piled high with the kind of second-hand material that might be found at a flea market back home. Rummaging through some of the items on this table she found an old leather album, frayed at the edges, the cover worn. Gingerly opening it, she found a wealth of old black and white snapshots affixed with yellowed tabs on coarse black paper: scenes of farmers pitching hay onto ox-drawn carts, of pipe-smoking elders seated before thatched huts, and later in the album, of handsome young men looking jaunty and carefree in their Polish military uniforms. This was the old Poland, but a Poland that still existed in its people. And she was one of them.

She remembered the pictures Mickey had sent her from England and France, of how they had spoken of visiting, together, the places he had seen in Europe. Soon, she vowed, they would take those trips together—to England and France, to Poland, beyond that to a whole world neither of them had ever seen. Knowing this album would bring back many memories and also initiate new experiences, she placed it gently in the crook of her arm, then turned toward the front of the store, craning her head to find a salesclerk.

Very late that night Evie, restless, turned in the narrow bed, having to reach several times for the *pierzyna* that had slipped to the floor. She had spent a wonderful last evening with Antek and Marysia, Stasiu and Gienek, sharing dinner with them and with Marysia's Tadek, who had arrived late that afternoon and was staying the night. He and Marysia would be taking her to the Warsaw airport very early the next morning.

Soon she would be back in Winston Estates, taking home with her so much more than she had brought. She would take with her many visions: of deep, dark woods; of an enchanted, candlelit evening; of a stone well that united generations. She'd take home memories of many people and of countless illuminating conversations. She'd take home the presents she had found in the shop and two very special prized possessions for herself.

Looking at her watch, she realized the night was almost over. In just an hour she would have to rise and ready herself for the trip home. But she could sleep on the plane, and when she awakened she'd be home.

Home. She was going home, and leaving home. But she looked forward to her journey. After all, she had so much to do.

Discussion Questions

1. In the preface to *One Amber Bead*, Sofia and Wladislaw come to the United States in search of the American Dream. What did they find on their arrival? In what ways has the pursuit of the American Dream changed for Evie and Mickey?

2. What personality characteristics do the cousins Evie and Jadzia share? How are they different?

3. Early in the novel, Apolonya tells Jadzia "You always have a choice." When Nazis come to Niedzieliska to take prisoners for their labor camps, Apolonya makes a dramatic choice. What, in her character, caused her to make that choice?

4. Both Evie and Jadzia experienced loss early in their lives. How did the loss of her mother affect Evie? How did the loss of Apolonya affect Jadzia?

5. World War II is the setting for approximately half of *One Amber Bead*. How was the war experienced differently by those living in the United States, in Poland and in Germany? How did her war experiences change Evie? Jadzia?

6. Although Evie was engaged to Mickey and Jadzia was in love with Antek, both women experienced affairs during World War II. Did this cause you to judge either or both women harshly? Why or why not?

7. What characteristics of Polish culture stood out for you? How did Polish culture change when it became Polish-American culture?

8. Weddings play an important role in *One Amber Bead*. What was the significance of Evie's refusal to participate in the Money Dance and the *Oczepiny* (the unveiling ceremony) at her wedding? Of Penny's decision to include those customs in her wedding?

9. Antek and Mickey are both complex characters. On the whole, would you describe Antek's character more positively or more negatively? Mickey's?

10. In the politically incorrect 1950's and 1960's, Polack jokes were very popular. What do Evie's and Mickey's different reactions to these jokes say about their feelings concerning their Polish ancestry?

11. Nineteen sixty-eight was a watershed year for Poland and the United States in that both countries experienced political upheaval and unrest. How did political differences affect both Jadzia's and Evie's relationships with their children? With their husbands?

12. Jadzia's trip to America gave the cousins new insights into each other's character, including the fact that each had kept secrets from the other. Had Jadzia not confessed her indiscretion with Wilhelm, would Evie have talked about her relationship with Charlie?

13. Why did Jadzia reveal the story of her love affair with Wilhelm, but withhold the incident which ended it?

14. Evie's trip to Poland gives her new insights into both her own and her cousin's life. How did these insights change her?

15. Did Evie over-react to the knowledge that Alfons was really Antek, the love of Jadzia's early life?

16. What role does the theme of forgiveness play in *One Amber Bead*?

17. Discuss the significance of the gifts Evie chose to take back to America with her. Do they indicate a change in her attitude toward her own family? Toward her Polish heritage?

18. What is the significance of the last four sentences of the novel: *Home. She was going home, and leaving home. But she looked forward to her journey. After all, she had so much to do.* Do you believe Evie's trip to Poland will change her life in any significant way? Why or why not?

About the Author

A long-time career of teaching creative writing and literature led Rebecca Thaddeus to the conviction that she could write a novel herself, and One Amber Bead is the result. The novel is based on the lives of her mother, a daughter of Polish immigrants, and her mother-in-law, who emigrated from Poland after World War II. Rebecca lives on a century-old farm in northern Michigan and is currently working on her second novel.

Visit Rebecca on Facebook and at writewiz1@msn.com.

CPSIA information can be obtained at www.ICGtesting.com
Printed in the USA
LVOW010721161111

255215LV00003B/9/P